First edition August 2021

71-75 Shelton Street, Covent Garden,
London WC2H 9JQ, UK

ISBN 9781801161381

Becoming Selfish

Volume 1

Liz Tomforde

Cherry Publishing

Subscribe to our Newsletter and receive a free ebook! You'll also receive the latest updates on all of our upcoming publications!

You can subscribe according to the country you're from:

You are from...

US:
https://mailchi.mp/b78947827e5e/get-your-free-ebook

UK:
https://mailchi.mp/cherry-publishing/get-your-free-uk-copy

CANADA:
https://mailchi.mp/96b9df3ed1ca/newsletter-canada-cherry-publishing

AUSTRALIA:
https://mailchi.mp/f7093b3c6c1a/newsletter-australia-cherry-publishing

Dedication

To my dad, who's no longer around to see this happen but would get a total kick out of the fact that his daughter is a published author.

Prologue

Logan

I may have had one too many cups of coffee. My heart feels like it's beating out of my chest, but I'm going to assume it's due to the caffeine intake and not because I just saw a sign that said Minneapolis is only twenty miles away. I was too anxious to stop at a hotel and sleep last night, but now I wish I had. It would have given me about eight more hours to try to calm my nerves.

What am I doing? I've never even been in the snow before. What made me think I could handle living in it? I guess we'll cross that bridge when winter hits in a few months.

The drive hasn't been too bad, and I had fun mapping it out from California. I stopped as often as I could, taking in some of the most beautiful parts of the country. I've never been able to travel much before, and now all I want to do is see new places. After I got my first taste of travel during my study abroad last semester, I haven't stopped thinking about all the cities I want to visit.

Last semester was the most fun I've ever had, and the freest I've ever felt. It was a weird time in my life, and I was working through a lot of grief, but going abroad was exactly what I needed. I even met my best friend when I was in Spain. You know, when you meet someone and you just get a feeling that they're going to be in your life forever? Well, I've never had that feeling before, but that's precisely how I felt when I met Marc. He helped pull me out of my misery and made sure I lived my life to the fullest while I was overseas.

It was the first week of classes abroad, and I was overwhelmed. The whole idea of doing a semester in Spain was such a last-minute decision for me. I'd never even been out of California before, let alone the country. It was the middle of the night, and I couldn't sleep, mostly due to jet lag, partly due to nerves. I'd gone downstairs to the shared living room, hoping to catch part of a basketball game on TV. Since the time difference was so drastic, I hadn't been able to watch any NBA games since I got there. I was trying to be as quiet as possible since it was three o'clock in the morning, but much to my surprise, someone was already sitting on the couch watching the exact game I was coming to see.

We sat on the same couch in awkward silence for a few minutes, both watching the game. I didn't want to stare at the stranger, but I was curious what the guy next to me looked like. His skin was a deep tan, and his hair was jet black. He seemed comfortable leaning back on the couch with his feet up on the coffee table, but he also looked confident. I sat there stiffly on the edge of the couch with my hands tucked under my legs. I didn't feel scared that I was alone in a dark room with a strange man in a different county. He didn't give off that vibe. In fact, I instantly felt more comfortable around him than most people I know, and he hadn't even said a single word to me yet.

As if he could hear my thoughts, he said, "Honestly, how does Harden get away with that many steps every time? How is that not a travel?"

Just like that, I knew I liked this stranger already because I had that same thought every time I watched the Rockets play. Without taking my eyes off the TV, I added, "Not only that, but he also draws a foul every time."

The tan boy gave a little chuckle under his breath, and turned to me. "Hey, I'm Marcus," he said while reaching out his hand for me to shake.

"Logan." I returned his handshake.

"Logan. That's a cool name for a girl. Where are you from?"

"California. You?" I detected a bit of a mid-western accent.

"Minnesota. So, I take it you're a basketball fan," he assumed while pointing towards the TV. "Do you have a team?"

"Not really. I'm just a fan of the sport in general."

He nodded his head and sighed in defeat as the Rockets drew another foul on the screen.

The Kings were playing as well. Judging by the look on his face, paired with the fact that they were already twenty points down, I assumed that was his team.

"King's fan?" I asked.

"Yeah." He sighed. "It's rough. They had this amazing team when I was growing up, so they tricked me into becoming invested in them, but they've sucked ever since."

I gave him a knowing smile. "Oh yeah. I remember White Chocolate and Chris Webber."

His face was plastered with shock and surprise. "Who the hell are you?" He laughed.

I leaned back on the couch and put my feet up on the coffee table, realizing I had never felt so at ease around a stranger before. We continued to watch the game, every once in a while complaining about a bad call, but we mostly sat in comfortable silence. It was almost five o'clock in the morning when the game ended and we headed back to our dorms, but I kept thinking about the stranger walking next to me and about how I had hoped we could hang out again. I had a hard time trusting people or letting many people into my life, so the next thing I said surprised even me.

Once I reached the girls' wing, I turned his way. "Hey, Marcus. Would you want to be friends?"

He chuckled and replied with a simple, "I thought we already were?"

I shot him a grateful smile before heading down the hall when I heard, "Hey, Logan..." I turned back to face him. "You can call me Marc. That's what my friends call me. You know, since we're friends now."

He was giving me shit already. It made me feel a little better since I kind of felt like an idiot for asking him to be my friend like I was a kid on the playground in preschool. I smiled at him but also rolled my eyes, so he knew that I knew he was giving me a hard time. He returned a knowing grin and headed down the boys' hall.

I remember lying in bed that night and feeling hopeful that I just met someone who would be a friend to me while I was in Spain.

And I was right.

Marc and I spent every day together that semester. We did our school work together, we explored the city together, and we would sneak downstairs in the middle of the night to catch as many NBA games as possible. Our relationship wasn't like that of siblings, but it was platonic, and there was never a question about that. I'd never had this close of a friendship with a guy before, but it almost didn't matter that he was a guy.

Marc not only became my best friend in Spain, but he became the best friend I've ever had. He told me all about his life in Minnesota. How his parents live in Indiana but own a house close to his campus, so they often visit. His mom married his stepdad when Marc was only three, and he has a stepbrother who is the same age named EJ. EJ plays hockey for their school and is well loved on campus, it seems. Marc also told me all about the girlfriend who broke up with him just two weeks before he left to study abroad and how they were together for three years. He had a feeling that she was cheating on him, and when he confronted her, instead of defending herself, she just broke up with him.

I told Marc I knew how he felt. I told him all about my ex-boyfriend. How I got back from seeing my mom in the hospital to find a woman's bra on his bedroom floor. I told him I knew it wasn't mine because I didn't own anything that red and lacy. I told him how, when I confronted my ex about it, he not only confirmed that he was cheating, but that it was with my closest friend at the time. I told him that I not only lost my boyfriend and my friend that week, but that was also the week that I lost my mom. I told him how a few weeks later, I packed up all my things and came to Spain to study abroad. I told him that it was my first time out of California and how I never wanted to go back.

So, I didn't.

That's a lie, I did. But only for a short time.

I had to go back for about two months to handle my parents' finances and sell my childhood home. After that, I packed up my car and started my drive to Minneapolis to begin grad school. Marc convinced me to move and get my MBA at the University of Minnesota, where he did his undergrad and got accepted into the graduate program. To be honest, it didn't take much convincing. I wanted to get the hell away from California and all the memories I had from there.

So here I am, less than twenty miles to my exit. In the fifth state I've ever been to, all of which were visited while on this drive. I'm anxious as hell, excited to see my best friend, but mostly nervous. Up until eight months ago, I had never really been on my own. I felt like I was because I was the one taking care of my parents when each of them was sick, but I've never truly been on my own. I've never gotten to think about me and only me. I always had an ailing parent to worry about or a boyfriend who only cared about what *he* needed. It feels pretty freeing not to have to think about anyone besides myself. But it also feels selfish. I've never used that word to describe myself before, but maybe that's exactly what I need to be. Selfish.

Chapter 1

Logan

This campus is enormous. It's so much bigger than the small state school I graduated from back home. It takes me a good thirty minutes of driving around campus, stopping to ask for help on three separate occasions to find my dorms. The graduate school housing seems to be in a quieter part of campus, and I'm thankful for that. It's not that I mind noise and other people partying; it's just not what I'm into.

Pulling into a parking space, I grab my phone out of my purse to check the email about housing, needing to remind myself of my dorm number.

"C-13," I say aloud in the hope that it'll stick in my mind. It shouldn't be that hard to remember—thirteen is my lucky number.

Along with my housing email, I have a missed text from Marc from about two hours ago.

M: *I can't believe you're going to be in Minnesota today! I know you're still a ways away, so let me know your ETA when you can. I'm planning to move into the dorms around 2:00. Let me know when you're here so I can help you. See you soon.*

I check the clock on the dashboard. It's only 11:27. I want to tell Marc that I'm here already, but I don't want him to rush over to help me unload my car because I can do it on my own.

***L**: Hey! I'm actually already here. I didn't feel like stopping last night, so I just drove straight through. I don't need help unpacking, so don't rush over here. I'll see you around 2:00.*

I put my phone back in my purse and throw it over my shoulder. Grabbing just the essentials, I lock the car and head inside.

The first floor of the building is spacious and well lit. Desks line the walls under the windows and pool tables crowd the entryway's right side. There are also two large couches, a coffee table, and a giant TV hanging on the wall.

Each side of the entryway has a staircase, and next to one of them is an elevator. I take the elevator, hoping that there will be some indication from the buttons what floor 'C-13' might be on. I step inside and, just as I had expected, some of the buttons are lettered instead of numbered. I press 'C' and wait for the doors to close.

Right as the door is about to shut, someone yells, "Hold the door, please!"

I put my hand between the closing doors to stop them, and a few seconds later, when the doors fully open again, a girl who looks about my age comes rushing into the elevator with her hands full.

"Thank you so much," she huffs, out of breath.

"No problem. Do you need help carrying any of that?" I eye the pile she's carrying in her hands.

Glancing down at her arms full of stuff, she shakes her head. "Oh, no. I'm good."

"What floor do you need?" I ask while looking at the lettered buttons.

"C. I think? Is that even a floor number?" she laughs.

"Yeah, it is. That's where I'm heading too."

We ride in silence as I stare at the numbers and letters changing, indicating the floor we are currently on. "1...2...A...B..." The elevator dings at what seems to be the fifth floor. Why they don't just number them all? I have no idea.

The doors open, and the girl with her hands full tries to exit the same time as me, but we can't both fit through. Giving each other an awkward laugh, I tell her, "Go ahead."

"Okay," she says and walks through the doors.

I didn't expect her just to say, "okay." I kind of expected her to say "oh no, after you" or something to that effect, because that's what I would have done. But I like that she just said "okay" and walked out. She's confident it seems, and doesn't feel the need to play the 'pretend to be polite' game.

I follow out behind her, and since her hands are so full, she moves slowly, so I quickly catch up and pass her. I scan the doors of the hall to find C-13. The even numbers are on the left side, and the odds are on the right. C-9, C-11, and finally C-13.

Opening my purse to pull out the envelope that has my orientation information inside, I grab the key out of the envelope and put it in the doorknob. Before I can unlock it, I hear a voice behind me.

"Neighbors, huh?"

It's the girl with the full hands from the elevator. She's across the hall, nodding her head at the placard that reads, 'C-12.'

I smile at her. "Looks like it. Small world."

She smiles back at me, and I realize then just how pretty she is. She's stunning, actually. She has long dark hair and a natural olive tone to her skin. She's not wearing much makeup because, quite honestly, she doesn't need to. Her brows are naturally bold, and her teeth are perfectly white. She's wearing a black spaghetti strap top and a gold choker necklace with a small dangling 'A' from it.

"I'm Ali. Ali Bertoli." She reaches out her hand to shake mine, and as she does, she drops one of the bags she was carrying.

"I'm Logan Leo." I shake her hand and offer a smile in return. After I remove my hand from hers, I reach down and pick up the bag for her, mostly because I doubt it would've been possible for her to bend down with her hands so full, and I hold it out to return it to her.

"Thank you. I'm refusing to make more than two trips downstairs, so I'm left looking like an idiot while I try to carry everything I own in my arms."

I chuckle at her candid response, catching an accent in her voice. Her last name is probably Italian, but her accent is not.

"Where are you from?" I ask my new neighbor.

"New York. How about you?"

"California."

Her eyes widen. "Really? I love California! LA is so much fun."

Most people seem to assume I mean southern California when I tell them I'm from the state.

"Actually, I'm from up north. About an hour north of San Francisco. Where they make wine."

I usually add in the last part because people get excited about that fact. Even if they have no idea where I'm talking about, 'wine country' sounds appealing.

"Oh, cool! I've never been to northern California before, but it sounds nice, and it's probably beautiful."

I give her a half smile. "Yeah, it's nice." I don't mention that I plan on never going back.

"What part of New York are you from?"

"Brooklyn."

The accent makes total sense now. I've never been to New York before, but of course, I know where Brooklyn is.

I realize then that her hands are still full, and she probably wants to get inside so she can set it all down.

"Sorry, do you need help unlocking your door?"

Her eyes widen with gratitude. "Yes, please! My key is on my wrist."

I cross the hall, and she bends down, so her wrist is level to the doorknob. She can't very well take her hand away from the stuff she's carrying, so I awkwardly grab the key that's on her bracelet and stretch it as far as it'll go. I unlock her door, opening it as wide as I can for her.

"Thank you! You're the best."

"No problem. Let me know if you need help getting the rest of your things from your car."

Why is that my first instinct? I'm supposed to be spending this time thinking about what *I* need and doing what *I* want. And here I am offering to help a stranger who hasn't even asked for it. Not that I want to be rude, I just need to start thinking about myself a bit more before thinking about everyone else. I've never done that before, and it's been harder than I thought it would be. I mean, I still have a full car to unload on my own, and here I am, offering to help a stranger get her things from hers.

"Thanks, girl, but you probably have your own car to unpack," she repeats my selfish thoughts exactly.

I give her a slight smile, cross the hall to my room, and unlock the door. When I enter, I'm shocked to see just how large it is. I've never experienced the college dorm room lifestyle, but this doesn't seem like an average dorm room. I knew it was going to be a little different because the grad school housing is single dorms—no roommates. But I had fully assumed that it would be the size of a shoebox since it was a single, but man was I wrong. A queen bed covers the furthest wall from the door, and there's a small side table next to it. The bed is pushed against the corner to maximize space, making the room look even more massive than the images I saw online. Across from the bed, there's a dresser, and next to that, a desk. The only drawback to this dorm room is the bathroom situation. The bathrooms are communal, which makes me a little nervous. I've never shared a bathroom with anyone before, and especially not with guys.

Crossing the room, I set my pillow and purse on the bed, and place my water bottle on the nightstand. I grab my phone out from my bag to find a text waiting from Marc.

M*: Woah, you made good time. Okay, well, I'm grabbing the rest of my stuff from EJ's house. I'll be there soon. If you want help, I can force him to come with and unload your car. Don't say no just to be stubborn.*

I roll my eyes while smiling at my phone. Marc knows me way too well, but that's not going to change the fact that I can unpack on my own. Plus, I haven't met his stepbrother yet, and from what he's told me, he's not the nicest person to people outside of his family. Marc loves him, obviously, but I don't need to be asking favors from someone like that. The last thing I need right now is to have to deal with some asshole relative of my best friend.

L: *Marc, I'm good. I've almost finished already. See you when you get here.*

A little white lie isn't going to hurt anyone. Ever since I met Marc and filled him in on the last few years of my life, he's been overly protective of me. I've never had someone want to look out for me, but then I'm also independent and have never felt like I needed it. It is nice to have someone care about your wellbeing, but I'm just used to taking care of myself.

Chapter 2

Eli

I can't believe it's finally my senior year. Well, super-senior year. Whatever, it takes most people five years to graduate anyway. Not that I give a shit how long it takes to get my degree, I'm just here to play hockey. After I had to redshirt my sophomore year because I broke my ankle, I took my time with classes and made my semesters as easy as possible since I knew I had to be here for five years. Unless the league called me up early. I would leave in a heartbeat, no matter how close I was to graduating.

This year is going to be the best for sure. I barely have any real classes to take, so I can enjoy my final year, play hockey, and party. The only shitty thing is that Marc isn't going to be living with me this time. We lived together in the hockey house for the last four years, even though he wasn't on the team. The only time we've ever been apart was last semester when he went to Spain to study abroad. Those few months were absolute shit without him. He's my only real friend, and I couldn't be happier that he's back even though he's going to be living in the grad school dorms, while I'll still be in the hockey house. Knowing him, he'll be over here most the time anyway.

Today is when he officially moves out, even though he wasn't here last semester or this summer. I didn't leave this summer; I had too much training to do. This year is my last shot at getting called up to the National Hockey League, and I can't have any distractions.

"Hey man, the last of my stuff is loaded in the car. I'm going to head out." Marc peeks his head in through my door, pulling me out of my thoughts.

"Alright, man. You coming tonight?" I get off my bed to hug him goodbye. A manly hug. The kind where you just swing one arm over their shoulder and give them a quick tap with your fist.

"Yeah, for sure. I wouldn't miss your first party of the year. I'm bringing Logan by the way."

Marc made a new friend while in Spain, which doesn't surprise me. He's friends with everyone. Not like me, where people want to say they're friends with me, but in reality, they don't give a shit about me. Most everyone thinks I'm just some selfish hockey player with an attitude who gets with any chick he wants. Which, to be honest, is mostly true. But I care about people too. I just haven't met anyone who I care about that isn't related to me.

Anyway, Marc made a new friend named Logan. He hasn't shut the fuck up about him since he got back, which makes me think that this guy is actually cool and someone Marc sees as a real friend. Marc is friendly to everyone, and everyone loves him, but he's picky about the people he keeps close to him.

Somehow, he convinced this guy to move all the way from California to attend grad school here. Who in their right mind would leave California's weather to live in Minnesota? Besides the fact that this guy is clearly out of his mind, I hope he's cool since he will most likely be spending a lot of time around here with Marc.

"Cool. Sounds good. By the way, Patrick is moving into your old room. I don't remember if I mentioned that or not."

Marc rolls his eyes at the sound of Patrick's name. "Fuck that guy."

I couldn't agree more. "Well, you're the one leaving me to live with the asshole," I remind him as I try to guilt-trip Marc into staying.

He chuckles. "Yeah, well, I'm not turning down living by myself in grad school housing to spend another year in a party house with a bunch of dudes. Did I mention that there are coed bathrooms?" He smirks, wiggling his eyebrows a couple of times.

I huff out an arrogant laugh. "Yeah, I get it. You're going to be surrounded by grad school chicks all the time. Meanwhile, I'll be here hosting every party this year and offering my bed to any girl that might need a place to crash." I raise my eyebrows back at him, giving him a knowing look.

I don't mean my actual bed, but Marc understands that, so I don't feel the need to clarify. He knows I don't allow anyone in my room, let alone my bed. If I'm going to fuck someone, it definitely isn't going down in here, and there's sure as shit not going to be a sleepover afterward.

"Okay, okay." He raises his hands in defeat. "Trust me, EJ, I know how many girls you can pull. But this is my first year being single, so if you can try not to sleep with every girl you lay your eyes on, that would be great," he says in a somewhat condescending tone.

"Well, if you're trying to find a chick who hasn't been with me, you might want to start with the incoming freshman class," I add with a smug smirk.

"Speaking of chicks, is Lauren coming tonight?"

I can't fucking stand that girl. I didn't like Lauren the whole time her and Marc were dating, and I hated her even more when she broke up with him. I know she cheated on him; I just don't have any proof.

"I'm assuming she'll be here. She's at every party, but I can kick her out. Trust me, I don't mind."

"Nah, it's cool. I can't avoid her forever. Might as well rip the band-aid off tonight."

"Alright, as long as you're sure?"

"I am." Marc turns to leave, but he quickly pops his head back in to say, "Also, Logan is new here, so try not to be too much of an asshole tonight," then ducks out before I have a chance to respond.

If this Logan dude doesn't have enough of a backbone to take a little shit from his best friend's stepbrother, I don't think I'm going to want him around much.

Once I'm alone again, I start to clean up my room a bit, not that anyone is going to see it. No one is allowed in here, especially on a party night. But the cleaner I can make it, the better I will hopefully sleep. I've tried everything to sleep better, but nothing has done the trick. Having a clean room helps me turn off my brain a bit at night, but it's never truly off. It's always overthinking and overanalyzing about my future, worrying about my next game, wondering if I'm ever going to get that call from the league. My sleep has gotten worse the older I've gotten, and the further my dream of playing in the NHL has become. After I broke my ankle three years ago, I've been anxious. I always assumed I was guaranteed to play in the big leagues at some point, as did everyone else, but after my injury, it's been a giant question mark. The only thing that's helped me sleep better is alcohol, but I try to avoid going overboard on that when I'm in season or training.

Speaking of alcohol, I grab my keys and head out to buy drinks for the party tonight. I don't plan on drinking since I have training in the morning, but I'm one of the few guys that lives here that's over twenty-one and can buy alcohol without using a fake ID.

Chapter 3

Logan

By the time I've unloaded my car, Ali and I have passed by each other three more times. On the trips down to the parking lot, I've learned that she's also starting her first year of grad school to get her MBA, and she's excited to hear that I'm doing the same. She also asked if Logan Leo is my real name because she thinks it sounds like an actor's name. I don't think she remembered that part about me not being from LA, but I informed her that it is indeed my real name and that my dad was adamant on the name, Logan, whether I was born a boy or a girl.

Ali is wearing a tight black crop top that barely covers her bra and it's paired with plaid pants that are tight around her ankles, inside of Doc Marten boots. Her vibe is edgy but effortless. Her entire stomach is exposed, and she looks absolutely flawless.

She fills me in on her family life. The oldest of three girls, her parents are married and living in Brooklyn, as are both sets of her grandparents. She likes to work out, but she also loves to eat, which are two of my favorite things as well.

Ali also adds that she doesn't have a boyfriend because she doesn't believe in them, which I find interesting.

"What do you mean you don't believe in boyfriends?"

"I just mean, why tie yourself down to one person when you can experience a whole world full of people?"

We both close our trunks. Ali's goal of only taking two trips ended up turning into five. As we head back into the building, I say, "Yeah, I guess so. I've never thought of it that way before. I'm not one to date around a lot. I've only ever had one boyfriend."

She turns to me with a shocked expression. "What? But you're like, hot. I would think guys would be all over you?"

I don't think anyone has ever called me hot—even a girl. My cheeks warm. "I don't know. I've never really been out to meet a lot of guys. I had a pretty hectic home life until last year, so I've just kind of been a homebody."

"So, you have the same boyfriend now?" Ali asks.

"Oh no. We broke up around Christmas last year. He cheated on me. I'm still trying to get over some of that."

Her eyes widen again. "What a piece of shit! And an idiot!" She takes a deep breath. "Well, now you have me as your wing-woman, and we're going to meet some new guys this year. But no boyfriends. Just experiences."

The number of times she's mentioned 'experience' makes me more and more aware that I have none. I had only dated my ex, Zac, for about nine months. At that time, my mom had gotten really sick, and my focus was all on her. I probably wasn't the best girlfriend for him, but I honestly did the best I could.

We met in class during my junior year of undergrad, in one of the very few classes I had on campus. Most of my classes were online, because I needed to help my mom out after my dad had suddenly passed away during my senior year of high school. When I met Zac, I was mostly shocked that he was giving me the time of day. My life was not that of a typical college student, and his definitely was. I didn't go to the parties that everyone went to, I didn't attend the football games, and I didn't even spend much time on campus. So honestly, I had no idea why Zac was interested in spending time with me. Our relationship was pretty surface-level, and I don't think I ever fully trusted him to show him my real life at home.

When I finally did let him in, he ran. Well, he cheated. And to be honest, I don't blame him. My life was a handful even for me at the time, and he couldn't handle it, which I understood. I just wish he would've told me with his words rather than finding another woman's bra on his bedroom floor. My heart knew there was something I couldn't trust in him, and my body recognized it too. Physically we never did much because I didn't feel comfortable enough to give him that part of me. Again, I don't blame him for cheating.

Ali and I reach our dorms, going our separate ways to unpack the rest of our belongings. I'm almost done making my bed when I get a knock on my door.

Chapter 4

Logan

Opening the door, I find the one person I'll never get tired of seeing.

"Logan!" Marc hugs me, picking me up at the same time. I tend to forget just how tall Marc is. I thought I was tall at 5'8", but he's at least 6'2" and can pick me up with ease.

"Hey!" I wrap my arms around his neck. I've missed my best friend for the last two months. We've talked every day, but it's just not the same.

"Dude, we're on the same floor. How sick is that?" he states while placing me back on my feet.

"Really? Where's your room?" I peek my head out into the hallway.

He points about three doors down on the opposite side of the hall. "C-8. Right there."

"Damn. That's closer than when we were in Spain. That's awesome!" I'm beginning to think that they put all of the first-year MBA students on the C floor.

"Do you need help unpacking anything?" He looks around my completely unpacked room. "Never mind, you're good." He laughs. "You don't have plans tonight, do you?"

"Marc, I don't know a single soul in this entire state. Do you think I have plans tonight?"

"Yeah, my bad. Okay, well, you do now. We're going to EJ's house for their kickoff party."

He says EJ's house, but I'm pretty sure that's where Marc used to live too. From the stories he's told me, it's where all the hockey players live and it's a total party house.

I hesitate. I'm not really into parties, and this seems like an extreme way to start off the school year. "I don't know, Marc. I don't know if I'm in the mood to go to a party. I've been driving for days."

He shakes his head as if he's trying to unhear what I just said. "No, Logan. You're going. I told you that things would be different from what you're used to when you got here, and that starts tonight. It's the first Friday of the school year, and you don't have classes until Monday. You still have a few hours to get a nap in beforehand. You're going to this party."

I can tell there's no point in fighting it, he's adamant about me going and having fun.

"Party? Did I hear someone say 'party'?" A voice from the hallway asks.

I lean my head around Marc to find Ali standing in the doorway with her shoulder effortlessly leaning against the frame.

I chuckle to myself because I've already experienced the confidence that is Ali, and I can tell that all three of us are going to this party, whether or not I want to.

"Yes, you did. And if I'm going, so are you," I say to the girl I just met a few hours ago. "Marc this is Ali, Ali, this is my best friend, Marcus."

"Nice to meet you." He reaches out his hand to shake hers.

Her eyes wander his frame, and her gaze lingers slightly longer than is usual for a casual once-over. Is she checking him out? I find it a little odd, only because I've never thought of Marc in that way, but she clearly has no intention of being discreet about it.

She returns his handshake with a sly smile on her face that's borderline mischievous. "Yeah, you too," she says, biting her bottom lip in a somewhat seductive way. Oh yeah, she's definitely checking him out.

I look at Marc, who, if the color of his skin allowed him to, I believe, would be blushing right now.

"Alright then," he says awkwardly, while looking down at the hand Ali is still holding onto.

Oh, he's so uncomfortable right now, and I find it hilarious. I've only known Marc to be completely confident and comfortable in who he is. It's something I admire about him, but this is the most flustered I've ever seen him, and I'm loving it. He's watched me be the awkward one during our friendship, but now the tables have turned.

"Well, I'll let you two get ready. We can head out around nine if that's cool?" Marc asks while rubbing the palms of his hands on his pants. Is he sweating?

I silently nod in agreement and give him a grateful smile.

"Can't wait," Ali states as she leans her head against the doorsill, keeping her eyes locked on Marc.

She's got to know that she's making him nervous.

"Cool. See you guys then." Marc nods his head, looking at the floor, and keeps his head down the entire time as he exits the room.

Ali rushes into my room, closing the door behind her. She turns around to face me with her mouth wide open in shock. "Um excuse me. Who is the hottie?"

"Marc?" I question with a laugh. "That's my best friend. We met in Spain during a study abroad semester last year. He's the reason I moved out here. He did his undergrad here as well."

She sits on my bed without asking. "Okay, but like more than friends? Or potentially more than friends?"

I suspect my face has a look of shock and confusion plastered on it. "You mean us? Oh no-no-no. Definitely not. He's my strictly platonic friend. To be honest, I don't even think about the fact that he's a guy. It's not like that."

She crosses her legs, making herself even more comfortable on my bed. "So, would you mind if I was interested?" Ali asks with a somewhat nervous and questioning smile on her face.

I make my way to my desk chair and take a seat. I don't know how to answer that question. I don't have any interest in Marc in that way, but I do feel protective of him. He just got cheated on by his long-term girlfriend, and the last thing I want for him is to have his heart broken by a girl from New York who was just looking to add him to her list of new experiences. But maybe he would be okay with that? I don't know where his head is at when it comes to relationships at the moment, so I'm not going to be the one to stand in the way.

"You do you. Just so you know I think he's more of a relationship type of guy, but maybe he would be down for something more casual. I'm not sure."

She stands up, seeming to be satisfied with my answer. "Good to know. Well, now the big question. What are we wearing tonight?" she asks with a mischievous glimmer in her eye.

Chapter 5

Eli

The house is packed tonight, which is not much of a surprise since we throw the best parties on campus. I recognize most everyone here so far, but I'm hoping there will be some new girls coming through tonight. I don't necessarily feel the need to hook up with a random chick, but it's nice to keep my options open. I still haven't decided if I'm going to drink or not, so I'm sticking to water in my red solo cup for now.

I wander through the house, getting stopped at least five or six times. It's mostly girls wearing close to nothing, being desperate, or guys who want to talk about the upcoming hockey season. Not that I mind either of those situations usually, I'm just not really in the mood to deal with it tonight. I haven't been sleeping well at all, and I'm exhausted. I probably shouldn't have agreed to host this party, but we always throw a kickoff party the weekend before school starts. I've had so much anxiety about this upcoming season, knowing it's my last one if I don't get called up by the time it's over, which has been affecting my sleep a little too much lately.

I get stopped again, this time by a blonde wearing a skin-tight red dress. Her cleavage from her fake tits could not be more in my face as she grabs my arm, raking her long nails down my bicep. I instantly recognize her.

"Hey, Maddison," she says, giving me a smirk.

"Alyssa." I roll my eyes. I don't feel like dealing with her tonight even though she is an easy lay.

"Missed you this summer." She cocks her head to the side while continuing to graze her nails over my arm. "How was this dreadful town without me?"

"Quieter," I state matter-of-factly.

She licks her lips, biting down on her bottom one. God, could she be any more obvious? I realize then that she thinks I meant quieter because she wasn't screaming my name while we were in bed. She is the loudest girl I've ever been with, which can be kind of hot sometimes. But what I meant is that it was quieter because I didn't have to hear her annoyingly high-pitched voice saying 'Hey, Maddison,' at every party she's at. And she's at *every* party.

Anyone who knows me through hockey calls me by my last name, Maddison. My family calls me EJ, which is short for Eli James. I guess that's fine, but I just want to be called by my name, Eli. I rarely meet many people that don't know me through hockey, and even if I do, as soon as they hear people calling me Maddison, they start to call me that too.

Alyssa's long nails are still raking my arm. I look her up and down, contemplating giving her the attention she's so desperately seeking. Just then, I hear someone yell "EJ" from across the room. My eyes dart to the front door to find Marc waving me over.

"Gotta go." I grab Alyssa's hand and remove it from my arm. If I change my mind about her tonight, I'm sure she'll still be around.

I bob and weave through the crowd of people, getting stopped by a couple of guys trying to get me to join their beer pong game. Once I make my way through the mass of students, I hug my brother.

"Really, dude? Did you get more popular while I was gone last semester?" He's giving me shit. He knows how annoying I find it when people pretend to know me because they assume I'm going to play professional hockey one day and want to be my friend. But little do they know that I may never play professional hockey at this rate.

"Very funny," I say sarcastically.

I look down at the short brunette next to Marc as she scans the room, twirling a piece of her hair between her fingers. The spunky attitude radiating off of her isn't Marc's usual type, though, she's hot as hell, so I guess she's everybody's type. Even though I can't keep my promise to Marc about not attempting to sleep with every girl I lay my eyes on, I can keep my promise when it comes to the one girl he came here with.

"Hey, I'm Eli." I reach my hand down to her to shake.

Just then, I hear "Maddison!" from somewhere in the kitchen. I turn my head to see who it was, but I have no idea who said it, I honestly don't care, and the house is too packed to find out.

"Maddison, huh?" the short girl asks, cocking her head to the side.

"Yeah, its Eli, or you can go with Maddison if you prefer." I'm still holding out my hand for her to shake it.

She places her small hand in mine. "Yeah, I think I'll go with Maddison."

Of course she will.

"I'm Ali."

I look at Marc, waiting for him to introduce me to his date, but he doesn't say anything. Why is he being so awkward?

"So, how do you know my brother?" I motion between the two of them.

"Brother? You guys are brothers? You look nothing alike." Her head is on a swivel, looking back and forth between us.

We often get that question when we tell people we're related. Marc's deep tan skin and my pale complexion are a dead giveaway that no blood ties exist between us. My brother and I share a knowing look, laughing to ourselves.

"We're stepbrothers. My dad married his mom when we were kids," I explain while Marc stays silent.

"Oh, cool," she says, nodding and seeming to understand the situation better. "So, is there a place where I can grab a drink around here?"

"For sure. The kitchen is fully stocked. Marc, you can show her where it is." Hopefully, if Marc gets a drink in him, he will loosen up. He's being oddly stiff. I know he's only really been with Lauren, so he's a little out of the game, but he can do better than this.

"You drinking tonight?" he asks me.

"Haven't decided yet. So far, just water." I hold up my red solo cup in a 'cheers' motion.

We give each other a little head nod as he and Ali make their way to the kitchen. I'll catch up with him at some point later on in the night.

I scan the room, unable to decide what I want to do or who I want to talk to. Maybe I should've gone with Marc and his date. I'm honestly pretty bored already. It's all the same girls who are used to throwing themselves all over me and every other guy in this place, and I've never understood why chicks wear the tiniest outfits they own with the highest heels they can find to these parties. By the end of the night, they all have their shoes off, and the floors of this house are usually covered with sticky alcohol and vomit. Realizing that if these are the type of people I'm dealing with tonight, maybe I *should* just start drinking.

The downstairs bathroom usually has a line and is pretty gross, even this early on in the evening, so I head upstairs to take a piss before I officially decide what my plan is for the night. As I make my way to the stairs, I get stopped a couple more times by people I kind of recognize, but honestly have no idea who the fuck they are, nor do I care to find out.

Once I finally make it to the stairs, I take them two at a time, needing to get the fuck out of this living room and away from these people even if only for a minute. I realize I'm still rushing when I get to the bathroom door, not because I have to piss, but because I just need to breathe for a second away from everyone else's eyes.

As soon as I reach for the handle on the bathroom door, it opens and someone knocks into me as they're trying to leave the bathroom in a hurry, which causes me to spill my drink all over my shirt.

"Shit! Oh my god! I'm so sorry!" they say, covering their face with both hands.

"Look where you're going next time," I growl. I'm not in the mood for this shit tonight. I lift my eyes off my soaked shirt to see who it is that just pissed me off.

The girl standing in front of me is tall, with pretty hair. It's a dark red color, the kind of red that you can tell she dyes it, but it looks so good and shiny. It's down and curled, but pulled to one side. Her collarbone is inked with a small handwritten tattoo on it, though I can't read it from here, and her skin looks smooth with a natural golden glow to it. Her eyes are almost almond-shaped and a deep shade of emerald green. Her dark gray T-shirt highlights her chest perfectly, and her baggy jeans with holes at the knees make her look casual and effortless. She has a few bracelets on and a watch. An Apple Watch it looks like. She's probably into working out; she looks like she works out. My eyes continue to trail down her body, finding a pair of black Vans on her feet, and I smile to myself as I think about all the girls downstairs wearing those ridiculous heels.

My final verdict is that this girl is absolutely gorgeous.

"Yeah. Okay. You're right. My bad. Sorry again," she states with disinterest, trying to make her way around me. I'm blocking the doorway, not on purpose, but because I'm a tall guy and take up a lot of space.

She's thrown off by the edge in my voice. I try to think back to what she was responding to, but I'm a little taken aback by how pretty this girl is. What did I say to her before? Oh yeah, I was an asshole and told her to look where she was going next time. Nice one, Eli. You idiot.

"No, I'm sorry," I begin, hoping I can prevent her from leaving. I'm not one to apologize for anything, but if it means she will stay,

I'm willing to give it a shot. "I shouldn't have said that. I didn't mean it. You don't have to look where you're going. Ever. You're welcome to run into me anytime." I shoot her my most convincing smile, hoping that my charm will change her first impression of me.

"I'll remember that next time I try to apologize for spilling someone's drink on them." She smiles, pointing to my wet shirt.

It seems to be working.

She has a perfect smile. It's a little shy but perfect. Dimples indent both her cheeks, though the one on the left is more prominent, drawing my eye right to her mouth. I can't stop staring at her mouth. Her lips look soft, and I wouldn't mind feeling them against mine.

Snapping out of my trance, I glance down at my shirt. "Don't worry about my shirt. It's just water."

As I look back up at her, we lock eyes. God, she's pretty. I have no idea what to say to her right now because my brain is in a fog and I can't seem to think straight. I'm never like this around girls.

"So, uh, are you new here? I don't think I've seen you around before," I lie. I *know* I've never seen this girl before. I would've remembered.

"Yeah, actually, I am. I'm starting grad school on Monday," she replies.

Beautiful *and* smart. Goddamn. "Cool. Well, I'm going into my last year here, so if you need help finding your way around, I know the campus pretty well at this point." I let out a halfhearted laugh. God, could I be any more awkward right now? "I'm Eli, by the way," I tell her as I reach my hand out towards her, hoping my palm isn't too sweaty from the nerves.

"Logan," she states while returning my handshake.

As soon her hand touches mine, a calmness washes over me. It's the calmest I've felt in a while.

Chapter 6

Logan

His hand is large and strong. The arm that's reaching out to me is covered in tattoos, almost like he's wearing a sleeve of ink. His skin is taut from the muscles underneath, and they cause his dark green T-shirt to be a little tight around his biceps. His wet shirt sticks to his abs, making him look like he should be modeling for an ad targeted towards women. He's tall, really tall. He's got to be 6'4", at least. His dark brown hair is messy and unruly, causing him to have to push it out of his face repeatedly, and his rosy cheeks play off the paleness of his skin. His warm mocha eyes pour into me as I check him out, noticing that his other arm doesn't have any tattoos. It makes me wonder if there are any more on the rest of his body. My eyes continue to wander over his frame, noting his dark blue jeans and gray Converse.

This guy is ridiculously attractive, and I get the sense he knows it.

My hand is still in his when someone asks, "Are you using the bathroom? Or can I get in there?" I hadn't noticed we were still standing in the bathroom doorway, where I spilled his entire drink down his shirt.

"Oh, no. It's all yours." I quickly pull my hand away from Eli's as we both move out of the way.

The stranger walks into the bathroom, closes the door, and leaves us standing there awkwardly facing one another.

"Well, I better go find my friends." I point over his shoulder towards the stairs.

"Oh. Yeah. For sure." He moves out of the way so I can get around him.

“It was nice to meet you,” I quietly add, giving him a small smile as I walk past him.

“Hey, Logan?” I hear from behind me. I quickly turn my head back in his direction. “Am I going to see you again tonight?” A not-so-subtle smirk forms on his lips.

Okay, I’m blushing now. “Um, I don’t know. I’m not planning on being here too long.”

“Well, I’m pretty sure you owe me a drink.” He points at his shirt, a playful smile covering his mouth.

“I’ll keep that in mind.” My cheeks begin to heat as I turn back to the stairs.

Okay, that guy is charming, and Ali is going to be so excited when I tell her I just got hit on. Or at least I think I just got hit on? Regardless, it doesn’t matter because I’m not going to entertain it. This guy can get any girl he pleases, and I get the vibe that he’s used to getting what he wants. As much fun as Ali claims it is to experience different men, that’s just not me. And I don’t want to think about any guys right now. I just want to think about me.

Making my way downstairs, I realize the house has gotten even more packed while I was upstairs. This place is so big that I’m going to have a hard time finding Marc and Ali, but I begin my search by making my way through the crowd towards the kitchen. I figure that would be a good place to start looking, seeing as that’s where the alcohol is kept. Thankfully, when I make it there, I find Marc talking to a couple of guys, though I don’t see Ali anywhere. He spots me and waves me over.

“Hey, you good?” he asks with a bit of concern on his face.

“Yeah, don’t worry about me.” I shoot him a look that says, ‘stop being so protective.’

“Can’t help it.” He laughs. “Logan, these are some buddies that I used to live with here, Cam and Patrick. Guys, this is Logan.”

“Hey,” I lift my hand in a small wave towards them.

The blond one looks my body up and down. "Hey, I'm Patrick. Where are you from?"

"California." I won't elaborate.

"Mmm, Cali. Very nice." He continues to drag his eyes up and down my body, lingering a little too long on my chest. "So, is this your girlfriend or something? What about that chick from New York?" he asks Marc but keeps his eyes focused on me.

Apparently, Ali was here recently, so she can't be too far. The way this Patrick guy is eyeing me makes me want to leave this conversation as quickly as possible to go find her.

"No. Logan and I met last year in Spain. I convinced her to enroll in grad school out here. And that other girl is just some chick I met today who lives on my hall." I glance towards Marc out of the corner of my eye. I kind of thought he liked Ali? Maybe I was wrong, or perhaps this is just the way he talks around the guys.

"Good to know because she was hot," says the shorter one with copper hair. Cam, I think, is his name.

Marc slightly tenses up next to me. Patrick hasn't stopped eye-fucking me since I got here, and I could not feel more uncomfortable. Since I can tell we both want out of the conversation, I turn to Marc. "Hey, let's go grab a drink," I suggest, even though I can see he has a full one already.

He looks down at his cup but catches on quickly. "Yeah, I could use another. See you guys later." He nods to the boys.

"See you around, 'Cali,'" I hear the blond call out to me as we walk away towards the keg on the other side of the kitchen.

"Gross," I say in disgust once we are out of earshot of them.

"I know. Sorry about that. I gotta play nice with them since they are still EJ's housemates, but please stay away from them. Especially, Patrick, I don't like or trust that guy."

"Trust me, not a problem." I grab a red solo cup from the stack on the counter.

"You drinking tonight?" Marc asks while raising his eyebrows in surprise.

"No, probably just water." It's not that I don't drink, I just don't do it often. I don't enjoy the taste, so I only drink when I want to get drunk. With classes starting on Monday, tonight is not that night.

I turn away from Marc to fill my cup with water from the sink as I hear him yell, "Hey EJ! Over here!" loud enough to be heard over the crowd. I turn around with my cup full, excited to finally meet the stepbrother he's told me about, but when I do, I find the tall boy with brown eyes and a wet shirt standing next to Marc.

Then my entire cup of water hits the floor.

Chapter 7

Eli

Still in a daze from the encounter I had outside the bathroom, I make my way downstairs and head to the kitchen to get myself a new drink. I keep my eyes peeled for the pretty girl from upstairs, but I haven't spotted her yet, and I find myself hoping she didn't leave already. She was super hot, and usually, I'd try to hook up with a girl that looks like that, but she doesn't seem like the type of girl I'm used to pursuing. I can't quite put my finger on what it is, but I do know I want to see her again.

I push my way through the group of people crowding the entrance to the kitchen. Right then, I hear Marc call my name from across the room, close to the sink. I give him a nod, so he knows that I heard him, before I start heading in his direction. When I make it to him, I bump my fist with his as my eyes wander to the girl next to him with her back towards me, facing the sink.

I'd recognize that burgundy hair anywhere.

She turns to face me with an expectant smile, but as soon as her eyes lock with mine, her expression changes from excited to shocked.

Then she drops her cup of water, and it splashes all over the floor.

Wow, this girl is clumsy.

I look down at the wet ground and back up to her face. "I believe that's two for two," I say to her with my most flirtatious smile.

She's stands frozen in shock until she registers the mess she just made. A blush warms her cheeks as she looks down on to the wet floor. "Shit. My bad!" she apologizes before reaching down to pick up her empty cup. She frantically looks around, spotting the paper towels sitting on the counter next to the sink. Before she can use them, Marc takes them from her hand and puts them back where they came from.

"Don't worry about it. Honestly, a puddle of water on these floors is the cleanest they've ever been," he reassures her.

Does he know her?

Marc points to her while looking at me. "EJ, this is Logan."

I know that, but how does he? "Yeah, I know. We met upstairs." I keep my eyes locked on hers. She still has that shocked look on her face. "But how do you guys know each other?" I motion my finger between them.

"Dude, this is Logan," Marc states again. "Logan from Spain?" He looks at me like I'm an idiot.

Just like a lightbulb got flipped on, everything clicks. Holy fucking shit. *This* is Logan? Marc's friend Logan? But she's not a dude. This is the Logan that he spent last semester watching basketball games with in the middle of the night and shooting the shit? What the fuck?

Now my face shares the same shocked expression as hers.

"Hi," she says without breaking her eye contact from mine.

Well, her brain seems to be working just fine, but mine is currently not. "But, you're not a guy," I state aloud, accidentally.

She chuckles and thankfully doesn't seem to be offended. "Thanks for noticing?"

Marc smacks my shoulder. "Dude, what the fuck?"

I don't even look at him. I can only look at her. I cannot believe this is the person he's been telling me about since January. Logan seemed cool and all when I assumed she was a guy, but now that I know she's not, I'm a little confused as I think back and try to remember the stories Marc had told me about her. Now that I know his Logan is the girl that took me by surprise when I met her upstairs, I don't know what to think.

Is he into her? How could he not be? But I think he would've mentioned that she was a girl if he was. He never gave me any indication that his new friend wasn't a guy. He just told me that they kicked it all the time, watched sports, and did their schoolwork together.

While I'm lost and confused in my thoughts, the spunky brunette from earlier returns, pulling my attention back to the present.

"There you guys are!" she bursts while swinging an arm around each of Marc and Logan's shoulders. She's pretty short, so she's on her tippy-toes trying to do so. She cocks her head towards Logan. "We're gonna go play beer pong with a couple of cute boys I just met." Her voice sounds like she might be a little tipsy already.

Logan seems apprehensive. "Oh, I don't know if that's a good idea." She shakes her head. "I'm not even drinking tonight."

Is she not? I just assumed she would be. Everyone else does during these kinds of things. If and when I decide to be sober at a party, I'm usually the only one.

"Nope. You're playing. I'll drink for both of us," Ali commands, grabbing Logan by the wrist and pulling her to the living room.

My eyes follow Logan out of the room, and right before they turn the corner, she looks back, briefly making eye contact with me. Before I know it, she's out of sight, but definitely not out of my mind.

Chapter 8

Logan

Ali has pulled me into the living room without my mind catching up to what just happened. I can't believe that cute guy—Eli—from upstairs is Marc's stepbrother, EJ. Thinking back on the stories Marc had told me about his brother, I know Eli is a hockey player, can be a bit of an asshole, but is well-loved around campus, especially among the ladies. Most of these facts line up with the first impression I'd gotten from our encounter outside the bathroom. But, Marc has also told me what a great guy EJ is once you get to know him, though he doesn't let many people close enough find out.

Regardless of all that, he's off-limits. I hadn't put too much thought into what could've happened with the guy I met upstairs, but now that I know he's Marc's brother, anything that could have been is definitely off the table, which is for the best. I don't need to be thinking about anyone else's feelings at the moment.

Ali steers me to a table covered in sticky liquid. Beer, I assume. Ten cups are lined up in a triangle shape on each side of the table, and each cup is about half full of beer. Looking to the other end of the table to see who our opponents are, I'm not so pleasantly surprised to find the guys from the kitchen earlier, Cam and Patrick.

I glance back at Ali. "I really don't want to play," I plead.

"You're playing. I need you to wing-woman for me. See that guy over there?" She nods her head in Cam's direction, a devilish smirk sliding across her lips. "I think he's cute. So, suck it up, buttercup, and play a round with me." She places a ping pong ball in my hand.

I've played this game before, but only once at a party that Zac took me to. I only went to two parties with him when we were in college, neither of which were as big as this one. Not even close.

Ali shoots first, but her ball doesn't even hit the table.

"Well, shit!" She giggles, twirling around in a circle before leaning into me. She's clearly tipsy already. Having her drink all ten of these cups is a terrible idea.

I stand on our side of the table, lining up my elbow the way Zac taught me. I release the ball, and to my surprise, it lands in a cup towards the back, closest to where Patrick is standing.

"Yes, Logan!" Ali throws her arms up and around me.

Patrick picks up the cup and raises it to me in a 'cheers' motion while giving me a mischievous smirk. He drinks the liquid down in one gulp.

The game continues, and Ali still hasn't made a shot, but I've made nine. Thankfully, she's only had to drink two of the cups of beer. I line up my elbow, shooting towards the final cup, and when it plops into the beer, I proudly smile up at the boys across the table who just lost.

"What the hell? You're so good!" Ali exclaims, hugging me again. This time I hug her back. I'm glad she made me play. That was fun.

Cam picks up the last cup he has to drink, but before he does, he says, "Okay, we just got hustled for sure. Rematch."

Patrick chimes in, "Yeah, no way I'm going out like that." He looks up to me. "Cali, I know you're lying to me. You've played this more than once. Line up those cups; we are going again."

Ali's eyes plead with me. I can tell she's having fun, and so am I. She's been flirting with Cam the whole time, he's been flirting right back, and I'd imagine something will happen between them tonight.

I look at her then back to the boys waiting for my response. Patrick has a devilish grin as he stares at me. “C’mon Cali, one more?” he coaxes.

I wouldn’t say I like that he keeps calling me ‘Cali’ but it doesn’t bother me enough to correct him. “What the hell,” I give in, throwing my hands up in defeat. “If you guys want to lose again, let’s do it.”

Patrick keeps his stare on me as he sets up the cups again. I don’t love the way his eyes linger on me, but it doesn’t gross me out the way it did when we were in the kitchen.

Chapter 9

Eli

I'm left standing in the kitchen with Marc, wondering who Logan went to play beer pong with. I still can't wrap my head around the fact that she's the new friend that Marc hasn't stopped talking about. How did I never catch on to the fact that she was a 'she'?

"Why the hell didn't you tell me that Logan was a girl?" I ask my brother.

"I didn't know that I had to, and it doesn't really matter that she is."

"Of course it matters." I swat him on the shoulder. "I had assumed you were hanging out with some bro from California for five months while you were in Spain. Now I learn that it was a girl the whole time? Not to mention the fact that she looks like *that*?" I nod my head in the direction Logan had walked off. "You could've been banging her the whole time, and I wouldn't have had a clue."

I wonder if he did?

"Don't talk about her like that, man," Marc snaps. "She's not just some piece of meat."

Okay, he's being overly sensitive about her. "Wait, are you into her?" I ask, finding myself hoping that he says no.

"Dude, no. It's not like that. I probably never mentioned that she was a girl because I don't think of her in that way. She's just my friend." He pauses. "But I am protective of her. She's been through a lot, and I don't want you messing with her the way you do with every other girl on campus."

She's been through a lot. What does that mean? Mess with her like every other girl on campus? Is that how my brother sees me?

"Is that really how you think of me, man?"

He sighs. "No, you know what I mean." He gives me an apologetic look. "I know you're not looking for anything more than a hookup, and that's fine. I honestly couldn't give a shit what you do with any other chick—more power to you. But Logan is not like the girls you're used to. She's cool, and she's my friend, and she's already dealt with too much bullshit in her life. I convinced her to move here so she could have a fresh start, and I don't want the first thing that happens to her here is my own brother breaking her heart." He takes a deep breath and downs the rest of his beer, giving me a second to process what he said.

It's clear how much he cares for her, and as much as I don't want to agree with him, I know he's right. I'm not looking for anything more than a hookup, and if he's this adamant about me staying away from her, then I will. His friendship is way more important than some random girl, regardless of how intriguing she is.

"You're right," I tell him, nodding my head. "I'll stay away from her."

He rolls his eyes at me. "You don't have to stay away from her, EJ. You can still be her friend. She's great and one of my favorite people, so I know you'll like her too."

Little does he know that completely staying away from her is my only guarantee to keep my promise of not hooking up with her.

"Anyway," he changes the subject. "Have you seen Lauren? I was hoping to talk to her at some point tonight."

"Nope," I respond, keeping it as short as possible. I can't stand that girl, and I don't want my brother going near her again.

"EJ..." he drags out my name, insinuating that I'm lying to him. Which I am.

I sigh in defeat. "Yeah, I saw her a little bit ago. She was on the back deck with some of the guys from the team."

"Thanks, man. I'll catch you later." He pats me on the shoulder before heading towards the back door of the house.

Chapter 10

Eli

I spend the next couple of hours working the room and talking to a bunch of people I don't give a shit about. I haven't seen Marc since he left me to find his ex, and I haven't spotted Logan since she left the kitchen to play beer pong. I've decided to stick to my plan of not drinking tonight, and it's making this stage of the party harder to get through sober, since everyone is pretty drunk and not making much sense. Sometimes I wonder why I even throw these parties when I don't like the majority of the people who show up anyway, but I guess I do it because it's what people expect me to do.

It's late, and I have to be up early for training tomorrow, so I should go upstairs and get some sleep. Well, at least *try* to get some sleep. Over the last couple of hours, people have either reminded me that it's my last season this year or asked if I've heard of any teams looking to call me up to the NHL for their season. Both of which have caused the anxiety I've been trying to avoid feeling all night to seep in.

As I make my way through the living room to get to the stairs, I hear yelling from the far side of the room where the beer pong table is. It's not actually yelling, I realize, but extremely loud cheering. Looking over, I find that Logan and Ali are playing. Have they been playing this whole time? I head towards them to see who their opponents are, only to discover it's Cam and fucking Patrick. I involuntarily roll my eyes.

There's a crowd that's gathered, watching the game. I stay hidden towards the back but, because of my height, I can see just fine. Standing a ways behind Cam, my sightline is perfect to see everything Logan does. She tosses her hair over her shoulder, perfectly lines her elbow up with the table, and prepares to launch the ball across it.

She has a drink in her other hand, from which she takes a sip. She must have decided to switch to something harder than water, but I don't care that she's drinking; I just hope no one forced her to. Namely, Patrick.

"Six, Patty! You're about to lose six times in a row!" someone in the crowd yells.

Have the girls won five times already? That's fucking awesome. Scanning the players, I notice that Logan doesn't seem drunk at all, Ali appears to be about the same level of buzzed as she was when I saw her in the kitchen, and both boys look pretty hammered.

"Fuck! I know! Cali has been hustling us this whole time!" Patrick yells back to the crowd.

Did he just call Logan, 'Cali'? I hate that. Why does he have a nickname for her already? He doesn't even know her. I realize that he's spent more time with her than I have because they've been playing this game for so long, but fuck, he doesn't know her.

Scanning the table, the girls still have seven cups sitting in front of them, whereas the boys have only one. Logan can win it on this shot.

"It's not my fault that you're both terrible at this game!" Logan yells back to him, and it makes me smile. She seems tough; I like that.

As the last word leaves her mouth, she shoots the ball across the table, and it lands perfectly in the final cup. The crowd drunkenly cheers. A couple of people start chanting, "Six! Six! Six!" as Logan puts her cup down and takes a bow. She and Ali are both laughing, and she looks happy. It makes me smile.

This feels weird. Outside of my family, I've never cared if someone else was happy. But I think back to what Marc said about her having a hard life, whatever that means, and I'm glad that she's happy at this moment.

"One more! C'mon!" Cam drunkenly yells out, holding onto the table just to keep himself upright. There's no way he could handle losing another game.

I start heading towards the stairs to go to my room, but I look back for a second to get one last glimpse of Logan for the night, and she catches me doing so.

"Sorry guys, I think I'm done for tonight," she tells them without breaking eye contact with me.

She picks up her cup from the table and starts walking in my direction.

"Where the hell did you learn to play like that?" I ask her when she makes it over to me at the base of the stairs.

"I have absolutely no idea," she giggles. "I've only played once before, and I was terrible then. So, this must've just been luck."

I smile down at her. "Well, you're impressive nonetheless."

Her eyes lock with mine, and a blush warms her cheeks. I find myself unable to stop staring at her. Her emerald-green eyes are mesmerizing. The ink on her exposed collarbone catches my eye, and now that I'm close enough, I can see her tattoo more clearly. It's small and handwritten. I think it says 'I love you.'

I wonder who wrote it. Does she have a boyfriend?

She catches me staring and flips her hair over her shoulder to cover up her tattoo. Maybe she doesn't want me to ask about it, or perhaps she doesn't want me to know that she has a boyfriend.

"Are you done for the night?" Logan quickly glances up the stairs.

"Yeah, I need to get to my room."

She reaches out her cup to me. "Well in that case, this is for you."

Taking her cup, I look inside. It's just water.

"I've owed you a new one all night, and I couldn't stand being indebted to you any longer." She gives me a playful smile, and I can tell she's been planning to use that line on me for a while.

God, she's charming. This promise to Marc is going to be hard to keep.

I laugh under my breath before taking a sip. There's a bit of her chapstick on the rim—vanilla, I think.

"Maddisoooon," a drunk guy slurs while coming down the stairs, but I have no idea who he is. He begins to fall into Logan when he reaches the bottom, but I grab him and hold him upright with my empty hand.

"Maddison, this season, we're going all the way. Don't you agree?" he drunkenly asks.

"Definitely," I quickly state with a nod.

The last thing I want to talk about right now is hockey, and I don't want this guy around Logan any longer than he already has been.

"You should go talk to Patrick about this season." I motion in the direction of the beer pong table.

"Patty!" the drunk guy exclaims as I help him go on his way.

Looking back at Logan, I shake my head.

"So, Maddison, huh? How many names do you have?"

"Too many," I explain. "Maddison is my last name."

"Oh. Then, where does the 'J' in EJ come from?" She cocks her head to the side.

"My middle name is James. Eli James. EJ for short," I try to explain my family's nickname.

"Got it."

"So, what's it going to be then?"

"Huh?" She gives me a questioning look.

"Which name are you gonna pick? There are plenty of options." I scratch my brow with my thumb before putting my hands in my pockets. Why do I feel nervous? I already know where this is going.

Everyone chooses to call me Maddison. Maybe it rolls off the tongue better, I don't know. She might choose EJ since she's heard

Marc refer to me that way already. That might be a little weird, though, since only my parents and brother call me EJ.

"Hmm, I think I'll go with Eli," she says.

"Really?" I ask, surprised. "Why, Eli?"

"Because that's what you introduced yourself to me as. So, that's what I'm going to call you." She shyly smiles up at me.

My body instantly relaxes. I've noticed she's had that effect on me so far. I didn't expect her to say that, and I didn't expect her to be so cool. Something about her just puts me at ease.

"Have you seen Marc around?" Logan asks, changing the subject.

"Not for a couple of hours. I think he went to find his ex."

She rolls her eyes. Glad to see we are on the same page about that.

Logan's head is on a swivel, looking around the room.

"Do you want help finding him?" I ask.

She shakes her head. "No, I'm good. I don't want to keep you." She nods towards the stairs with a bit of a questioning look in her eye.

Is she insinuating that there's a girl who is waiting for me upstairs? Would that bother her?

I decide to ease her mind just in case. "Just going to bed."

Her shoulders seem to relax a bit. Or I could just be imagining it. "Well then, I hope you sleep well, Eli." She gives me a sweet smile. "I'm gonna go find Marc so we can head back to the dorms."

And with that, she turns to leave. As I start up the stairs, I turn around to look back at her, but she's nowhere to be seen. I take another sip of the water gave me. The rim still tastes like vanilla, and it's my new favorite flavor.

Chapter 11

Logan

Making my way through the house, I continue to search for Marc. I haven't seen him for most of the night, and I need to find him so we can get back to the dorms. Ali is nowhere to be found, which I'm assuming is because she's off with Cam somewhere. I didn't intend to stay here so late, but I actually had a really good time. This night was the most fun I've had in a while.

Continuing through the house in search of my friend, my mind wanders back to Eli. He's obviously gorgeous, charming as hell and, if I'm being honest, he's been stuck in my head most of the night. Typically, I wouldn't think twice about a cute guy I randomly met, especially right now when I just want to focus on me, but between the things Marc has told me and the impression he gave me tonight, I find myself intrigued and confused about him.

After an unsuccessful forty-five minutes of looking for Marc, I start to get a bit frustrated at myself for staying so late with no way to get home, regardless of the fun I had. The house is beginning to clear out, but I wouldn't trust a ride from someone after most the party guests have been drinking all night. Asking for directions would also be pointless. This campus is enormous and I had a hard enough time finding my dorm in broad daylight, let alone trying to find it in the middle of the night with directions I received from a drunken stranger.

As I turn the corner to check a room I've already searched three times, a guy stumbles into me, spilling his beer down the front of my shirt. I close my eyes, hoping it's my imagination, and that did not just really happen.

"That's just great," I sigh, the cold moisture seeping through the fabric.

"Oops!" he drunkenly laughs before continuing to stumble through the house.

Turning on my heel, I head straight towards the kitchen to clean myself off. I reek of beer, regardless of the fact I didn't drink any, and my clothes are becoming sticky. I grab the paper towels next to the sink and dampen one under the faucet, but while I try to wipe my shirt clean, I'm distracted when I hear Eli's name.

"You know how Maddison is."

I look over and see a blonde talking to two of her friends. She's leaning over the counter, and it causes her chest to stick out and appear larger than it already is.

"When has that boy ever turned down sex? Especially from you, Alyssa," one of them asks her.

"I know, but he's already in his room," she whines, causing her to sound desperate as she explains him to her friends. "He doesn't let anyone in there. I've been hooking up with him for years, and I've never slept in the same bed as him, let alone even *been* in that room." She has her heels in her hand, and the mascara on her eyes has made its way underneath them, making her drunken state even more noticeable.

"Whatever, it's just the first weekend of the year. It's not like we don't have the rest of the school year to hook up," Alyssa says, trying to convince herself that she doesn't care while standing up straight and tugging at her dress.

He's never spent the night with a girl? That does seem odd. What does he do—just has sex with them and leaves? Not to mention it's not even in his own room. The conversation I just overheard lines up with the impression I had of Eli before I met him, but it doesn't align with the guy I met tonight. Maybe that's part of his game; he knows how to use his charm to convince you he's someone who he's not.

Just as I finish eavesdropping and wiping at my shirt, an arm swings around my shoulders. Twisting my head to the side, I find

Patrick's face so close to mine that I can smell the beer wafting on his breath.

"Hey Cali, I've been looking for you," he drunkenly slurs, licking his lips.

"Well, here I am," I plainly state as I continue to try and clean my clothes.

Thanks to the hours we spent playing beer pong, I'm not as alarmed by him as I was when we initially met in the kitchen at the beginning of the night. Regardless of that, I remember Marc's warning about him.

"Whatcha up to?" he asks, his gaze wandering down to my shirt. Or my chest, I can't tell.

"Just looking for Marc. Have you seen him?"

"Nope, not for a while. I can help you look, though," he offers with his arm still draped over me.

As much as I don't want to ask for his help, I might need it. Ali is nowhere to be found, and Marc is my only way of getting back to my dorm tonight. He's the only person I trust to walk with me. Patrick lives here, so he knows this house and where I might be able to find him.

"Actually, that would be great."

A smile creeps across his lips. "Have you tried upstairs?"

"Not yet." I shrug his arm off my shoulders.

In the belief that Patrick knows this house better than me, I follow him upstairs in search for Marc. I've already scoured the downstairs numerous times, but I've avoided looking up here in the fear I would walk in on someone hooking up, or worse, walk in on Eli hooking up with someone.

When we reach the top of the stairs, Patrick turns to me and says, "You know what, it's getting late. Why don't you just crash in my room for the night, and you can find Marc in the morning." He has a sneaky smile on his lips as he nods in the direction of what I assume is his bedroom.

I stay tight to the railing as he leans in closer. I can now tell just how drunk he is by him slightly falling into me. I guess losing six games of beer pong will do that to you.

"That's okay. Thank you, though. I'm just going to find my way back to the dorms," I say while tightening my grip on the rail.

"C'mon Cali, it'll be fun. Just stay with me," he repeats, running his fingers down my arm before grabbing ahold of my elbow.

Marc's warning about him starts to flash through my mind like sirens going off. My heart begins to thump against my chest, and my knuckles are turning white thanks to the tight grip I have on the stair railing.

"Patrick." I keep my tone stern but even. "I said no, thank you," hoping I can break through his drunken state of mind and make him understand.

I try to yank my arm away from him, but his grip on me has gotten even tighter.

"I said, stay with me. You'll have a good time, and I'm not going to take no for an answer." He looks me dead in the eyes with a blank expression as if he's not even there.

I think the fuck not.

I look around the hallway, but no one is around, and I'm scared for myself at this moment. Typically, I can handle myself, but Patrick is a big guy and much stronger than me. If he doesn't leave me alone, I can't protect myself.

"Get the fuck away from her!" someone yells from down the hall.

I instantly recognize him by the sound of his voice and when I turn his way, the sleeve of tattoos down his arm is the first thing to catch my eye. Eli stands in his doorway, his size taking up most of the threshold. He doesn't have a shirt on and is only wearing a pair of boxer briefs. If I wasn't so scared, I would allow myself to admire his body a little longer, but right now, I'm just grateful for his timing.

Chapter 12

Eli

I lie in bed, trying to fall asleep to no avail. It's getting quieter, meaning the house is beginning to clear out, but my mind continues to wander back to Logan as I lick my lips and taste the vanilla that still lingers there from her drink. God, I wish she wasn't Marc's friend.

As I'm lost in my thoughts, voices echo right outside my door—both of which I recognize.

"C'mon Cali, it'll be fun. Just stay with me," I hear Patrick say to who I assume is Logan judging from the ridiculous nickname he's given her.

Is she going to stay with him? Does she want to?

"Patrick. I said, no, thank you." She answers my question, and a wave of relief washes over me until I recognize the edge in her voice. She sounds panicked. She sounds like she might need help.

I jump out of bed as I hear him tell her, "I said, stay with me. You'll have a good time, and I'm not going to take no for an answer."

A knot instantly forms in my stomach, knowing that she might be in danger. As soon as I swing my bedroom door open, the first thing I see is the grip Patrick has on her arm, and her white knuckles holding onto the stair railing for dear life. She's scared.

"Get the fuck away from her!" I yell.

Patrick turns my way, Logan too, but he doesn't let go of her.

"Get the fuck away from her," I warn once again as I stalk towards them. My eyes narrow as I stare at Patrick, my expression flooded with anger. I want to kill the bastard, and tonight he's finally given me a reason to lay hands on him.

"Fuck off, Maddison," Patrick slurs. "I never get in the way with the chicks you're fucking."

Bile rises in my throat for more than one reason. There's no way in hell anything was willingly going to happen between Logan and Patrick tonight.

"What the fuck did you just say?" I grab him by the collar of his shirt and pin him to the wall, his feet dangling a few inches from the floor. "Did you just say you were going to fuck her? Because what I heard was her telling you no."

Patrick doesn't answer, mostly because he can't. I have him pinned to the wall so firmly that his face is turning red, and his eyes are wide with fear.

Good. He needs to learn he can't mess with her. I mean, she's Marc's best friend, and he would kill me if I let anything happen to her. Which is the only reason I'm out in the hallway about to start a fight wearing only my boxer briefs. That and, if I'm being honest with myself, I couldn't stand the thought of someone hurting her.

Not that I would ever be okay with any woman feeling scared or pressured but knowing that Logan was in that position makes me sick.

"Logan, go in my room and close the door," I forcefully tell her without turning to face her as I continue to stare Patrick down.

As soon as I hear my door close, indicating she's safe inside, I pull his collar back before once again slamming him into the wall. "Stay the fuck away from her," I sternly warn while staring him in the eyes. The anger pulses through me, my nostrils flaring on my exhale as I drop his shirt.

Patrick slumps to the floor. "What the fuck, man? She's just some random chick. Calm the fuck down!" he says with panic in his voice and fear in his eyes as he grasps at his throat.

That pisses me off even more, and I rethink if I should connect my fist to his jaw, but decide for now to just leave him be. I stand over him, waiting for him to get up or try to come at me, just wanting another reason to beat the shit out of him. But he doesn't try anything, so I turn back to my room and slam the door behind me.

Chapter 13

Eli

Once I shut the door, I turn and find Logan standing in the middle of my room with her arms crossed, her eyes wide, and her breathing ragged. She looks a bit frightened at the moment, understandably so. Not sure if she's scared of Patrick or me, I cross the room to stand in front of her, hoping I can bring her some comfort.

"Hey, you okay?" I softly ask, bending my head down, and causing my eyes to be level with hers while placing my hand on her arm. My shoulders instantly relax as soon as I touch her. I didn't realize how tense I was from the adrenaline still coursing through me.

She gasps and quickly flinches, but then seems to calm when she remembers it's me and not Patrick touching her. "Yeah, I'm okay." She exhales as her shoulders settle. "Thank you. I'm sorry you had to do that. I know he's your friend."

"Oh, no. Fuck that guy." I shake my head. "He just...He lives here, and we play on the same team, but we're not friends. He's kind of the worst."

She chuckles and uncrosses her arms, seeming to feel more comfortable now that she's not in any danger. "Well, thank you again. I need to go back to my dorm and get some sleep." She points towards the door. "Have you seen Marc?"

"I haven't. I have a feeling he probably went home with Lauren." I roll my eyes, and she does the same, which causes me to smile. "Do you want me to walk you back?"

Logan's gaze takes a long lingering wander down my almost fully bare body. "No," she sighs. "But thank you for offering. You were sleeping, and you've done enough for me tonight already. I can figure it out from here." She makes a move towards the door, but I step in front of her, stopping her in her tracks.

"I wasn't asleep, and I can't let you walk back to your dorm alone right now. It's the middle of the night, and that's a thirty-minute walk. Not to mention it's pitch-black outside. Would you even know your way back?" I doubt she would since she just moved here, and this campus is huge.

She looks defeated as her shoulders sag and she lifts her eyes towards the ceiling. "No, probably not. But I don't know what else to do. Everyone is drunk and, not to be rude, but your couches are gross, and I refuse to sleep on one of them."

That makes me laugh because she's right, but I would also never allow her to sleep on one. Especially with how many people usually end up drunkenly crashing downstairs after every party.

"Sleep in here," I say before my mind catches up to my mouth.

I've never let anyone sleep in my bed before, and now I'm suddenly aware that this girl is standing in the middle of my room when no one is usually allowed in here. I often feel a rush of anxiety when someone tries to intrude on this space. It's my one place on campus where I can be myself and not deal with the outside pressure from everyone else, but with her here, I feel an overwhelming calm in my room. And I suddenly don't want her to leave.

"I mean, only if you feel comfortable. You can have the bed, of course. I'll sleep on the floor," I add.

She looks around the room, confused. "But I thought no one was allowed in here?"

"Where did you hear that?"

She blushes. "I overheard a girl talking about it with her friends downstairs." She quickly glances away, seeming to be embarrassed for eavesdropping.

Her rosy cheeks make me laugh. "Well, whoever she was, she's right. Usually, that's the case, but you're Marc's friend, and he would kill me if I let you walk back to the dorms right now." I lie to her about my real reason for wanting her to stay.

"Are you sure? I don't want to invade your space."

"Yes, I'm sure. It's no big deal," I respond, hoping she will indeed stay and invade my space.

After taking a moment to think about her decision, she responds. "Okay... I appreciate it, Eli. Thank you." She gives me a grateful smile.

Hearing my name coming off her lips sounds so good that at this point, I think I would do just about anything to hear her say it again.

Chapter 14

Logan

We stand in the center of his room, awkwardly glancing at each other, unsure of where to go from here. I pull my gaze away from him, noticing how clean his place is. Judging from the state of the rest of the house, I did not expect his room to be this tidy. His bed is large and pushed up against the back wall, centered under the window. There's a bookshelf to the left filled with trophies and awards, and his desk is on the right wall with his laptop sitting open alongside a framed picture of him, Marc, and who I assume are their parents. His walls are mostly clear besides a calendar above his desk, filled with writing, and a mirror on the back of his door.

Once I've thoroughly analyzed his space, my eyes wander back to his body. I'm reminded that he's shirtless as my stare lingers on his muscular chest before it makes its way down his tattooed arm. Now that he's standing so close, I can make out more of the details. They're all in black ink, which I find beautiful and straightforward. A large and sprawling oak tree takes up most of his upper arm. Intertwined underneath is a rose, but it's not just any rose. It looks vaguely familiar, but I can't place where I know it from. Next to the rose is delicate and graceful handwriting. I think it's a name. Elizabeth, maybe. Is that a girlfriend? Or an ex? Perhaps *she's* the reason he doesn't sleep next to anyone? Regardless, I feel incredibly uncomfortable looking at it, so I peel my eyes away before I finish analyzing the rest of his tattoos.

Eli senses this and appears to feel as uncomfortable as I do at this moment. He uses his other arm to hold onto his tattooed one, covering the rose and the name with his hand. He scratches at his brow and says, "Um...so. Go ahead and take the bed," while pointing in that direction. "Also, I have training early in the morning, so you might hear my alarm go off, but I'll be as quiet as possible," he explains while making himself a makeshift bed on the floor with only a single pillow and blanket.

"Let me sleep on the floor," I offer. "Especially if you have to get up early. You shouldn't have to sleep on the floor. This is *your* room."

"I would never let you sleep on the floor," he tells me, shaking his head and giving me a questioning glance. His eyes are flooded with sincerity.

His gaze starts to wander my body, warming me from the inside. This feels nothing like when Patrick was eyeing me earlier in the kitchen. This is welcome.

"What happened to your shirt?" Eli asks while pointing to my soaked top.

I had almost forgotten that I'm covered in beer. "Some drunk guy spilled his drink on me." I awkwardly shrug.

"Three for three. You're a clumsy one, Logan." He gives me a playful smirk.

The way he says my name sounds like honey coming off his tongue. It's slow and deep and sounds better than when anyone else has ever said it.

"This time wasn't my fault." I hold my hands up in defense. "And one could argue that you were to blame for the other two."

"Oh, no, no, no! I don't think so!" He shakes his head at me. "You just can't seem to keep ahold of your drink when you're around me," he teases, both of us laughing.

A sudden rush of guilt takes over when I remember I'm flirting with Marc's brother. I avert my eyes from his and wipe the smile off my face.

He seems to notice my regret. "Um...let me grab you something to sleep in. You can't wear that to bed."

"That's okay, I'm fine."

"Logan," he interjects, "don't be stubborn. No reason to be uncomfortable all night wearing jeans and a wet shirt."

He sounds like Marc, and I begin to wonder what Marc has told him about me. Does he know about my parents? Does he know about my ex? I suddenly feel less comfortable around him, knowing that he might know more about me than I do of him.

Eli walks over to his closet, pulling out a T-shirt and handing it to me. I hold it up, noting just how large it is. It's going to be a dress on me, which is probably why he didn't offer me any pants. The shirt is maroon with yellow writing on the front that says, 'The University of Minnesota Hockey.' I flip it over to see his last name towards the top, printed in large font, and underneath is a number thirteen.

"Thirteen, huh?" I question.

"Yeah, it's my lucky number."

My eyes widen with surprise, a shy smile covering my lips. "Mine too."

He returns the grin while continuing to maintain his eye contact with me. His eyes are beautiful, and I find myself not wanting to go to sleep so I can continue to stare at them all night.

After a beat, he scratches his brow with his thumb, seeming nervous. "Sorry, I'll um...I'll turn around so you can get changed," he says as he turns to face the wall.

It causes my smile to grow. Eli seems like such a gentleman. I don't see the guy that I've heard all the stories about. He may typically be an asshole, and he not let many people close, but he hasn't treated me in a way that would make me believe either of those things are true.

Undressing myself, leaving on only my underwear, I fold my clothes in a neat pile. He seems to keep his room tidy, and I don't want to add any mess. I throw his shirt on to cover my naked body, and I was right; it comes down to my mid-thigh and is loose on me.

I could tell Eli was a tall and muscular guy, but the size of his shirt confirms it.

"All good, thanks," I tell him, indicating that I've finished changing.

He turns around, eyeing my pile of folded clothes first. Realizing that I left my bra on top, my eyes widen in embarrassment. Why did I do that? He pulls his stare from my pile of clothes to look at me. His eyes drag up my body from my legs, lingering a beat on my chest, and finally to my face. I can see his pupils dilate from here, his mouth slightly parted. Suddenly, I feel my cheeks warm.

At this moment, I become hyper-aware that I'm standing here in nothing but his T-shirt and my underwear, while tight black boxer briefs are the only thing that covers his chiseled body. I've never felt my body being pulled like a magnet to someone else's before, but I'm drawn to him. I had never felt this type of attraction even towards Zac, and I've only known Eli for a matter of hours. My eyes widen as I gulp, remembering that this beautiful boy is my best friend's brother. Turning my head away from him, I ignore my inappropriate thoughts as I climb into his bed, covering my body with his blankets like a shield to keep me away from him.

Chapter 15

Eli

I can't believe she's in my bed right now. I can't believe I allowed anyone to be in my bed. I lie on the floor with only my pillow and blanket, doubtful that I'll get any sleep down here, but I honestly don't care. The thought of her wandering around campus alone in the dark is enough to make me want to sleep on the floor for the rest of the school year if it means she will be safe.

I've been lying here for at least thirty minutes lost in my thoughts. Usually, my mind is racing with anxiety and unanswered questions about my future, but tonight all I can think about is the girl lying in my bed. The way she looked in my shirt is like something I've never seen before. She looked perfect, and I can't seem to get the image of her in my clothes out of my head, but then I'm not sure that I want to. Glancing at the clock on my nightstand, it reads 3:35 in the morning, and I need to be up at 7:00 for training. I turn over and close my eyes again, hoping for at least an hour or two of sleep.

She must notice my restlessness because I hear her whisper, "Eli, are you still awake?"

I try to sit up and look at her, but my room is pitch black. "Yeah, are you okay?" I whisper back to her, hoping she's not having trouble falling asleep.

"Yeah. I just woke up and saw you moving around, that's all."

I place my head back down on my pillow, relieved that she's alright.

"You don't have to, but you can sleep up here if you want," she sweetly offers, continuing in a hushed voice. "I feel bad that you're down there."

I've never slept in the same bed as a girl before. I've never wanted someone else to witness my unrest as I toss and turn all night. I've never trusted someone to be vulnerable enough to sleep next to them. As I contemplate what I should do, my body begins to pull itself off the floor before my mind has fully decided.

"Are you sure?" I ask with a shaky voice, sitting up partway.

"Yes."

I get up off the floor and grab my pillow, walking softly towards the other side of the bed, trying to be as quiet as I can, hoping that Logan can fall back to sleep quickly. Pulling the covers back slightly, I'm reminded that neither of us is wearing much. I slide into the bed, being careful not to touch her. As much as I want to feel the warmth of her body against mine, I'd rather her feel safe and comfortable with me.

I lie on my back with my head on my pillow and my eyes facing the ceiling, my arms down at my sides. Logan is sleeping on her side with her back facing me and her legs pulled up to her chest, making herself as small as possible, and I hope it's not because she feels weird with me being next to her.

As if she could hear my thoughts, Logan rolls over and lies on her back as well. She extends her legs down and drapes her left arm over her stomach as her arm closest to me lies flat on the bed by her side. I smile to myself, sensing the ease she feels.

My mind is racing, knowing that she's so close to me. After about ten minutes, I hear the steady rhythm of her breathing, indicating that she's fallen back asleep. A smile creeps across my lips at the sound. I've never cared much about making sure someone else feels comfortable, but with this girl I met only hours ago, I want nothing more than for her to feel that way with me. I think back to what Marc said about her dealing with a lot in life already, and I want her to feel cared for. I want her to feel protected.

I keep my distance remembering Marc's request to stay away from her, even though I can feel my body pulling itself towards hers. I stay on my side of the bed, though I can sense her hand only inches from mine. I just want to feel her and the calmness she brings me. Holding my breath, I begin to inch my hand towards hers, moving slowly not to wake her. Once our hands make contact, my pinkie just barely grazing hers, I let out a sigh, close my eyes, and instantly feel relaxed and content. So much so that I fall asleep right away.

When I wake up to my alarm only a few hours later, I look to her side of the bed and around my room, but she's nowhere to be found. My shirt is folded and placed on the pillow that she was using, and they both smell like vanilla. I don't know when she left, but I do know that that was the best night's sleep that I've had in weeks.

Chapter 16

Logan

I wake up the next morning to a text from Marc, apologizing for having disappeared and asking me where I am. It's a quarter to seven when I text him back to say I'm still at the house where the party was held. He offers to pick me up, so I quietly change out of Eli's shirt and back into my clothes before I quickly make my way downstairs, ensuring that Marc won't find me in his brother's bed. I don't know how Marc would feel knowing I spent the night with Eli, it's not like anything happened, but it's not worth adding that complication into our friendship.

Getting into Marc's car at seven o' clock on the dot, I notice that he's still wearing the same clothes from the night before.

"Soooo," I begin to tease him. "Where did you end up last night?" I question, even though I already know the answer.

"Yeah, I know I'm an idiot. But I'm too hungover to hear about it right now."

"Okay, okay. I won't say too much, but I will remind you that you deserve to be treated better than the way Lauren treated you." I put my hands up in surrender as he shoots me a sideways glance. "Okay, that's all. Promise."

He chuckles. "Anyway, I am sorry for bailing on you last night. I shouldn't have left you alone without a way to get home."

I shake my head, casually brushing his comment away. I don't want him to feel bad, and if I'm being honest, when I think about where I slept, I didn't mind not being able to make it home last night.

"So, did you have to crash on one of those nasty couches?" he asks laughingly.

I chuckle awkwardly, not sure if I should tell him the truth. It's going to sound worse than it actually was. Instead, I decide only to answer the question he asked me and not elaborate. "No way. Those things are disgusting."

Thankfully, he seems too hungover to ask more probing questions about my night. The drive back to the dorms is quick, and we both stay silent for most of the ride.

When I get back to my room, I change into pajamas and climb into my bed, feeling the need for more than the few hours of sleep I got. Before I doze off, my mind drifts back to Eli and wonder if he woke up in time for his practice. He barely got any sleep. I hope he's doing okay. I shake my head, annoyed at myself for worrying about a boy that I don't even know. I need to focus on me, and school, and the sleep I need to catch up on before Monday. So, I turn off my brain and close my eyes.

The rest of the weekend goes by quickly. Ali is vague about her hookup with Cam but guarantees me it was a one-time thing and that next weekend it would be someone new. She asks if anything exciting happened to me that night, and I tell her no. She and Marc are awkward towards each other anytime they both end up in my room at the same time. Marc and I go over our class schedules, which line up perfectly with one another's except for the creative writing elective I added, just for fun. Marc invites me to go back to Eli's house to hang out, but I decline, knowing its safer to keep my distance. I just don't think Marc would approve of the way I've been thinking about his brother.

Before I know it, it's Monday afternoon and I'm almost finished with my first day of classes. The only one left is my creative writing elective, which I've been looking forward to all day. I walk in to find a large lecture hall that's still mostly empty. Of the people here, I don't recognize anyone from my other classes, which doesn't surprise me. Not many grad students would elect to take an undergrad class just for fun.

I make my way towards the front and sit in the third row. I'm excited to be here, but not enough to sit in the very front and risk being called on to answer a question. After about fifteen minutes, a professor walks into a now mostly filled lecture hall. He looks to be in his mid-thirties and is dressed casually in a T-shirt and jeans. He places his backpack on the desk and bends down to re-tie his sneaker. I can already tell just from his demeanor, that this class will be laid back, which is a welcome change from my rigorous grad school schedule.

"Alright, everybody," he booms from the front of the class. "Take a seat if you haven't already. My name is Professor Kenneth Brown, but for the love of god, just call me Kenny." A laugh erupts from the group of students.

"This is your creative writing elective. I'm assuming if you're here, it's because you didn't get into any of the pottery-making classes or the ones where you get to take pictures all day." He earns another small chuckle from the crowd. "I don't believe in grading creative papers on a traditional scale. If you turn in your work on time, with the correct subject matter, and it's grammatically legible, you'll pass. If you don't, you'll fail. Pretty simple."

He walks to the first row of students and hands one of them a piece of paper. "That's it for today, but before you go, make sure you sign in next to your name on the log sheet. It's in alphabetical order, so it should be easy to find your name. Grab a syllabus on your way out, and I'll see you all next Monday." He heads back to his desk and places a stack of syllabi on it. Kenny relaxes back in his chair, kicking his feet up on the desk as he waits for the class to sign in and leave.

I remember this about my undergrad classes. We usually got dismissed quickly on the first day. So far, grad school classes have been diving in right away, so I'm thankful for an early release after a long day.

Sitting up close to the front has its perks as the roll sheet reaches me reasonably quickly. I scan through the names until I find Leo. I grab my pen to sign, but before I can, my eyes wander to the name directly below mine.

Maddison.

Chapter 17

Eli

I make my way to my last class of the day, creative writing. I had to take one elective this semester to graduate next, and this was the only one that fit in with my practice schedule. I'm dreading it.

Walking in with only two minutes left until class starts, I spot an empty chair towards the back of the mostly full lecture hall and take a seat. The professor enters and looks to be about ten years older than me. He explains how the class is going to work, and thankfully it seems pretty easy to pass. I'm not one to be creative, and writing is not my specialty, so the easier it is to get through this class, the better.

Thankfully this week's class only lasts for about five minutes. I just have to wait for the log sheet to make its way to the back row so I can get out of here. At least now I have about an hour to kill before training. It's just a weight-lifting session, but still, it's important. I need to build as much muscle as I can before the season starts, and I've been working towards it all summer.

Slumping back in my chair, my eyes wander the room until they land on a girl with dark red hair towards the front of the class. I perk up, recognizing her instantly. She signs the log and then begins to look around the room until her green eyes lock with mine, a sweet smile on her lips. She offers me a small wave, and I do the same in return. She must've seen my name on the sheet because I could tell she was looking for me. Suddenly this class just became a lot more interesting.

Logan stands and heads towards the exit after grabbing a syllabus from the professor's desk. I'm still sitting here waiting for that damn log sheet to make its way back to me, and for the first time in my college career, I'm wishing I would've sat towards the front so I would've gotten out of here a lot sooner.

She's almost to the exit. I say a quiet "fuck it" under my breath as I decide to get up and follow her out. Before I leave, I stop by the fourth row of seats where the log sheet currently is and snatch it from a kid that looks so small I'm assuming he's a first-year. He seems scared as he offers me his pen to initial next to my name.

I swing by the desk where Professor Brown is chuckling and shaking his head at me as I give him a shrug and a sly smile, grabbing a syllabus from his desk. I rush out the door, spotting Logan ten yards away, about to cross the street.

"Logan!" I yell to stop her. God, do I sound desperate or what?

She turns around and smiles when she recognizes it's me. "Hi. What's up?"

I'm out of breath, not because I just chased her down, but because of how she looks right now. She's wearing a dark green sweater that hangs off her shoulders, and the green causes her red hair to appear even more vibrant. Her jeans and shoes look like the same ones she was wearing at my house the other night, and her hair is up in a high ponytail that perfectly shows off her face, though a few pieces have fallen down around her eyes.

"So, creative writing..." I begin, trusting my brain will find a way to form a sentence. "Why are you taking an undergrad class if you don't have to?"

She shrugs. "I thought it would be something fun to do. So far, it seems a little more casual than my grad school classes." She laughs under her breath, and I do the same, mostly from nerves.

I stand in front of her awkwardly, not knowing what else to say. I've never been this lost for words around a girl before, and I don't understand why I can't seem to get my brain to think of something to spit out. Thankfully, she speaks before I have a chance to.

"Thanks again for letting me crash at your place the other night."

"Of course, anytime."

"I don't plan on having to do it again," she tells me as my chest stings. "I mean, I'm just not really into parties, and I went to that one because Marc begged me to go. But I don't think it's going to become a regular thing," she adds, trying to soften her blow but without success.

"Well, even though they're not your thing, you're welcome to come anytime," I inform her, trying to hide my disappointment.

She smiles, nods, and glances around. "Actually, I'm headed to meet up with Marc now. There's a game about to start that we've been looking forward to watching. Do you want to come?"

"Where are you meeting him?"

"Some bar on the other side of campus."

"Double G?" I ask, already knowing the answer.

"Yes, that's the one."

Checking my watch, I realize I don't have enough time to make it across campus and back in time for training, but I quickly contemplate skipping my workout just to spend more time with this girl.

I've never blown off a workout, especially this close to the beginning of the season, and especially not to hang out with a girl. I need to get my head on straight, and being around Logan is making it hard to do so.

"Sorry, I have training," I tell her, confident in my decision.

"Okay. Next time maybe?" she asks with a hint of disappointment in her voice. Enough to make me rethink my decision.

"Yeah, maybe."

"Well, good to see you, Eli." Her disappointment shifts, a smile donning her pretty face as she walks off in the opposite direction.

I love hearing her say my name. It sounds better each time.

"Yeah. You too, Logan," I add, but she's too far away to hear me.

Chapter 18

Logan

I start making my way to the main bar on campus, Gopher's Grove, but I've learned that the students here like to refer to it as Double G. I make the walk confidently, remembering the route I saw on the campus map. This weekend I spent time looking it over to better familiarize myself with my new home. I also made sure to figure out the quickest route back from the hockey house to my dorm in case I ever got stuck there again.

Double G is pretty crowded for a Monday evening. It's the first day of classes, so I would have assumed people would be studying, but instead, most everyone is out grabbing a beer. I spot Marc through the crowd sitting in the back left corner at a table for two.

He stands to greet me. "Hey!" he says while hugging me.

"Hey! How much of the game did I miss?" I ask, looking up at the closest TV.

"Still in the first quarter. Nothing too exciting yet."

"Perfect." I swing my backpack over the back of my chair, and we both take our seats.

"How was creative writing?" Marc asks while keeping his eyes glued to the game.

"Short."

"Still happy about adding it on to your grad school schedule?"

"Yeah, I think so. It's only once a week, and the professor seems chill. Plus, I think it'll be a good creative outlet for me."

He nods his head in agreement but keeps his eyes locked on the TV.

"Actually," I continue, "your brother is in my class."

My words cause him to pull his stare away from the TV and look at me. They widen, his mouth slightly gaping open from shock.

"EJ? EJ is in your creative writing class?" He begins to laugh in disbelief.

"Yeah, I was surprised too."

"He must've needed an elective to graduate, and this is probably the only one that fit into his schedule. Because, let me tell you, creative writing is *not* an EJ kind of class."

I laugh along with him but keep myself from adding onto the conversation, wanting to avoid outing myself to my best friend that I'm more than curious about his brother.

Before I have the chance to change the subject, Marc questions, "Did you talk to him?"

"Yeah, I did, actually." I quickly glance up to Marc, trying to gauge his reaction with no luck. "I invited him to come along, but he said he had practice or something." I keep my statement as casual as I can while looking down at the menu.

"He pretty much always has a practice or training of some sort. And he would never skip it just to hang out with us." He continues to look over the menu, and thankfully, he doesn't seem too bothered or concerned by my admission.

My heart sinks a bit at his words, but I'm not surprised by them. Eli seems extremely focused on his hockey career, and I doubt he would let anything disrupt that. Not that I would want to.

I think quickly about how to change the subject. I don't want Marc to assume that I only want to discuss his brother, but he continues anyway.

"I'm glad you guys have a class together. I think you'll like him when you get to know him." He pauses. "Well, if he *lets* you get to know him. He can be a hard one to crack, but don't let his tough exterior put you off, he's a good guy deep down."

Marc's response put me at ease. I know I don't need his permission to spend time with his brother, but I appreciate it. Although, I do want to tell him that I'm so confused by his description of Eli. His brother has been nothing but sweet towards me, and I haven't once seen this "tough exterior" or him being a "hard one to crack." The only time I saw any signs of this was when he grabbed Patrick, but that was only to protect me.

As I'm about to respond, the server approaches our table with a beer and an iced tea in hand. I decide to keep my inquiries about Eli to myself, and I'm thankful that the conversation has been interrupted without me having to do so.

"I assumed you weren't drinking, so I ordered you an iced tea," Marc explains.

The server sets the drinks on the table. "You assumed correctly." I smile up at my best friend.

Marc and I order a bucket of wings to share and spend the next couple of hours watching the game and enjoying each other's company. I could hang out with him all day, and we would never run out of subjects to discuss. I just ensure that for the rest of tonight, none of those subjects include Eli.

Chapter 19

Eli

Tuesday started about the same as Monday did. I woke up early to get in an hour on the rink before classes began. Tony, the maintenance guy, made me a spare key so I could come by in the mornings to skate before he runs the Zamboni over the ice for evening practice. After getting a workout in, I suffered through my classes while not really paying attention to any of my professors. The class I was dreading the most is now the only one I look forward to, but of course, that's only once a week, and now I have to wait until Monday for creative writing.

As I walk out of my final class of the day, I spot Marc leaning up against a post right outside the door. That's weird; I'm pretty sure he has his own classes right now. Noting the expression on his face, worry instantly floods me. Is everything okay? Are our parents okay? Is Logan okay? I surprise myself by internally asking that last question.

I walk up to him with confusion on my face.

"Hey," he says solemnly.

"Okay, who died?" I ask with sarcasm, trying to lighten the mood.

He doesn't respond. He just looks down towards the ground. Fuck. Someone *did* die.

"Marc, what's going on?" My heart begins to race. Something is seriously wrong right now. I can feel it in the air between us.

"It's your dad. He's...well, he's in the hospital."

"My dad?" My stomach drops and my knees begin to feel weak.

"Fuck. I mean...I mean, Jamie. Not your dad. Not *our* dad."

I haven't heard my birth father's name in years. Taking a deep breath of relief, I try to process what this means and how I feel about it. How am I supposed to feel?

"What's wrong with him? Is he going to be okay?" I ask my brother.

He looks back towards the ground. Marc has never been good at giving bad news. He's too nice to have to deliver such terrible words.

"No, EJ. I don't think he's going to be okay." He looks up at me with pity in his eyes. "His liver is failing, and by the sounds of it, he only has a couple of days left."

I look down to the same ground my brother was staring at because I can't look him in the eye. "How do you know?"

"Dad." He pauses. "He's been calling you, but I think your phone must've been on silent during class. He got ahold of me and asked me to come and find you. He needs you to call him."

Marc has always called my dad, "Dad." His own was never around because he left before Marc was even born. When our parents married, we were only three years old at the time, and mine was the only father he had ever known. I, on the other hand, have always referred to Marc's mom as Mary. It's not my mom's fault that she's no longer around, so I reserve the title of "Mom" for her.

As far as my birth father goes, he's a piece of shit and never deserved to be referred to as "Dad." He left me as soon as my mom died. When I was only six weeks old, he decided that drinking was more important to him than me, so he asked his dead wife's brother to adopt me. Twenty-two years later, and nothing has changed.

I don't know how to process this information or how I should feel about it. I've always hated the guy. He would send me a card on my birthday when he was sober enough to remember, but besides that, I've only seen him a handful of times in my life. How sad can you be that someone is dying when you never even knew them? Not to mention, the things that I did know about him I hated.

Grabbing my phone from my bag, I have five missed calls from my dad. I start dialing. As soon as I hear the tone of his voice, I head towards my car to go back to my house. I can already tell that he's going to want me to pack a bag and head home to Indiana, even though it's the last thing I want to do right now.

Chapter 20

Logan

I spot three seats together towards the front of our economics lecture. Taking the middle of the three, I place my bag on one chair and my jacket on the other to reserve them for Marc and Ali. Marc left our last class early when he got a call from his dad, but I doubt he would miss another in the first week of school. That's just not like him.

As the class is about to start, I begin to worry that something is wrong with Marc. I glance around, but he's nowhere to be found. Ali rushes through the doors, waving at me when she spots me towards the front.

"Hey, girl! Thanks for saving me a seat," she says as I pull my jacket off her reserved seat. "Where's Marcus?" She motions towards the empty chair on my other side.

"I'm not sure. It's not like him to be this late." I glance around the room again.

Quickly pulling out my phone before class begins, I find a long text waiting for me from Marc.

M: *Hey. Long story, but I'm not going to make the rest of classes today—family emergency. EJ's birth dad is in hospice care. I think we are heading back to Indiana early in the morning so that EJ can say goodbye. Is there any possible way that you could bring me our assignments when you're done with classes tonight? We are staying at our parents' place ten minutes from campus before we head home in the morning. I would really appreciate it. I don't want to fall behind on our first week, but this is a priority.*

My eyes widen as I read his text. Eli's birth dad? I had no idea he was adopted.

"Everything alright?" Ali asks with a concerned look on her face as she notices me focusing on my phone screen.

"I'm not sure." I shake my head, looking down at my phone. "Sounds like something is up with Eli's dad."

"Eli? Who is Eli?"

I look at her, confused. "Eli," I repeat again, but with no response.

"EJ?" Still nothing.

"Maddison?" I try for the third time to connect the dots for her.

"Oh! Marcus' brother."

I nod but find myself a little annoyed at her for not knowing his name. It's not her fault, though. I doubt she's had him on her mind since their first meeting the way that I have.

I quickly type my response to Marc as the professor finishes setting up his desk.

L: *Of course. I hope everything is okay. Thinking of you both. Please send me the address when you can. I'll see you tonight.*

I remember Marc telling me about his parents' house that's close to campus. His parents come up and stay on the weekends during Eli's hockey season to watch his games. I'm assuming Eli wants to be alone and that's why they're staying there tonight.

Marc responds quickly with the address, followed by, *You're the best. I owe you.* Which, of course, he does not. I would do anything for him, and at this point, I think I would do anything for his brother too.

Class begins, but I have a hard time focusing. My mind wanders off to Eli, wondering how he's doing. Does he have a good relationship with his birth father? Is he sad right now? I sit through thirty minutes of class without taking in a single word the professor says. My mind is only thinking about Eli. This is precisely what I wanted to avoid this year. I wanted to be selfish and not worry about anyone else, but right now, I don't care about myself or this class. I just care about the tall boy with brown eyes who hasn't left my mind since Friday night.

Chapter 21

Logan

The drive to Marc's parents' house isn't too long. Although, in the last couple of minutes, the weather has begun to take a drastic turn for the worse. I'm not used to these kinds of thunderstorms in California, and driving in them is scary. As I pull up, the rain has begun to beat down even harder. I open the driver's side door, and the wind is so strong that it swings the door open, almost hitting Marc's car parked next to mine. Grabbing his assignments from the passenger seat, I place them under my crewneck sweatshirt to keep them dry and make a quick dash for the house. Just as I knock on the front door, a thunderous boom erupts, and a flash of light burst through the sky.

Shit. That one felt close.

Marc answers the door, and the smile on his face quickly changes to a look of shock when he sees the state of the weather outside.

"Oh my god! Get in here." He urges me inside. "When did that start?"

"During the last few minutes of my drive." I wipe my wet shoes off on the entryway mat.

He quickly glances outside one last time before closing the front door.

I take the papers out from under my sweatshirt, wanting to give them to Marc as quickly as possible and be on my way.

"Here you go." I hand him his assignments, which had gotten a little damp. "Sorry. I tried to keep them dry."

"Don't even worry about it. I just appreciate you bringing them all the way over here," he says as he places them down on the entryway table.

"Of course." I pause for a moment to look around the foyer of his parents' home. "This house is so nice."

"Yeah, it's worked out great for my parents to have a place to stay when they visit."

"Have you or your brother ever lived here?"

He shakes his head. "No, we both wanted to have the college experience of living on campus, but it's nice to come out here when either of us needs a night away...like tonight." He nods his head towards the living room where I assume Eli is.

"How's he doing?" I ask, referring to his brother.

He shrugs. "He's okay, I think. To be honest, I don't really know. He hasn't said much about it."

I nod my head in response, and we both stay silent for a moment, unsure of what to say next.

"Okay, well, I'm gonna take off." I move to hug him goodbye, but he stops me.

"What? No. No way. I can't let you drive right now." He furrows his brow. "Come hang out, at least until the storm passes."

Marc starts walking towards the living room, expecting me to follow, but I don't want Eli to see me right now. I shouldn't be here. This is a very personal time, I would know, and I doubt he wants some random girl in his space.

I try to get Marc's attention. "Wait, Marc. No, no—no," I say in a whisper, but my hushed voice is too quiet for him to hear.

"Marcus!"

He turns around with a questioning look on his face. "What's wrong?"

"I just...I don't think I should be here. Your brother doesn't need some stranger hanging around right now."

He rolls his eyes at me, but lightly laughs. "You're not just some stranger. Come on, just hang out until the storm passes. It'll be fine."

He continues to the living room as I reluctantly follow behind.

Chapter 22

Eli

We came to my parents' house to get away from everyone back at the hockey house. I didn't feel like seeing anyone tonight, but as soon as Logan walks into the living room, I seemed to have changed my mind.

She looks great, per usual. Her hair is up in a messy bun on top of her head, and the vibrant red is a bit darker from the rain outside. She's wearing a plain gray sweatshirt that looks to be two sizes too big on her and a pair of tight black pants. They're the kind that girls usually wear to do yoga. It's the first time I've seen her wear anything tight, and they show off her toned legs perfectly, not to mention her ass. No matter how shitty of a day I just had, I'm happy to see her.

"EJ, you remember Logan from the party the other night?" Marc asks, walking into the living room with Logan following behind. He takes a seat on the chair across from me.

Do I remember? I haven't stopped thinking about her.

"Yeah. Hey," I quickly say.

"Hey," she quietly responds.

"Oh, wait. You guys have a class together too. I forgot."

Logan stays standing awkwardly in the entryway of the living room.

"You can sit down." Marc laughs while pointing to the other end of the couch I'm sitting on. "Do you want anything to drink?" He stands, making his way towards the kitchen.

"Maybe just water," she meekly responds before taking a seat on the couch.

There's a good three feet between us, but I already feel better having her near me.

Once Marc is out of earshot, I turn my head slightly to her. "Hi," I say again, this time with a little more warmth in my voice.

"Hi." She smiles back at me as her shoulders relax. Her voice is much lower than usual. I can tell she's trying to be cautious around me. "How are you?" she asks, just as Marc comes back into the room.

He sets a bottle of water in front of her. He then places one in front of me, next to my whiskey glass, that I have yet to decide if I'm going to drink. If I were ever going to use alcohol as a distraction, tonight would be the night.

"I'm fine," I snap. I want to talk to Logan, but I don't want Marc to notice how comfortable I am around her already.

The room has fallen silent because of my short response. Marc retakes his seat, all three of us avoiding eye contact with one another. I decide to break the tension since I'm the one who caused it in the first place.

"I don't know. I don't know how I'm doing." I glance up at Logan. "I don't know how I'm supposed to feel."

She nods, seeming to understand me though I'm making no sense.

My gaze shifts over to Marc, but he's still looking down at the ground, unsure of what to say. Not that I blame him; this is a life event that neither of us has navigated before. When I look back to Logan, her green eyes are full of compassion and understanding, unwavering as she keeps her focus on me. She doesn't seem to be fazed by the weight of this conversation at all.

"Our parents want me to go back to Indiana to say my final goodbyes to my birth father." I glance down to the floor quickly. "What do *you* think I should do?" Looking up, my eyes lock on Logan so that she knows it's her advice I'm asking for.

Logan pauses, stunned that I would want her input. Her mouth slightly parts as she turns to Marc, and he seems just as surprised that I'm opening up to her this way. He gives her a meaningful glance as they have a quick conversation without using words.

She takes a deep breath, shifting her attention back to me. "I don't know your situation, but if it were me, and I had the chance to go back in time and say goodbye to my father, I would do it in a heartbeat."

My mouth gapes open in shock. Her father? I look at Marc, a knowing smile covering his lips. He quietly stands up and leaves the room, giving her and I space to talk alone. He had to have known this about her past. Is that why he asked her to come over? She could've easily emailed his assignments to him.

Turning back to Logan, she averts her eyes from mine.

"How did he pass away?" I softly ask her.

"He had a heart attack during my senior year of high school. I was in class when it happened, so I didn't get a chance to say goodbye." She finally looks up at me, her strength evident through her eyes.

Suddenly, I feel a deeper connection to this girl than I already had. She has a depth to her that I knew was there, but I didn't know why. Marc has mentioned multiple times that she has had a hard couple of years, but for some reason this feels like just the tip of the iceberg.

"I'm sorry."

"It's okay. I'm fine," she brushes it off.

I laugh to myself at her toughness. "Yeah. I know you are."

A few moments of silence fall between us before I ask again, "So, you think I should go then?"

She shrugs. "I'm not sure, Eli. I know what I would do, but I don't know your history with him."

I take another deep breath. "Do you want to know?"

She looks at me, surprised that I've offered this information to her. "Only if you want to share. I don't want you to feel pressured to tell me anything that you don't want to."

"I don't feel any pressure," I assure her by shaking my head, grateful for her thoughtful response.

She shoots me the most genuine smile. Her dimples are as clear as day as she waits intently for my words.

"As you've learned, my dad is not my birth father. He's actually my mom's brother...which technically makes him my uncle, but he will always be my dad. My mom died during childbirth with me. My birth father, Jamie, was married to my mom, and from the stories I've heard over the years, he was a pretty good guy. But, once my mom died, and he was left alone with me, he couldn't handle it, I guess. So, he started drinking, and over time it consumed him. My dad tried to help by getting him into rehab, but Jamie didn't want to go. Instead, Jamie asked my dad to adopt me because he couldn't handle the responsibility anymore."

I take a moment to catch my breath after word-vomiting all over the place. I've never told this story before, but it felt good as the words came off my tongue. I look to Logan, her mouth parted and her eyes wide. Not with judgment or with pity. I think she's just trying to process everything I just told her.

I eagerly wait for her response, but instead of hearing words, I feel her arms wrap around my neck. I didn't expect her to hug me, but the warmth of her cheek pressed up against mine instantly settles my nerves over telling her my story. Snaking my arms around her back, I close my eyes. Her skin smells like vanilla, and her body fits perfectly in mine.

"You didn't have to tell me all that," she whispers in my ear as we continue to embrace.

"I wanted to," I assure her as her lips form a smile against the skin of my neck.

She pulls away but continues to keep her eyes on me. Logan sits in the space that was previously empty between us, with her legs crossed underneath her. Her arm casually drapes over her leg, but her hand is resting on my thigh. She seems even more comfortable around me now than she did before.

"I think you should go to Indiana," she tells me with confidence.

"Really? Even after everything I just told you?"

"Especially after that. But I don't think you should go for Jamie. I think you should go for you."

I look at her, confused.

"It could be a good opportunity to let go of some of your anger towards him. Don't get me wrong, you have every right to be upset with him, but it could be the only chance you have to thank him."

I pull away to create distance between us, a bit shocked by her answer, and to be honest, a little annoyed. I feel her hand slip off my leg. Part of me misses her touch, but most of me is frustrated by her opinion. Did she even listen to what I just told her?

A scowl forms across my face as I furrow my brows. "Thank him?" I ask, my voice louder and laced with confusion and anger.

Logan remains perfectly calm, looking me dead in the eyes. "Yes. Thank him. If Jamie didn't recognize that he was going to be a shit father and ask your dad to take care of you, you would have a drastically different life than the one you have today. As selfish as he seems to be, that was one thing he did out of selflessness."

My expression softens, and my shoulders relax as I take in her words. "I've never thought of it that way," I tell her as my frustration towards her begins to dissipate. "Maybe you're right." I scoot closer to her, back to where I originally was, but she keeps her hands crossed in her lap.

She cocks her head to the side and gives me a smirk, fully showcasing her dimpled cheeks. "I usually am," she chuckles, breaking up the serious tone of the conversation.

I laugh along with her, which is the first time I've laughed since my phone call with my dad this afternoon. How did she do that? How did she completely understand what I needed to hear, but also challenge me to think differently than how I was used to? I've never had someone speak to me with such candor before. After taking a bit more time to process the words she said, I realize that she *is* right. Suddenly, some of the anger I have towards my birth father begins to melt away, making me feel lighter. Whatever has caused Logan to have the wisdom to help shift my perspective, I'm grateful for it. I'm grateful for her.

Chapter 23

Logan

Marc walks back into the living room, looking sleepy and wearing his pajamas. I glance down at my phone to check the time, seeing that it's already after one o'clock in the morning. I hadn't realized it had gotten so late. Besides noticing the time, I have a text message waiting for me from my ex, Zac. My stomach drops, but I decide not to read it yet. Right now is not the time. I can feel the way Eli needs me in this moment, and for the first time in a long time, I'm happy to take care of someone else.

Marc lets out a long, drawn-out yawn. "I'm heading to bed. Logan, you should just crash here. It's late, and the storm hasn't gone anywhere yet."

Looking out the window into the darkness, I see that he's right. If anything, it's only gotten worse.

"EJ, will you show her the guest room whenever you guys go to bed?"

"Yeah, for sure."

Marc begins to head upstairs but stops in his tracks, turning to face us. "So, quick question for you. Are we going to Indiana tomorrow?" He raises a single brow while questioning his brother.

Eli takes a deep breath before responding. "Yeah. I think we should."

Marc glances at me, shooting me a thankful smile. "Alright, see you guys in the morning."

Eli grabs the water in front of him, and I realize he has yet to touch the brown liquid next to it. I don't know if he changed his mind about wanting a drink or forgot that it was sitting there. Either way, he leaves it untouched.

"Do me a favor?" he asks, turning to me. "Please don't tell anyone about what I just told you. No one knows any of this about me."

I look him in the eyes with as much sincerity as I can. "I would never share your secrets."

His brown eyes soften as his lips form into a grateful smile, drawing my eyes right to them. They're perfectly pink and slightly full. If this were any other moment, and we weren't talking about his dying father, I might have tried to kiss him. As shocking of an admission as that is for me because I've never been one to be forward, something about the way I am around Eli is different. I feel like I can be myself around him.

We continue to chat for the next hour or so about more lighthearted topics. Eli asks me if I enjoyed Spain. I tell him I loved it and want to travel more one day. He's shocked when he learns that I had never left California until then. He shares all the places he's been, mostly for hockey, and how I would love some of those cities, regardless of how cold they could get. I tell him I've never been in the snow before, and he laughs before reminding me that I'm in for a shock. He continues to tease me by threatening to take away my keys soon because he doesn't trust a Californian to drive once the first snow falls.

Neither of us make it to a bedroom to sleep. Instead, we fall asleep curled up, with Eli's feet towards my head, and my feet towards his. He takes up most of the couch with his size, but I don't mind being sandwiched between his legs and the back of the sofa. He keeps his arm draped over my legs the whole night and uses my shins as a makeshift pillow. I can't imagine it's very comfortable for him.

It was innocent, the way we slept, so I doubt that Marc would've been bothered if he found us that way. Regardless, when I wake up, I leave before he has a chance to.

Chapter 24

Logan

The boys have been in Indiana for a couple of days. I’ve missed having Marc around, but it’s given me a chance to spend time with Ali. My first impression of her was that she was a wild child with a ton of confidence, and she’s proven me correct. I’ve grown to admire those aspects of her personality in the short time that I’ve known her. Just in the week that we’ve been neighbors, she’s begun to pull me out of my shell, and I’ve enjoyed having a girl friend again. My last female friendship didn’t end so well when I found out she was sleeping with my boyfriend, but Ali seems like the most loyal friend I could ask for.

It’s a little after seven o’clock on Thursday evening when Ali barges through my door for our nightly “study” session. She doesn’t knock before entering, but I’ve learned to appreciate how comfortable she is around me. She always brings her books with her, but we have yet to open one up and study while she’s here.

“What’s up, my friend?” She walks in and places her books on my desk.

“Not much, just finishing up emailing Marc today’s work,” I tell her as I sit cross-legged on my bed and close my laptop.

“How’s he doing?”

“Good, I think. He’s been busy with his family, so we haven’t really talked much. He only reaches out when he has questions about our assignments.”

A knowing smile dances across her lips. “I’m not talking about Marcus. I’m talking about his brother.”

“Um, I don’t know how Eli is doing. I don’t really know him,” I tell her as my cheeks begin to heat.

"Mmm-hmm, okay," she says with a condescending tone and a devilish grin.

"What?"

Ali takes a deep breath. "Logan, you're my girl, so I'm going to be honest with you. I know you like Maddison."

My eyes widen, and my lips part. "I don't even know him," I remind her, trying to change her mind.

She laughs. "Yes, you do. I saw the way you were looking at him when I walked into the kitchen at his party, and I saw your reaction to Marcus' text about Maddison's father. I don't blame you, girl. He's a tall drink of water. A deliciously tall drink of water." She pinches her fingers and thumb together, kisses them, and tosses it away dramatically like the true Italian that she is.

Her description of him is spot on. "Are you sure *you* don't like Eli?"

She rolls her eyes at me. "He's hot, but not my type, and don't change the subject. You like him, right?"

I sigh in defeat. "I don't know. I know I shouldn't. He's Marc's brother, and from what he's told me, Eli sleeps around a lot, and that's just not what I'm into." I pause for a moment. "I don't know why we are even having this conversation. The guy can have any girl he wants," I add, hoping to end the topic with that.

It doesn't work. "Okay, first of all, look at you." She eyes me up and down. "If you don't think you're exactly what he or any other guy would want, you're wrong. Secondly, who cares if he's Marcus' brother? If Marcus is your real friend, I doubt he would care if you had feelings for Maddison. Lastly...okay, yeah, I've heard he does sleep around a lot, but maybe that's just what you need? Maybe getting laid by a super hot guy would be good for you?"

I stay quiet, not wanting to answer the last part of her question.

"What? You're telling me that you *don't* want to have sex with him?"

I bite my tongue, giving her a blank stare. This is the part I hate about girl-talk; they always pry into your personal life. Marc would never ask me this.

"Wait. Logan..." Her voice is laced with confusion, and I know where this conversation is going. "Are you? Have you never..."

I stay silent for another moment, not sure if I'm ready to divulge this information to a girl I've only known for a few days. On the other hand, she's going to figure it out eventually so I may as well get it over with now.

"No," I tell her, breaking the awkward silence between us. "I haven't."

She raises her brows in surprise. "Can I ask why?"

Leaning back on my headboard, I attempt to make myself as comfortable as I can during this uncomfortable conversation. "Well, I didn't want my first time to be with a random stranger. I wanted it to be with someone I loved. Zac was my only boyfriend, but I don't think I ever loved him. I also somehow knew I couldn't trust him, so I never had sex with him." She stays silent, so I add, "Then he slept with my friend, so I guess I was right."

"Honestly, fuck him." She shakes her head in disapproval, then pauses for a moment before continuing. "But I actually think it's cool that you've waited. I've never slept with someone I had any real feelings towards, but I bet it would be even more amazing. Whoever you choose is going to be a really lucky guy." She smiles sweetly at me.

Not many people know that I'm a virgin; it's not something I choose to bring up in conversation. But I've never had someone understand my view on it the way Ali is right now. It's refreshing not to feel judged for my life choices, and it makes me appreciate her friendship even more.

I look at her gratefully, and she seems to understand that I want to change the subject. "So, what are we ordering for dinner?" she asks while pulling out her phone to see what's available nearby.

Just then, my phone dings as a text message comes through. Zac's name appears on my screen, causing my stomach to drop. He's texted me a few times over the last couple of days, and every time I see his name pop up, my skin crawls with anxiety.

"Is that Marcus?" Ali asks without looking up from her phone.

"No, actually, it's Zac."

Her eyes shoot up from her screen, her face plastered in shock and disbelief. "Excuse me, what?" she asks. "Why is he texting you?"

"I don't know. He's been texting me a little bit lately," I shyly answer.

"And have you been responding to him?"

I look away from her, afraid to see the judgment that will undoubtedly be plastered across her face. "Sometimes," I lie. I've answered him *every* time.

"Logan!" she scolds. "Why would you do that? He's a piece of shit!"

"I know, I know, but I don't know. We have history, and it's easy with Zac, I guess."

"Yeah, easy to get cheated on!" she yells, which makes me laugh.

"But seriously, girl, please don't go there again. You've got to respect yourself more than letting some frat boy treat you that way."

"How did you know he was in a fraternity?" I ask, confused.

"With a name like Zac, I just assumed."

I decide not to respond to him while Ali is here. It's not that I necessarily want to be with Zac again, but I've been a little homesick lately. Not from missing California, but from missing my home...my parents. And Zac knew my mom, so I feel some sort of comfort when I talk to him.

We spend the rest of the night eating pizza, watching a new Netflix movie, and talking about boys. Ali brings up Eli a few more times, but I change the subject. Now that she knows I may be catching feelings for him, there's really no use in lying to myself about it any longer.

Chapter 25

Logan

I think Fridays are going to be my new favorite day of the week. I only have one class today, and it doesn't start until eleven, so I got to sleep in later than usual. As I'm putting my books in my bag and getting ready to leave for class, I hear a knock at my door, which is a little odd, since Ali refuses to knock and Marc is still out of town.

"Come in," I shout over my shoulder as I finish zipping up my bag with my back to the door.

"Hi," I hear them say.

I instantly recognize his voice.

Turning around, I find Eli standing in my doorway with his hands in his pockets. He looks as handsome as ever and taller than I remember. He's wearing a gray hooded sweatshirt that says 'U of M Hockey' on the front paired with black sweatpants that hit just above his ankles, like joggers. He also has on a pair of running shoes and a backward baseball hat. He looks comfortable, casual, and so freaking sexy.

Once I close my mouth to keep myself from drooling, I respond. "Hi. I didn't know you guys were back yet."

"Yeah, we just got back into town. I was just dropping Marc off," he tells me before slowly eyeing me up and down, his lips slightly parted.

I nod my head in silence, finding myself lost for words at the fact that this boy is standing in my room right now.

"He um..." He clears his throat. "He told me where your room was. That's pretty cool you guys live so close."

"Yeah. It's really convenient." I suddenly feel parched and swallow so loudly that I'm sure Eli must be able to hear it from where he's standing. "And Ali is right across the hall, there." I point towards her room, trying to push back my inappropriate thoughts about Eli being in my space.

He nods his head but doesn't seem to care about her proximity. "Sorry to barge in like this," he changes the subject. "I know you have to get to class, but I um...I just wanted to thank you for the other night." He scratches at his brow with his thumb—a nervous tick of his I've picked up on.

"Thank me? For what?"

"For what you said." He pauses to collect his words. "It really helped me change my perspective on everything. It helped me to let go of some of the anger I was holding onto."

Judging by his averted gaze, Eli is uncomfortable sitting in this vulnerability right now.

I eye him, trying to gauge his emotions. "Did he—" I begin to ask, but he cuts me off.

"Yeah. Jamie passed away yesterday morning," he softly answers my unasked question.

"I'm sorry, Eli. Are you okay?"

He takes a deep breath. "Yeah. Yeah, I think I am. I was able to say goodbye to him, and I even told him I was grateful for his decision to give me up to my dad for adoption." He pauses for a moment. "Which, in turn, made my dad cry like a little baby when he overheard Jamie and I talking." He lets out an awkward chuckle, and his words make me smile.

"Anyway, I just wanted to swing by and say thank you for the other night, so... thanks." He gives me a shy grin, his brown eyes locking with mine.

"Of course."

"Also, I know it's not really your thing, but there's going to be a party at my house tonight, and I just wanted to let you know you're welcome to come."

As tempting as it sounds to go to his house again tonight, I should be responsible and stay home to study. I don't need another weekend of trying to catch up on sleep because I went out partying on a Friday night.

"Thanks, but I think I'm going to stay in tonight. I need to do some studying." I quickly nod my head as if I'm trying to convince both him and myself.

A flash of disappointment spreads in his eyes. "Okay. Well, I'll let you get to class." He motions towards the backpack in my hand. "See you around, Logan." He offers me a half-smile before turning to leave my room.

I'm almost annoyed at myself for trying to be responsible. It is only Friday, and I have the entire weekend to study.

"Hey!" Marc says a few moments later as he pops his head through my open doorway. "You ready for class?"

"Yes, I am." I grab my bag and swing it over my shoulder. Locking my door behind me, we start the walk to our business lecture.

"I missed having you around here," I tell Marc with a light smack to his shoulder.

"Yeah, me too, I missed being here. It was an exhausting couple of days."

"How is everything?" I ask him with genuine curiosity. "I mean, I know Eli's birth father passed, but how are you both doing?"

As Eli's name leaves my mouth, Marc looks at me out of the corner of his eye. I've never called Eli by his name in front of Marc before, and he probably assumed I would call him 'EJ' or 'Maddison' like everyone else does. Hopefully he doesn't find it weird that I call his brother by a name that no one else seems to refer to him as.

"I'm assuming EJ stopped by your room this morning?"

I silently nod my head in response.

"Yeah, he was asking where you might be." He pauses. "But to answer your question. I'm doing fine. I never liked Jamie much, especially how he treated his relationship with EJ. And as far as EJ goes, he's doing surprisingly well. Whatever you said to him the other night seemed to really resonate with him. He seemed a lot less angry towards Jamie, and I think they even had a real conversation before he passed."

He nudges my shoulder. "So, thank you. For whatever you said to him."

"Can I ask you a question?" I ask my best friend.

"Of course."

"Did you really need me to bring your assignments over the other night? Because I could've easily emailed them to you like I did the rest of the week." I glance up at him suspiciously.

He laughs as I catch him red-handed. "Well, I was happy to see you regardless, but honestly, I didn't know how to help EJ. I know the situation with your parents was different, but I've never dealt with losing someone before. I thought maybe you could help him."

His sweet answer makes me smile. He's such a considerate person, and he loves his brother dearly.

"I'm sorry if you felt pressured to tell him about your dad, that wasn't my intention."

I shake my head. "I didn't at all. I'm glad I could be there for him. And you."

We continue our walk in silence for a few more moments.

"So, party at the hockey house tonight. You down?" Marc asks me, changing the subject.

"I don't think so. I'm going to stay in and get some studying done."

"For real?"

"But you should take Ali. You know she won't turn down a party," I add, trying to take the attention off of me.

“Yeah, maybe.” He avoids eye contact, just as he does every time I bring her up in conversation.

By the time we make it to the lecture hall, it’s almost entirely full already. I’m typically at least fifteen minutes early to every class, so I hadn’t realized we were running behind. Spotting Ali towards the middle of the room with two empty seats reserved next to her, I point Marc in her direction, and we make our way over, just as the professor enters the room.

“Thanks for saving us seats.” I take the chair closest to her, putting my backpack at my feet.

“No problem. Hey, Marcus,” Ali says shyly, smiling up at him.

“Hey,” he flatly answers before taking his seat.

They’ve been awkward around each other since they met. Ali tends to be shy when he’s around, which is unlike her, and Marc is almost mute when she’s near. They’re my two closest friends, so I’m going to make it my mission for them to get comfortable around each other.

My phone ding in my bag, but I ignore it.

“Ali, there’s a party at the hockey house tonight. You should go with Marc,” I tell her as Marc stiffens in the seat next to me.

“Are you going?” she asks me.

My phone dings again.

“No, I’m going to stay in and study.”

Another ding.

Reaching into my bag, I grab my phone while Ali scolds me on my decision for the night. “What? That’s ridiculous, Logan! It’s Friday night, and this is the first week of classes. I know you don’t have that much studying to do.”

“Thank you, Ali! That’s what I’m saying,” Marc chimes in on the other side of me.

I wanted my friends to be cool with one another, but I didn’t need them to gang up on me.

As I grab my phone, I find three texts from Zac waiting. Ali must notice that I'm facing my screen away from her because she asks, "Is that Zac again?" before rolling her eyes.

"What?" Marc booms. "Why the hell would he be texting you?"

I sigh. "It's a long story. I'll fill you in later."

As the professor finishes setting up his things in the front of the room, I see Marc shaking his head out of the corner of my eye.

I read the last text from Zac to myself.

Z: *Logan, please give me another chance.*

I take a deep, resigned breath. "Fuck it. Let's go to the party tonight. I could use a distraction," I tell my friends, and both of them attempt to suppress their victorious grins.

Chapter 26

Eli

I started drinking at around six o'clock today. That was a little over four hours ago, so you could say that I've been feeling the effects for a while now. I had an emotional couple of days, and the alcohol is helping to take the edge off. The house is crowded, unsurprisingly so, but I don't give a damn about a single person here. I've been looking towards the door for the last hour waiting for Marc to come through. I was hoping Logan would've come if I invited her, but my plan didn't seem to work.

"Maddison!" I hear my name in a pitch so loud it could break a glass window.

"Hey, Alyssa," I say with indifference, keeping my eyes focused on the door.

"What's wrong?" She sticks her bottom lip out in a pouty way. I can tell by how she's asking it's to be seductive, not because she actually cares what's going on with me right now.

"Nothing." I pull my arm away from her grasp.

Most of her body is on display, and her heels are so high that she's added five inches to her short stature. Before last week, I would've taken her into a random room and fucked her, seeing her look like this while she hung all over me. I can tell that's what she wants me to do right now, but ever since I met Logan, I haven't been able to think of anyone else besides that green-eyed girl.

As the front door opens, someone calls out my brother's name, and Marc walks into the house with Ali following closely behind. Then, I see *her*.

As Logan walks in, it's as if time slows down, and she's moving in slow motion. My mouth gapes, and I can literally feel the air being taken away from my lungs. She looks insane tonight, in the best way possible. Her hair is down and lightly curled, and I can see the dark red color shining from here. Her skin-tight black shirt accentuates her chest perfectly, and it's tucked into a pair of black jeans that hug every curve of her body. Her form-fitting all-black outfit is completed with a pair of black boots that make her legs look a mile long. She always looks stunning, but tonight she's turned up the dial, and I'm finding it difficult not to stare.

Once I do pull my eyes from her, I realize that every guy in here is having the same reaction. It's annoying that anyone else would be looking at her because they don't even know her. If I would've known that she was coming tonight, I probably wouldn't have started drinking. She's all the distraction I need.

"Who is that?" Alyssa asks me in a tone that sounds less than thrilled.

I don't answer her, but instead, I start making my way towards Logan. Getting stopped by a few people, I quickly brush them off and continue on my path. I know I'm relatively buzzed right now, but the closer I get to her, the further she seems to be. I glance down for a moment, and when I look up again, she's gone. Marc is missing too, but Ali is still standing by the door.

"Hey, where did my brother and Logan go?" I ask her once I make it to the entryway.

"I think they went to the backyard." She nods towards the other side of the house.

I turn to head towards the back door, but Ali pulls me back by the arm.

"Oh no, you don't. They need to have a little best friend heart-to-heart. Just give them a minute." She pats my shoulder, as if I were a good boy for staying put.

The conversation they're having outside is making me worry. Is Marc telling her to stay away from me? He knows my reputation, and from his point of view he would just be looking out for her, but I'm different around Logan. I hope he would recognize that. I would never treat her the way I have the random girls from my past.

“What’s going on?” I ask Ali, panic clear in my voice.

“Nothing about you, chill out.” She rolls her eyes in exhaustion.

She’s feisty as hell, and her New York accent matches her attitude perfectly.

“What’s that supposed to mean?”

She sighs. “It just means that I saw the way you were staring at her in the kitchen last week. I know what’s going on in that head of yours, but don’t worry, Marc is clueless. He’s just talking some sense into her right now because she’s been texting with her ex.”

“What?” I ask, much louder than I intended to.

“Okay. Apparently, that was the wrong thing to say.” She nods her head, realizing her mistake. “Let’s go grab you a drink. While we are at it, let’s get me one too. I have a feeling we’re both going to need one tonight.”

Chapter 27

Logan

“Okay, remind me never to leave the house with you while you’re looking like *that* again,” Marc says, shaking his head.

“What? What’s that supposed to mean?” I ask, pretending to be offended, but unable to hold back my laughter.

“It just means...” He looks around, giving dirty looks to any guy who glances our way. “That I’m probably going to end up getting into a fight tonight because these pervs won’t stop looking at my best friend.” He mockingly shields my body with his.

“Alright, Marc.” I pull him down by the arm to sit next to me on the back yard’s patio furniture. “Don’t worry. I can take care of myself.”

“Mmm-hmm,” he hums, jokingly putting up his fists towards a random guy who walks by as if he were going to fight him. Marc must not notice that the guy is holding his boyfriend’s hand and not checking me out in the slightest.

“Okay, what did you want to talk to me about,” I ask, changing the subject.

He takes a deep breath. “Zac.”

“What about Zac?” I look at him as blankly as possible, trying not to give away the uncertainty I feel about this topic.

“Why are you texting him?”

I sigh. “I don’t know. I guess it’s just easy to fall back into that pattern with an ex.”

I avert my eyes from Marc’s judgmental glare.

“Well, you shouldn’t even be giving him the time of day. Not after what he did,” he starts to slightly raise his voice. “What has he been saying?”

“That he wants another chance.” I look at him meekly.

"And what did he say when you told him abso-fucking-lutely not?"

I stay silent.

"Don't tell me you're thinking of getting back together with him?" His voice is even louder now.

"I'm not." I pause. "I don't know." I close my eyes, wishing I could get away from this moment. Marc is going to be disappointed with that answer.

"Logan, I love you, but that's the dumbest thing I've ever heard you say. He's a huge reason why your life was so difficult back in California!"

His words spark a fire in me. "You're one to talk! You just hooked up with your cheating ex last week!"

His face falls at my words, instantly flooding me with guilt. "Fuck. Marc, I didn't mean that. I'm sorry." I shake my head.

"No, you're right." He looks up at me, his voice soft. He pauses a few moments before asking, "How would you feel about me wanting to be with Lauren again?"

"Wait, do you?"

"Just answer the question," he says without answering mine. "What would you say to me if I told you I was going to get back together with her?"

My eyes widen at the thought. "I would tell you there's no way in hell I would let you do that!"

He stays silent, obviously wanting me to elaborate on my thoughts with more sincerity.

I feel sad for him just thinking that he could ever put himself back into that relationship. Lauren was horrible to him. "I would tell you that you are better than being with someone who would cheat on you. I would tell you how important you are to the people who love you, myself included. And I would tell you that you deserve to be someone's priority, not just their option."

The words coming out of my mouth sound like some pretty good advice I should probably take.

His eyes soften. “That’s exactly how I feel about you possibly taking Zac back. So, could you do me a favor and take your own advice? Please?” He cocks his head, a sly grin forming on his face.

Oh, he’s good. And he’s right. I know he’s right. I know that my entertaining the idea of Zac was dumb. I guess I was just missing home. That because he knew about my life back in California, and had met my mom, it was almost like he was a part of the family I was missing with my parents being gone. But, to be honest, he never respected that part of my life. The part of me losing my dad and caring for my mom when she was dying. He was never there for me, not the way Marc has been. Marc didn’t even know my parents, and I can see how much respect he has for me and my situation. Marc is more my family now than Zac ever was. My mom would’ve absolutely adored this friend of mine. And that makes me smile.

“Marc, I love you, you know that, right?”

“Yeah, me too, Logan. Me too.” He nudges his shoulder into mine.

Chapter 28

Eli

I'm on my second drink in the kitchen with Ali, and I've learned that she's actually not as annoying as I'd initially thought. My brother hasn't said much about this girl, but I think that she could be good for him. She's confident and speaks what's on her mind. Marc needs someone like that to challenge him, unlike Lauren. Lauren had the 'damsel in distress' thing going on, but Ali seems like she can handle her own.

Speaking of Marc, he and Logan have yet to come back from their talk outside. I'm about two minutes from ignoring Ali's warning and going to find them. If Marc doesn't talk some sense into Logan about texting with her ex, then I will. I don't even know the guy or why they broke up, but I'm not too fond of the idea of her talking to anyone else.

From another room, a high-pitched voice calls out my name. I close my eyes, trying my best to ignore it while taking another sip of my beer.

Ali laughs at my obvious annoyance. "Who the hell was that?"

"Just some chick. Her name is Alyssa, and she's annoying as fuck," I tell her before downing the rest of my beer.

"Maddison! Come drink with us!" Ali chuckles as Alyssa's squeal echoes from the other room.

"Come on." Ali hands me another drink. "Let's go get you even more buzzed and distract you from the fact that your brother is probably talking shit about you to your girlfriend right now in the backyard," she says sarcastically, tugging on my arm to follow her towards the living room.

"Not funny."

To be honest, it's kind of nice to have someone who knows how I feel about Logan. I've been trying to hide it from Marc, and I've tried to deny it to myself as well, but now that's it's out in the open, even to just one person, it feels nice.

Once we reach the living room, I spot a group of people who I'm less than thrilled to hang out with. Standing around a table are Alyssa, Cam, Patrick and Lauren. I stop in my tracks before we reach them, and Ali loses her grip on my arm. Confused, she turns around to look at me, silently asking why I stopped walking.

"I don't think this is a good idea," I whisper, trying to make myself small so no one from the table can spot me. But I'm 6'4" and Ali is as tiny as it gets, so I look like an idiot attempting to hide behind her.

"Why? What's the big deal?" Before I can respond, she adds, "Stop being such a wuss," and rolls her eyes. She continues to the table as I reluctantly follow behind.

"What's up, Ali?" Cam asks with a little too much excitement in his voice as we approach the group.

"Hey," she answers with much less enthusiasm. "Hey, Patrick," she adds, turning to the guy I would like nothing more than to punch in the face right now. A few more drinks, and I just might.

He nods to greet her before his eyes dart to mine and quickly look away.

Good. Patrick better be afraid of me. I'm still pissed off about what he tried to pull last weekend with Logan. I haven't said a word to him since, and I don't plan on changing that tonight.

The six of us silently stand around the table before I realize that the girls don't know each other yet.

"Ali, this is Alyssa and Lauren." I point in their direction. "Girls, this is Marc's friend, Ali."

Lauren shoots Ali a dirty look, but I don't think Ali catches on or knows who she is. This will be a fun dynamic to watch. I laugh aloud at my internal dialogue as Lauren shoots me the same dirty glare.

A flash of dark red hair catches my eye, and I glance up to see Marc and Logan walking towards the table. Finally. Making eye contact with her for the first time tonight, the stillness she brings me just by entering the room settles me. I can't help but smile, seeing her here, in the same way that I can't keep my eyes off of her. There's no way that Marc won't notice how I'm staring at Logan, though I'm starting to care less and less if he does. She returns the same enthusiastic grin, her dimples evident from here, until she looks down at my side and her face suddenly falls. Following her eyes with mine, I realize that Alyssa has her hand in my back pocket, and her arm snaked around my waist. She's clinging onto me with her chest pressed up against my side while giving Logan an evil territorial stare.

Chapter 29

Eli

Fuck. I didn't even notice Alyssa hanging all over me. I must be drunker than I thought. Logan has yet to look away from the girl at my side as I pull Alyssa's arm off of me and create some space between us. But it's too late. Logan looks back at me, with confusion and a hint of disappointment on her face.

Out of the corner of my eye, I can see Ali shake her head at me before giving Logan a sympathetic smile.

"Hey, man," Marc says, greeting me with a hug, entirely unaware of the fuckup I just made.

"Hey." I hug my brother, never breaking my eye contact with Logan. She does not look too happy right now.

"Hi, Logan," I say with as much joy in my voice as I can, but trying not to sound too desperate for her attention.

"Hey," she responds with complete disinterest.

Fuck.

I know it's lame, but whenever we greet each other, it's always with a 'hi' and never a 'hey.' I sound ridiculous, but it's something I've noticed and reserve in my head only for her, whether or not she's realized it yet.

"Logan, this is Alyssa and...Lauren," Marc informs her, pausing before saying Lauren's name.

She seems to catch on as her eyes widen, looking back and forth between Lauren and Marc. "Oh. Hey," she says, completely uninterested in either of the girls.

She dislikes them already, and it makes me like *her* even more. The distaste for Lauren, I'm assuming, is because of her past with Marc. And with Alyssa, it's because of the obvious current situation I've gotten myself into.

I chuckle at her flat greeting to the girls, but she glares at me when I do. Okay, so maybe she dislikes all three of us right now.

Even though she seems disappointed by seeing Alyssa with her arm around me, it's kind of nice to see her get jealous. It gives me more information about where she stands and how she feels about me. I was hoping that we were on the same page, and judging by her reaction to another woman hanging on me, now I'm sure we are.

Patrick leans over to say something in Logan's ear but she scoots away to create distance between herself and him. My whole body tenses at the sight of her being uncomfortable. She shakes her head in response to whatever he said to her, causing him to be frustrated. If he tries anything with her tonight, I will kill him.

I look at Marc to see if he noticed Patrick trying to talk to Logan, but he's entirely focused on his conversation with Ali. My eyes shift to Lauren and I can't help but smirk at her obvious annoyance at the two of them being so close.

"Let's do some shots!" Alyssa yells out enthusiastically.

The group seems to be on board with her idea as they grab shot glasses and begin filling them with vodka. Logan doesn't make a move, so I assume she's not drinking tonight, which makes me wish I didn't start drinking in the first place. I would've had just as good of a time, if not better, hanging out with her completely sober, so I decide to hold off on the liquor as well.

"What? You're not drinking, new girl?" Alyssa asks Logan, condescendingly, while holding up a bottle of vodka in her hand.

"No, I'm good," she states matter-of-factly, before her gaze shifts to me.

I don't care if she does or doesn't drink, but if she's not, then I don't want to drink anymore either. Even though seeing her with a few drinks in her would be fun, I don't want her to feel pressured either way.

"Then why are you even here?" Alyssa snaps, giving her the most judgmental glare possible. "Honestly, you don't belong here. If you're going to be so fucking boring, then you should just go home." She leans into me slightly while pointing to the door.

God, she's such a bitch. I should tell her that right now.

Logan seems taken back by Alyssa's sharp words. I need to defend her, but before I get the chance, Ali interjects. "Watch your mouth, bitch!"

Everyone's eyes go wide as Ali says my thoughts aloud.

"What did you just say to me?" Alyssa asks, taking a step towards her.

They're both small women, so I'm not sure how this fight would go, but I'm assuming Ali would kick her ass. She seems scrappy as hell.

"You heard me." She pauses, taking an equal step towards Alyssa. "Leave my friend alone. If she doesn't want to drink, then she doesn't have to. So why don't you just mind your own goddamn business." She takes another step forward. "Also, I'm from Brooklyn, and I *will* fuck you up if you really want to go right now."

I'm standing between them, but I wouldn't stop them if they wanted to fight. I would love to see Ali put her in her place, considering how she just spoke to Logan.

"Fuck you!" Alyssa yells as she steps back to her original spot, sensing that she's no match for the little New Yorker.

"Fuck you." Ali returns to her spot beside Marc. "Fucking puck bunny," she adds calmly, but loud enough to hear, before taking her shot of vodka.

I've heard the term before, in reference to the girls that sleep around with the hockey team, but I've never heard it said aloud to someone's face. Ali has known her for all of five minutes and just said what everyone has always wanted to say to her.

I like that Logan has a friend like her. She seems loyal.

Marc looks down at her, giving her a thankful smile for defending his friend. She returns the soft grin with a wink.

I knew something was going on between those two.

Chapter 30

Logan

"Well, cheers to that!" Cam says, breaking the awkward silence as he lifts his shot and pours it down his throat.

Everyone follows suit except Ali because she already took hers, and Eli. I'm not sure why he didn't take a shot. He has a drink in his hand and, judging by the redness of his eyes, he's been drinking for a while. I could care less that he's drinking tonight; if anything, it makes me want to join him.

After dealing with the Zac drama over the last few days and walking in to see that blonde hanging all over Eli, I'm starting to wish I'd joined in on taking a shot. The more I think about the fact that this girl, Alyssa, is one of Eli's hookup buddies, the more I need a drink.

The vodka is sitting in the middle of the table. I grab it and take a chug straight from the bottle. It burns like hell going down my throat. I haven't had a drink in a while, and I almost forgot how much I dislike the taste.

My eyes connect with Eli's as I put the bottle down. I can tell he was watching me the whole time as his mouth shifts from being gaped open in shock to a devilish grin. He slowly licks his lips as if he's trying to taste the alcohol on mine.

It sucks that he has a girl hanging on his every word right now, but it's hard to keep my poker face when he looks so damn good. He always does, though. He's wearing the same baseball hat he had on earlier, but this time it's facing forward and shadowing some of his face. However, I can still see his soft brown eyes and dilated pupils from here.

“Damn, girl. Okay!” Ali says to me, referencing my drinking straight from the bottle. “I guess we *are* drinking tonight,” she laughs.

I feel warm from the shot already.

Marc starts filling up three more shot glasses. “Another?” I ask him as he hands one to me and one to Ali, keeping the third one for himself.

“Hell yeah, another!” He holds up his shot glass, ready to cheers. “I haven’t gotten drunk with you since Spain.”

I blush at the memory of my drunken nights abroad. Marc had to hold my hair back on more than one occasion while I vomited into the toilet. You can thank the sangria for that. The fact that he’s excited to drink with me again is surprising, to say the least.

Ali has her shot glass up in the air touching Marc’s, waiting to add mine into the cheers.

I sigh in resignation, picking up my glass from the table to connect it to theirs.

“Fuck it,” I say before downing the vodka. It still burns, but slightly less this time.

My face contorts from the taste of the vodka, and Eli catches it. He still has the same smirk on his face as he shakes his head at me, chuckling.

Us both being drunk tonight is going to be fun.

Patrick scoots closer to me again before leaning down to whisper in my ear. “Logan, can I please talk to you in private for a second?”

When he asked me the same thing a few minutes ago, I shot him down quickly. I don’t want to talk to him, especially after what happened last week, but those vodka shots are already wearing down my inhibitions.

I look from Eli, whose face looks stern and concerned, back to Patrick, whose eyes are pleading with me. I’m going to need another drink to get through this conversation, so I take another swig from the bottle. That one didn't burn at all.

"Fine, let's go." I put the bottle down and start to walk away from the table, careful not to look in Eli's direction.

I go far enough from the group so that no one can hear our conversation, but close enough that Marc and Eli can see me if, for some reason, I should need them.

"What?" I ask Patrick harshly, crossing my arms in front of me.

He seems taken aback by my tone as he struggles to form the words. "I just wanted to apologize for last week. What happened upstairs...that's not like me. I was really drunk." He shakes his head, his eyes full of remorse.

"Being drunk is not an excuse," I plainly state.

"I know. I know it's not. I just..." He pauses, looking for the words to say. "I just wanted to say that I'm sorry and it will never happen again."

I pull my eyes from him, turning back to look at Eli. Judging by his tense muscles and rigid jaw, he's on edge that I'm alone with Patrick again.

I take a moment to absorb Patrick's apology. Maybe it's the alcohol, or maybe it's the fact that I don't want to hold a grudge against Eli's roommate, but I decide to forgive him for now.

"It's okay." I pause. "Well, it's not okay, but don't let it happen again, or I will never speak to you," I say as sternly as possible. "And I'll tell everyone I know what you tried to do." He nods his head while listening to me.

"Not that I know many people, but you get the idea," I add as he laughs at my awkwardness.

"I promise it won't happen again." He smiles down at me and leans in for a hug before I can even register what's he's doing. I don't like him touching me, and I have no desire to hug him back, but I don't know how else to get out of this situation. So, I uncross my arms that are sandwiched between our bodies and quickly pat his back so that it'll be over.

After our uncomfortable embrace, I glance over at Eli, and his expression has changed from worried to pissed off.

Keeping my head down, I start walking back towards the table as Patrick follows behind. When I look up, I'm careful not to let my eyes wander to Eli's face; I don't want to see the disappointment in his eyes. When I do look up, I look to Marc, and his face is plastered with confusion. He doesn't look concerned, because I don't think he knows what happened upstairs last weekend, but he does look suspicious as to why I would be off talking to Patrick alone.

"It's nothing, don't worry about it," I reassure Marc, but loud enough for Eli to hear.

Ali looks from me to Marc to Eli, then back to me again, but stays silent. There's an obvious tension among the three of us.

"I wanna play beer pong!" Alyssa whines, putting her hands on the table and sticking her chest out.

"I'll play!" Patrick chimes in. "Cali, you're on my team," he adds, nudging my shoulder with his.

"No, I don't think—"

"Great. Maddison, you're on my team then," Alyssa states, interrupting me while wrapping her arm around Eli's and looking at me as if she just won the unspoken contest we have going.

My eyes dart to Eli, who is glaring at me, clearly still annoyed that I was talking to Patrick. I can't tell if he wants to play or not, but if he's playing with Alyssa, then there's no way that I'm not.

"Fine. Let's play," I tell her, alluding to more than just a game of beer pong.

Chapter 31

Eli

I have no desire to play beer pong right now, but there's no way in hell that I'm letting Logan hang out with Patrick alone, especially after she's been drinking. I have no idea what they were talking about, but seeing her laughing and hugging him rubbed me the wrong way. I know I'm probably overreacting due to the amount of alcohol I've consumed, but if she wants to flirt with him right in front of me, two can play that game.

I begin setting up our side of the table with ten cups forming a triangle shape, filling them with beer, and keeping an eye on our opponents. Patrick looks desperate, eager for Logan's attention by cracking jokes, trying to make her laugh. It works, but I can't tell if she's flirting with him or just being polite.

"Maddison, you shoot first," Alyssa tells me while biting her lip and grazing her fingers down my bicep.

I glance up at Logan, and she rolls her eyes in annoyance. Good. Now she knows how I feel.

Grabbing a ping pong ball off the table, I line up my first shot. Regardless of how drunk I am, I'm always good at this game. I look across to Logan, and without breaking eye contact, I shoot, and my ball lands into a cup somewhere in the middle of their triangle.

Logan shakes her head, a sly smile forming on her lips as she picks up the cup I made and drinks it down after taking the ball out.

"Baby!" Alyssa screeches loud enough for the whole house to hear. "Nice shot!"

Logan's mouth slightly parts hearing the nickname Alyssa has given me. She has never called me 'baby' before, so I don't know why Alyssa would start now, except to piss off Logan, which seems to be working.

It's Alyssa's turn to shoot. Standing at the end of the table, she bends over slightly, sticking her tits out. She shoots and misses the table entirely. I find myself desperately wishing she was good at this game, and not just because I'm competitive, but because it would be over that much sooner if she were.

"Cali, you shoot first," Patrick says, picking up a ball and handing it to Logan.

If I have to hear that nickname come out of his mouth one more time, I might just lose it.

Alyssa's nails rake down my forearm as she grabs my hand, lacing her fingers through mine. She's acting overly territorial tonight, but I'm not hers to own.

Before I can separate my hand from hers, Logan spots us and her face falls. Guilt rushes through me for making her witness Alyssa's obvious advances without putting a stop to them. I was letting her flirt with me in the hope that it would make Logan a little jealous after I had to watch her get friendly with Patrick. But, him hugging her and making her laugh is nowhere near as bad as how I'm allowing Alyssa to act towards me right now.

That is until Patrick puts both of his hands on Logan's shoulders, massaging them as he says, "You got this, Cali, just focus."

Okay, now I'm really pissed off. Logan doesn't even flinch or push him off her. I don't know if it's the alcohol she's consumed or if she actually likes him touching her, but if she wants to be all over him, then I'll welcome Alyssa's passes towards me.

Logan shoots and makes her cup—of course. I had no doubt she would after recalling her win streak last week.

"Hell yeah!" Patrick rings out, throwing a fist in the air. "Let's go!"

Now I'm the one rolling my eyes.

Grabbing the cup she made, I hand it to Alyssa to drink. If I have much more to drink, I'm not going to remember the rest of the night.

Alyssa takes the cup, being sure to graze my hand with hers as she does. I watch as Logan catches the contact between us out of the corner of her eye.

Patrick walks up to the table and sinks his first shot as well. Logan holds up her hand to give him a high five, and he connects his hand with hers before swinging his arm around her shoulder and leaving it there. Her eyes nervously dart to mine, and I can feel the heat rising in my body as my anger is about to boil over at the sight of him touching her so casually.

Instead of saying the words that are on my mind, I decide to retaliate in the one way that will make Logan feel as terrible as I do right now.

Standing behind Alyssa, I wrap my arm in front of her, across her shoulders. Her small hands grab a hold of my forearm, and judging by the expression on Logan's face, I'm sure Alyssa is smirking at her right now.

The game continues, and each time Patrick pisses me off by touching Logan in some way, I answer back by flirting with Alyssa. I don't care if she doesn't reciprocate Patrick's advances; the only thing that makes me feel better right now is making Logan feel worse. I know I'm being an asshole, but I'm too drunk to care.

We only have one cup to make while Logan and Patrick still have three. It's my shot, and I've barely missed any tonight. Lining up my elbow to the end of the table, I bend my knees, and release the ball. As soon as it leaves my hand, I know it's going in. The 'plop' that echoes through the room confirms my suspicions.

Before I can look up at Logan and give her a victorious grin, as I have with every shot I've made tonight, two small hands on either side of my face pull me down. Suddenly, there's a pair of lips on mine. They're firm and cold, but I recognize them instantly. As soon as my drunken mind catches up with my body, I pull away from Alyssa. That was too far.

"What the fuck?" I ask loudly with a look of disgust on my face.

She seems confused, and I don't blame her. I've been flirting with her all night to get Logan's attention, so it's no surprise she got the wrong idea.

Logan...fuck, please tell me she didn't see that.

Looking across the table to our opponents, Patrick stands alone like the loser he is. Judging by Logan's absence, she did, in fact, see that kiss.

Chapter 32

Logan

I should have never come to this party. I should've just stayed home and studied like I had planned to do. I know the alcohol is making me more upset than I should be right now. If I were sober and thinking clearly, I would remind myself that I was warned about Eli. I would talk myself down off the metaphorical ledge I'm on by remembering that I've only known him for a week, and that I'll be able to forget about him in another. Except, even if I were sober right now, I would know I was lying to myself. I don't think I'll be able to forget about Eli for quite some time.

I bolt from the living room, eager to get as far away from him and Alyssa as possible. Seeing her lips on his stirred something inside me, and I feel like I'm about to lose it. I'm not going to cry. I never cry, but the vodka is making me more emotional than I should be right now.

As I'm rushing towards the back door, a small hand grabs my arm.

"Hey, you okay?" Ali asks, concern evident on her face.

"Yeah. I'm good. Just grabbing some air," I lie while plastering on the fakest smile I can muster.

She gives me a half-smile and releases my arm. I don't think she bought my lie, but she's not trying to fight me over the truth either.

I reach the back door and step onto the deck as the September air begins to cool me down. I'm warm from the anger and booze, so the chill in the air feels good against my skin.

Looking up towards the night sky, I fold my arms across my chest and close my eyes. Taking a moment to collect my thoughts, I try to think logically about how I'm feeling.

On multiple occasions, I was told that Eli slept around a lot, and I was even warned that he can be an asshole. Neither of these things should surprise me, but the guy I got to know over the last week was different from the picture painted for me by everyone else's opinions. I really thought he was different around me.

I laugh aloud at my ridiculous thought. I'm an idiot.

My coming here for school was to focus on myself for a change. I was supposed to come here and study, spend time with my best friend, and not let another stupid boy make me feel like I'm not good enough. I've been here for seven days, and I've already failed miserably. Honestly, I shouldn't even be upset right now. It's not like I can be what Eli needs. He wants a hookup, that's clear, but I'm not a hookup type of girl. I've never even had sex before, though he doesn't know that yet.

"Logan." I hear his voice behind me before I feel his hand on my shoulder.

"Go back inside, Eli." I pull away from his touch.

Without turning to look at him, I begin walking around to the side of the house. There are too many people on the back deck to make a fool of myself in front of.

The side alley of the house is narrow but empty, and there's not much light, which is a good thing. I don't want him or anyone else to see how upset I am right now.

"Logan, what's wrong?" Eli asks, ignoring my request for him to leave as he follows me into the alley.

"Nothing. Just leave me alone." I continue walking away from him.

"No."

"What?" I stop in my tracks and turn around to face him.

"No, I'm not going to leave you alone," he says, standing a few feet away from me with his arms crossed. "Is this because I kissed Alyssa? Well, she kissed me, but you know what I mean."

I scoff at his arrogance. "Not everything is about you, Eli." I refuse to let him know he's right.

"You were the one all over Patrick, so you have no right to be upset right now," he retorts, raising his voice.

"What?" My eyes widen as I take a couple of steps towards him. "Are you kidding me?" I shake my head. Now I'm the one with the raised voice. "I barely talked to the guy! He was apologizing for being a drunken asshole last week!" I motion towards Eli, "Sound familiar?"

He rolls his eyes and adjusts his hat in frustration, turning it around, so the brim faces the back.

I could not be more annoyed with him right now. He's mad at *me*? He thinks *I'm* the one in the wrong here?

Turning away from him, I continue down the alley. I don't know where I'm going, I just know that I need to get away from him.

Before I leave, I turn and add, "And just so you know, the only reason I even forgave him was because he's *your* roommate, and I didn't want living with him to be awkward for *you*!"

"I don't give a shit about having to live with him!" Eli yells, walking towards me, leaving only about a foot between us. "I don't want you talking to him!"

"Well, I don't want you talking to Alyssa!" I snap.

"What?" His eyes widen in surprise.

Shit. "Nothing."

"Logan, what did you just say?" Eli lowers his voice, stepping towards me again, and closing the gap between us completely.

I stay silent.

He takes a deep breath, lowering his voice. "Listen, you have all the power here, so if you don't want me talking to Alyssa or anyone else for that matter, all you have to do is say something."

I pause for a moment, absorbing the words he just said. He's only inches from me, but I know I couldn't have heard him correctly.

"What?" I ask in disbelief.

"You heard me."

All I have to do is tell him that I don't want him to be with anyone else. Of course, I don't want him to be with anyone else, but I'm not sure I can give him enough of what he's looking for to ask that of him.

Looking away from him, I shake my head. "I don't know, Eli. I don't know what I want," I lie.

He puts his finger under my chin, lifting my face to look at him. His lips are only inches from my mouth, and his brown eyes are soft as they try to read mine. "Yes, you do, Logan," he says in almost a whisper. "And I know what I want, so the ball is in your court."

Chapter 33

Logan

My gaze bounces from his eyes to his mouth and back again. Eli's lips are so close to mine that I can feel the heat radiating off them, causing me to no longer remember why I was so upset with him. All I can think about is how it would feel to have his mouth on mine. I have to know.

My tongue slyly wets my lips as I lean up. He meets me partway, gently pressing his mouth to mine. His lips are warm and soft, causing my stomach to tighten and my lungs to be short of air.

Our kiss starts slow and sweet, being sure to take in every moment and every movement, but I need more. I wrap my arms around his neck to pull him down closer to me as he opens his mouth slightly, deepening our kiss. My tongue connects with his, pulling a deep groan from Eli's throat. Our innocent kiss quickly picks up momentum as he wraps his arms around my lower back and presses himself into me. Our bodies could not get any closer, but they mold together perfectly. His tongue dances around mine as I inadvertently release a low moan, but it just feels so good. *He* feels so good.

Eli takes my noises as a cue to go further, but I'm not complaining. He lowers his hands under my butt and lifts my legs, wrapping them around his waist. I tighten my arms around his neck, causing our bodies to be pressed together so firmly that I swear I can feel every one of his muscles through his shirt. He carries me to the side of the house with ease and presses my back against the wall, being careful not to separate his lips from mine. His mouth feels feverish in its movements, wanting more as I run my hands from his neck up to his hair.

Forgetting Eli was wearing a baseball cap, I knock the brim slightly, causing it to fall over his eyes. He breaks our kiss for a moment, unable to contain his laughter. He releases a hand from the underside of my thigh, while pressing me harder into the wall to keep me up and attached to him. Not wanting to be bothered by his hat, he takes it off and tosses it to the ground.

Eli looks back to me while our kiss is paused, searching my face, and out of breath. His expression goes from playful to serious as he looks at me thoughtfully. There's not much light in the alley, but enough that I can look down at his swollen lips, begging them to reattach themselves to mine. Before he reconnects our mouths, he whispers a soft, almost inaudible "Come here," and it's the hottest thing my ears have ever heard. My eyes flutter closed from the pressure of his mouth on mine again, his tongue expertly moves with mine, and his lips stay soft but firm enough to set the pace.

I can tell he knows exactly what he's doing.

Then, as I feel my body begging for more, I'm reminded that he, in fact, *does* know exactly what he's doing. He does this all the time, he is notoriously known for getting around, and I refuse to be just another one of his many conquests. I can't be. I can't give him what he wants. I don't know how to be somebody's casual hookup, but I do know that's all he's looking for.

Recalling how he behaved with another girl just moments ago, I pull my face away from his. He leans in to continue, but I tell him to stop, admittedly without much conviction behind my words. He ignores me by attaching his lips to my neck, working them over the sensitive spot below my ear. It feels incredible, the moan that I accidentally release confirms it, but I can't do this. This is a bad idea, and I know it.

"Eli, stop," I repeat, this time much more assertively.

"What's wrong?" His voice is soft as he pulls his face away to look at mine, searching for an answer to his question.

"This is a bad idea."

"What?" he asks, his expression showing both confusion and concern.

He gently sets me back on my feet and moves his body away from mine, but only by a few inches.

"Is this because of Marc? I'll explain it to him. I don't think he'll care." Which only reminds me that kissing my best friend's brother is another reason to add to my list of why this can't happen.

"This was a mistake. I'm sorry." I cover my face with my hands to avoid looking at his disappointed face. "I can't...we can't. I'm sorry. I shouldn't have done that," I continue without saying the actual words that I'm trying to convey.

Removing my hands from my face, I look at Eli. He starts to back away from me as his expression begins to shift from confused and sad to angry and hurt. I want to explain to him as gently as I can that I can't give him what he's looking for, but before I'm able to form the words, he retaliates.

"Why are you even here?" he spits.

"What?" I look at him, confused.

"Why the fuck are you even here, Logan? You don't belong here." His brows are furrowed with disgust. "Alyssa was right. You *should* go home." He pulls his gaze away, unable to look me in the eyes. His words are sharp and said in a way that is meant to hurt me.

I swallow hard, trying not to cry. I can't remember the last time I cried, but the last few minutes have been so overwhelming that I'm on the verge. But I refuse to shed a tear over this asshole as he shoots venom at me with his words. Eli doesn't deserve to see me affected by him. Instead, I shake my head at him in disappointment as he reveals his true colors to me and turn on my heel to head back into the house.

As I rush inside, I can hear him just a few steps behind me. Ali is the first face I see as soon as I walk through the door, and she looks from me to Eli with worry plastered on her face.

“What’s going on?” she asks me, clearly concerned.

“Nothing. I’m going home. Tell Marc I left.” I try to keep my face neutral as not to worry her with my current state of emotions.

“I’ll go with you,” she insists.

“Ali, stay. Please. I’m fine. I’m just tired.”

She takes a moment to ponder her decision then nods her head in agreement. I can tell that she once again doesn’t believe the words coming from my mouth but doesn’t fight me on them either. She and I are just as stubborn as one another, and she knows that I won’t allow her to follow me home.

I turn on my heel, rushing towards the front door to leave, when I hear Eli’s voice behind me.

“Alyssa.” He pauses. “Come upstairs with me,” he says loud enough for half the house to hear him, but I can tell the volume was meant solely for me.

Turning around, I find Eli’s eyes locked on mine as he wraps his arms around Alyssa’s shoulders and leads her towards the stairs to take her up to his room.

Chapter 34

Eli

I tear my eyes away from Logan's as I reach the base of the stairs. I wanted her to see me grab Alyssa, and now that she has, I can't look at her any longer.

I'm numb, but not from the alcohol, as I remove my arm from Alyssa's shoulders and reach for her hand instead. Her long nails graze against my hand, her fingers interlocking with mine. This feels wrong, but I repress the nagging ache in my chest as we continue up the stairs. I don't know what the fuck just happened, but I do know I need a distraction right now, and Alyssa can help with that.

Once we reach the upstairs hallway, she makes a beeline for my bedroom door, pulling me behind her.

"No. Not in there," I tell her, gently yanking her back.

She turns around and sticks out her bottom lip, pouting. "But why not?" she whines in her annoyingly high-pitched voice.

"Because no one is allowed in my room. You know the rules."

"Fine." She rolls her eyes with a dramatic sigh. "Where are we doing this, then?" She bites her lip and cocks her head as she runs her fingernails from my chest to my pants' waistband. She reaches for the button above my zipper and unfastens it without breaking eye contact with me.

I have no fucking idea where the open rooms in this house are now. I can't recall who all moved in and out this semester, but I don't want to waste time to find out.

Spotting the bathroom across the hall, I nod my head in its direction. "In there," I tell her.

She looks at the door down the hall, then back to me, her lips tugging up on one side of her mouth in a smirk. Wrapping her hand around the bottom of my shirt, she leads me towards the bathroom.

As we near it, I'm suddenly reminded of the night I met Logan. She ran into me, spilling my drink down the front of my shirt, in this very bathroom—in this very doorway. I remember the flurry I felt in my stomach and the lack of oxygen in my lungs when I saw her for the first time. I can still picture her embarrassed face perfectly as she apologized for being clumsy. She was so sweet and so flustered. That is, until I was an asshole to her, just like tonight.

I don't know what went wrong in that alley. Everything was amazing. We were amazing. I didn't even give Logan a chance to tell me why she thought we were a mistake or why she regretted kissing me. Maybe I could've eased her worry instead of validating her regret, but I was so focused on my bruised ego and hurt feelings that I decided to try to make her feel as terrible as I felt in that moment. What the fuck is wrong with me? To be honest, I've never had a woman turn me down like that, and I reacted in the worst way possible. I've only known Logan for a week, but that's long enough to know that she deserves more respect than what I treated her with tonight.

I lick my lips as I think about her, remembering how it felt to have her mouth on mine, trying to taste her still. The mixture of vodka and vanilla lingers, but only slightly. I don't want the taste of Alyssa to take away what's left of her.

Alyssa reaches for the door handle, but I stop in my tracks, causing her to lose her grip on my shirt. "Wait." I shake my head. "I can't do this."

"What are you talking about?" She turns around to look at me, confused.

I close my eyes and take a deep breath. "I can't do this. I'm sorry."

“What? But we do this all the time...” she adds, still equally confused though her voice has begun to rise in volume, sounding flustered.

I stay silent instead of answering. My own thoughts aren’t making much sense even to me right now, let alone to someone else.

“What the fuck, Maddison! Is this because of that new girl?”

She’s clearly upset with me, and I don’t blame her. I’ve been stringing her along all night as I tried to get Logan’s attention. I feel a bit guilty, but honestly, Alyssa will be onto someone new as soon as I leave this bathroom.

I unapologetically shrug, ignoring her question. “Sorry, Alyssa,” I tell her plainly, without an ounce of remorse in my voice.

As I re-button my pants, her mouth falls open in shock. I turn on my heel and hurry down the hall, needing to find Logan and apologize for treating her the way I did. I need to hear her out and try to understand her reasoning for stopping our moment.

I rush down the stairs, taking them two at a time while looking around the crowded living room for her, but I don’t see her anywhere. I spot Marc and Ali talking between themselves in the back corner of the packed room, so I make my way through the crowd, pushing without apology, and ignoring anyone who calls my name.

“Marc!” I shout, out of breath, as I approach my brother. “Have you seen Logan?”

Ali glares up at me, shaking her head before she walks away, leaving Marc and me alone. She’s clearly pissed off, but I don’t really care about her opinion of me. I’m trying to salvage the only opinion I seem to care about besides my brother’s.

“What did you do?” Marc snaps.

I’m taken aback by his harsh tone. “Nothing, man. Chill. Where is she?” I ask again.

"Ali just told me that she looked upset and went home." He pauses for my response, but I stay silent. I don't want him to know how I treated her. I'm not even sure I'm ready to tell him I kissed her, but I'm definitely not prepared for him to know what a dick I was to his friend.

"What the fuck did you do, EJ?" he asks again, this time his voice is even louder.

My defensive mode immediately kicks in. Even though he's right, I don't like that he would assume her being upset was my fault. "Nothing! She was probably just tired or something and left. I don't know," I lie.

Marc shakes his head at me, clearly not believing my words. "You know, you can be a real selfish prick sometimes, EJ. She's my closest friend here, and the *one* person I've asked you to be nice to, and you can't even do that?" His face is full of disappointment but also hurt.

We don't argue much, but when we do, usually it's because I'm in the wrong and don't want to admit it. Marc is almost like my conscience—he calls me out on my shit when I need it. It's annoying as hell, and sometimes I just don't want to hear it. I know I fucked up with Logan. I don't need him making me feel worse about it.

"Fuck you!" I spit back at him, hoping that the harsh words will make me feel better.

"Fuck you, man," he calmly responds, shaking his head as he knocks his shoulder into mine and walks away, leaving me alone with my guilt.

She can't be too far ahead of me. I was only upstairs for a few minutes before realizing what a massive mistake I was about to make. If I run fast enough, I should be able to catch her before she gets to her dorm. I don't like the fact that she walked home alone and drunk, and it's my fault that she did. Let's add that to my list of fuckups for tonight.

Running in this cold air is beginning to sober me up. Between that and the argument I just had with my brother, I'll hopefully be sober enough to apologize clearly and explain to her why I said what I said. I was just hurt; I didn't mean it. If I were in my right mind at the time, I would never have told her to leave. She's the only person that I actually *want* to have around, and I just royally fucked everything up.

I still have yet to see her by the time I reach her dorm. Did she make it here already? Worry begins to take over, thinking that something may have happened to her along the way.

Jogging into the elevator, I press the button for her floor, feeling anxious. It seems like a lifetime since I was last here, when in fact it was just this morning that I was inviting her to that stupid party.

Once the elevator opens, I rush to her door and knock, but she doesn't answer. The concern increases ten-fold, as I start to believe that something *did* happen to her on the way back from my house. My stomach is in knots thinking that she could be in any danger. But wait. Maybe she never actually left my house? Perhaps she's still there. And Patrick...Patrick is still there. The thought of them together causes my stomach to sink until I see a light pop on, shining through the crack under Logan's door.

She still hasn't answered, but at least I know she's home.

I change my knocking to pounding as I call her name. "Logan!" I shout with no response. "Logan. I know you're in there, please just talk to me for a second."

Nothing.

"Logan, I know I fucked up. Please, open the door!" I say louder as I continue to pound my fist against the wooden barrier.

Just as I'm about to hit the door once more, it swings open.

"What the hell do you want, Eli?" she asks loudly, her eyes wild, anger clear on her face.

"I just...I want to..." I stutter. All the words that I recited on my way over here are suddenly slipping my mind. I can't seem to think straight now that she's standing in front of me.

She tries to close the door, but my arm is firmly pressed against it, holding it open.

She rolls her eyes and lets out a deep sigh. "Eli, I'm going to bed. I don't want to do this right now."

"Do what?"

"Whatever it is that you're trying to do." She looks away.

"I'm trying to apologize." I bend my head slightly to make my eyes level with hers. Maybe if she has to look directly at me, she'll feel sorry for me and listen to what I have to say. "Listen, I'm an asshole. I didn't mean anything I said. I don't even know why I said it." I shake my head.

She doesn't respond, so I continue.

"And taking Alyssa upstairs..." I pause, searching for the right words. "I didn't...we didn't...nothing happened, just so you know." I hope she believes the sincerity in my voice.

"I don't care," she says flatly as she pulls her eyes away from mine. My heart drops to my stomach, hearing those words leave her mouth.

"Yes, you do." I try to make eye contact with her again, but she's avoiding me. I need to look into those green eyes of hers so she can assure me that she didn't mean what she just said; that she *does* actually care. Even if she doesn't say the words, her eyes will tell me for her.

"No, Eli. I don't care," she states. "Because you showed your true colors tonight. You're exactly who everyone warned me you would be." She looks at me again, but her eyes don't show me any of the validation I was hoping for.

"What does that mean?" I back away, creating space between us.

She sighs. "It just means that I know you're used to getting whoever and whatever you want, but I'm not playing your game anymore." She stares at me, emotionless. I don't think she's even upset anymore.

"No, Logan, it's not like that—" I begin to explain myself and my actions, but she interrupts me.

"It's exactly like that. Go home, Eli. I'm done." And with that, she turns away, closing the door in my face, leaving me in shock from her words.

I didn't think the conversation would go this way. I was sure she would forgive me; they always do. But, once again, Logan has proven to me she's not like any girl I've met before. I have to fix this, but I don't know how.

I place my hands on either side of her doorframe as I ponder my next course of action. As soon as I see her light turn off, I say a quiet, "Fuck," as I rest my forehead on her door, realizing that she is, in fact, done with me. Inhaling a deep breath, I start my lonely walk home.

Does she really see me the way everyone else does? I've only known her for a short time, but she's the first person, outside of my family, that I've begun to open up towards. But, maybe she's right. Maybe I am the man everyone considers me to be. I was a total asshole to her tonight, and for what? Because she hurt my feelings? What the fuck is wrong with me?

As I approach my house, the argument I had with Marc replays in my mind. I need to apologize to him, but I don't think I have it in me to do it tonight. Besides, I doubt it would mean much coming from me tonight. The house is still packed with people as I make my way upstairs, but I ignore anyone who tries to stop me as I go straight to my room and lock the door behind me. There's no one here I want to talk to tonight. The one person I actually want to talk to will probably never speak to me again.

I lie in my bed knowing I won't fall asleep, but for once, it has nothing to do with anxiety over hockey or my career, and everything to do with a green-eyed girl who has taken up occupancy in my head, rent-free.

Chapter 35

Eli

My alarm went off at seven o'clock this morning, but I've been up, tossing and turning, most of the night. The alcohol has worn off, and the hangover has begun to set in as the pressure pounds against my head. The way my night ended has not sat well with me, and I've been going over what went wrong, ever since.

My phone dings on my nightstand, and I grab it to see a couple of texts waiting for me—two from Alyssa, and one from Tony, the maintenance guy. Unfortunately, nothing from my brother, which I assume is because Marc is still pissed off at me from our argument last night.

Without looking at the texts from Alyssa, I delete them, but read the one from Tony.

T: *Maddison, we are working on the glass paneling at the rink today, so if you're coming to skate, can you wait until 9? Thanks.*

I usually try to get to the rink by eight o'clock on the weekends, hoping to get in some time on the ice by myself, so I guess now I have an extra hour to kill.

As I lie in bed, I contemplate using my hour to get some sleep and quickly realize it's a futile plan. My mind has been going all night. I hop out of bed and start putting my hockey equipment into my gym bag, being sure to grab my skates, pads, and helmet. I glance at the clock; I've only wasted five minutes.

I know what I need to do with my extra time, but I have to swallow my pride in order to do it. I need to apologize to Marc for how I acted last night, and while I'm there, maybe I can convince Logan to talk to me.

I dress quickly, throwing on a pair of basketball shorts, a long-sleeved T-shirt, and running shoes. Before I leave my room, I spot a baseball cap on my desk, and I throw it on, hoping it will hide the lack of sleep that's surely evident on my face.

The drive to the grad dorms is only a few minutes from my house, so I should have plenty of time to apologize before I need to get to the rink. The stereo blares as soon as I start the engine, but I shut it off. I need to use these few minutes to think about what I'm going to say to both Marc and Logan.

The common area of the grad dorms is packed with students. There are guys playing pool and girls sitting around the tables, chatting. I've been to these dorms a few times this week already, but have yet to see anyone out of their room. I guess grad students hibernate until the weekend comes around.

I get in the elevator, head to the C floor, and begin a different type of walk of shame down the hallway. Without thought, I pass Marc's dorm and head straight to Logan's. Marc will forgive me eventually; we are family, but Logan I'm not so sure about, and our conversation is the one that's weighing heavier on me.

I knock on the door and wait for her to answer, but she doesn't. I contemplate if I should start pounding like I did last night, but my sober mind is much more aware of how rude that was. I'm probably here too early for a Saturday morning. She did get home late last night. I knock one more time just to be sure, careful not to hit the door too loudly and wake her up, knowing that would put me in even more hot water.

Still no answer.

A voice from down the hall calls out, "She's not home right now."

I turn around to find my brother standing in his doorway, halfway between the hallway and his room, looking in my direction.

"Hey," I say sheepishly, not knowing where we stand at the moment.

"Hey," he responds flatly.

I start walking towards him as I begin my apology. "About last night—"

"Don't worry about it. We were both drunk," Marc cuts me off, shaking his head.

"No, you were right. And I shouldn't have talked to you like that. My bad, man." I give him an apologetic grin and hold my fist out to him.

He pounds my fist with his. "It's all good, man. Want to come in?" he asks, nodding towards his room.

Following him inside, I take a seat on his desk chair, while he lies on his bed with his arms casually crossed underneath his head.

"So, you're looking for Logan?" he asks without an ounce of judgment in his voice.

I slump over, leaning my elbows on my knees, and take a deep breath.

"Yeah. I need to apologize for something." I keep my eyes away from his. I don't want to see him disappointed with me again.

"Eli James Maddison is apologizing?" He slowly says my name, pronouncing every syllable. "I've lived to see it all."

"Hilarious, man." I look down, shaking my head.

"I'm just giving you a hard time. When did you get so sensitive?" He throws a pillow in my direction, hitting me in the face with it. "I don't know when she'll be back, though. You should just text her."

I pick up the pillow and toss it back at him, missing intentionally. "I don't have her number."

Marc reaches for his phone to airdrop Logan's contact info to me. Getting her number has proven easier than I thought it would be. When I hear my phone ding, I pick it up, eager to save her information.

"Leo? That's her last name?" I ask while looking down at my phone, but Marc doesn't respond.

When I look back up at him, he's no longer paying attention to me as he mindlessly scrolls through his phone. Since he seems distracted, I take this as a prime opportunity to ask him some questions without raising suspicion.

"So...what's her story?" I try to make it seem as if my question is impromptu.

It doesn't work. Marc sets his phone on his bed and eyes me carefully, silently asking me to elaborate.

"You've said she's had a tough life, but you've never explained." I shrug, trying to keep my expression casual.

Marc shakes his head. "I don't know, man. It's not my place to say. She's not really one to open up. She's a lot like you in that way, actually." He pauses a moment before expanding on his thoughts. "It's her story, and I think that she should be the one to decide if she shares it." He gives me an apologetic smile when he refuses to answer my question.

I stay silent, unsatisfied with his response, but trying to be understanding.

He must sense my unrest as he continues. "I mean, you know about Logan's dad. I'm surprised she told you about that as quickly as she did. It took her a good three months to share anything with me," he says, trying to reassure me about my lack of knowledge of the girl.

"Yeah. I guess so. I'm just trying to figure her out," I explain.

I never ask Marc for this kind of information; I typically could care less. He knows me well enough to know that if I'm asking, it's for a good reason. That reason being, she's all I've thought about since the day I met her, but he doesn't need to know the exact details.

He sits up, putting his back against his headboard, stretching his legs out in front of him, and gathering the words he's going to say next.

"Look, all I'll say is that she is probably the toughest person I know. She's dealt with more at our age than someone should have to." He shakes his head. "I wanted her to come out here so she could have fun and be a normal twenty-two-year-old for once. She's been taking care of other people most of her life. I just wanted her to take care of herself for a change."

He didn't elaborate much, but it's enough to appease me, for now.

"You're a good guy, Marc," I remind my brother with sincerity.

He rolls his eyes, a small laugh rattling in his chest. "Yeah. I know."

I laugh along with him, both of us obviously finished with the heart-to-heart shit.

"So, how bad did you fuck up?" he asks with an amused smile, crossing his arms in front of his chest and changing the subject.

"Pretty bad."

"She's stubborn as hell too, or at least she tries to be, so good luck getting her to forgive you anytime soon."

"Yeah," I sigh. "I've begun to learn that about her."

A few moments of silence linger between us, before he adds, "You're both adults, and you guys can do what you want, but she's going to be part of my life, and therefore yours too, even *after* you sleep with her, so you might want to think about that before you do." He gives me a knowing look.

"It's not like that."

"EJ, I know you, man. It's always like that with you." He looks at me plainly, no sarcasm in his voice.

Since I got to school, I've had a reputation for sleeping around and moving on quickly. To be honest, I've enjoyed living up to it. I've never wanted the responsibility of having a girlfriend. My mindset has served me well because I've never had to worry about someone else's well-being, and my focus has always been able to be on hockey with no distractions. Lately, though, I've been toying with the idea that maybe things can be different, maybe I can have both. Something about Logan makes me want to have both. But, if my own brother doesn't think I can change, what makes me believe that I can?

That's enough self-reflection for one day. It's Marc's turn to get grilled. I can't be the only one taking all the heat here.

"Anyways, what's up with you and that Ali chick?" I ask.

"What are you talking about?" He looks at me, conveniently confused by my question.

"Mmm-hmm. You think you know me so well, but I know you too, man. I saw you two making eyes at each other last night." I relax back in my chair, resting my hands casually behind my head, so I can enjoy watching my brother squirm.

He scoffs. "Not a chance. She's not my type." He shakes his head so quickly it's as if he's trying to convince himself of his words.

"Well, maybe she *should* be your type. I think she would be good for you. She's way cooler than Lauren, that's for sure."

"Yeah, yeah." He waves me away. "Still not gonna happen."

I check my phone for the time. It's already half-past eight. I stand up and stretch my legs as I begin to make my way out of his room.

"Alright, I gotta head to the rink. The boys are throwing another party tonight, you coming?"

"Obviously." He shrugs his shoulders at my ridiculous question.

"Cool. See you then." And with that, I leave and close the door behind me.

Before heading to the rink, I swing by and grab my gym bag out of the bed of my truck. I decide to leave my car at Marc's place and just walk to practice. The walk isn't too far, and the weather is still warm enough. I'm glad I wore shorts today because it'll be too cold before long to do so.

There's a weight lifted off my shoulders now that I've apologized to Marc. Now, I just need Logan to forgive me, and things will be back on track. I'm glad I have her number, but I'll wait until after I skate to shoot her a text, otherwise I'm just going to be checking my phone every five minutes for her reply.

On the way to the rink, I pass by a large window of the campus gym and casually glance inside while continuing my walk. I do a double-take when I notice Logan in the far corner of the gym, where the punching bags are. There are four other heavy bags, all occupied by guys; she's the only female around. I walk a little further down the window pane to get a better look at her, being sure to stay out of her sightline. As I near, my mouth parts at the sight of her. She's wearing those tight yoga pants again with only a sports bra on top. She has boxing gloves on, her red hair is in a high ponytail, and her body is glistening with sweat. She continues to throw combinations on the bag, hitting hard and with technique. She looks more coordinated and confident than any of the guys around her, and she is without a doubt the sexiest thing I've ever seen.

I don't want her to see me; I just want to admire her for a moment longer. She's strong and can obviously take care of herself. But, on a deeper level, I think back to what Marc mentioned earlier about her always having to take care of other people, and it makes me wonder, has anyone ever taken care of *her*? If I hadn't fucked up so badly, maybe that could've been my responsibility.

Chapter 36

Logan

"Hey, bitch!" Ali exclaims as she bursts through my door without knocking.

"Bitch? Really?" I turn away from the pile of laundry on my bed to give her a sarcastic, skeptical glance.

"Yeah. Okay, I was giving it a shot. Didn't like the way it rolled off the tongue. Probably won't use it again." She shrugs.

Shaking my head, I chuckle at her candor as I go back to folding my clothes.

"Anyway, I came by looking for you this morning, and you weren't here. Did you end up spending the night with a certain freakishly tall hockey player?" She wiggles her brows suggestively.

"Nope. I was at the gym."

She eyes the sweat-soaked clothes on my body. "You're kidding me. How the hell did you work out this morning? I have *the* worst hangover." She sighs dramatically, plopping down in the seat at my desk.

"Yeah. Well, I sobered up pretty quickly last night."

"What the hell happened between you and Maddison? Last I saw, he was running out of the house, and I assumed he was coming to find you."

"Yeah, he did." I shrug. "But I don't really want to talk about it." I continue to fold my clothes, being sure to avoid eye contact with her.

"You know me well enough to know that I'm not going to stay out of it, so you may as well just fill me in now," she tells me with determination in her voice as she leans back in my chair and folds her arms across her chest.

I stop distracting myself with laundry and turn to her as I say, "He's a jerk. I don't know what else to say. One minute we were kissing and the next—"

"Excuse me, what?" she interrupts. "Back up. When the hell did that happen?" She sits up, looking at me with her eyes wide, shocked by the bombshell I just dropped.

"When he and I were outside, right before I left," I explain.

"Oh. My. God! And how was it? I feel like he probably knows what he's doing."

"Oh, trust me, he does." I quickly nod in agreement. "It was amazing. The hottest kiss I've ever had." My cheeks begin to heat as I recall the moment Eli pinned me against the side of the house with his muscular body.

"So, what was the problem then?"

I sigh. "I just got in my head, I guess. He's looking for a casual hookup, and as you know, I'm not. Not to mention, he's Marc's brother. So, I stopped it before it went too far, but I think he got offended. I was having a hard time explaining myself, but he was *such* an asshole about it. Then, as you saw, he took that Alyssa girl upstairs and probably had sex with her." I turn back towards my bed to continue working on my laundry, not wanting Ali to notice the disappointment that's surely evident on my face.

"They didn't have sex," she states matter-of-factly.

"Okay, well, whatever they did together upstairs."

"No, Logan. He didn't do anything with her. He came back downstairs almost as soon as you left."

I can tell by the expression on Ali's face that she's being honest and sincere, as she tries to assure me of her words. Maybe Eli *was* telling me the truth? I didn't believe him when he told me that nothing happened between him and Alyssa last night. After dealing with Zac, my first instinct was to assume that Eli was lying, but regardless, it doesn't matter.

"Well, either way, I don't care. I'm done thinking about that boy. Or any boys for that matter. I need to focus on myself."

"Mmm-hmm," Ali hums as she gives me a knowing look.

"What?"

"Nothing," she says in a sing-song tone.

It's obviously something.

"But I do think you care, more than you want to admit," she quickly adds.

I knew it wasn't nothing.

I stay silent. I don't know what to say to Ali right now. I had written Eli off in my mind, and I figured Ali would be on board with my decision, but she doesn't seem to be.

"Look," she continues. "I'm not okay with Maddison treating you the way he did last night. That whole 'taking Alyssa upstairs' thing was a dick move. But I do know he likes you...a lot. I don't think he's used to having feelings for someone, and he obviously doesn't know how to handle said feelings, so maybe you should cut him some slack on this one?"

Um...likes me a lot? Are we talking about the same hockey playboy? Eli doesn't do feelings. He does hookups, which is precisely the reason I stopped ours last night.

"Whose side are you on?" I ask, surprised by her suggestion.

"Yours! Obviously. But you and I are the same, in that if someone did that to me, I would never forgive them, solely because I'm too stubborn. I'm just saying if you *want* to forgive him for being a dumbass, maybe you should let yourself forgive him. After he apologizes and explains himself, of course."

I was sure that Ali would be cursing Eli's name after I told her what happened. I assumed she would pick up her metaphorical feminist torch and burn down these dorms if I suggested forgiving him. Instead, she's encouraging me to give him another chance.

I want to. I really want to, but I know it's not a good idea. The only relationship I've ever been in, I was cheated on. Why set myself up for another obvious heartbreak? Eli has girls falling at his feet for a chance with him, and what? He's going to give that up to be with someone as inexperienced as I am? I don't think so. He doesn't know how to be committed, and I don't know how to be casual. He'll probably leave as soon as he gets what he wants. I know Ali is trying to be a good friend, but I don't think she realizes that me admitting that I want to give Eli another chance is just setting me up for failure.

"Anyway—" I begin to change the subject before being interrupted by a knock at my door.

"Hey." Marc pops his head in my doorway.

"Hey, come in." I nod towards my room, hoping he didn't overhear any of mine and Ali's conversation.

"Marcus," Ali flatly greets him without looking in his direction.

"Ali," Marc responds in the same uninterested manner.

They are so weird around each other.

Marc gently swats my shoulder. "Everything okay? You left without saying goodbye last night."

"Yeah, sorry. I was just tired." I eye Ali, silently begging her not to mention what happened with Eli.

"Okay." He draws out the word, scrunching his brows together.

I can tell Marc knows I'm lying, but I have a feeling he doesn't want to press the issue until we are alone.

"Well, I'm going back to the hockey house tonight. You coming?"

I shake my head. "I'm going to sit this one out. I need to catch up on some studying and sleep."

He understandingly nods. I'm sure he knew I was going to say no before he even asked.

"Ali, you in?" he asks, offhandedly.

"Can't tonight. I have a date."

"What?" Marc and I ask at the same time. My question is filled with excitement while his is asked in shock.

"With who?" I grill.

"You know that guy, Dylan, from our class?"

"The kiss-ass who raises his hand every five fucking minutes during a lecture?" Marc questions, his inquiry full of judgment and disgust.

"Yep," she states proudly.

"He's cute!" I reassure her.

"He seems lame," Marc adds.

"Stop." I playfully smack him in the arm. "That's exciting. But I thought you don't do boyfriends?" I turn my attention back to Ali.

"I don't." She shrugs. "But I will do free dinners with cute boys."

I roll my eyes and shake my head, laughing at her honesty.

"I like dating, I just don't want to be in a relationship, that's all," Ali explains as she quickly glances in Marc's direction.

My phone dings, but I don't see it anywhere around me. Feeling around under my pile of laundry, I hear its sound again, and find it wedged between a stack of clean folded shirts and a pillow on my bed. There are two texts on my screen, both from the same unknown number.

I swipe my finger across the screen to open and read them.

Unknown: *Logan?*

Unknown: *Hi.*

The only people I text, besides Zac, are both sitting in my room, so I don't know who it is, though I can make an educated guess.

"Who is that?" Ali asks once she sees the confusion set in on my face.

"I don't know," I tell her, shaking my head. "I don't know this number."

"There's a good chance that's EJ," Marc slowly tells me, guilt heavy in his tone.

"What?"

"Well..." Ali interrupts, standing from my chair. "That's my cue to go." She looks between Marc and me before turning on her heel and leaving the room.

"I gave him your number. He came by looking for you this morning," Marc adds sheepishly.

"He did?"

I figured that Eli was only remorseful because of the alcohol coursing through his veins. I didn't expect him to try to apologize again in the light of day.

"I just figured it was easier for him to text you, rather than him continuing to swing by and try to apologize for whatever shit he pulled last night. Sorry if I overstepped."

"It's fine, really," I reassure him.

Turning my attention back to my phone, I hover my thumb over the keys, ready to type my response to Eli, but I'm not sure what to say. Between my conflicting feelings and my conversation with Ali, I'm confused, to say the least. After a moment, I decide not to respond at all, as I click the lock screen and toss it back on my bed.

I catch Marc watching my movements out of the corner of my eye. "You know you can talk to me about anything, right? Even if it's about my brother."

"I know. But there's nothing to talk about." I give him a forced smile, trying to look convincing.

"Okay. Since you're too stubborn to tell me what's going on, I'm going to pretend that I believe you, for now." He starts heading towards the door before adding, "And Logan?"

"Yeah?" I turn to face him.

"You should really shower. You smell terrible," he says, with a playful smile on his face as he eyes my sweaty workout clothes.

I grab my pillow from my bed and chuck it in his direction. "Yeah. I know, asshole!" I laugh. "Everyone keeps coming into my room and bugging me!"

"Love you," he adds as he walks out of my room, proudly chuckling at himself.

"Love you too, jerk." I shake my head and return to folding the pile of clothes on my bed with a smile plastered on my face.

My phone dings again. I pick it up to see yet another text from Eli's unsaved number, and my smile disappears.

E: *Can we talk?*

Without responding, I hold down the power button and shut my phone off. I don't know what to say to him, so I decide not to deal with it today.

Typically, I speed through my shower routine so I can get back to the security of my dorm room as quickly as possible. I have yet to get comfortable with the idea of coed bathrooms, not to mention the fact that the only thing protecting my naked body from the rest of the world to see is a thin and flimsy shower curtain.

However, today I decide to take my time. I let the hot water wash over my sore muscles from this morning's boxing session while I clear my head. I usually do my best thinking while in the shower, but today I decide to tune out, turn my mind off, and not think about anything.

Once the hot water runs cold, I shut the faucet off and wrap my towel tightly against my body before leaving the protection of the shower walls. Upon exiting, I realize my worry is for nothing, because there's not a single soul around. Usually, these bathrooms are packed, but I'm assuming most students are spending their Saturday afternoon doing things that are a little more exciting than what I have planned.

Back in my room, I throw on my comfiest outfit: an old tattered sweatshirt of my dad's, a pair of running shorts, and my coziest socks. I spend the rest of my day exactly as I had scheduled. I put my clean clothes away, take a quick nap, and study for my upcoming week of classes. Ali provides an impromptu fashion show because she needs help choosing an outfit for her date. We decide on a chunky sweater paired with a mini skirt that shows off her legs perfectly. The weather is still warm enough to get away with exposing a little skin, but cold enough that the sweater won't look out of place.

Marc conveniently swings by my room as Ali is using my mirror to put on her final touches. She's finishing her makeup by applying a coat of mascara, but besides that, she is dressed and ready to go, and she looks great.

"Woah!" Marc exclaims once his eyes land on Ali.

"I'll take that as a compliment," she quips matter-of-factly while continuing to primp herself in the mirror.

Marc slowly pulls his eyes off of her and turns his attention to me. "Logan, I'm heading out. You sure you don't wanna come?"

"Nope, I'm happy here. I'm looking forward to watching TV and going to bed early," I inform him from my bed, which I'm sure has an indent from my body at this point. I haven't gotten up from this spot in hours.

"Alright. Sounds good. Let me know if you need anything."

"I won't," I add playfully, trying to remind Marc of my independence.

"Ali." He bids her farewell.

"Marcus," she responds flatly while continuing to work on her mascara in the mirror.

As soon as I know that Marc is far enough down the hall that he is out of earshot from me, I ask, "Why are you guys so weird around each other?"

Ali pulls her focus from the mirror and turns to face me. "What are you talking about?" she questions. "We're not...we aren't weird at all."

"Mmm-hmm," I hum, unconvinced, but she expertly changes the subject.

“Okay, final look. What do you think?” She stands and twirls in a circle to give the full effect.

“I think that Dylan is a very lucky guy.”

“Damn right, he is,” she states confidently. “Okay, I gotta go meet him downstairs. I’ll see you tonight when I’m back.” Grabbing her purse, she swings it over her arm. “Actually, you know what, let’s just assume I won’t see you until tomorrow,” she gives me a suggestive wink.

I laugh and shout, “Have fun!” as she hurries out the door.

And with that, I’m left alone. I assume most people my age wouldn’t be caught dead in their room alone on a Saturday night, but I welcome the solitude. There was a time in my life that I didn’t get much of it. All I want to do is get take-out for dinner and eat it in my bed while finding something binge-worthy to watch on Netflix. *That* is what I like to call a wild Saturday night.

Hours pass, and I’m stuffed full from eating an entire half of an extra-large pizza. I was sure to get a bigger size than I needed, knowing that Marc will enjoy it as a hangover cure tomorrow. The halls have been pretty quiet for most of the night, and I haven’t heard a single voice in the dorms for a while now. I’m sure everyone is out having fun, celebrating the completion of the first week of grad school. Personally, I consider being lazy and watching TV just as fun, if not more, which is why I’m currently on my fourth episode of *New Girl* tonight.

I peel myself off the bed, needing to fill up my water bottle. I throw on my slippers to head down to the common area, bottle in hand. No one is around, but the halls are still fully lit, causing my eyes to painfully adjust to the fluorescent lighting.

I fill up my bottle with the filtered water, and as soon as I turn the corner to head up the stairs, I spot Eli coming through the lobby doors.

My body is frozen in place. Part of me wants to believe he's here to see his brother, but Marc is at the hockey house right now, and I know in my gut that he's here to see me.

After a bit of fumbling through the entryway, he pauses, and Eli's bloodshot eyes meet mine.

"Hi," he says, seeming surprised I'm downstairs right now. Or here in front of him. I'm not sure.

"Eli." My statement comes out in almost a whisper as my voice is a bit hoarse from not speaking for so long. "What are you doing here? Marc is at your house."

"What are *you* doing here?" he slurs, trying to sound charming with his rhetorical question, but he just comes off like a mess.

"I live here," I reply sarcastically. "Are you drunk?" I scrunch my face and squint my eyes, trying to get a better look at his face from across the lobby.

"No," he scoffs as he scratches at his brow with his thumb.

I roll my eyes at his response. He's definitely drunk. "I'm going to bed," I tell him as I beeline it for the elevator.

As I step inside, I spot the sadness on Eli's face, standing in the middle of the lobby. I try to ignore the ache in my chest as I press the button for my floor.

Before the doors can fully close, Eli rushes over and stops them with his hand.

"Can I come up?" His question is full of desperation as he holds the doors open with his hands on either side.

The light hits him just right as he stands in the threshold. God, he looks good. Of course, he does. He always does. And the fact that he looks so good when I'm supposed to be upset with him just annoys me even more.

"I don't think that's a good idea," I tell him, trying to hold my ground.

"Please," he pleads, his red-rimmed eyes softening as he looks at me.

I keep my stare on him as the confusion begins to set in. “Why aren’t you at your party?”

“Why aren’t *you* at my party?” he asks drunkenly, leaning against the elevator frame, once again trying to be playful.

I contemplate not answering his ridiculous question, but he continues to stare at me smugly, silently waiting for a response.

“You know why. I’m done with parties for a while.” I pull my eyes from his and push the close button, wanting to get away from him before my walls begin to break down.

In my peripheral view, I watch his face fall a bit from my direct response. What did he expect, though? That I would go over to his house again and pretend as nothing happened?

I’m hoping my somewhat harsh answer will cause him to leave, but instead, he stands up straight and asks, “Can I please come up and talk to you?”

I’m trying to avoid looking directly into his warm brown eyes. The tone in his voice sounds desperate, but I don’t want to give in to him. He’s used to getting what he wants, and I don’t want to be another girl he can walk all over and expect to be forgiven so easily.

“I really don’t think that’s a good idea. You should go home, Eli.” This time there’s less determination in my voice than before.

“You’re telling me you’d rather me drive home...*drunk* than let me stay and talk to you?” He cocks his head and gives me an arrogant smile.

“I thought you said you weren’t drunk,” I reply smugly just as the elevator starts to annoying beep at us, thanks to Eli standing in the way of the door.

His face softens, losing its cocky edge as he chuckles and shakes his head. “You’re annoying,” he teases as he steps inside the elevator with me, the doors closing behind him.

“What are you doing here?” I ask him directly, turning to face him. I don’t want to joke around with him, his charm is already beginning to wear at my resolve, and I'm not ready for my walls to be broken down just yet.

"You weren't responding to any of my texts." He shrugs as we ride the elevator up to my hall.

"I turned my phone off." I direct my attention to the closed doors, straight ahead.

"Oh. Why?" he asks. I can see his reflection through the metal, noting the hurt on his expression as he looks down at me.

"Because I wanted to be left alone." I look him straight in the eyes. "Which clearly didn't work," I add, as I once again turn my attention ahead, facing the doors. I know I'm being mean right now, but I don't know how else to keep my defenses up against him.

Thankfully the elevator stops on my floor, and as soon as the doors open, I dash out of there, speed walking down the hall, trying to get away from him, and needing to create some distance from the magnetic pull he seems to always have on me.

"Logan, please," Eli begs from down the hall behind me.

I slowly turn to face him with my hand on the doorknob to my room. He's still standing in front of the elevator with desperation coating his face.

"I don't want to talk, Eli. All I want to do is watch my show in peace," I explain as my shoulders drop. Even though the words tell him one thing, I can sense my body language is saying the complete opposite.

"Then we don't have to talk. Can I at least just stay for an episode and sober up? Then I'll go. Promise." His request is laced with sincerity, but there's also a bit of desperation in his voice.

I know it's a bad idea. I know I should make him leave. But, as annoyed as I am with him right now, I still want him near me. It feels good to have him in my space. I want to give in, but I feel disappointed in myself that I'm not stronger when it comes to this boy.

"You might not want to stay. You don't even know what show it is yet," I add, not knowing what else to say to hold him off.

"Logan, I don't give a fuck about the show."

"Fine," I sigh. "You can stay. But only for one episode." I try to sound stern as I avoid looking in his direction, walking into my room, but I can sense his presence following behind me.

I plop myself back on my indented bed, making myself comfortable once again.

Out of the corner of my eye, I can see a proud grin spread across Eli's face. He closes my door before standing directly in the center of my room, asking for permission to sit on my bed with me.

"The floor seems like a good spot for you," I tell him without sarcasm, keeping my eyes ahead on the television.

Eli lets out a little chuckle, making himself as comfortable as he can on my floor.

"Can you turn it up?" he asks, nodding towards the television.

"Really? You're probably not going to like this show."

"Like hell, I'm not! I love Schmidt." He keeps his eyes locked on the TV screen and there's not an ounce of sarcasm in his voice.

I laugh to myself, shaking my head. He's wearing me down with his charm, and I find myself beginning to be okay with it. All my instincts to keep him away falter when he's this close to me. As requested, I turn up the volume before taking a pillow from my bed and tossing it in Eli's direction, being sure to hit him with it. He doesn't turn around to face me, but from the view I have of his profile, I spot a grin spread across his lips before he places the pillow on the ground and lays his head on it. He crosses his legs at his ankles and folds his arms across his chest. He looks far too comfortable for a guy who probably shouldn't be here right now, but I'm glad he is, nonetheless.

Chapter 37

Eli

There is no way that I'm going to admit to Logan that I've already seen this season of *New Girl*...twice. In the same way, I'm not going to admit that I didn't actually drive here, but instead walked. It'd be way too easy for her to kick me out if I told her.

I didn't know what else to do besides show up here and see if she'd forgiven me yet. I texted her multiple times with no response. Marc rolled his eyes at me when I asked him to double-check that he sent me the correct number. I started drinking as a way to distract myself, but it didn't work. It only made me think of her more as I found myself, once again, making the walk to the grad dorms.

She still seems somewhat upset with me and hasn't spoken a word since I sat down, but we've already watched three episodes, and she hasn't asked me to leave yet. There's no way in hell that I'm going to be the one to bring it up. Maybe she's beginning to forgive me, and perhaps she wants me here. I decide to test my theory.

"You know, Logan, it's rude to make your guests lie on the floor," I teasingly guilt her, hoping she will allow me to sit on the bed with her.

"You're not a guest. Guests are welcome," she responds harshly though I think I detect a playful tone in her words.

I turn to look at her, hoping eye contact will help my case. "C'mon Logan. It's uncomfortable down here. Let me just lie on the bed."

She rolls her eyes and shakes her head at my obvious desperation. "Aren't you sober yet?" She tries to suppress her smile, but her dimples are making their appearance regardless.

“Nope, still drunk,” I state with a sly grin on my face. I’m not really drunk anymore, but I don’t want to give Logan any reason to make me leave.

She laughs under her breath at my blatant fib. “I know you’re full of shit right now, but fine. Stay on your side of the bed, though.” She tries to sound stern, but the slight tug at the corner of her lips gives her away.

Proudly standing up, I grab the pillow off the floor and toss it back on the bed. I begin to climb over her body, to the other side, being sure to take my time and admire her as I do. I pause midway, with my hands on either side of her shoulders, flat against the bed, and my legs straddling hers. I haven’t had much of a view of her since the room was so dark, but now, hovering over her, I can see her in all her glory. She’s stunning, somehow even more beautiful than she was last night. She doesn’t have a stitch of makeup on, and her hair is down in its natural wave. She’s just wearing an old sweatshirt and a pair of shorts, but she looks absolutely perfect. My lips part as I allow my gaze to wander, taking in every stunning inch of her body.

She must notice me taking my time climbing over her because when my eyes finally make it to her face, she’s knowingly shaking her head at me and trying to suppress a smile.

“My bad,” I tell her in my most seductive voice with my lips only inches from hers. I give her a devilish smirk and unwillingly make my way to the other side of the bed.

She chuckles and shakes her head again as she says, “You’re hella dumb,” in a playful manner. The fact that she doesn’t give into my typical advances is frustrating but intriguing.

“Hella? Watch out Logan, your northern Californian is coming out,” I tease from the opposite side of her bed as I continue to use my charm to try and break down her walls.

As we continue to watch the show, my focus shifts to her body that is now less than a foot from mine, and I feel calm for the first time today. I didn't realize how exhausted I was from my lack of sleep last night and the stress I've been feeling, wondering if Logan would ever speak to me again. Now that I'm here, in her bed, with her so close, I can finally relax.

I turn to lie on my side, facing her, partly to be more comfortable, but mostly to have a better view. Her arm is casually draped in the space between us, and I can almost feel the warmth from her body, even from here. Deciding to test my luck, I cautiously move my hand to touch her. I place it on her tanned forearm and gently hold on to her, needing to feel her. She doesn't even flinch or try to move away, and I feel like the luckiest son of a bitch in the world because of it. I release an embarrassingly loud sigh of relief, feeling her warm skin against mine. My body begins to melt into the mattress from the calm that her presence brings me, and I don't even finish one more episode before I find myself drifting off to sleep.

Opening my eyes, I expect to find Logan next to me, but she's nowhere to be seen. Glancing down at my empty hand, I begin to wonder where she is and how long I've been asleep. I reach into my pocket for my phone to check the time. It's 2:15 in the morning. The light from my screen illuminates the room just enough that I can see rustling on the floor.

"Logan?" I whisper.

"Yeah?" she responds, confirming that she left me in the bed alone to sleep on the floor.

"Why are you sleeping down there?"

She doesn't answer, so I continue. "You shouldn't be sleeping down there. Let me. I don't want you on the floor." I begin to sit up and swap places with her.

"It's fine, Eli," she tells me as she remains still on her makeshift bed.

She's so stubborn. I don't know how many times I'll have to ask her to sleep in the bed for her to actually do it. I have to force myself to keep from going over and picking her up, throwing her over my shoulder, and placing her in the bed myself. But I know the real problem is not her stubbornness, but the fact that I have yet to apologize for my behavior at the party.

"Logan?" I lie back on her bed with my eyes focused on the ceiling.

"Yeah?"

"I'm sorry for how I treated you last night." I recall the look of disappointment and hurt that donned Logan's beautiful face as I spit angry words at her and swung my arm around Alyssa's shoulder. I shake my head, trying to erase the memory, but knowing I'll never forget the way Logan looked at me.

She doesn't respond, so I decide to continue. "What I said to you, I didn't mean it." I close my eyes again as I try to muster up the words I need to say. "And trying to make you jealous, that was just really immature of me."

"Why did you do it then?" she asks, her voice soft and without judgment or anger. Her sweet tone coaxes me to continue being vulnerable with her.

"I don't know. Because I'm an idiot, I guess." I pause as I search for the right words. "I don't know how to be around a girl like you. I've never met anyone like you before," I truthfully confess.

"What do you mean 'like me'?" she asks, seeming genuinely confused.

From the bit of moonlight coming through her window, I see her shift on her side to face me.

"You have this...old soul, like you know more about life than most people. You have your shit together, and you don't fall for my usual tricks."

She chuckles. "I wouldn't say that I have my shit together. Far from it, actually."

"Well, regardless, I find myself constantly wanting to be around you, and I feel a little out of my element here. I don't know how to handle feeling this way." I pause again. Something about her makes me feel like I can be completely open as I ask, "Why did you stop our kiss last night? Was it something I did?"

"No. Of course not," she admits. She sits up and faces me, crossing her legs underneath her. Getting up to sit up on the edge of her bed, I lean forward and face her, with my elbows resting on my knees. I can't see much of her face, but from what I can tell, she's being genuine and seems like she's having a hard time saying the words that she wants to say. "That kiss was...it was great." A slight smile forms on her lips at the memory. "It's just that I think you're looking for something that I can't give you." Her face falls.

"What do you think it is that I'm looking for?" I ask, my curiosity piqued.

"A casual hookup."

My eyes widen for a moment at her direct response. "Normally, you'd be right, but that's not how I think of you." I pause for a moment, deciding whether I should just lay it all out there, but at this point, it feels like I have nothing to lose. "I like you, Logan. More than I've ever liked anyone, and it's freaking me out. I don't know what to do about it."

She sighs heavily at my confession. "Eli, I think maybe it's just the chase. I don't think you know what you're saying." She looks at me as if I've gone crazy. Maybe I have.

"Like hell, I don't. Logan, you can't tell me how I feel about this thing between us. You're more than just some random hookup to me." My voice is desperate and my eyes pleading. How does she not see how much she means to me already?

"You don't even know me. I doubt you'd feel that way if you did." She pulls her gaze away from mine.

"I'm trying to get to know you, but you don't make it very easy," I tell her softly. I don't want to guilt her, but it's true.

"I can't do this." She shakes her head.

I pause, not knowing what to say to her. Why is she fighting against this so hard? I know she feels the chemistry the same way that I do. I've never been this vulnerable with someone, and she's just shutting me down with every response.

"Who hurt you?"

"What?" Her eyes widen as she looks back at me. Even with just the dim moonlight coming through the window, I can see the color drain from her face.

"Who hurt you so badly that you can't trust how you feel about me enough to give me a chance? I know I fucked up last night, but this is more than that." There has to be something or someone one who fucked with her head that's causing her not to trust herself around me.

She stays silent, pulling her eyes away from my intense glare.

Fuck. I don't know how to get through to her. I don't know how to get her to trust what I'm telling her.

"Logan, I want this. And I don't mean in just a sexual way. I want whatever this is." I motion between us. "This isn't just some game to me. Please, just give me a chance," I beg. I've never begged for anything, but I'm not above it when it comes to this girl.

"You're Marc's brother," she counters, trying to find a reason to resist our connection.

"Who gives a fuck?"

She shakes her head. "I don't know, Eli. I think we should take a step back and try to be just friends."

"No! I don't want to be just friends," I say louder than I intended to, shaking my head in denial.

"Eli..." she pleads.

"Logan..." I don't want to give in to her, but it's not like I can force her to look at me as more than a friend if she doesn't want to. My stomach drops at the thought. I wait for her to take her words back, but she doesn't.

“Fine.” I pause, looking down to the ground, defeated.

“Fine,” I repeat. “But will you at least just sleep up here? I don’t feel like a very good *friend* having you sleep on the floor,” I add, hoping to change the tone of this shitty conversation.

She chuckles before giving in. “Fine. Scoot over.”

She grabs her pillow and blanket from the floor as I move back onto the side I was initially sleeping on. She takes her spot back and lies down with her eyes on the ceiling and her arms at her sides. Even though her rejection hurts, I still feel better having her close.

If she feels for me even a fraction of what I do for her, how could she suggest that we be just friends? From the moment I laid my eyes on Logan, friendship has been the furthest thing from my mind. Between the longing looks and that passionate kiss last night, I can’t believe this is what she really wants, and I don’t want the night end like this.

Deciding to test her resolve, I start moving my body closer to hers. Her breathing begins to quicken the closer I get. I place my head on her shoulder and drape my tattooed arm across her waist as her body completely stiffens under my touch. One of her arms is pinned underneath my weight, but the other is lying limp next to her body, unsure of what to do.

“Eli...” she tries to warn me, but the word comes out ragged, giving away her real emotion.

“What? Friends cuddle,” I state confidently, not moving from my spot.

After a moment, her chest heaves in a silent laugh then relaxes into the mattress, but she doesn’t move away from me. I reach for her hand and place it on my arm that’s across her waist, silently asking her to hold me. She stills for a moment, but then her fingers begin to lightly trace the tattoos on my arm. My eyes flutter closed from her touch as her vanilla scent fills my nostrils. My senses are in overload, and god, does it feel good. I need this. I need her. If I could sleep like this every night, I would be the happiest man in the world.

Minutes of silence pass between us, and I'm almost asleep again from Logan's gentle stroke when she softly asks, "Who is Elizabeth?"

My eyes shoot open at the sound of the name before I look down at my arm. She's delicately tracing her finger over the tattooed word, repeatedly. In the past, I've been able to avoid answering this question. Typically, when women see it, they either don't want to know why another woman's name is tattooed on my arm or, if they do ask, I ignore the question until they let it go. With Logan, I feel the need to share. Maybe it's because she already knows about my family, but I want her to learn whatever she wants to know about me.

"Elizabeth is my mom," I tell her. "I'm named after her. Eli is for her."

She remains silent but continues to trace her finger over my tattoo, and I'm glad she can't see my face right now. I'm not used to being this open with someone, and it makes me feel a little uneasy. Instead of asking more questions, she pulls out her arm that is sandwiched under my body, wraps it around my shoulder, and begins to gently stroke my shaggy hair. She softly kisses my forehead, resting her lips there, and putting me at ease. My eyes close at her soft touch, and I decide to continue on with my admission.

"That's why I like that you call me, Eli. You're the only one who does."

She stops her movements as she asks, "Why don't you just ask people to call you by your real name?" Her lips still graze my forehead, and the warmth of her breath tickles my skin as she speaks.

“I don’t know. So many people call me ‘Maddison’ that at this point, it’d be hard to change. And I kind of like that you’re the only one who calls me by my real name. I like to hear you say it.”

I feel a smile form on her lips against my skin. I consider asking her about the tattoo she has on her collarbone, but I don’t want to ruin the moment. I also keep myself from informing her that friends don’t hold each other like this and that friends don’t give sweet lingering forehead kisses, but I’m not dumb enough to think that my smart remarks won’t ruin this. Logan doesn’t ask any more questions. Instead, she continues to stroke her fingertips against my arm and keeps her other hand burrowed in my hair as we lie in her bed, holding each other until we both fall asleep.

Chapter 38

Eli

Waking up to the vibration of my phone ringing in my pocket, I pull it out, with my eyes still shut, hoping that I can go right back to sleep if I don't open them too much. I squint one eye open to look at the bright screen and find Marc's name flashing across the top. I decline his call and toss my phone back on the bed. I'm not going to let his call ruin the best night of sleep I've had all week.

Closing my eyes, I reach my arm out to pull Logan to my chest, but when I feel for her, she's not there. Opening my eyes, I quickly realize that she's not in bed at all. I glance around the room and back to the floor where I found her hours ago, but she's nowhere to be found. This is now the third time that Logan has left me in the morning, and waking up to her being gone is almost as bad as not getting to sleep with her at all.

My eyes adjust to the sun peeking through the window as I roll out of bed and put my shoes on. If she left before I was awake, I doubt she would want me to still be here when she returned. I don't know what happened; I thought everything was okay. I know she said she just wanted to be friends, but after sleeping the way we did, I hoped that Logan had changed her mind. But now, I think she may be regretting our sleepover.

Realizing this is the first time I've been alone in her room, I take a moment to glance around quickly. Her closet is open, packed full of clothes, which doesn't surprise me. Even when she's dressed casually, Logan always looks stylish and put together. Her desk is clear besides a few papers on top of her closed laptop, and above her bed is a map, the kind where you scratch off the states you've visited, but she only has six scratched off. Two of them are

California and Minnesota, and I remember when she told me that going to Spain was the first time she had left her home state.

Her small bookshelf is jam-packed with the most random collection of books. They include everything from *Little Women* by Louisa May Alcott, to *The Book of Basketball* by Bill Simmons. This girl is truly an anomaly, and those two books remind me of precisely who Logan is. A feminine beauty with a tomboy attitude.

There's a single framed photo on one of the shelves. It's the only photo in her room, which I find strange since most girls' rooms are plastered with pictures. This photo is simple and worn. It's a picture of a couple, who I assume are her parents. It occurs to me that she has never mentioned her mom before, and I wonder if they're close. Her mom is beautiful, just like Logan, but I see more of her in her dad's features. He has the same striking green eyes.

I've been snooping for a little too long, but I'm just trying to get a glimpse into this girl's life. Logan could be back anytime; I have no idea when she left, so I grab my phone and shove it back in my pants' pocket before quickly straightening up her bed. After one last glance around her space, I leave her room, hoping it won't be the last time I'm here.

On my way to the elevator, I knock on Marc's door, hoping he might want to grab breakfast, but he doesn't answer. He's probably with Logan, wherever she may be.

The walk back to my house isn't too bad. The air is getting colder by the day, so I move quickly to warm my body. As I walk by the campus gym, I have an instinct to glance inside, remembering I got to see Logan in there yesterday. I slyly peek into the large window, and sure enough, there she is, inside by the free weights section. Once again, she's the only female in that corner of the gym and is surrounded by meatheads throwing heavy weights around. She looks completely unfazed by anyone around her and seems fully confident in her movements. A slight smile forms on my lips as I find myself being proud of her for being such a badass and not letting any of these dudes intimidate her. Her hidden confidence intrigues me that much more, but I continue on my way, not wanting her to catch me lurking or in awe.

So, she left me in bed to go to the gym. Maybe that's just her morning routine, or perhaps she needed a way to decompress after the last two nights. Either way, I understand, as most of my mornings are spent trying to clear my mind while on the ice. Sometimes it's my only safe haven.

As I reach the front lawn of my house, I find cups scattered all around, a couple of people passed out on the front porch, and one of our beer pong tables knocked over on the grass. I make my way up to my room, stepping over sleeping bodies in my path and trying to avoid the pools of spilled liquor.

Once I make it to the upstairs hallway, a girl leaves Patrick's room, down the hall from mine. Her back is to me as she quietly closes his door and begins to tiptoe away. I recognize her as soon as she turns to face me. Her eyes lock with mine, causing her to freeze. It's Marc's ex, Lauren. I shake my head in disappointment as she adverts her eyes from mine and hurries down the stairs. I knew she was an idiot, but hooking up with Patrick? She's worse than I thought.

Opening my door, my eyes widen in surprise finding a body lying in my bed. As I begin to make my way over to grab the stranger by the collar and throw them out, they turn over to face me. Realizing that it's only Marc, I sigh in relief. But it makes me wonder if he knows that Lauren was fucking Patrick just a few feet away.

"Hey, I just called you," he says with a raspy voice.

"You better not have had a girl in here with you," I warn, though I'm more concerned that he may have heard what was happening down the hallway.

"What, do you think I have a death wish? I know I'm the only one allowed in here." He sits up on my bed. "Where were you last night? I couldn't find you."

I lean back against my dresser with my arms crossed against my chest, facing him. "I went to a friend's house," I say as casually as I can.

"Logan?" he asks, raising his brows.

I don't answer, but instead, avert my guilty eyes away from his gaze and scratch my brow, trying to cover my face inconspicuously.

"Next time, maybe try to come up with a better lie than being at a friend's house. You and I both know that I'm your only real friend."

"I'm not lying. She told me last night that she just wants to be friends. So technically, I was at a friend's house." I try to come off smug, but my tone just sounds dejected.

"Wow, I knew that girl was smart." He chuckles.

"Shut up," I tease, trying to go along with my brother's banter, but it doesn't work. I know my expression looks as defeated as I feel right now.

Marc eyes me for a moment as confusion sets in. "What's the big deal? So what? There's one girl in the whole world who doesn't want to sleep with you. You'll be onto someone new next week."

I shake my head. "It's not like that, Marc, that's what I've been trying to tell you." I look him in the eyes and hold his gaze, trying to get him to understand what I want to say.

His mouth gapes open, seeming taken aback by my words, both spoken and unspoken. "So...what? You want a relationship with her?" He looks at me with his eyes wide. "EJ, you've never even dated someone before."

"I don't know. I haven't really thought that far ahead, but I do know I like Logan. I like her a lot." My expression is pathetically desperate, I can feel it.

"Well, I didn't expect you to say that. I don't think I've ever heard you say that about someone before." He pauses, surprised by my admission, and searching for the right words. "I don't know, man. Maybe her wanting to be friends is for the best? At least that'll make things less complicated for me." He chuckles, trying to lighten the mood.

It doesn't work. If anything, my expression goes from desperate to pitiful.

"Look," Marc begins. "I don't know what to tell you, man. If she wants to be just friends, there's not much you can do about that. But I want you to be happy. I want both of you to be happy, however that may look."

I nod my head in agreement, forcing a smile on my face.

"But, if she changes her mind and you do something shitty to her, I can't have your back on this one," he continues. "I just got her to stop talking to her asshole of an ex. I don't need to add your name to the list."

"So, she's not talking to him anymore?" I ask, with a touch too much excitement in my tone.

"I don't think so."

"What happened between them anyway?"

"I'll let her give you the details, but he was a piece of shit." He ends the conversation with that, getting out of my bed and putting his shoes back on. Marc doesn't answer my prying, but maybe her ex is why she won't trust her feelings for me.

"Anyways, thanks for letting me crash in your bed." He reaches his fist out for mine.

I pound my fist with his as I say, "I didn't let you. You just did it anyway."

"Same thing." He shrugs. "You hungry? Wanna go grab some breakfast?"

"Yeah, for sure, that sounds good." I grab my truck keys off my dresser.

"One thing, though," he adds as we begin to walk out of my room, "can you try to talk about something other than Logan today?" He gives me a knowing glance.

"I'll try," I tell him with a laugh as I close my bedroom door behind me.

And I do try. I try to spend my entire Sunday avoiding the topic of Logan. I try to stop checking my phone every thirty minutes to see if she's texted me. I try to concentrate on my workout when I go to the gym later in the day, and I try not to imagine her lying next to me when I go to bed at night. I try and fail miserably on all counts.

Chapter 39

Eli

I rush out of my physiology lecture as soon as it's over. For the first time in my college career, I'm determined to be early to a class as I make my way to creative writing. I'm hoping to get there in time to sit with Logan. I didn't talk to her at all yesterday, and I'm still confused as to where we stand after Saturday night. After my confession, I didn't want to bombard her with texting her all day to check-in, but man, was I tempted.

I've almost made it to the lecture hall when I spot Cam and a couple of guys from the team, just ahead. The last thing I want to do is stop and chat with them right now, but there's no way to avoid it as they're in my direct walking path.

"Shit," I say under my breath when Cam spots me. I try to avoid making eye contact with him and continue on my way, but it doesn't work.

"Maddison!" he says as he jogs up to me. "What's up, man?" He pats me on the shoulder.

"Not much, just running late to class," I tell him as the rest of the group approaches. I attempt to make my way around them, but Cam grabs my arm to stop me.

"Why are you in such a rush, man?" He looks at me, confused. "Since when do you give a shit about getting to class on time? Hang out for a minute."

"I can't, I really gotta go." I glance towards the lecture hall.

He looks at me with both surprise and confusion on his face. Typically, I would seize any excuse to be late to a class or even miss it. And it's not that I don't want to hang with Cam or the rest of the guys, and thankfully Patrick isn't with them, but this is the *one* class I'm actually looking forward to.

"Alright, see you at practice tonight, I guess." He shrugs, dejected, and confused.

I stop in my tracks, looking up towards the sky as my shoulders sag. "Shit, I forgot tonight was our first practice."

"Dude, what is up with you? You've never forgotten about a practice before."

"Nothing. It's nothing." I shake my head. "Senior classes are just a bit more overwhelming than I planned," I lie as I look towards the lecture hall once again. "Speaking of, I really do have to go. I'll see you guys tonight," I tell the group, jogging to my class.

"Don't forget about alumni weekend on Saturday, man!" Cam shouts in the distance.

Without turning around or slowing down, I shoot him a thumbs up in the air.

Shit. I completely forgot that tonight was our first official practice as a team. How could I have forgotten? This season has been weighing on my mind ever since we lost in the playoffs last year. This final season is way too crucial for me to lose focus, and I have Senior Showcase in Chicago in a couple of months. It's going to be riddled with NHL scouts. If I'm not on my A-game, my career is fucked.

With only two minutes to spare, I walk into creative writing and spot my biggest distraction sitting in the fourth row. Unfortunately, I'm too late, as all the seats around Logan are taken, so I find an empty chair a few rows behind her. It's been eating me up, wondering where we stand, so I decide to text her and see if I can gauge her reaction.

E: *Thanks for saving me a seat, friend.*

I hear the ding on her phone from here, as she reaches into her bag and pulls it out. I notice a slight grin form across her lips as she reads my text message. That has to be a good sign, right?

Logan scans the room until she spots me. Relief washes over me as her green eyes lock with mine, cocking her head to shoot me a sweet smile. I give her a quick wave and try to hide my giddy expression as she returns her focus to her phone to type her response to me.

L: *Sorry, friend. The guy next to me was super intimidating when he asked if he could sit there.*

I look to the guy sitting beside her, who is not in the least bit intimidating, and recognize him as the freshman I snatched the log sheet from last week. She turns around to me and shrugs while giving me a playful smile. Could she be any more charming? I shake my head at her in mock disappointment as I try to suppress my grin.

Before I can respond and continue our banter, Professor Kenny walks in and places his things on the desk, next to his computer.

"What up!" he booms from the front of the class.

He stands front and center as he begins. "Alright, let's get into our first paper. As you saw on your syllabus, that I know you all read in its entirety." The class chuckles at his sarcasm. "This week's assignment is titled 'Passions'. Now, this is not some telenovela-type paper where I want you to write me some horny script. This paper is about *your* passions. What drives you? What wakes you up in the morning? What keeps you from sleeping at night? I want to know what makes you, you."

Well, this is going to be an easy one. A couple of pages about my love for hockey should be a breeze.

"Your paper is due next Monday. I want five pages written about your passion in life. Now, I know I said this class would be easy, but I can't make it *that* easy. You're not going to be writing about yourself. You're going to be writing about one of your peers, another student in this class."

A girl in the front row shoots up her hand to ask a question, but Kenny ignores it.

"No, you cannot pick your partner for this assignment," he answers her unasked question. "I already have you assigned."

The girl slowly lowers her hand back down.

"I don't care if your BFFFF is in this class." The crowd chuckles. "I don't want you to write about someone you already know. This paper is to get you to learn about someone new. Open up your perspective on another person's life. Find out what makes you different, and find out what makes you alike."

I glance down to Logan, praying that somehow I got partnered with her, knowing my chances are slim as this class is filled with a hundred or so students.

"You're assigned in alphabetical order," he adds.

Fuck yes. My odds just got better. I know that 'Leo' and 'Maddison' have to be near each other on the list.

Kenny walks back over to his computer and projects the pairings on the big screen hanging in the front of the room. The list begins with 'Aarons' and 'Adler' then 'Anderson' and 'Barr.' I scan the names until my own name catches my eye somewhere in the middle of the screen. I swear I'm the luckiest son of a bitch in this room because I'm partnered with the name above mine, 'Leo.'

Logan turns around to face me. She shakes her head in disbelief with a sly grin on her face. I can tell that she's wondering to herself if I somehow planned this, even though there is no way that I could have. Knowingly shrugging my shoulders, I flash my cockiest smile and pretend that I did indeed have a hand in this.

Kenny places a piece of paper on his desk. "Take the rest of the class to find your partner and exchange numbers, or Instagrams, or tweets, or whatever the hell you kids do now." He earns another laugh from the crowd. "You can use the remainder of the hour to interview your partner now, or you can do it later this week. I don't really give a shit. But I want your paper turned in by the beginning of class on Monday. Don't forget to sign in before you leave." He taps the paper on his desk before taking a seat in the chair behind it and pulling out a book to read.

The class erupts with students calling out their own name or their partner's name, and the room is so loud that I can barely hear myself think. I grab my bag and walk down to Logan's row just as she's gathering her things. When she spots me in the aisle, I gesture towards the exit, and she nods in agreement before following me down to Kenny's desk to sign in. I'm in front of her, but I move out of the way to let her sign before taking my turn.

The cold air hits me as soon as we walk outside, and I cross my arms tightly to keep the warmth in. Logan is only wearing an oversized graphic T-shirt and baggy jeans with holes in them, and she's somehow made her tomboy outfit look sexy and feminine. But as good as she looks, I know she must be freezing. By the time we are only ten yards away from the building, about to cross the street, her arms are covered in goosebumps, and her nose is beginning to turn red.

When we stop to wait for the light to change at the crosswalk, I say, "Alright, Miss 'I'm from California, where it's 72 degrees year-round', why aren't you wearing a jacket?" I take mine off and wrap it around her shoulders.

"It wasn't cold when I left this morning." She shrugs, her teeth chattering as she holds my jacket tightly to her body.

"Welcome to Minnesota, where you don't know what the hell the weather is going to do."

"Well, thank you," she says, referring to my jacket as she slips her arms through. It's way too big on her, but still, it looks better on her than on me.

The crosswalk light turns green, and we begin to walk again.

"So, how much did you pay Kenny to pair us up?" she teases.

"You don't even want to know," I banter back with her, sarcastically shaking my head.

We stop walking when we make it to the other side of the street.

"So, when do you want to do this? We can do it now, or we can get together later this week?" she asks.

"How about later?" I suggest, knowing that if we make plans, I'm guaranteed to see her again before next Monday. "I have our first official practice soon, and I don't want to rush my opportunity to ask you all of my burning questions." I give her an arrogant smirk as I put my hands in my pockets, hoping to warm them.

"We will see about that," she teases, but I can sense the unrest she has at the thought of my prying. "When is good for you?"

"Tomorrow?"

"I can't. I have a late class on Tuesdays. And Thursday I have a study session planned with Ali." She ponders for a moment. "Wednesday?"

"Wednesday is no good for me. We have weight lifting before a two-hour skate. How about Friday night, after my practice?"

"Are you sure you want to waste a Friday night working on our assignment?" She seems unconvinced.

"There's nothing else I would rather be doing," I say in a sarcastic tone, but in reality, I'm not joking, not even in the slightest.

"Okay, that works for me."

"I'll meet you at your place then, around nine?" I ask, hoping for the opportunity to be in her space again.

"Perfect." She gives me a sweet smile, locking her green eyes with mine. God, how badly I want to lean down and press my lips to hers, but I can't. I still don't know where her head is at when it comes to us.

After a moment, she breaks our eye contact and begins to take my jacket off to return it to me. "Oh, no. Keep it. I'll get it when I see you Friday," I tell her as I hold my hand out to stop her. Even though I'm freezing right now, I would rather her be warm.

She gives me a grateful smile as she pulls my jacket back on and holds it tightly against her body.

"What do you have planned for the rest of your night?" I ask, avoiding the question I really want the answer to.

"I'm headed to Double G to meet up with Marc and Ali."

"Look at you. You sound like a local," I say with pride, trying to mask the cold chatter of my teeth.

"I try." She shrugs, a blushing grin on her face. "Okay, well, have a good practice, Eli. I'll see you Friday." She quickly grazes her hand against my arm, instantly warming my entire body, before she turns on her heel to leave.

If I don't ask now, I'm going to drive myself crazy, wondering, until Friday. "Logan!" I shout louder than I needed to as she's only about ten feet away from me.

"Yeah?" She turns back to face me.

"We're good, right?" I nervously scratch at my brow with my thumb.

"Yeah, why wouldn't we be?"

"I don't know." I shrug, looking towards the ground. "You left early yesterday morning, so I wasn't sure." I shyly glance up at her. God, I sound pathetic.

She begins to walk towards me. "I went to the gym. Sorry, I should've told you, but I didn't want to wake you up." She reaches out to put her hand on my arm again, instantly soothing my concern.

"So, we are good then?" I ask for confirmation.

"Yes, we're good." She nods and tells me again, giving me the reassurance I need. "See you Friday." She bites her bottom lip in an attempt to hold back her grin, but her dimples give away the fact that she finds my neediness amusing.

"And on Friday, are we still going to be just friends?" I tease, pressing my luck, and hoping that she has finally come to her senses.

"To be determined," she says, though the flirty smirk she shoots me over her shoulder as she turns to leave tells me that she's already made up her mind.

I watch her walk away, with her dark red hair blowing in the wind and my jacket sleeves hanging down, past her arms. She is literal perfection, and I could stare at her all day.

I don't even recognize myself anymore from the thoughts I'm having as I shake my head and pull my phone out to check the time. Fuck, I have to get home and grab my gear for practice tonight or I'm going to be late. Looking back up, I make sure to capture one last glimpse of the stunning girl with dark red hair as she walks away from me.

Chapter 40

Logan

"How was creative writing?" Ali asks, before finishing off her second beer.

"It was...interesting," I vaguely tell her, looking down and scanning the menu in my hands.

I seem to have piqued her curiosity as she sits up straighter in her chair and suggestively asks, "Oh, how so?"

"Well..." I begin as I look around Double G for Marc. He left for the bathroom a couple of minutes ago, but the bar is so packed tonight that I assume he will be waiting in line for a while. "I got paired up with Eli for an assignment. We have to interview and write a paper about the other person."

"How much did he pay your professor to make that happen?" She laughs at herself as she sits back in her chair.

"That's exactly what I said!" I slap the menu down and laugh along with her.

"Well, that will be fun, right?" She pops her shoulder. "You said things were good between you two after he came to your room and apologized for the other night."

"Yeah, it's all good between us, but I don't know," I sigh. "I'm afraid if I spend more time with Eli, I'm just going to end up liking him even more than I already do."

"Okay, so what's the problem? You like him, and he *clearly* likes you. He made it pretty apparent that he's interested in more than just a hookup, and we all know that your whole 'I just want to be friends' act was bullshit anyway," she says, causing me to chuckle at her brutal honesty.

Eli's confession on Saturday night rocked me to the core. I didn't expect any of those words to come out of his mouth.

"I find myself constantly wanting to be around you."

"I like you, Logan. More than I've liked anyone, and it's freaking me out."

"Logan, I want this."

To say that I was stunned is an understatement. I tried to keep Eli at bay. I tried to resist him and the way I feel about him, but it was no use. He told me he wants me, and it was said in a way that meant more than just sex. Now that he's made it clear that he doesn't just see me as another random hookup, I can finally admit just how much I want that boy too. I threw out the 'let's be friends' thing as a last desperate Hail Mary, hoping to stand my ground against him, but I'm pretty sure Eli knew I was full of shit as soon as I relaxed under the weight of his perfectly chiseled body on top of mine and fell asleep with him in my arms.

I spent all day yesterday wondering if I would hear from him, and slightly concerned that my 'friends' act had driven him away for good. I had a hard time sleeping last night, anxious over the fact that I knew I would get to see him in class today.

"Actually," I pause, "I don't know if there is a problem." I cock my head to the side as I think about Ali's words. It all suddenly seems so simple. "I guess now the only problem is that Marc doesn't know."

"Oh, he knows," she adds, nonchalantly.

"What?" My eyes widen in shock.

"He knows." She casually shrugs.

"*What* does he know?"

"Well, he knows Maddison likes you. He told me earlier that Maddison wouldn't shut up about you yesterday. So yeah, Marc knows." She pauses. "Well, he knows Maddison's side of things."

"And what did Marc have to say about that?" I ask, trying to sound indifferent, but inside I'm a nervous wreck about my best friends' opinion of me possibly being with his brother.

"Not too much, but I don't really know. You should talk to Marc about it."

"Talk to me about what?" Marc asks as he approaches the table and retakes his seat. He doesn't seem too fazed, so I doubt he overheard the last part of our conversation.

Ali and I eye each other momentarily, as I contemplate being honest with him and laying everything out on the table.

"About...what kind of wings we're ordering tonight." I decide to be a coward instead.

"Buffalo, obviously. What kind of question is that?" He looks at me in mock disgust, shaking his head in disappointment.

Ali rolls her eyes at my lack of bravery as I avoid the topic of Eli for the rest of dinner.

Back at our dorms, Ali splits off to her room as I head into mine.

"Hey," Marc calls from down the hall. "Can I talk to you for a second?"

"Yeah, of course." I nod towards my dorm, silently inviting him to come inside.

I take a seat on my bed, trying to make myself as comfortable as possible. Though I can tell by the tone of Marc's voice that this conversation will be anything but comfortable.

"What's up?" I ask, as coolly as I can.

"Okay, I know this might be weird for you...and for me." Marc begins to pace the length of my room. "But I wanted to talk to you about EJ."

I had a feeling this was coming, though I was trying to postpone it as long as possible.

Marc keeps his eyes averted from mine as he continues. "I'm not going to lecture you about why I think it's a bad idea or anything like that. I just wanted to tell you that if the only reason you told EJ that you wanted to just be friends with him was because you were worried about me, then don't be. I just want you to be happy." He stops pacing and looks at me with sincerity in his eyes.

"Even though..." He continues to walk. "He's an idiot, and I'm worried that he's going to fuck it up," he tells me, and I can't help but laugh.

"So, am I right?" He pauses again while eyeing me with concern. "Were you just worried about what I would think?"

I take a deep breath and pull my gaze away from Marc's. "How did you know?"

He sighs. "Because I know you..." he states, "And today, Ali informed me of what an idiot I am when I told her how impressed I was that you were immune to EJ's charms."

The image of Ali lecturing Marc at Double G before I got there makes me laugh out loud.

"Well, it wasn't just because of you, Marc. There were other reasons, too. But more recently, yes, I was worried about what you would think."

"I think it's going to be kind of weird to see you guys together in that way," he quickly says. Then softens his blow by adding, "But if anyone can get my brother's head on straight, it'll be you." He gives me a half-smile.

A moment of silence lingers between us as I absorb everything Marc just said. I've been trying to avoid this conversation because I was sure he would scold me for being ridiculous, like the way he did when he found out that I was texting with Zac. But I should've known that Marc would be understanding and almost even on board with the idea of me spending time with his brother. If there's one person that Marc loves more than me, it's Eli.

"So...what did he say about me?" I tease, knowing that he won't divulge any information, but trying to lighten the mood.

"Oh, hell no!" Marc shakes his head. "I'm staying out of it." He throws his hands up in defense.

I tilt my head to the side, smiling up at my best friend as I try to contain my laughter. He really is such a good guy, and I'm lucky to have him. Eli is too.

"You know there's nothing that'll ruin this, right?" I motion between Marc and myself, referring to our friendship. "In case that's something you're concerned about."

"Yeah, I know." He gives me a thoughtful grin. "But, if he does anything to make you upset, you let me know, and I'll kick his ass," he adds, without sarcasm.

"I can handle myself."

"Oh, I know!" Marc pretends to shadow box me, then nudges me in the shoulder. "But you don't always have to take care of yourself. That's why I'm here. I got your back."

Chapter 41

Eli

I've been looking forward to tonight all week. Even though the start of the season has kept me busy with longer practices and team meetings, the days have felt like they've dragged on not being able to see Logan. But it's Friday, and I finally get to see her. I haven't had an opportunity to lay my eyes on her beautiful face since Monday. I did try to casually run into her between classes, knowing her schedule because it happens to be the same as Marc's, but my timing never worked out. I even swung by Marc's room a couple of times for no particular reason, hoping she would be there, but she never was.

I've tried to avoid texting her too much, hoping that my absence would cause her to miss me and realize that she feels just as strongly for me as I do for her. Though, judging by our few flirty and banter-filled text exchanges this week, I have a feeling that she's already come to that conclusion.

I was going to go straight to her place after practice, but I decided to swing by my house first and grab something to sleep in, in the hope that I'll get to stay with her again. I haven't had a decent night's sleep since I was last with her, and the memory of her warm body next to mine is the only thing that got me through those sleepless nights.

As I pull up to my house, my truck vibrates from blaring music before I notice the crowd of people spilling out onto the lawn with red cups in their hands. There wasn't supposed to be a party tonight, but it's becoming more apparent, the closer I get to the house, that there is. The alumni game is tomorrow afternoon, and we always host a massive party for all the graduate players afterward. Since we have to play tomorrow, tonight was supposed to be a night off from drinking for the team, even though tomorrow's game is just for fun.

When I open the front door, the first person I see is the last person I wanted to. "I've been waiting for you." Alyssa grabs my hand and cocks her head as her lips lift in a seductive smirk.

Ignoring her words, I pull her hand off mine without responding to her advances. I sure as shit learned my lesson last week.

I spot Cam just a few feet away in the kitchen. "Cam!" I yell over the music. "What the hell is going on?" I look around the packed house, frustrated.

"Maddison!" he shouts as he approaches, handing me a beer.

"There wasn't supposed to be a party tonight. We have to play tomorrow."

"Chill out, Captain. That game doesn't matter." Cam rolls his eyes. "Don't look at me; I didn't know this was going down. I just got home ten minutes before you did." He holds his hands up in defense before proudly looking around the crowded house. "But Jay is in town, and he's the one who made this happen."

"Jay is here?" I ask, surprised. I didn't expect him to be in town until tomorrow. I would've never made plans if I'd known he would be here, simply because I know he won't let me get away without partying with him.

"Yeah, man! I don't know where he ran off to, but he's around somewhere," Cam tells me excitedly, before chugging the rest of his beer and heading towards the keg for a new one.

Jay was a senior here when I was a freshman. I wouldn't necessarily call him a friend, but he was sort of a mentor to me in my first year. He was the 'big man' on campus until he graduated, and I filled his role. I followed in his footsteps when it came to how I played on the ice as well as the reputation I earned among the ladies. He was on the way to play professionally when he blew out his ACL his senior year, and ever since, Jay has made it his mission that I would live out the dream that he would never have.

I set the beer down that Cam gave me on the closest surface I can find and make my way towards the stairs. I try to move quickly so that Jay and the rest of the guys won't notice me. I just need to get to my room, grab a change of clothes, and slip out of here unnoticed. I'm looking forward to hanging with Jay, but that can wait until tomorrow as I had initially planned.

The stairs are only a few feet away as I barge through the crowd when I hear someone say, "Where do you think you're going, kid?"

There is no way to get out of this now. I sigh in defeat as I turn around to give my old mentor a hug. "Jay, what's up, man?" I swing my arm around his back for a quick embrace.

"Not much, just waiting for your scrawny ass to get here and have a drink with me," he says as he playfully punches me in the shoulder.

"I haven't been scrawny since my freshman year, and we both know it."

"Hey, I heard you got named Captain today, man. Congrats." He lifts his drink to me in a cheers motion before taking a chug from the cup.

"Thanks, man. But it's not that big of a deal. I've been Captain for the last three years." I glance up towards the stairs, wishing I would've made it up there before getting recognized.

"Well, it's a big deal every year, so come have a celebratory drink with me." He nods towards the kitchen. "It's not every day that U of M's greatest hockey player of all time comes back to town," he teases, referring to himself.

"Pfft. You know I took that title a long time ago, right?"

"Mmm-hmm. We still have to see about that." He finishes his drink. "You get called up to the NHL, and I'll proudly hand over my title," he says, causing my anxiety to seep through again.

Since I met Logan a couple of weeks ago, the unease I feel about my unknown future has decreased. She's been a distraction for me in both good and bad ways, but without her here to pull my thoughts in a different direction, suddenly, all I can think about is the pressure sitting on my chest caused by Jay's words.

"C'mon, let's grab a drink," Jay insists as he starts towards the kitchen.

"I can't, man. I have plans."

He stops in his tracks, turning back to face me. "What plans? Cancel them," he states as if my course of action should be obvious.

"I can't. It's for a school project."

"Absolutely not." He shakes his head at me. "Since when do you give a shit about school, especially on a Friday night?"

"Since now." I shrug, trying to stand firm against him.

"Is there a chick involved? You trying to get laid tonight? Just have her come here."

"No, it's nothing like that," I quickly tell him, shaking my head. Even though there is a girl involved, there's absolutely no way in hell that I'm letting Jay near Logan tonight. I don't need him to know about her yet. He'll be the first to remind me that I don't need any distractions outside of hockey—right before he tries to sleep with her.

"Well, then I'm sorry, kid, but you're staying," he says with finality, but I don't budge.

He pauses before changing his tactic. "At least stay and have one drink with me. I haven't seen you for months, Maddison," he pleads with a softer, less demanding edge.

I don't know if it's the pressure I feel to fulfill this status quo of being who everyone thinks I am, or if I just feel bad leaving Jay hanging that causes me to agree.

"Fine." I sigh. "One drink. Then I have to go." I've always had a hard time saying no to Jay, and apparently tonight is no exception.

"Cam!" Jay shouts to him over the crowd causing my teammate to hurry over like a dog being called to their owner. "Take Maddison's phone and keys until he has a drink with me. He doesn't need them." Jay keeps his stare on me, testing me.

"Jay, no. I said I'd stay for one." I roll my eyes at his antics. He's being ridiculous now.

"Yeah, well, let's just make sure you keep that promise." He shrugs. "Cam." Jay nods for him to take my belongings.

"Sorry, Maddison," Cam apologizes with plenty of guilt and fear in his eyes. If there is one person he's more intimidated by than me, it's Jay.

I sigh in defeat, knowing there's no use in fighting it. Jay's not going to let this go until he gets his way. He never does. I may as well get it over with now.

"Let me just send a quick text," I tell them both as I pull my phone out and type a message to Logan.

E: *Hi. I'm running a little late, but I'll be there soon.*

I had planned to be at Logan's by nine, and it's only eight-thirty now. I should be able to make it there in an hour. Thirty minutes late isn't too bad.

I have no idea what time it is, but I do know that I've had way more to drink than the one I promised Jay. Every time I try to leave, he stops me at the door and puts another beer in my hand. He and the rest of the team won't let me out of their sight long enough to make a dash for it, and I'm trying not to cause too much suspicion over my desperation to leave. Typically, I would never consider leaving if Jay was in town; I used to idolize the guy, but I currently have a more important person I need to see. I've been keeping my eye out for Cam so I can get my phone back and call Logan, but he's nowhere to be found.

"One more," Jay says, pulling me away from the door, yet again.

"No, man. I can't. I really have to go this time." I pull my arm from his grip.

"Since when do you leave a party? What is going on with you?"

"Maddison..." Alyssa slurs in her high pitch voice as she walks by, grazing her nails down my arm, and for once, I'm thankful for her interruption.

"Well, hello there," Jay says in a low tone as his eyes follow her every move.

"Hey." Alyssa bites her lip as she continues to walk away, making sure to sway her hips more than usual, knowing Jay has his eyes on her.

"Whoa!" Jay drunkenly exclaims. "You're telling me that you're going to leave when *that* girl is here?" He nods in Alyssa's direction, his eyes wide.

"That's exactly what I'm telling you," I state matter-of-factly, finally fed up with his bullshit for the night.

"Have it your way, kid. I'll be enjoying myself tonight." Jay rubs his hands together, wandering off to follow Alyssa.

With Jay preoccupied, I make my break for the door. I still have yet to spot Cam and get my phone and keys back, not that I could drive. I'm way over the legal limit. I might not always make the smartest decisions, but I'm not enough of an idiot that I would drive drunk. But, I would like my phone back so I can check the time and let Logan know that I'm on my way. The walk is going to add an extra thirty minutes on to my arrival time, so I'll worry about my things tomorrow. I guess she will find out that I'm on my way when I get there.

"Hey, man..." I say to the first person I spot once I make it outside. "What time is it?"

"Maddison!" the guy shouts, though I have no idea who this stranger is. "This season is going be sick, right?"

"Yeah, for sure," I brush him off. "The time?"

"Oh. Yeah." He pulls his phone out of his pocket. "It's only twelve-thirty."

Fuck.

Chapter 42

Logan

"I thought you were supposed to be working on your paper with EJ tonight?" Marc asks from the hallway as he passes by my open door.

"Yeah, we are, but he texted that he's running a little late," I inform him from my spot of the floor in my room, surrounded by my laptop and notes, where I've been sitting and waiting for Eli.

I assume that he got stuck at practice later than he had planned, which is no big deal. I'm just looking forward to seeing him tonight. I've been looking forward to it since Monday, and thankfully, I've been so busy with school that this week has flown by. This will be the first time I get to see Eli since my conversation with Marc about my feelings for his brother, and I'm excited to spend time with him, guilt-free.

I've only texted with him a few times this week, and I would be lying if I said that I didn't miss him.

"Are you sure you don't want to bail on my brother and watch the Raptors game with me?" Marc playfully suggests.

I chuckle as his attempt. "I can't. But make sure you record it. I want to watch it tomorrow."

"I'm going to order a pizza. Want me to get a bigger one so we can share?"

"No, I'm okay. Thanks though. Eli should be here soon." I glance down at my phone again. It's already nine-thirty.

"Ali!" Marc yells, standing in the hall between our rooms.

"Yeah?" She shouts back to him while sitting at her desk and working on schoolwork.

When Ali and my doors are both open, we can see perfectly into the other's room, so we keep them that way most of the time. That way, we can hang out without actually having to leave the comfort of our own spaces.

"Want some pizza? I'm going to order one," Marc asks.

"Yes, please! Pineapple for me!"

"Gross," he says to me as we both shake our head in disgust.

Marc and Ali have seemed a little more comfortable around each other this week, and I think my plan to make them friendly towards one another is finally starting to pay off.

"Well, the game is going to start soon, so I'll be watching it in my room," Marc informs me as he turns on his heel to head back to his dorm.

He quickly turns around and pops his head back in my doorway. "Have fun, but not too much fun," he adds with a playfully pointed glance, causing me to laugh at his empty threats.

I've texted Eli twice now with no response. I hope nothing happened to him, but I'm starting to have a bad feeling. It's already eleven, and he was supposed to be here at nine. I know he texted earlier that he was running late, but I figured he would've called if he was going to be *this* late.

As my concern grows, I decide to go down to Marc's room and see if he's heard from his brother.

His door is closed, so I gently knock and hear a distant, "Come in!" being yelled my way.

Walking in, I find Marc sitting on the edge of his bed, eyes fully focused on the game. Ali is here too because they shared a pizza, but she's sitting towards the top of his bed with her back against the headboard, scrolling her phone, and not giving the basketball game on TV a second glance.

"Perfect timing, the Celtics just tied it up with two minutes left," he tells me, without pulling his gaze from the game. "You and EJ done already?"

“No, actually, he never showed up,” I tell them both as Marc’s focus leaves the television, and Ali pulls her attention away from her phone. “I was wondering if you’d heard from him?”

“No, I haven’t. Let me call him.” Marc looks utterly confused as he grabs his phone from his bedside table and dials his brother.

“Have some pizza. We have leftovers,” Ali says, pointing to the large pizza box sitting on Marc’s dresser. I’m sure she’s hoping food will bring me some comfort. And she’s right, it usually would, so I open the box to grab a piece, but there are only pineapple slices left. No, thank you.

“That’s weird. It went straight to voicemail.” Marc looks at me then back to his phone, puzzled.

“Do you think he’s okay?” I ask as panic begins to set in.

“He’s fine.” Ali looks down at her phone, shaking her head in disappointment.

“What do you mean?”

She sighs. “You remember that blond chick from the party? The one I wanted to fight?”

“Alyssa? Yeah, hard to forget.”

“Well, I started following her on Instagram, you know, so that I could despise her from a distance. Anyway, look at her latest picture. She just posted it.” Ali holds up her phone for me to get a better look. “The location is tagged as ‘The Hockey House,’” she adds with caution.

My eyes scan the photo as my lips part in shock. It’s a selfie of Alyssa puckering her lips in her signature ‘more makeup, less clothing’ look. And there he is, standing a few feet behind her with a drink in his hand. Eli is looking off, talking to someone out of frame, so I doubt he even knows this picture exists for anyone to see. But here it is, right in front of my eyes.

“I’m going to kill him,” Marc says, looking at the photo over my shoulder.

“He’s an idiot,” Ali adds, sympathetically.

I almost don't hear either of them. My ears are buzzing, my head is spinning, and I can't seem to pull my eyes away from the picture on Ali's phone.

"It's fine. I'm fine." I try to convince myself as I shake my head, pulling myself out of the daze I'm in.

"Well, hang out with us and watch the game," Marc quickly suggests, searching for a way to make me feel better.

"No, it's okay. I think I'm going to go to bed." I start to head towards the door, knowing that there is no way in hell I'm going to be able to sleep, but needing to be alone.

"Are you sure?" Ali asks, unconvinced.

She and Marc are both eyeing me as if I am a bomb about to go off, but I don't react to disappointment in that way. I've had plenty of disappointment in my life, and I know how to handle myself and my emotions. Let's just add Eli's lying ass to that list of life's disappointments.

"Yeah. I'll see you guys tomorrow." I turn to give them a convincing smile, but I'm sure they notice how forced it is.

Closing Marc's door behind me, I take a deep breath once I'm alone in the hallway. I close my eyes for a moment to collect my thoughts when I hear Marc tell Ali, "He's a fucking idiot."

I actually feel worse tonight than I did after last week's party. I expected more from Eli after his apology and confession last weekend. I thought he was sincere when he told me how he felt, but in reality, he was full of shit. And once again, he has shown his true colors.

I haven't looked at my phone for a while now. Every time I checked it and saw the lack of missed calls or texts from Eli, my stomach dropped in disappointment, so I figured it best to keep myself from looking at all. I've laid here in bed for a couple of hours, with my eyes locked on the ceiling, unable to sleep.

I really thought he was different with me, but once again, I shouldn't be surprised that he's proven everyone else correct. Am I really that naive that I keep allowing boys to lie straight to my face? If my relationship with Zac taught me anything, it was to spot the red flags early on, and Eli is waving his red flags all over Alyssa's Instagram.

My room is pitch black, except for the small amount of fluorescent light coming from the hallway through the gap under my door. When the space around me suddenly gets a bit darker, I snap my head in the direction of my door to find the shadow of two feet facing my room.

Somehow, I already know it's Eli. I locked my door tonight in case he came by because I didn't want my anger with him to dissolve as I'm sure it would once I saw his face.

Sitting up in my bed, I anxiously await his next move, and because of the stillness around me, I can almost hear my own heartbeat accelerating in anticipation.

I hear Eli take a deep breath before gently knocking on my door.

"Logan?" he softly says.

God, I missed his voice.

"Logan, will you please open up? I'm sorry that I'm so late." He knocks again, this time a little louder.

I stay silent. As much as I want to let Eli in and look into his whiskey brown eyes, I need to hold my ground. I'm not a weak person, but I can be when it comes to this boy. Instead, I walk closer to the door to be near him, but I stay quiet so that he doesn't know I'm awake. Even though it pains me to hear the desperation in his voice, I need to remember how little he cared for me when he left me waiting for hours. I'm not even mad at him. I'm just disappointed.

"Please. I know I fucked up. Can I just talk to you for a minute?" he asks, his voice rising in volume as he jiggles on the doorknob before realizing it's locked.

He lets out a loud sigh, followed by a small thud, which I assume was his forehead resting against the door. "Fuck," he says under his breath.

I hear him lean his body against the door, and judging by the lack of light coming into my room, I assume he slid himself down to the ground and is now sitting with his back against it.

"Maddison? What the hell are you doing here?" I hear Ali ask, outraged.

"Nothing, Ali. Go back inside," Eli says, trying to brush her off and keep her out of his mess.

"You have some nerve showing up here! You were supposed to be here hours ago!"

I stay close to the door to hear Eli's excuse as Ali defends me, but I also remain quiet. I don't want anyone to know that I can hear their conversation.

"Yeah, I know. I fucked up," Eli responds, sounding defeated.

"You should just go back to your party."

"How did you know about that?"

"It's all over Instagram, you dumbass!" she shouts. I can just picture the look of disgust on her face right now.

"Okay, okay. I'll handle my brother," Marc chimes in out of nowhere, trying to calm her down.

"I can explain what happened," Eli tells him with desperation in his voice.

"She's right, EJ, you are a dumbass." I can hear the frustration with his brother through his words. "What the fuck, man?"

"Fuck. I don't know what's wrong with me," Eli says with so much sadness in his voice that the tone hurts my heart.

Marc lets out a heavy sigh of disappointment. "Let's go. You can sleep it off in my room."

The light begins to peek through the crack under my door as Eli stands up.

“I told you I wasn’t going to have your back if you fucked up,” Marc reminds his brother.

“Yeah, I know. I don’t know how I’m going to fix this one,” I hear him say in the distance as they walk back to Marc’s room.

Chapter 43

Logan

I slept terribly last night. Actually, I don't even know if I did sleep. When my alarm went off this morning, as a reminder to get ready for the gym, I was already awake. I continued to snooze it for another hour, hoping I would get just a bit of sleep, but it never came.

I don't even have the energy to get a workout in, which is very unlike me. I have the whole day to make it happen, but I don't have the motivation today. I feel defeated. It's not like Eli and I are together, but it doesn't mean that I feel any less disappointed and let down by his actions last night.

The only plan for my Saturday is to study. I was supposed to go to Eli's hockey game with Marc, but I don't think that's the best idea after how last night went down.

As I drag myself out of bed, I stand up straight and stretch my arms towards the ceiling. My joints pop, every muscle in my body sore from lack of sleep. The only thing that will make my aching body feel better is a long shower. The hot water will feel good against my muscles, and hopefully, it'll clear my mind too. For once, I'm looking forward to taking my time in there as I remember how empty the coed bathrooms were last weekend.

Covering myself with my robe, I grab my toiletries and towel, heading on my way. Thankfully the showers are down the hall in the opposite direction from Marc's room. I don't want to risk running into Eli today.

When I walk into the bathroom, I'm disappointed to see more than a few people in here. It's much more crowded than it was last weekend, but still less so than on school days. I hold my robe tightly against my body as I search for an empty shower stall. Most are taken, but I find one towards the middle of the row as I step inside and put my toiletry bag down. I double-check that the shower curtain is fully covering the opening before removing my robe and hanging it on the hook right outside.

The water starts cold, but it quickly turns warm. I turn the dial to the hottest setting and let the steaming water beat down on my body. Closing my eyes, I put my face directly under the stream as I try to clear my thoughts about the night before, but before I can even begin to relax, I hear Eli's name being called.

"Maddison! What's up, man!" I hear some guy say with excitement, but there's no response.

Shit. I didn't think Eli would come in here to shower. I knew he stayed in Marc's room, but I assumed he would've gone home when he woke up this morning.

"Hey, Maddison. Fancy seeing you here," some chick says. I roll my eyes at her tone. This guy has girls fawning over him all the time and, quite honestly, it's getting annoying.

Again, he doesn't respond.

I can just imagine her gawking at his perfectly chiseled body while his towel hangs low on his hips, barely covering his manhood. The image almost makes me dizzy, that is until I remember that I'm upset with him.

"Logan! Logan, are you in here?" he yells out.

What the fuck?

"Logan!" Eli shouts again, looking for me.

I poke my head around the curtain to see Eli pacing the shower stalls as he calls my name. He's fully dressed, shoes and all, with no intention of showering, and it's evident that he's here to find me.

"Eli? What the hell?" He snaps his head in my direction, his expression instantly shifting from frantic to relieved when his brown eyes lock with mine.

"I went to your room to talk to you, and you weren't there..." he begins as I roll my eyes and close my curtain to continue my shower. "Logan, I really need to talk to you." I stay silent, wishing the squeal from the shower head would drown out his pleading voice.

"Please, let me just explain what happened last night," he adds, panicked.

There's plenty of chattering voices in the bathroom from people whispering amongst themselves. I'm sure they're just as shocked as I am that U of M's star hockey player and most notorious playboy is publicly apologizing in a coed bathroom.

"I stopped by my house after practice to grab a change of clothes before I was headed over to meet you. I had no idea there was a party going on."

I stay silent, still waiting for the apology portion of his explanation.

"Anyway, an old buddy of mine was there, and he wouldn't let me leave until I had a drink with him," he tries to rationalize.

"A drink doesn't take four hours!" I snap from my shower stall.

"I know. I know it doesn't." He sighs. "Every time I tried to leave, he would stop me. Trust me, the only place I wanted to be last night was with you."

My eyes widen, and my lips part as I'm taken aback by his sweet words. Not just that he's saying them, but also that he's saying them in front of a crowd.

"You could've called." This time when I speak, my voice has less anger behind the words.

"They took my phone. And my keys. Cam still has them, actually," he says, his voice soft. "Please, Logan. I was looking forward to seeing you all week, you have to believe me."

I stay silent again, not sure what to think. I want to believe him, I do. It's just that I have a hard time trusting people after everything Zac put me through last year.

“I’m sorry. Please give me another chance,” he adds, his voice laced with sadness and desperation.

I’ve had the luxury of having my bedroom door and now a shower curtain to block my view of Eli when he’s upset. He’s hard enough to say no to as it is, let alone when he’s right in front of me. After a few moments, I take a deep breath and open the curtain just enough to peek out at him, knowing that I’m tempting myself by looking into his soft eyes. But, when I glance around for him, he’s already gone.

I take another few minutes to rinse my hair and gather my thoughts. If Eli is telling me the truth, I shouldn’t be that upset with him. Sure, he probably could’ve handled the situation better, but if what he’s saying is true, it’s not as bad as the scenario I played out in my head of him being with another girl.

Shutting off the water, I reach out for my robe, being sure to keep it wrapped snugly against me before leaving the stall. When I walk out, I have about ten different sets of eyes on me with whispers and giggles floating around. They all seem to be just as shocked and amused by Eli’s admission as I was.

Finding an empty sink to place my toiletries in front of, I grab my brush and smooth out my hair.

The girl using the sink next to mine looks up at me through the mirror, impressed. “Damn, girl. What the hell kind of spell do you have Maddison under?” she asks, shaking her head and laughing in amusement.

I can’t help but laugh with her, recalling how ridiculous Eli must’ve looked standing in the coed showers fully dressed and confessing his feelings to a shower curtain for everyone to hear.

I shyly glance back up in the mirror as I tell her, “I have absolutely no idea.”

Chapter 44

Eli

I bolt from the bathroom as quickly as possible. The sheer number of eyes on me while I tried to apologize to Logan was a bit unnerving, but part of me doesn't even care how stupid I looked. I just needed her to know how sorry I am. I don't know what I'm going to do if she doesn't forgive me...again. I really need to get my shit together if I want to have a shot with this girl.

I wish I could've gotten a better read on her in the bathroom. It's so hard to know what she's thinking when I can't see her face. Her green eyes are usually so telling that it's as if I can almost read her thoughts when I look into them, but here I am, having no idea where I stand, yet again.

Making my way to the elevators to go back home, I pass by Logan's room and realize I left her door open when I came by looking for her only a few minutes before. She should be back soon, and I need to see her, face-to-face, and apologize again.

Slipping inside, I take a seat on the edge of her bed and wait for her. But I don't make myself too comfortable because I'm in hot water at the moment, though I always feel at ease when I'm in her space. I keep my head down with my hands interlocked and my elbows resting on my knees. I probably look like I'm in time-out, and to be honest, I feel like it too.

A few minutes later, she hurries into her room wearing only a thin robe that clings to every curve of her body.

"Eli, what the hell?" Logan asks with exhaustion when she finds me sitting on the edge of her bed. She closes the door behind her.

I know I should respond, but I can't. I know I should look into her eyes so I can see what she's thinking, but I can't. All I can do is stare at her naked body—the one that's covered only by the thin fabric wrapped about her. Her hair is damp from the shower, and I can smell her fresh vanilla scent from here. My mouth has gaped, I know this, but I can't seem to help it. She's absolute perfection in every sense of the word, and she doesn't even know it.

She catches me staring, so she tugs at her robe, making sure it's covering her body completely. When I realize I'm making her uncomfortable, I break out of my daze and close my mouth. Uncomfortable is the last thing I want her to feel around me.

"Sorry." I pull my eyes up to meet hers, but I still can't read her expression. She tears her gaze away from mine as her cheeks begin to blush.

She stays silent. Maybe she doesn't know if I'm apologizing for staring, startling her, or for the actual apology I need to give her, and honestly, I don't know either.

"I just...I wanted to apologize. Face to face," I begin, but I still can't get a read on her. "I know I fucked up. I'm so sorry about last night. I did try to leave, but I probably could've tried harder, and I'm sorry about that. I really did want to be here, and I know I keep fucking up, but I hope you can forgive me. I've never done this before, and I obviously suck at it." I look at her with remorse and hope all wrapped into one, but again she stays silent with her eyes pulled away from mine.

I stand up to leave, looking her in the face one more time, hoping for some relief from my guilt when our eyes finally connect. They ultimately give way, and I can almost see the walls breaking down behind them as she lets out a deep resigned sigh.

"Eli," she says.

God, I love the way my name sounds coming off her lips.

"Don't let it happen again."

A weight lifts off my chest as I take an embarrassingly deep breath of relief and give her an appreciative smile.

"It won't," I reassure her.

A few moments pass as we awkwardly glance back and forth at each other, unsure of what to say. Maybe I should leave, but I really don't want to.

"You're coming to the alumni game with Marc, right?" I ask, breaking the silence.

"I don't think so. I need to work on my paper for creative writing."

I look at her, confused. "But we haven't talked about it yet. You won't even know what to write."

She shrugs. "It's due Monday, and I'm sure I can come up with a few pages. Hockey, right?"

"Well, what would I write about?" My voice begins to sound frantic. "I want to do this assignment the way we are supposed to."

I honestly have no idea what I would write about because I really don't know anything about this girl, except for how I feel about her. I was hoping this assignment was my opportunity to get a look into what makes her who she is and have some of my questions answered about her past.

"Well, you had your chance to do that last night," she snaps. She's still hurt by my not showing up, and I can't blame her. She takes a deep breath before changing her tone. "I'm sure you can write whatever you want. I doubt that Kenny will even read it."

I shake my head at her in disagreement. I honestly don't give a shit about the actual paper; I just want to spend time with her. I want to know her, I want her to know me, and this assignment is the perfect opportunity.

"After the game, I want to take you somewhere."

"Eli..." she begins to object.

"Logan, please," I plead. "Just say you'll come with me. I think it will help you understand me a bit better." I pause a moment for her response, but she's still standing her ground and not giving in. "I want you to understand me."

She inhales a deep breath as every feature on her face softens. "Okay, fine. I'll go."

"I'll be here at five-thirty. Promise." I know I have the biggest shit-eating grin on my face right now because I'm getting my way, but I don't care. "Dress warm."

"Where are you taking me?" she asks with suspicion, but the sly grin forming on her lips tells me she's in, regardless.

"You'll have to wait and see," I playfully tell her while trying to hold back my excitement.

I give her one last look up and down before I leave. I don't even try to be sly about it as I bite my bottom lip, roaming her body with my eyes. And once my gaze makes it back to her face, she doesn't even try to playfully scold me for my staring. She just lets me take her in. I get the feeling she likes me looking at her just as much as I do.

Taking the image of her perfect body and wet hair, I lock it in my mind and leave for my game, reeling about the fact that I get to see her again as soon as it's over.

Chapter 45

Logan

When Marc swung by my room before he left for the alumni game, I didn't mention that I had plans to see Eli afterward. He didn't even ask if I wanted to come along; he just assumed that I was done with Eli's bullshit and wouldn't want to see his brother. Which maybe I should be, but I can't seem to shake the guy. He's already begun to occupy space in my mind and heart, and I don't know if I'm going to be able to stop it. Maybe I don't want to stop it.

It's a few minutes until five-thirty, the time that Eli said he would be here. I'm trying not to get my hopes up that he will even show, let alone be on time, but I did do my hair and makeup in anticipation, so I guess you could say my hopes are already there.

I hear a knock on my door and look at the clock. If this is Eli, not only did he show up, he's early.

Opening the door, I can't hold back the smile plastered on my face when I see Eli standing in my doorway.

"Hi."

"Hi," he says in return with the same expectant smile.

I doubt he's noticed it, but whenever I greet him, I always say 'hi' instead of 'hey' or 'hello.' It's a stupid little thing I reserve in my mind only for him.

He doesn't say anything. He just stares at me, which is fine by me because I can't help but stare right back at him. I swear, every time I see Eli, he gets more handsome. It's like god made him the most attractive man I've ever seen so that I would forgive all the stupid shit he does. Because right now, I'm starting to forget why I was even upset with him last night.

He's wearing his hockey sweatshirt again with jeans and Converse. He has his hat on backward, reminding me of the night we kissed, and I accidentally knocked it off. The memory heats my cheeks as a laugh slips from my lips.

"What's so funny?" He asks while laughing with me, but not knowing why.

I shake my head as I try to hold back my giddy smile. "Nothing."

"You look...beautiful," he tells me, his tone quickly changing from playful to serious.

My cheeks warm once again. They've got to be beet red at this point.

"Thank you," I shyly respond.

I'm really not looking all that great, but I'll take the compliment. Honestly, I had no idea what to wear because Eli didn't give me any indication as to where we are going. Plus, Ali went to the game with Marc, so I didn't have her here to help me pick out an outfit. But I'm happy to see that my decision to dress on the casual side was the right move. My jeans, hoodie, and Vans seem to match Eli's intentions for tonight perfectly.

Though, I do hope I dressed warm enough. Marc told me that there was a massive party at the hockey house tonight, so I know we won't be out too late because Eli will need to get back. Thinking of the temperature suddenly causes me to remember Eli's jacket that he lent me on Monday after class. As much as I don't want to return it to him because it's filled my room with his masculine scent, I grab it off my chair to give to him.

"Almost forgot about your jacket." I hold it out for him.

"Keep it. You might need it tonight. I don't know how cold that California blood gets."

"I'm from *northern* California. It gets cold there. I'll be fine," I inform him, playfully rolling my eyes at his concern.

"Mmm-hmm," he hums, unconvinced. "Do you drink coffee?" We exit my room and I lock the door behind us.

"I'm a grad student. Of course, I drink coffee."

"Okay, good. I'm taking you to my favorite coffee shop," Eli tells me as we get in the elevator.

I look at him, confused. "That's the place you're taking me that will help me understand you better?"

"No. That's just a pit stop, but I need some caffeine. I didn't really sleep last night," he tells me before realizing what he's saying.

"That makes two of us," I respond shortly without looking in his direction. When the elevator opens on the main floor, I step out before him.

"Shit. That was stupid of me to say."

"No, it's fine." I shake my head. "I'm trying to forget about last night. I shouldn't keep bringing it up."

Eli opens the lobby door for me as the chilly September air hits me. I instantly cross my arms in front of my chest, needing to keep my body warmth in. If this is how cold I am at the end of September, I can't imagine how I'll handle the weather come the middle of January.

Eli notices me shivering and wraps his arm around my shoulder, pulling me into his body as we walk towards his car.

"Told you that you were going to get cold," he reminds me as I laugh to myself, leaning my body into him even more.

He surprises me by placing a simple swift kiss on the top of my head, and suddenly my entire body is ignited. Every inch of my skin tingles with warmth. I'm definitely not cold anymore, but there's no way I'm leaving his embrace until we reach his car.

When we do, he opens the passenger side door of his truck for me to get in. The step-up is high, but I'm tall, and my legs are long, so I jump in with ease. He closes the door behind me before getting in on the driver's side.

His sleek black truck is so nice, and it has all the bells and whistles. It's masculine and sexy without trying too hard, just like Eli.

"So, are you going to tell me where we are going?" I ask as the engine purrs.

"Not a chance." He gives me a sly smirk before looking into the rearview mirror to pull out of his parking space.

His devilish grin is going to be the death of me. And that backward hat—so hot. Unfortunately, his sweatshirt sleeve covers his tattoos, but regardless, he's still so freaking attractive. One hand holds onto his truck's steering wheel while the other arm casually drapes on the center console between us, and he looks more at ease and relaxed than I've ever seen him.

His brown eyes never leave the road, but somehow he catches me admiring.

"What are you staring at?" He keeps his eyes forward, holding back his cocky grin.

"Nothing." Quickly pulling my eyes from him, I look out my passenger side window, slightly embarrassed he caught me red-handed.

He lets out a knowing chuckle and continues to drive.

"Are we getting close?" I ask as I look at the clock, realizing we've been on the road for almost an hour.

"Yep. It's the next exit," Eli tells me as he continues to drive.

A minute later, he pulls off the freeway, and after a few turns, he parks in front of a small coffee shop. The shop is quaint and quiet, but the town is even quieter. I haven't seen more than five other cars on the road since we pulled off the freeway. I have no idea where we are or what town we are in, but I don't care. I'm just glad I get to be here with Eli.

Eli opens my passenger side door, holding his hand out to help me out of his truck. When we approach the coffee shop, he opens the door again, and it makes me wonder if he's always this polite to the girls he spends time with.

The coffee shop is even smaller inside than it appeared outside. There are only three tables in the lobby and one barista working behind the counter. I have no idea how Eli found this spot in the first place, but I find it interesting that he drove me over an hour to get coffee here.

"Hey Trev," Eli says to the man behind the counter with his back towards us.

Trev peeks over his shoulder, his eyes widening in surprise. "Eli? I didn't expect to see you for a couple more months." His voice drips with excitement as he quickly walks around the counter to give Eli a hug. "You know the ice isn't frozen over yet?" he asks, seeming just as confused as I am.

I don't know if I'm more shocked that this guy just called Eli by his real name, or that Eli hugged him with as much enthusiasm as Trev had.

"I know. I just wanted to stop in. How's Stacey?" Eli places his hand on Trev's shoulder. His eyes are bright, seeming at ease in this place.

"She's good, man. Baby is due around Christmas."

"That's awesome. Can't wait to meet the little guy. And Ian?" I've never heard Eli be this kind and relaxed towards anyone back at school. I'm so confused as to what is going on and who Trev is.

"He's great. Growing like a weed. And he can't wait to skate with you again," Trev says before turning his attention to me. "And who might this be?"

"Shit. Sorry, this is—"

"I'm Logan," I interrupt, holding my hand out to greet Trev.

"Yes, this is Logan," Eli beams as he smiles down at me.

"Logan." Trev says my name, dragging out the 'n.' "Nice to meet you. I've never had the chance to meet one of Eli's friends before." Trev eyes Eli, as Eli begins to nervously scratch at his brow, feeling put on the spot.

So, he's never brought anyone out here before. Wherever *here* is. But this place seems important to Eli for some reason, and the fact that I'm the only person he's ever brought here makes my heart flutter.

"What can I get you, young lady?" Trev asks, walking back behind the counter. Trev doesn't look more than ten years older than me, so I find it funny that he would refer to me as "young lady."

The menu board is pretty sparse, so I try not to be too difficult.

"Can I have a latte?"

"Of course," Trev says before looking to Eli. "Black? Large?"

"Please. Can we get them to go today?" Eli hands him a twenty-dollar bill.

"No problem." Trev returns fifteen dollars in change, but Eli puts it in the tip jar and slips in another twenty when Trev turns around to make our drinks.

I don't know who this guy is or why Eli is so sweet to him, but it makes me melt to see Eli this way. He's shown his kindness to me, but I'm happy that someone else gets to see this side of him too.

"You think we can get tickets to a game this year?" Trev asks Eli, handing him his black coffee.

"Of course, anytime. I'll even show Ian around the locker room. Just let me know when you guys can make it out to Minneapolis."

"Thanks, man. Ian will be stoked to see you out there on the ice." Trev hands me my latte, which has the most delicate and beautiful foam design on top.

"Who is Ian?" I chime in, unable to keep my curiosity at bay.

"Ian is my son," Trev informs me.

"Yeah, and he's a little five-year-old stud," Eli adds.

"Yeah, well, that's because he's been hanging around you too much." Trev motions towards Eli. "Eli taught him how to skate last year, and now my kid is obsessed with being just like him. He even asks us all to refer to him as Maddison instead of Ian."

"Uh-oh. You might wanna get that kid's head on straight before it's too late," I tease.

Eli gives me a mock look of shock, but the corners of his gaping mouth begin to pull upwards.

"Watch it." Eli playfully knocks his hip into mine.

"Damn. I like this girl. Calls you on your shit," Trev says, impressed.

"Yeah, tell me about it." Eli rolls his eyes, but the smile on his lips remains.

"I'm glad I finally got to meet one of your friends," Trev continues. "I'm going to need you to come back, okay, Logan?"

"She will be," Eli states without hesitation, and my heart does that flutter thing again.

We say our thank yous and wave our goodbyes as we head out the door of the small and sweet coffee shop.

I hold on tightly to my hot latte, trying to steal some of the warmth from the cup, and I'm a little annoyed that Eli was right about my inability to handle the Minnesota chill.

Eli quickly jogs to the truck ahead of me, opening his door, but he doesn't get inside. Instead, he grabs his jacket as well as a beanie and a blanket that he must have stashed in the back seat.

"Where are we going?" I ask him, confused, as he walks back to me with his hands full.

"There." He nods towards the distance, behind the coffee shop.

I turn around, but all I see is a broad field with a line of thick trees in the distance.

"Trust me," Eli says, giving me his most convincing smile and holding open his jacket for me to put on. But I don't think he realizes that asking me to trust someone is not as easy as it sounds.

Slipping my arms through the jacket sleeves, I alternate my latte between hands. He pulls out the camel-colored beanie he had stuffed in the pocket and gently puts in on my head, covering my ears and instantly warming me up.

"Better?" he asks, both of his hands lingering on the sides of my face, his eyes bright as he looks at me.

"Much." I smile at him gratefully, keeping my eyes locked with his.

He doesn't pull his hands away. Instead, he keeps them cupping my face. "You look so much better in my clothes than I do."

"Not a chance. You look good in everything," my mouth tells him before my mind catches up. My eyes widen in embarrassment, hearing my internal dialogue spoken out loud.

Eli's lips turn up into a grin as he searches my face for a moment. He seems like he might kiss me, but instead, he clears his throat and pulls his hands away from my face. "Ready?" he asks.

"For what exactly?"

"You'll see." He tries to hold back his smile as he grabs my arm and loops it around his.

Chapter 46

Logan

The closer we get to the line of trees, the more confused I become.

"Did you bring me out here to kill me?" I ask Eli, only somewhat kidding. We are in the middle of nowhere, Minnesota, and the coffee shop is getting smaller and smaller behind us.

"I wouldn't tell you if I did." Eli laughs, shaking his head at me when he notices me stop in my tracks. "You're ridiculous. Come on."

When we reach the edge of the forest, Eli releases my arm but glides his large hand down until it's holding mine. Every nerve in my fingers ignites at once as he leads me through the maze of towering pines.

I follow closely behind him, and after a few minutes of weaving through the massive trunks, he releases my hand and moves out of the way. "Okay, we're here," he says.

It takes a moment for my eyes to adjust to the bright reflection of the sun beating down on the water, but once they do, I'm greeted with one of the most enchanting scenes I've ever laid eyes on. There's a lake that's not too large, entirely surrounded by a thick forest of trees. It's perfectly silent aside from a few birds chirping off in the distance. The sun is lingering just above the tallest pine, making its way toward setting, causing a gorgeous reflection on the water to illuminate the secluded space. Only a few feet of bank separate the tree line from the water, so I walk down to the edge and place my fingers in the lake, instantly regretting it. The sun might be beating down, but the water is so cold that it will probably freeze over in just a few short months.

"It's beautiful," I tell Eli as I stand, turning to face him, with the water and sun at my back. I tightly grab ahold of my latte, trying to warm my hands again.

He's still standing up at the top of the shore, close to the tree line.

"Yeah, it is," he says, staring directly at me. I'm not sure if he's referring to the scenery or me, but I don't ask him to elaborate.

"So, you brought me to one of Minnesota's ten thousand lakes?"

"Actually, it's a pond. It's too small and shallow to be considered a lake."

"So, why the pond?" I walk back up towards him, standing directly in front of him.

He looks around for a moment. "Here. Come here." He grabs my hand again, leading me to a small bench on the bank of the water. It's the only man-made thing among the stunning scenery.

I take a seat as he unfolds the blanket in his hands and places it on my lap before sitting down as close to me as he can, tucking himself under the blanket as well. His eyes are locked on the pond as he gathers his thoughts. Eli takes a sip of his coffee, followed by a deep breath before he begins.

"I want to tell you something that I haven't told many people before. I'm hoping it'll give you a better glimpse into who I am, not just who everyone at school thinks I am."

He looks to me with anticipation as I nervously nod my head in response.

"When I was in high school and being recruited by colleges, I was basically a shoo-in to get called up to the NHL within a year or two. I know that sounds super fucking arrogant, but it's the truth, and everybody knew it. But then, during a preseason game at the beginning of my sophomore year of college, I was illegally thrown into the boards. I shattered my ankle and tore a bunch of ligaments. I couldn't walk, let alone skate. It was fucking awful." He tries to shake the memory away.

"I had to take that season off to heal and rehab, and I was really struggling. Physically, obviously, but even more so mentally. Scouts weren't interested in me anymore, and all of a sudden, my future was up in the air."

He glances up to me, maybe trying to gauge my reaction, I'm not sure. But he quickly shifts his eyes back down to the ground before continuing.

"I felt this insane pressure to get back to normal, so much so that I started suffering from panic attacks almost daily. Practically every night, I would wake up in a sweat. I couldn't sleep anymore. It consumed me. For the first time in my life, I didn't feel like I was going to be good enough again."

Eli lifts his eyes to mine again, but I don't know what to say. I'm shocked to learn that he was struggling so badly. He always seems so cocky and proud when it comes to playing hockey, but in reality, he has literal panic attacks, agonizing over the fact that he might not be good enough.

He averts his gaze from mine again as he continues. "When my ankle was somewhat healed and I was cleared to skate again, I fucking sucked. Like I was so bad that I could barely even stand on the blade. I was so weak, and I was doing physical therapy, but it was excruciating, and it wasn't working. I just felt too much pressure from everyone at school to get back to where I was before, that I couldn't get my mind right to focus on healing my body."

I can see the worry beginning to form on his face as he tells me his story. I don't want to interrupt, but I do want to calm him down. Taking his hand in mine, I lace my fingers through his. His hands are so large and strong that they almost entirely engulf mine, but I love the way it looks, my hand in his. It looks like it belongs there. He gives my palm an appreciative squeeze before taking a deep breath, calming his nerves.

"When you asked me why I brought you here, it's because this place has become especially important to me, and I wanted to share it with you. During the time that I was trying to rehab, I felt so defeated, and my mental state was so weak, that I made the decision to stop playing altogether. I was going to give up my scholarship and call it quits. I got in the car to drive back to Indiana and tell my dad, but I ended up pulling off for a pit stop and randomly finding Trev's coffee shop. Trev was cool, and no one was in there that day, so I ended up sitting and talking to this stranger for hours. It was weird, it was the first time I opened up to someone outside of my family, but because I didn't know Trev, there was no pressure to be the guy that everyone back at school knew. I didn't tell him everything, but I filled him in enough for him to know that I was struggling. He brought me back here and showed me the frozen pond. He offered it up to me if I wanted to start doing my physical therapy out here, away from the pressures of everyone on campus. His parents own the property, and no one else knew it even existed."

I turn my body on the bench so that I'm fully facing Eli, even though he continues to look ahead. Keeping our intertwined hands in my lap, I graze my thumb gently across his to encourage him to keep talking.

"I decided to give it a try and see if I could get my mind right as I tried to heal my ankle. I came out here every morning before class and basically retaught myself how to skate from scratch. I felt like I could actually breathe and get away from the anxiety I have when I'm back on campus, and it worked. After six hard months, I was back, and better than ever before the next season started. This place has kind of become my safe spot, and I come out here whenever I need to get away. It's one of my favorite places in the world."

He takes a deep breath before taking a sip of his coffee, keeping his eyes averted from mine. Clearly, this is the most vulnerable Eli has ever felt. I can see it in his expression.

"No one knows about this. Only Trev and his wife and son know that I come here, not even my own family. I keep it private, so it doesn't get tainted by outside noise. You're the first person I've ever told, let alone brought here," he adds, waiting for my response.

My heart skips a beat at his words. The fact that he wanted to share this place with me makes me speechless. So, instead of saying anything, I reach up and turn his chin to face me, looking from his eyes to his mouth and back again. I can't help myself as I press my lips to his, the warmth of his mouth igniting my whole body. He stays still for a moment as if my kiss took him by surprise before I move my hand to the side of his face, pulling him into me. As he catches on to what's happening, Eli sharply inhales, parting his lips, and deepening our kiss. His mouth presses tightly to mine, and I can feel how much he needs me in this moment. He's warm, and his lips are soft as they explore mine.

Moving his hand to the back of my head, he pulls me closer. We keep our kiss simple but passionate, and after a few moments, I pull away but keep my hand on the side of his face, stroking his shaggy hair with my fingertips, and looking into his warm brown eyes.

"Thank you," I tell him, "for bringing me here." I gently kiss his cheek before drawing away.

Eli shakes his head while a surprised smile forms on his lips. "Well, I didn't expect that," he laughs. "So can I assume you're over the whole 'let's just be friends' thing?"

I playfully roll my eyes. "You knew I wouldn't be able to hold my ground on that."

He gives me a knowing smile.

"Do you even want to play professionally, or do you feel like that's what you should do because people are expecting it from you?"

"Oh, no. It's definitely my dream. It just feels a little more overwhelming now that everyone's expectations of me are so high. But, as soon as I get that call, I'm on the first flight out to wherever I'm needed," Eli casually states.

Oh, I don't like that. I don't like the thought of him leaving at any moment.

"Does anyone else know about your panic attacks?"

"Only my parents and Marc...and now you."

"And have you ever talked to anyone about how to deal with your anxiety?"

"Yeah, I've seen a few therapists. I was even put on a medication for the attacks, but it made my brain foggy and didn't work anyway."

"And you still have them? The panic attacks, I mean."

Eli chuckles at my string of questions, but I can't help it. I'm more than curious about this man that no one else seems to know.

"Yeah, sometimes." He shrugs. "I just try to deal with them when they start to come on. I try to focus on something else."

"And that's been working?"

"It has lately." He pauses. "Since I met you." He looks at me, no longer nervously keeping his gaze from mine.

My eyes widen at his words. "What do you mean?"

"Since I met you, I haven't been thinking about hockey too much. You've been a distraction, to say the least."

"And that's a good thing?" I ask, confused by his admission.

"I think so." His eyes search my face as his thumb gently caresses the back of my hand. "Do you remember the night you slept in my bed? The night we first met."

"Of course." How could I forget? That was the night he crept into my mind and didn't seem to want to leave my thoughts.

"That was the first time I had ever shared a bed with someone. I had never let anyone sleep next to me because I didn't trust anyone enough to allow them to see me if a panic attack came on in the middle of the night, but with you, I didn't care if you saw me like that. I just wanted you near me. The few nights I've slept next to you have been the best sleep I've gotten in a long time."

I swear my heart has dropped into my stomach from his confession.

“Why are you telling me all this?” I look at him, honored but confused. He’s so vulnerable with me, and it makes me feel good knowing that he can be open around me, but Marc has always said that Eli was closed off and doesn’t let people get to know the real him.

“Because I want you to know me. I mean, I want you to know anything that you’d like to know.” He looks at me shyly.

My heart is doing that flutter thing again. “I want to know everything.”

A small smile forms on Eli’s lips as he leans forward to gently kiss my forehead, leaving his lips lingering for a moment. He’s done that a couple of times now, and I love the gesture.

“About last night,” he sighs. “I had an old teammate of mine in town. His name is Jay, and Jay is the epitome of the pressure that I feel from the rest of the school to make it to the NHL. Sometimes, I just feel like I have to be who these people expect me to be. So I throw the parties, and I do stupid shit without thinking twice about anyone else. I’ve never cared about anyone before. Before you. But who they think I am is not who I want to be, so I’m working on it. I’m sorry again for last night, but hopefully, this helps you understand me a bit better.”

“It does,” I tell him with a grateful smile on my lips.

I’ve been attracted to Eli since the first moment I saw him, but now, seeing who he really is and getting to be one of the only people who does, makes me more attracted to him than ever before. All the concerns I ever had about falling for this boy are out the window because I don’t really have a choice anymore. I’ve already fallen.

Chapter 47

Eli

I feel an odd mixture of both relief and vulnerability after spilling my guts to Logan. I've never been so open with anyone before, but she makes me feel like I can be completely myself with her. Having her in my favorite place makes me love this pond even more. I never thought I would tell anyone about this spot, but now that Logan knows, I want her to be with me every time I come.

"So, now that you know way too much about me, we need to talk about your portion of the paper." I pause to take a sip of my coffee. "What's *your* biggest passion in life?"

"I don't really have one," she admits with a nonchalant shrug.

"What? Of course, you do. Everyone has something that drives them."

"I guess I'm the exception to the rule." She casually takes a sip of her latte as she continues to avoid the question.

"Well, that's not very helpful. What am I going to write about then?"

"I don't know. I doubt Kenny will even read our papers. You can just make something up," she suggests, keeping her eyes averted from mine.

"Logan, are you avoiding the question?" I playfully ask.

"No," she answers much too quickly.

"You are."

"I'm not, I just haven't felt passionate about something in a long time."

"Okay. Well, then what is something that you used to feel passionate about?" I just want to get to know this girl, but man, is she making it difficult.

She waits for a moment, deciding if she's going to appease my prying, then tells me, "I guess if I had to choose something, I would say that I was once passionate about playing basketball. But that's not really the case anymore."

"Well, that's cool. Were you any good?"

"I was a high school all-American and had a full ride to play for the University of Oregon," she casually replies.

I did not expect that. When I asked if Logan was any good, I didn't really care either way. I just wanted to keep the conversation going. But now that I know she was a total badass, I just find her that much more attractive.

"What? How did I not know this about you?"

"No one knows. Not even Marc."

"You're telling me that I know something about you that Marc doesn't?" I ask with my eyes wide. I'm about to get so fucking smug if I know something about this girl that my brother doesn't.

"You should feel honored."

"Oh, I do!" I tell her with way too much enthusiasm. "So, you played for Oregon, how was that?" Does she not realize how hot it is that she was a division one athlete? I know firsthand, the dedication that it takes.

"I didn't end up going there," she tells me, cutting off my thoughts. She pulls her gaze from mine, keeping her head down. "When my dad died in my senior year of high school, my life at home got pretty hectic, and I had to give up my scholarship. Instead, I stayed home and attended the local state school."

"Why?" I quickly ask.

"It's a long story." She shakes her head, obviously not wanting to divulge.

"Okay." Shit. I don't want to upset her. We've been having such a good conversation, and I don't want it to end because I ask the wrong questions.

"Do you miss playing?" I ask carefully.

"Sometimes, yeah. But it's been a while since I've even touched a basketball. My dad was my coach growing up, so sometimes the memories tied to playing make me think of him, which can be hard." She looks up into my eyes, seeming to feel more comfortable about opening up to me.

"How is your mom doing without him being around?" I ask, pressing my luck. She's never mentioned anything about the rest of her family, so I'm hoping this is my opportunity to find out, but her expression goes blank. I clearly struck a nerve.

"Sorry, I shouldn't have asked that." I shake my head. "I didn't mean to pry."

"No, it's okay." Her frozen expression softens, trying to ease my regret for asking. "Um...actually, my mom passed away last December." She holds my gaze, attempting to gauge my reaction.

Suddenly it's like all the pieces of the puzzle are beginning to fit together. Everything that Marc had told me about Logan having a rough few years. Her wisdom and ability to understand what I was dealing with when my birth father passed. Her independence. She's already lived through more life, and loss, than someone should have to deal with, especially at our age.

"I'm sorry. I shouldn't have brought anything up. I didn't mean for you to have to tell me."

"That's okay. You obviously didn't know." She gives me a slight smile as if she's trying to make me feel better when I should be the one comforting her.

"Were you guys close?"

"Yeah, she was my best friend." Logan's face begins to light up until she pauses for a moment, getting lost in her memories.

"When I was younger, my mom's kidneys started to fail—"

"Logan, you don't have to tell me if you don't want to," I interrupt. I don't want her to feel pressured to tell me anything when she's not comfortable. Just because I opened up to her, doesn't mean she owes me anything. I know how private she can be.

"I want to. I mean, if you want to know?" she asks, seeming unsure.

Looking up for a moment, she explores my face, searching for any hesitation from me, but there's none to be found. I want to be here for her. If she's willing to open up to me, then I want to hear everything she has to say.

"Come here." I motion for her to come closer. Lifting the blanket, I use my other hand to guide her hips onto my lap. She sits across my legs as I pull the blanket back over her to keep her warm, holding her in my arms. She fits perfectly against my body, and I feel at ease having her this close. Hopefully, my holding her brings her the same comfort that it does me.

"I want to know anything that you feel comfortable enough to share," I tell her.

She gives me an appreciative grin before resting her head on my shoulder and continuing. "My mom's kidneys were failing, and my dad was going through testing to see if he would be a match to donate to her, but he passed away before he could. That's when I decided that I would donate to her if I were a match, which I was. She was so low on the donation list that, at that point, I was her only chance of getting a transplant. I gave up my scholarship to stay home, and we had the surgery, but it didn't work. Her body rejected my kidney, even though we ran all the proper tests." She pauses as I tighten my grip around her body.

Could this girl be anymore selfless?

"Her health started to decline drastically from there. She was back on dialysis, and it was taking its toll on her body. I was taking care of her all day, every day, spending hours with her hooked up to machines, to the point where I barely had time for myself anymore. Even when I was healing from my own surgery, all I could think about was her. I was stressed out all the time. She was my only parent left, and we were so close, but I was always waiting for the other shoe to drop and for something else bad to happen. Her kidney issues were just the beginning of a laundry list of health issues that began to come up."

Her words begin to come out rushed and frantic, so I lift my head to glance at her, causing her to pause. Looking into her green eyes, I tuck a fallen strand of hair behind her ear and underneath the beanie. She takes a moment, gives me a thankful smile, and rests her head back on my shoulder before continuing.

"The worst of it was in her last few months. She was constantly in and out of the hospital, and each time I took her in, I thought that was it. I thought that was the time I was going to have to say goodbye. They had her on some extreme medications to keep her alive, which caused pretty some severe side effects. Her mind was so foggy that she didn't even know who I was most of the time. That's one of the hardest things I had to come to terms with is that my own mother didn't recognize me for the last couple of months of her life."

I rest my head on hers, wanting to be close to her and bring her comfort. She doesn't have to tell me this, and I can tell she's struggling with it, but I just want her to feel taken care of. She deserves to be taken care of.

"When it was near the end for her, she had been in the hospital declining for weeks. She was so sick at that point that I had to be the one to make the call and let her go, that we had to stop trying with all the meds. I think about that every day, wondering if I made the right decision. She was basically gone already, but still, I battle with that decision every day."

I honestly have no idea what to say right now. I'm way out of my element here, but I don't want Logan to feel alone in her grief. She's not even crying as she tells me about her mom. Has she ever had the opportunity to cry on someone's shoulder before?

"Did you have anyone to be there for you or to help you?" I ask, resting my head on hers, my lips brushing against her temple, and remembering what Marc had said about her always having to take care of herself.

"No, it's just me. I don't have any siblings, and the only family I had was my parents. I had a boyfriend at the time, but he definitely did not help the situation."

I want to get back to that boyfriend topic, but right now, I just want to remind Logan of how special she is.

"Do you know how incredible you are?" I lift my face from hers so that I can get a better look at her.

"I'm not." She shakes her head, laughing under her breath. Logan doesn't do a great job at accepting compliments, but I think it's because she's not used to hearing them.

"Logan, you are. You're the strongest person I've ever met." I look into her eyes, willing her to believe me. "I wish I would've known you then. I wish I could've been there for you."

"Me too," she says, giving me a half smile.

Bending down, I gently graze her lips with mine, wanting to thank her for trusting me. As much as I want to kiss her longer, it doesn't feel like the right time after the heaviness of our conversation. As if I wasn't already crushing on Logan enough, getting a glimpse into the woman she really is has done nothing but cause me to fall for her even more.

She nuzzles her head into the crook of my neck and wraps her arm around my shoulder. "So when you ask what my passion is, the truth is, over the last few years, I haven't had the time to find something that I feel that way about."

"Well, we're going to work on that." I tighten my grip around her waist. Though, I don't think she realizes she already has something that she's passionate about. You can see how much she cares for people and wants to take care of them. I saw it the night I told her about my birth father, I heard it just now when she spoke about donating to her mom, and I feel it every time I'm vulnerable with her. She might not realize she's passionate about it, and honestly, she's probably sick of having to care for everyone else around her, but it's who she is. It's ingrained in her.

It makes sense, Marc being so protective of her. He wants her to think about herself for a change instead of worrying about everyone around her. Now, I totally get it, and I couldn't be more on-board.

I know I don't deserve to be here with the strong and selfless girl in my arms, but I'm going to do everything in my power to take care of her and be who she needs. I get that she's independent and can take care of herself, but she shouldn't have to. She doesn't even see that she deserves the best the world can offer her—not that I think I necessarily am, but I'm going to try my hardest to be.

Chapter 48

Eli

I have no idea how long we've been sitting here, but I'd be happy to stay out here all night, holding Logan. This moment is the most content and peaceful I've felt in a long time, and judging by her slow and steady breathing, I think the same goes for her. The sun is almost entirely set, causing the pond to be overtaken with darkness, but still, I refuse to interrupt us. As if she could hear my thoughts, Logan speaks for the first time in a while, keeping her head nuzzled against my neck.

"We should get going," she says in an almost sleepy and sedated voice, her warm breath brushing against my skin.

"I don't want to."

"It's almost dark, and you have to get back for your party."

I almost completely forgot about the alumni party tonight. Jay and the guys will kill me if I'm not there, but I don't know if I care anymore. I just want to be wherever Logan is tonight.

"Come on." She stands from my lap, taking the blanket with her and wrapping it around herself.

A small whimper from the loss of contact escapes my lips, causing Logan to giggle at my neediness. I grab both of our empty cups and stack them within one another to throw them away back at the coffee shop.

"Hop on," I tell her as I turn my back towards her.

"Really?"

"Yeah, it's too dark to see through that maze of trees. I'd rather just carry you."

"Here, I'll hold the cups." She holds out her hand for our trash.

Logan gets on the bench and climbs on my back, wrapping her arms around my neck and her legs around my waist. I fucking love the feeling of her body against mine.

I start weaving through the trees while Logan holds her phone out to light our path. She bends down and gently places a single kiss on my neck, causing my whole body to be overtaken by goosebumps. I almost decide to put her down right here, pin her up against one of these trunks, and kiss her for a while. But I know she's cold, and I want to get the heat on in the truck for her as soon as possible.

When we reach my truck, I open her door, and she climbs in with ease. Her flawless long legs make the step-up look easy, and I can't help but admire her perfect ass as she does. I take the empty cups from her and toss them in the trash outside of the coffee shop. The lights inside are off, and Trev's car is gone, which isn't too surprising; It has gotten pretty late.

When I jump in my car, I quickly start the engine and crank the heat for Logan. She's going to have a tough time once actual winter hits if this is how she's handling late September. Before I back out of the parking space, I reach across the center divider and put my hand on Logan's thigh, partly to warm her up, but mostly because I want to touch her again. She places her hand on mine as her eyes dart to me, and suddenly the temperature in the truck feels like it went up another ten degrees.

"Thanks for bringing me here," she says sweetly as her eyes wander to my lips then back to my eyes again.

"Come here," I whisper, pulling her hand towards me, motioning for her to sit on my lap. I take off my baseball cap and toss it in the backseat, not wanting it to be in our way.

She climbs over the center console, straddling her legs around me. And fuck, does she feel good. Reaching behind her, I quickly kill the engine. I have a feeling it's about to get too hot in here to have the heat blasting at us from the vents.

As I bring my hand back, I place it on her hip and slide her forward, pressing her closer to me. I can already feel myself getting hard beneath her as my jeans are beginning to tighten, and it's not because I haven't had sex since I met her, but because it's Logan that's sitting on me. She places her hands on my shoulders and leans down, gently placing her forehead on mine, but she doesn't kiss me. Her lips stay only an inch or two above mine, and it's taking everything in me to keep it slow and savor every moment between us.

I look into her green eyes as she looks into mine. Reaching up, I remove my beanie from her head and toss it aside without breaking eye contact with her. A strand of hair falls into her face, so I tuck it behind her ear, keeping my hand resting there, on the side of her face. Her eyes flutter close at my touch, and I can feel the pulse in her neck quickening under my fingertips. My breathing accelerates, and my lips part, all thanks to the view I have of her wearing my jacket and straddling me in my truck. We haven't even kissed yet, but between her ever so slightly rocking on my lap and our mutually ragged breaths, I'm already insanely turned on.

My lips find their way to her neck, but still, I don't kiss her. I graze them against her skin as I take in her heavenly vanilla scent. My nose trails a line from the base of her neck to her jaw while my bottom lip drags behind, causing little bumps to form all over Logan's body, before I kiss the sensitive spot just below her ear. I pull back to look into her eyes, but I can't wait any longer as I lick my lips and crush them against hers. We simultaneously let out a pair of matching moans in relief. I part my lips and deepen our kiss as Logan's tongue grazes mine. I groan much too loudly, but I don't even care. The way my body responds to hers is like nothing I've experience before.

Logan's hands find their way into my hair, and she burrows them there, tugging gently at the roots. Moving both my hands to either side of her hips, I begin to ever so slightly rock them harder and faster against me. I'm really regretting my decision to wear jeans. I wish I could feel her better.

She moves her lips from my mouth to my neck, dragging them up to my ear until she gently nibbles and sucks on it. Her flushed cheek is pressed tightly to mine before she continues to trail wet kisses down the length of my neck.

I love watching her take control. It's sexy as hell.

"Fuck," I say in a low, raspy voice as my head falls back onto the headrest. The car is filled with heavy breaths and moans, and between her teasing lips and her hips' perfect movements, I'm about to explode.

Her lips find their way back to mine as I lean forward with her in my lap, needing to take control before her expert movements cause me to humiliate myself by coming in my jeans before we even really get started. I move my hands to her ass, squeezing tightly as I try to relieve some of the pressure building up in my body.

I don't think I've ever been this attracted to someone before, and I feel out of my element with Logan. Sexually, I'm plenty experienced, but I've never been with someone I care for this much. It's proven to be a much more challenging task to control myself than I expected.

Reaching my hands around to the hem of her sweatshirt, I begin to slide it up, needing to focus on her pleasure and suppress mine before I embarrass myself.

I keep my lips connected to hers when my hands reach the silky-smooth skin of her stomach. As they travel up, the beat of her heart quickens under my palm. She has a light layer of moisture forming on her skin from the heat inside this truck, and I'm sure my body's temperature matches hers. I want to get our clothes off as soon as possible. No, I *need* to get our clothes off as soon as possible so that I can see her perfect body in my hands. Luckily, the parking lot is pitch black, and there is no one within miles to see what's about to happen inside my car.

As soon as my fingertips reach the base of her satin bra, an alarmingly loud ring radiates throughout my truck. Logan gasps in surprise, disconnecting our lips in shock. The vibrating phone in the center console displays Marc's flashing name across the screen.

"You've got to be fucking kidding me," I groan, leaning my head down on Logan's chest as her body begins shake with laughter.

Taking my hands out from under her sweatshirt, I quickly decline his call.

"Sorry about that," I say in a raspy voice, dipping back in to kiss Logan, hoping to start again where we left off. But she leans back against the steering wheel and puts her hands on either side of my face to stop me.

"We should probably get back." She has an apologetic smile on her lips as my face falls in her hands.

I'm going to kill my brother.

"You have to get to your party," she adds.

"Will you come with me?" There's still a pressure throbbing against my jeans from her sitting on me.

She shakes her head. "No, I'm going to stay home and work on my paper." She soothingly brushes my fallen, shaggy hair away from my face.

My heart sinks in disappointment from her words. I don't want to go without her. I don't want to go anywhere without her. Fuck, what is happening to me?

She leans back in, gently kissing my lips as she tries to soften the blow of her not coming to the party with me before quickly climbing back into her seat and fastening her seatbelt.

Starting the engine, I adjust myself in my seat, hoping to hide the effect her body had on mine. I turn the heat back to cool in an attempt to defog the windows inside my truck caused by our heated moment. She reaches for my hand, intertwining our fingers, as she drapes both our hands in her lap. She gives me a sweet and innocent smile, vastly contradictory to the sex vixen who was just grinding on my lap moments ago, before casually looking out the window as if nothing happened.

I swear, this woman is going to be the death of me, but goddamn am I going to enjoy her slaughter.

Chapter 49

Logan

Thank god that Marc called when he did. If he didn't interrupt our moment, I don't know that I would have. My cheeks begin to heat as I remember the feeling of Eli's growing bulge beneath me. Tightening my crossed legs, I try to relieve the empty sensation. If this is just the tip of the iceberg as to what I've been missing out on, I'm done for. Eli is flawless, absolute perfection in the form of a man, and my body knows it. He has a magnetic pull on me, and I don't know how long I'll be able to fight it off for.

I have to tell him. He deserves to know that I'm a virgin before he gets in too deep. I need to give him a chance to call it off. It's only fair. I know how he's going to react, or at least I can assume. With the amount of sexual experience he has, it's probably going to scare him off, just as it has with most other boys before. Somehow, I hope it doesn't, though, because my heart is in it, and my body is following closely behind.

Something about how he held me while I told him about my mom broke down any remaining walls I had with him. He's really not the man that everyone else thinks they know. He's the man that only I get to know.

Eli's grip on my thigh tightens as he pulls up and parks in front of my dorm. I don't want him to leave and judging by the look on his face and the intensity with which he's holding onto me, I don't think he wants to either. We let out a pair of matching sighs, knowing he has to go to the alumni party back at his house.

"You're sure you can't come with me?" he asks again, trying to use his adorably pouty lip to sway my decision.

I sweep my hand across his forehead and graze his cheek with my thumb. "Sorry, ba—" I begin before stopping myself.

"What did you just say?" Eli asks, his gaping lips turning up at the corners.

"Nothing." My eyes are wide as I pull my hand away from his face and turn my blushing cheeks towards the passenger window.

"Were you about to call me 'babe'?" he teases.

"No."

"Logan..." He puts his finger under my chin, pulling my gaze away from the window to face him. "Were you about to call me 'babe'?"

"No," I smugly reply. "I was about to call you, 'baby'." I'm already caught red-handed. I may as well tell him the truth.

His eyes sparkle as his mouth forms into the most adorably happy grin I've ever seen.

"Say it."

I pause for a moment, contemplating if I want to go straight to the nicknames stage with him already. I never called Zac anything besides his name, but the way I feel about Eli is already incomparable to my relationship with Zac, so I decide to appease him.

"Baby." I look straight into his eyes and say it before biting down on my lower lip, trying to suppress my amusement to his reaction of the word. I don't think I've ever seen him so light and happy.

"Fuck, that sounds good coming from you. Say it again."

"Baby."

"Use it in a sentence."

I laugh aloud at his persistence. "You're ridiculous, baby."

He reaches across the center console and presses his smiling lips to mine, before leaning back in his seat and shaking his head in satisfaction.

I like seeing him this way, and I have a feeling that I'm the only one who ever has.

He leans across the center console again with his arm reaching out. Just as I think he's about to pull me in for another kiss, he reaches behind me into the back seat and pulls his laptop out of his bag before opening his door.

"What are you doing?"

"I'm coming with you," he states as if it should be obvious.

"Eli..." I drag out his name, silently telling him he doesn't have to do this.

"Logan..." he says my name in the same mocking manner.

"I don't want you to miss your party just because I don't want to go," I tell him, trying to reassure him that I'd be totally fine with him going. Even though, there is a nagging ache in my chest that doesn't want him to leave me. What is happening to me? I'm never clingy.

"You think I'm going to leave you after the night we just had, and after you just called me 'baby', baby? Besides, I really don't want to go. I would rather work on my paper upstairs with you." He gives me a soft grin.

God, he's beautiful. I'm in trouble.

"I really do need to work on my paper, though." I raise my eyebrows, shooting him a knowing look.

"Logan. Are you accusing me of wanting to come upstairs for a reason other than academia?" He quickly leans across and brushes his lips with mine. "I'm offended," he says in mock disgust before laughing at himself and getting out of the truck to jog over and open my door.

I'm still giggling as I climb out, but I'm not sure if it's because of his humor or the fact that he just seems so giddy right now.

As we walk into my dorm room, a blanket of heat instantly surrounds us.

"Logan, are you kidding me?" Eli hurries over to the thermostat to turn in down.

"I thought it might be cold when I got back."

"You're going to give me heat stroke, woman," he says as he peels off his sweatshirt, taking part of his shirt with it and giving me visual access to his perfectly chiseled abdomen.

My mouth gapes at the view.

He catches me staring and quickly pulls his shirt down to cover himself. He has a cocky grin on his face as he shakes his head. "I don't think so, young lady. We have schoolwork to do."

I'm really regretting making that rule in his truck.

Taking his jacket off, I drape it on the back of my chair where it belongs. I reach for the hem of my sweatshirt before remembering that I didn't wear a shirt underneath, only a bra. Sifting through my drawers, I pull out a pair of shorts and a cropped tee, wanting to change into something cooler and more comfortable.

"Turn around," I instruct Eli.

He eyes the clothes in my hands before giving me a very smug, "No."

"Excuse me?" My eyes light up at the thought of him wanting to watch me undress. I quickly recall just this morning I was standing here in only my robe, the spot between my legs aching, as Eli took in every inch of my body with his eyes.

"I'm not turning around." He shrugs, testing me as he puts his hands in his pockets.

I hold my ground and his gaze. Just as I see the flicker of hope cross his face that I might actually undress in front of him, I reach out to the wall and flip the light switch, instantly coating the room in darkness.

He chuckles from across the room before. "Well, fuck."

I quickly change and switch the light back on before turning around to my desk and grabbing my reading glasses that are sitting on top. Putting them on, I throw my hair up in a quick messy bun before turning back to face Eli.

"Are you kidding me?" he asks. My brows furrow in confusion before realizing from his gaping mouth and wide eyes, he's referring to me.

"How do you just look like that? You don't even try." He bounds over to me in two easy strides, grabbing the sides of my face before pressing his lips firmly to mine. My cheeks blush from both his compliment and show of affection.

"You're one to talk," I say as he pulls his lips away, lingering them just above me. "You roll out of bed looking like pure sex." After our night of confessions and vulnerability, I no longer feel all that nervous telling Eli exactly what I think of him.

"You really want to compare us, you little sex vixen?" His voice is deep and husky as his eyes begin to hood and darken.

Oh, he looks so hot right now, and my mind is racing with the dirty, dirty things I want him to do to me. Judging by the deep devilish stare on his face, I have a feeling he wants to do them just as badly.

I have to tell him, and I have to tell him soon.

Clearing my throat, I pull my face from his embrace, averting my eyes from his. "So, the paper..." I change the subject as I grab my laptop from my desk and climb up onto my bed. Resting my back against the headboard, I cross my legs at the ankles, hoping to ease the throbbing that's happening at the apex of my thighs.

Eli saunters over to the bed. Literally, saunters. He knows exactly what he's doing to me.

Before he stretches out next to me, I stop him with a hand on his chest.

"Maybe you should sit over there," I tell him, nodding towards the foot of the bed.

He laughs. "Really? You have that little self-control?" His smirk could not be more smug.

"It's not me I'm worried about." I'm lying, of course—it's definitely me.

He laughs under his breath, kicking his shoes off and begrudgingly sitting on the bed opposite me. His bare feet are next to my hip, and mine are next to his thigh. Pulling out my computer, I place it on my lap, trying my best to concentrate on my paper and not on Eli's beautiful body that's situated on my bed only inches from me.

His phone rings, but he declines the call without checking the caller ID. He continues to stare at his computer screen, but I don't hear him typing at all. I have a feeling he's trying to concentrate on not touching me as much as I'm focused on not touching him.

His phone rings again.

"Aren't you gonna answer that?" I ask, not looking up from my screen.

"Nope, it's probably just Jay wondering where I am." He declines the call again.

Eli's foot grazes my bare thigh, and my entire body ignites at his touch.

His phone rings yet again.

"Eli, maybe you should go to the party." I close my laptop to look at him.

"I don't want to." He picks up his phone and holds down the power button, shutting it off. "I want to be here with you," he continues as my heart flutters from his words.

He gives me a sweet lingering smile as I keep my eyes locked on his. It's taking everything I've got not to crawl over and throw myself on him right now.

"Paper," he reminds me, his mouth forming a cocky grin as he nods towards my laptop.

Playfully rolling my eyes, I open my laptop and continue writing. Or at least I pretend that I'm writing. Literally, I have two words typed out. 'Eli' and 'Maddison' are the only words on my otherwise entirely blank screen. I can't concentrate with Eli sitting on my bed.

His foot grazes against my bare leg again, and oddly, it's the sexiest thing. Who am I kidding? Everything this guy does is sexy.

I swallow as I try to keep my focus on the screen in front of me.

Eli places his hand on my bare foot next to his leg and slowly grazes his thumb across the top. Every nerve in my body is firing at once from his touch, and somehow this random gesture is turning me on. Why is this so hot? He's obviously not typing with just one hand, but I know if I look up at him, I'll be done for.

His hand begins to slowly glide up my leg, lingering around my ankle before moving to my shin. His calloused fingertips stroke against my skin, continuing to make their way up my body.

My pulse is quickening as I bite down on my lip, trying to keep my eyes locked on my laptop screen. I'm not even focusing on my paper anymore. I'm just focusing on not jumping the guy's bones right here and now.

Eli lets out a loud sigh. "Fuck it," he says as he closes his laptop and casts it aside. He gets up and crawls towards me, taking the laptop from my hands and closing it before tossing it to the other side of the bed. He makes his way between my legs, and they quickly open for him. He gently removes the glasses from my face, setting them on my bedside table before placing both his hands on either side of my body and leaning down into my ear, his nose and lips grazing my cheek.

"You're distracting me." His tone is low and raspy, causing me to gulp from his words. I literally hear myself swallow.

His warm tongue meets my neck as my eyes close, my head dropping back from the sensation. My hips jerk up to meet his, the bulge in his pants pressing against me as he groans. He sucks and teases my ear before continuing to trail kisses down my neck and my chest, over my t-shirt, before leaning up and feverishly pressing his lips to mine. I part my mouth, letting his tongue find mine. He's warm and soft yet firm, and I can't get enough of him.

Wrapping my arms around his neck, I pull him into me and slide down, lying flat on the bed. His mouth continues to search mine, and our breathing becomes ragged, wanting more. He presses his erection against my sensitive spot, and this time I'm the one who lets out a whimpering moan.

He pulls his lips from mine as they continue their gentle assault down my body. He peppers them across my neck, over my t-shirt but between my breasts, and finally to my stomach. He begins to pull my shirt up slowly, kissing my flushed skin and I can't get over how good his supple, warm lips feel pressed against me.

He lifts my shirt a little more before pulling back and staring at my stomach. Eli stops his kisses and looks down at me, unable to tear his gaze away from my middle. I feel the heat crawling up my skin as the self-conscious doubt consumes me, thinking that he might not like what he sees. I'm all too aware of just how many girls he's been with and how many girls he's probably comparing me with right now.

"Did it hurt?" he asks, keeping his eyes locked on my abdomen.

"What?" My pulse is racing.

"Did it hurt? When you donated your kidney."

Following his gaze, I find him staring at the four small scars scattered around my abdomen from where they removed the kidney I donated to my mom. His fingers begin to graze the marks gently.

I look back to Eli and realize his expression is not that of judgment or dissatisfaction, but one of care and concern.

"I was sore for a few weeks, but it wasn't particularly painful," I say, reassuring him.

His eyes soften as they finally break their stare, and he looks up to my face. His expression is filled with...I don't know. Adoration? Respect? Love? Maybe all three, but the way he's looking at me right now, no one has ever looked at me like that before.

He leans down and places a soft lingering kiss on one of my scars. His warm lips take their time before moving to the next. He continues until he loves on all four of them as I tilt my head back and look towards the ceiling, trying to keep the tears from falling down my face. I can't remember the last time I cried, but being encompassed with so much love and respect for the hardest thing I've done in my life is making me emotional.

He continues to kiss my body as he lifts my shirt up and over my head, tossing it to the ground. This no longer feels sexual. It feels like he's taking care of me, loving me, respecting me. He sweetly kisses up my neck to my cheek, catching a fallen tear with his lips, as he wipes another from my other cheek with his thumb. He traces soft, gentle kisses up to my temple as I turn my head and melt into him. I've never felt this way before. I've never allowed myself to be vulnerable with someone this way. For him to know these sides of me and what I've gone through, it's new and scary, but it feels good.

After Zac treating me the way he did and not understanding what I was going through with my mom, I promised myself that I would never let someone into that part of my life again. I thought I would keep it locked away like an old secret and pretend like my life was easy and normal from there on out. Even though Marc knows about what I went through, he doesn't know the depths of the toll it took on me.

Eli pulls away from me, keeping his face only a few inches above mine, close enough that I can look into his eyes. They're soft and a bit glossed over. He continues to stroke my cheek as he keeps his beautiful brown eyes locked and searching mine.

"I...like you so much, Logan," he says as if he's trying to hold himself back.

He places his forehead gently against mine, my heart racing from his words and embrace.

"I like you so much, too." I lean up and gently kiss his perfect lips, needing them on mine.

Chapter 50

Eli

I can't believe I almost just told Logan that I loved her. That would be insane, I've only known her for a couple of weeks, but however I feel about her, I do know that I've never felt this way before. She's the strongest person I know, but also the softest in the way she loves and cares for people, and I'm the lucky son of a bitch who gets to be included on that list.

I also can't believe I just almost cried in front of her. I absolutely never cry. Thankfully, I controlled it and kept it together. I want to be strong for her so she can let her guard down when she needs to, but it pains me to know that she was struggling alone last year.

Lying down on my side, I face Logan as I continue to stroke her cheek with my thumb until the few tears of hers stop falling. Usually, when girls cry in front of me, I want nothing to do with it, but with her, I feel honored that she would be so vulnerable with me. Knowing her private and tough nature, I would imagine that she doesn't cry very often.

"I need to tell you something," she says, breaking the silence. "And you're probably not going to like it."

My stomach instantly drops.

I swallow hard, brushing the fallen tendrils of hair behind her ear. "Okay," I say softly, but it comes out in more of a question form.

She pauses, making the beat of my heart pound harder against my chest. Something is wrong. I can feel it. What the fuck is going on?

She gives me one last longing look before closing her eyes, inhaling deeply, and saying, "I'm a virgin," on the exhale.

I let out a long sigh of relief. That's it? That's what she was worried about telling me?

"Okay," I state as I lean forward to kiss her lips while her eyes are still closed.

They instantly shoot open. "Okay? That's it?"

"Okay...yeah, that's about it." I nod my head.

"It doesn't bother you?" she asks, searching my face with confusion plastered on hers.

"Should it bother me?" I haven't been with a virgin since I was a sophomore in high school, but honestly, it doesn't bother me one bit. Surprising maybe, because look at her. She's absolutely stunning, and the fact that no one has tried to fuck her yet is mind-blowing.

"It bothers most guys," she states matter-of-factly.

"Well then, I guess I'm not most guys. I already told you this wasn't just about sex for me." I pull her closer, trying to keep my eyes focused on her face and not on her chest that's currently pressed up against me and spilling out of her black satin bra.

She pauses, seeming utterly lost and confused. "Do you have any questions?" Her grip tightens on my hip.

"Is there a reason you've waited?" I continue to stroke her hair.

"I just wanted it to be with someone that I feel a connection with. Someone I trust."

"You had a boyfriend, right? You guys never—"

"No," she cuts me off. "I didn't trust him, and for a good reason. He cheated on me." Logan pulls her gaze from mine.

"You're shitting me. What a fucking idiot." My voice and body temperature rise. How could someone hurt this girl like that? She's too good to be treated that way.

"I don't know. I get it." Her cheeks turn rosy. She's so bad at defending herself. She's literal fucking perfection, and she has no clue. "Honestly, I don't really blame him. I was in a weird headspace with my mom being sick, and I just couldn't get there physically with him."

"No, Logan. He's an idiot. There's no valid reason for someone to cheat. Anyone who would let you slip through their fingers is a fucking moron," I reassure her, wanting her to understand my words and how much she deserves.

It's all starting to make sense, her hesitation with me. Her not wanting to forgive me after I fucked up last weekend after we kissed. God, I feel even worse now than I already did. She has trust issues, and I basically told her not to trust me the second we got involved.

"Is this from him?" I ask, brushing my fingers across her collarbone. Stopping at her tattoo that says, 'I love you.'

"No. No, I never loved him." She shakes her head as relief washes over me. "I've never been in love before," she adds, looking into my eyes, trying to tell me more than just her words can. "This is my dad's handwriting. It was taken from the last birthday card he gave to my mom before he died." She reaches her hand up and places it on mine, covering the inked words, as her stunning green eyes pour into mine.

Everything in my body melts. I've wondered what this tattoo meant since the first night we met. I didn't think it would have such a sweet and sentimental meaning behind it. It represents the only two people she has ever loved, and I pray to god I'll get to be the third.

I hold Logan's stare before I lean in and kiss her jaw, trailing wet kisses down her neck until I gently place my lips against her collarbone, kissing the black ink. She reaches her hand up to the back of my head and holds me while I wrap my arm tighter around her waist. I nuzzle my forehead into the crook of her neck and just lie with her for a while.

Everything I've learned about Logan today has been overwhelming, but beautiful. It makes me sad that she's been scared to share these sides of herself with anyone, but I'm honored to be the man who gets to see the real her.

I wait a few minutes and bask in her embrace, filling my nostrils with her sweet scent, before changing the subject back to the prick that hurt her.

"So, this douchebag ex of yours...how long were you guys together?" I pull away to look at her.

"About nine months."

I'm trying to gauge her reaction to talking about her ex. I don't want to press her if it's difficult for her to talk about, but honestly, she seems like she doesn't give a fuck about the guy.

"And how did you find out that he cheated on you?"

"I went to his apartment the night I had to say goodbye to my mom, and I found my friend's bra on his bedroom floor," she states matter-of-factly.

"It was with your friend?" My eyes widen, and my mouth parts. This guy is the worst.

"Yeah," she says, without an ounce of sadness in her voice.

"And he wasn't with you at the hospital when your mom died?"

She shakes her head but stays silent.

"I fucking hate this guy," I tell her as my blood begins to boil. I wish he were here so I could take my anger out on him. He deserves a good ass-kicking for what he did to her.

Exhaling, I try to calm myself down. "But I'm also glad that he's such a piece of shit. We might not be here right now if he wasn't." I lean over and kiss Logan on the lips, then the cheek, then the collarbone before pulling away.

"So it doesn't bother you?" she asks. "That I'm all innocent and inexperienced."

"Logan, you're far from innocent. Sexually inexperienced, maybe. But, innocent? Your innocence was taking away the second you had to say goodbye to your dad so young, and then your mom. You've seen more of the shitty parts of life than most people ever will. And the inexperienced part I'm not worried about." I shake my head. "I'm a fantastic teacher." A sly smirk forms on my lips.

She laughs at my cockiness. "It really doesn't bother you that I haven't had sex yet?" I can tell she's not entirely convinced, and I get it. I have plenty of experience, but I couldn't care less that she hasn't. Honestly, I feel relieved that no man has ever been inside of her. She's going to be mine and only mine.

"No, Logan, it doesn't bother me. If anything, it's a fucking turn-on."

"What?" she asks, eyes wide.

"The fact that I get to go where no man has ever gone before...I'm getting hard just thinking about it," I add, only somewhat joking as I press my package against her.

"Eli!" She playfully swats my arm. Her expression half mortified, half amused.

"I'm just playing. But no, I promise you it doesn't bother me, even in the slightest. I'm excited that I'll get to be your first."

"Who says you're going to be my first?" Logan asks, giving me a smug look. She knows damn well that I will be.

"You're really over there trying to convince yourself that I'm not? Baby, you know there's no stopping this." I motion a finger between us before turning her onto her back and hovering over her.

"But only when you're ready. I'll wait as long as it takes," I add with sincerity as I look down at Logan and gently kiss her lips.

We've been lying here in bed, facing each other, with our eyes closed for a while now. If it weren't for Logan's fingertips, gently stroking my lower back, under my shirt, I would think she was asleep. I'm so content in bed with her that I would probably be asleep already if it weren't for her tits being pushed against my chest, distracting me.

"Logan?" I whisper with my eyes still closed, and my voice raspy. I gently stroke her hair and graze my thumb across her cheekbone.

"Mmm," she hums in acknowledgment, too tired to speak real words.

"I know we've had an emotionally draining night, and I'm trying to be respectful, so I'm going to need you to put a shirt on for me so I can do that." I open my eyes to get one last glimpse at her perfect tits pressed up against me, spilling out of her bra.

"What if I don't want you to be respectful?" she asks, her eyes still closed as my dick twitches at her words.

"What did you just say?" I lift myself to hover over her. She spreads her legs for me, allowing me to press myself down on her. My eyes hood over and my mouth gapes, looking down at her flawless body pinned beneath me.

"You heard me," she says as she continues to graze her fingers up my back, squeezing when she gets to my shoulder blades. Her pupils are dilated, and I can feel myself hardening already.

"What do you want me to do, baby?" I ask in a low husky tone as I gently rock my hips into her. She arches her back from the sensation, and I almost explode at the sight.

"Whatever you want to do," she whispers, looking into my eyes as her breathing accelerates.

"Don't say that." I shake my head, trying to push back the thoughts of all the dirty things I want to do to her right now. I know she's not ready to go there tonight, and I don't want her to feel pressured in any way.

"I need some guidelines here," I tell her in a breathy voice as I lean down and start to kiss and nibble at her neck, my hips continuing to rock into her.

She drops her head back, giving me better access to her neck and collarbone. "I don't want to give you guidelines."

So, she's trying to kill me tonight. Noted.

Her silky-smooth legs are on either side of me, hugging me, as I run one of my hands down the length of her soft thigh and squeeze her plump ass.

"Tell me when..." I kiss her exposed chest. "You want..." I drag my lips up her neck. "Me to stop," I whisper into her ear. I lean back to look into her eyes as I brush a stray hair away from her face. "I mean it, okay? You set the pace."

She nods her head but stays silent.

I look down at her lips. They're pouty and pink and fucking perfect. I run my tongue over her bottom one, and she tastes like a fucking dessert.

Logan snakes her hand around the back of my neck, pulling me into her, and wrapping her full lips around mine. Her tongue expertly dips in and out of my mouth, exploring me. She's a fucking fantastic kisser; she knows exactly what she's doing. Her bottom lip drags against mine, drawing out low moan from my throat.

I'm painfully hard right now, pressed against her tiny shorts. I'm never wearing jeans again; the fabric is way too thick. I want to feel her. I want to feel the warmth between her legs that I'm positive is there right now. I know she's as turned on as I am in this moment.

I pull my lips away so I can get a glimpse of her. Her cheeks are flushed, and her lips are swollen and glistening. Her eyes are dark, and her chest is moving quickly from her ragged breathing.

She keeps her eyes locked on mine as she reaches under the hem of my shirt, slowly peeling it up and over my head before tossing it to the ground. Her soft fingertips drag down my body, exploring every crevice. I've never had someone touch me this way, taking in every inch of me, but it feels so good. Her eyes wander the length of my torso as her fingers find their way to my lower ab muscles, stroking the V that falls into my jeans. My body shudders, knowing her hand is so close to my dick, even though my pants are a barrier between her skin and mine.

I look down at her chest, her perfect chest. They've been taunting me all night, her tits barely covered by that little black bra. I need to see them. I need to feel her in my palm. I slip my hand under her back as she arches up for me, bringing them right to my face.

Is she trying to make me come in my jeans right now?

Finding the clasp, I glance up at her, looking for any sign of hesitation on her face. I told her to tell me when to stop, and right now, she doesn't look like she plans on stopping me anytime soon.

I quickly unfasten the clasp with a deft flick of my hand, sliding one strap down her shoulder, followed by the other. My eyes widen when her tits finally come into full view. They're perky and full, but soft, and absolutely fucking flawless. I can't wait to feel them in my hand and in my mouth. My dick throbs against Logan's shorts as she slips her arms out from the straps and tosses her bra to the floor, all while keeping her eyes locked on me. I pull my gaze back to her face, trying to gauge any hesitation, but still, there's none.

"God, you're perfect," I remind her with my raspy voice.

I press my chest onto her warm skin, thankful for one less barrier between us, as my body melts into hers. Palming one of her perky tits, I reconnect my lips with hers, exploring her mouth with my tongue and her breast with my hand. I roll her nipple with my thumb, before pinching it between my fingers. Her hips buck up, pressing herself into my dick, as Logan releases a soft moan into my mouth.

Fuck, I love that sound. I want to hear it again.

Moving my lips to her neck, I bite and suck, being sure to leave a mark. The pressure building up between us is causing our moment to become more heated and frantic.

Squeezing her in my hand, I continue to move my face lower to her chest. Surrounding her taut nipple with my mouth, I suck and lick, then flick her with my tongue. She lets out a ragged and breathy, "Fuck," as she jerks her hips into me once again, arching her back.

I swear, this woman is intentionally trying to embarrass me by making me explode right now. So, I concentrate on making her feel good, teasing her with my tongue and grazing her with my teeth.

Just as I'm about to slip my hands into her tiny shorts and finally feel the warm wetness between her legs, a loud knock at the door stops my movements as Logan gasps and quickly sits up, pulling her body away from my mouth.

"Logan, it's Marc," comes the voice from behind the wooden barrier.

Is this a fucking joke?

Chapter 51

Logan

I can't help but laugh right now. This is the second time we've been interrupted by my best friend tonight, and Eli is pissed off about it.

"I'm going to kill him." Eli shakes his head as I continue to chuckle. "Seriously, he is such a cock-blocker." He glances in his brother's direction. We can see the shadow of Marc's feet through the gap under the door.

"Ignore him," Eli says, looking back to me then down to my exposed chest.

"I can't. My light is on. He obviously knows that I'm home."

"Fine, I'll deal with him." Eli peels his body off mine, quickly heading towards the door in frustration.

"Wait! I don't have a shirt on." I frantically sit up on the edge of the bed, crossing my arms to cover my chest.

Eli eyes me for a moment, before bending down and picking a shirt up off the floor. "Mmm, I know," he purrs in my ear before kissing my cheek and putting the shirt in my hand.

He holds onto the doorknob and looks back to me, waiting for me to get dressed. I slip the shirt over my head, but it fits more like a dress. Eli's eyes soften, and his smile grows when he realizes he handed me his shirt instead of mine.

"Damn," he breathes out, eyeing me as my cheeks heat.

After lingering on me for a beat, he returns his attention to his brother on the other side of my door.

"You're killing me, man," Eli says as he swings the door open.

Marc's expression goes from neutral, to shocked, to mortified as he looks from a shirtless Eli back to me, sitting on my bed, wearing his brother's tee. This shirt is so long on me he probably can't see that I'm wearing shorts underneath.

"Well, this is going to be in my nightmares tonight," Marc sarcastically says as he begins to chuckle awkwardly. I follow suit, giggling from the bed, my cheeks flushed from the whole situation.

Eli doesn't seem quite as amused. "We were right in the middle of something, if you know what I mean. What do you want?"

"Okay, just because I'm cool with you sleeping with my best friend does not mean that I want to hear about it." Marc holds his hands up. "Or see it for that matter," he adds as he closes his eyes and turns his head, a grimace covering his face.

Marc doesn't know that I'm a virgin. It's not something that has ever come up in conversation between us, and judging by the cocky smirk on Eli's face right now, he's loving the fact that he knows something else about me that his brother does not.

"I saw Logan's light on and was coming by to see if she wanted to go to the alumni party with me, but from the looks of it, I'm assuming that neither of you guys are going." Marc glances between Eli and me. "Why aren't you there? Jay is going to kill you," Marc adds, looking back at his brother.

"I didn't want to go." Eli shrugs. "But, don't tell Jay where I am, I don't need him to know."

"Why are you going so late?" Eli asks Marc, confused.

"I was busy," Marc responds, eyeing his brother.

"You should take Ali with you," I chime in from the bed.

"Yeah, Marc. You should take Ali with you," Eli agrees in a teasing tone as he gives his brother a sly grin.

Marc rolls his eyes in response. "So, you're really not going?"

"Nope."

"Good for you, man." Marc nods in approval. "Logan, study session tomorrow?"

"Yeah, let's do it. Noon?"

"Sounds good. Alright, love you both, but let's never do this again," Marc says as he motions between the three of us before turning to leave. But I have a feeling that Marc seeing his brother and me together is going to happen a lot more often than Marc is willing to admit.

Eli closes the door, locking it behind him before walking over to stand directly in front of me, between my legs. My hands find his abdomen as I gently graze my fingers over the ridges of muscle, releasing an involuntary yawn as I do so.

"Tired, baby?" Eli brushes a hair behind my ear and keeps his hand resting there, cupping my face. I lean into his touch and close my eyes, nodding in response.

"Let's get you to bed." He leans down and gently kisses my forehead.

"Will you stay with me?" I ask, looking up at him.

His sweet smile grows, his brown eyes softening as he nods in agreement.

"That was probably weird for Marc," I change the subject. "Last he knew I was still upset with you about last night."

"I explained it to him. I talked to him after my game and told him what happened and that I was coming to see you and try to fix things," he explains. "Trust me, though, I got the lecture of a lifetime."

I can' t help but laugh at the image of Marc trying to defend me by putting Eli in his place.

Eli takes a few steps back from me as he begins to unbutton his jeans. He pulls them down to his ankles before stepping out of them and giving me visual access to his perfectly toned body. The only part of him that I have yet to see is what's hidden behind his tight black boxer briefs, though I don't think it'll be long before I do.

My lips part as I admire the perfect specimen in front of me. If someone were to draw my ideal man, it would be Eli. Tearing my eyes away from him, I try to push back the thoughts of all the things I want him to do to me right now instead of sleeping. I reach for the hem of Eli's shirt to return it to him, but he stops me.

"You should probably leave that on. If I see your perfect tits again, there's no way in hell I'm letting you sleep tonight." His dark eyes flicker down to my covered chest.

I've never had someone speak to me this way, and it's a huge confidence boost knowing that my body is a temptation for him. But still, I chuckle at his lack of self-control as I reach for my phone on the nightstand.

"I'm going to the gym at eight tomorrow. Sorry if my alarm wakes you up."

"Perfect. I have to go to the rink in the morning, I can walk you on my way." Eli's chiseled frame climbs into bed behind me, getting comfortable under my sheets.

"Are you boxing or lifting tomorrow?" he casually asks as I sit on the edge of my bed, messing with my phone.

I turn, snapping my head in his direction. "How did you know that I box?"

His cheek is pressed into my pillow, but I can see it turn pink as his eyes widen, realizing the words he let slip. Eli is not often embarrassed, but he is right now, and it's adorable.

"I've seen you in the gym before. A couple of times," he confesses shyly.

My mouth opens in mock shock. "Eli, were you creeping on me?" I tease, trying to hold back my amused grin.

"Maybe." He shrugs. "I couldn't help it. You looked so fucking sexy dripping sweat in your tiny little outfit. Also, remind me not to mess with you. Have you always been into boxing?" he asks as I climb into bed, under the sheets, facing him. His hand finds my hip, pulling me closer as our bare legs intertwine beneath the sheets.

"I started getting into it when my mom was sick. It was kind of my only outlet. It was my one hour a day to myself, and I just fell in love with it. It helped clear my head."

He nods understandingly. “I get that. That’s how I feel when I have the ice to myself.”

Leaning across the small gap between us, Eli places his lips on mine and leaves them lingering for a moment before lifting his arm up and around my shoulders, silently ushering me to lay my head on his bare chest. His masculine scent fills my nostrils as I place my cheek on him. He’s warm and safe, and I don’t ever want to leave this spot. Judging by the tight grip he has on me, I don’t think Eli is going to let me.

My heart rate calms as my breathing slows. I’m moments away from sleep when Eli leans his soft lips onto my forehand, his warm breath tickling my skin as he speaks.

“Logan?” He whispers.

“Mmm-hmm,” I hum as I keep my eyes closed, ready to drift off to sleep.

“Please don’t leave before I wake up tomorrow. I hate it when you’re gone in the morning.” There’s an edge of desperation in his voice.

I don’t respond with words, but instead, I wrap my arms as tightly around his waist as his arms are around me, knowing he needs the reassurance. I didn’t think about the fact that it might bother him if I was gone in the morning, but it makes my heart flutter that he needs me here. I think I need him just as much, though, and that scares me a bit.

“Morning, baby,” Eli murmurs in my ear.

Keeping my eyes closed, I recall that I got to have Eli in my bed with me last night. My back is against his bare chest, and his arm is wrapped around me, under my shirt, gripping me firmly to him. Our legs are still tangled around one another, as Eli slides his bare foot against my smooth leg.

“Morning,” I say in a raspy voice. God, it feels good waking up to this man wrapped around me. “My alarm didn’t go off?”

"It did about five minutes ago, but you didn't wake up, and I just wanted to hold you for a few minutes longer." He leans down and gently kisses the back of my neck. The sensation makes me tingle as I squirm and back my ass into his morning bulge.

"Fuck," he groans in a low, raspy voice, resting his head against the back of my neck. "You can't do that. I have to be at the rink in twenty minutes, and you're going to cause me to miss morning skate if you do that again," he warns, even though he's gripping my hip and pressing my ass firmly into him.

Giggling, I turn around to face him, running my hands through his shaggy hair.

"Hi," he softly says as his warm eyes pour into mine.

"Hi." I lean up and press my lips to his and leave them lingering against him.

"Mmm, I like waking up to you," he tells me as his mouth grazes mine, his fingertips stroking my lower back, under my shirt.

"Me too," I tell him before quickly kissing him one last time and slipping out of bed.

Eli lets out a frustrated groan from my absence.

"You're going to be late," I remind him. "I'm gonna brush my teeth real quick, then we gotta go." I grab my toiletry bag and head off towards the bathroom, leaving a mostly naked Eli in my bed.

Now that I'm alone for the first time since yesterday afternoon, I can finally take a moment to think and clear my head. But when I try, all I can do is smile at myself in the mirror as I brush my teeth. I don't think I'm going to be able to wipe this stupid grin off my face for a while. Last night was amazing. Eli was amazing. I never expected him to accept me the way he did, especially with his reputation around campus. But that's not Eli. They don't know him.

I don't want to leave him right now, and that makes me nervous. I've never been clingy or dependent on someone, and I don't want to start now. As much as I want to be around Eli all the time, I need to make sure I keep my independence, because with how I feel about that boy already, I can easily see myself thinking about him and his needs and not about my own.

When we exit the lobby of my dorm, the cold air hits me, reminding me that the first day of October is just one step closer to winter coming in full swing. Thankfully, I'm a little more prepared today with my puffy black jacket zipped up over my workout clothes, keeping the chill out and the warmth in.

Eli jogs to his truck to grab his hockey gear before he returns to me, effortlessly sliding his large hand into mine, intertwining our fingers. This feels like a very couple-ly thing to do, walking hand in hand, but I love it. I feel safe and taken care of with him.

"So, can I come back over later?" Eli asks as we continue our walk towards the gym.

"I don't think today is a good idea. I have that study session with Marc later, and I still have to write the paper you wouldn't let me write last night." I squeeze his hand in mine. As much as I want to see him later, I have to get my schoolwork done, and his beautiful body is too much of a distraction for me.

"Plus, you need to work on yours, too," I remind him. "Did you decide what you're going to write about?"

"Yeah, I have an idea."

"Care to share?"

"Nope," he says, trying to hold back his grin as I playfully roll my eyes at his secrecy.

"So, I'm not going to see you until class tomorrow?" he guilts me, trying to change my mind. But I stand firm, knowing I need to make sure I take care of myself first and don't get caught up in spending all my time with him.

I look to him with an extreme pout on my face, sticking my bottom lip out as far as it'll go. "Sorry."

He laughs as he lifts my hand that's laced with his, kissing the back of it before pecking my exposed bottom lip.

The ten-minute walk to the gym is over much too quickly as the building comes into view around the corner. I'm already sad about saying goodbye to Eli even though I know I'm going to see him again tomorrow.

As we approach the rec center entrance, Cam and Patrick walk up at the same time with giant equipment bags slung over their shoulders.

"What's up, guys?" Cam asks enthusiastically. I've only met him twice, but he's always so kind and lively. I like his vibe.

Eli instantly drops my hand and puts his in his jacket pocket. I look down at my empty palm then back to Eli, but he keeps his eyes ahead, focused on his teammates.

"Hey, Cali," Patrick says as Eli stiffens next to me. Eli's mouth is pressed in a hard line, and I can tell he's trying to hold himself back.

"Hey," I quietly respond, still confused by Eli's urgency in releasing my hand from his.

"Where the hell were you last night, Maddison?" Cam asks, looking between Eli and me.

"I was busy," he quickly says, keeping his eyes straight ahead, refusing to look at me.

"Mmm-hmm," Patrick hums as he looks back and forth between us, obviously catching on. He licks his lips as his eyes rake down my body. "I missed you last night, Cali."

"Let's go, we're going to be late," Eli interrupts, ushering the guys towards the rink. "See you around, Logan," he casually adds as he walks away.

"Bye, Cali," Patrick says as he walks backward, facing me, with a flirtatious smirk across his lips.

I can see Eli's shoulders straighten and stiffen from here.

What the fuck was that? All the security I gained from Eli in the last twenty-four hours just flew out the window. Is he embarrassed to be seen with me? Is that why he let go of me and acted like we were almost strangers? The pit in my stomach grows as I watch the boy I was falling for walk away in the distance, not even bothering to turn around.

I'm in a daze as I wander into the gym. Was it really just about the chase for him? There's a buzzing in my head and my ears as I walk past the treadmills and head straight for the punching bags. Honestly, I wasn't even going to box today because I didn't have the need to work anything out on the bag. But now, all I want to do is wrap my hands as quickly as possible and work through the emptiness and embarrassment I'm feeling. I'm no stranger to feeling disappointed in life, but this one took me by surprise.

"Logan." I hear my name emanating from the treadmills as I stroll by. I turn to find Ali walking at a high incline on the treadmill closest to the aisle with one of her earbuds pulled out from her ear.

"You okay?" she asks, clearly concerned by my disoriented expression and gaping mouth.

I can't speak, so I just nod my head as I continue ahead to the punching bags directly in front of the cardio equipment. The gym is packed for a Sunday morning, but thankfully there is an unoccupied bag waiting for me. Pulling off my jacket, I toss it aside, leaving me in only my sports bra and leggings as I begin to frantically wrap my hands.

"Hey, Maddison!" a woman's voice rings out.

I look up to find Eli rushing towards me, slipping past anyone who tries to get in his way.

"Eli, what are you doing? You're going to be late," I remind him as he bounds towards me.

He doesn't respond, but instead, he grabs my face on either side and firmly presses his warm lips to mine. His tongue grazes against my surprised lips as I open them to give him access to my mouth. His movements are feverish but passionate, and he tastes as good as always, but I'm a little confused by his sudden display of affection. His tongue continues to explore my mouth as the whistles and shouts from the fellow gym-goers surround us.

He pulls his lips from me but keeps his forehead leaning on mine with his hands cupping my face.

"I'm sorry," he whispers only inches from my lips. "The guys on the team have never seen me with someone before, and I reacted in the worst way." He closes his eyes and shakes his head. "I'm not used to being with someone. I might need you teach me how to do this, okay?"

I nod my head against him as a small grin forms across my lips.

"Well, you're doing a pretty good job at it right now," I tell him, causing him to smile at my words.

He quickly pecks my lips again before leaning down to my ear.

"You look insanely hot right now, and I'm going to be picturing you in this outfit all day," he whispers before slapping my ass and walking away. He briefly turns back around to give me an arrogant smirk as my cheeks heat from his public display of affection.

The entire gym is dead silent. I'm assuming because most everyone is as shocked as I am that the university's most notorious playboy just made a somewhat public declaration of his feelings for me.

"Ali," Eli says to greet her, walking by her treadmill and out the door to head back to the rink.

Ali's mouth is gaped open in shock as he walks by her before she turns her attention back to me. Her jaw is practically on the floor, and her eyes shine with amusement.

"Shut. The Fuck. Up!" she excitedly shrieks, loud enough for the entire gym to hear.

Chapter 52

Eli

Morning skate went by quickly, but I miss having the rink to myself. Now that it's the regular season, I have to share it with the rest of the boys. My night with Logan played on repeat in my mind the entire time I was on the ice as I remembered the way her body molded into mine. At one point, Patrick pulled me from heavenly thoughts when he made some smart remark about how amazing Logan's ass looked in her tight workout pants. I mean, he wasn't wrong, but I don't want him or anyone else looking at my girl, so I made sure to hit him a little harder into the boards to teach him a lesson. Not that he knows that she's my girl yet, but he will soon enough.

The rest of my Sunday kind of sucked. I knew Logan was busy studying with Marc, so I didn't want to interrupt her. She's used to being independent, and I don't want to bombard her with my presence, but I'm having a hard time holding back. I just want to be with her.

Having to write my paper about her just made things worse. The more I thought about her and her selfless heart, the more I wanted to walk my ass over to her dorm to just be around her. I've never crushed this hard before, but then I don't even think crush is a strong enough word for it at this point.

It's like a switch got flipped inside of me after taking Logan to the pond last night. I've never wanted to make someone my girlfriend before, but after last night with Logan, all I want is to be the man who takes care of her. I'm done with all the stupid shit. The sleeping around and not giving a fuck about anyone besides myself. She's it for me. I don't know how to explain it, but I feel different today. Lighter almost—more myself.

When Sunday night rolled around, I couldn't help myself as I pulled out my phone to text her. I knew she didn't want me to distract her studies by being with her, but she never said that I couldn't text her. I lay in bed, wishing she was next to me as I typed out my message.

E: *I miss you.*

Not even a minute later, my phone buzzed, and as I looked at my screen, a giant shit-eating grin formed across my face.

L: *It hasn't even been a whole day yet.*

I can just imagine her rolling her eyes with a big, satisfied smile on her face as she read my needy words. I waited, staring at those three little dots as Logan typed another message to me.

L: *But I miss you too, baby.*

I grew up hearing my parents use pet names, and I've never really understood why you would. I mean, they're cheesy as hell, but when Logan uses them, I love it.

Her sweet text was enough to satiate me for the night. I knew I was going to sleep like shit, but it's not Logan's responsibility to take care of my sleep, even though the only time I get a restful night is when she's next to me. I don't want her to feel burdened to have me over all the time just because I can't make it through the night without her, especially when she's trying to focus on her schoolwork. I don't want to be a distraction for her. I want her to take care of herself for once. The thing that sucks about the timing is that I leave for Michigan this week for a preseason tournament, which means I won't get to sleep well again until next weekend.

Monday's classes dragged on, and I left my physiology class ten minutes early, so I was guaranteed to sit next to Logan in creative writing. Much to my surprise, when I got to the lecture hall, Logan wasn't there yet, so I picked a pair of seats somewhere in the middle of the room. Not so close to the front as Logan would prefer, but not towards the back where I would've chosen. Keeping my eyes glued to the door, I wait for her to walk in.

When she does, my mouth drops open at the view, and my shoulders instantly relax, just knowing that she's in the same room as me. Logan looks stunning, as per usual, but today she's radiating. Her hair is down and curled, and the deep red color looks fresh and shiny. She's wearing a dark gray, skin-tight skirt that hits just below her knee, hugging every curve. Her silky dark green top flows away from her body, but I know exactly what's hidden underneath. The green of her shirt brings out the green of her eyes, and I can see them beam from here. She looks like a sexy little businesswoman dressed liked this—*my* sexy little businesswoman. That is, until my gaze wanders down her perfectly toned legs to her shoes, finding a pair of old worn Converse on her feet. I can't help but laugh when I glance back to the matching pair I'm wearing.

She looks around the room, which I hope is because she's trying to find me, and when her eyes connect with mine, they soften. She gives me a sweet smile and cocks her head to the side when she realizes I've saved her a seat next to me.

"Hi," she says, sliding into the chair I had reserved for her.

"Hi," I say in a daze, totally mesmerized by my girl.

"You're late," I remind her in a teasing tone as she hurriedly pulls out her laptop and slips her jacket off her shoulders.

"And you're early. My oh my, how the tables have turned, Mr. Maddison," she jokes, which makes me grin. But it also makes my cock twitch to hear my formal name come out of her mouth while she's dressed like this.

"If you call me Mr. Maddison again, I'm going to have to drag you out of here, over my shoulder, and take you back to your bed."

She swats my arm as she giggles at my forwardness. "I had a marketing presentation for class that ran over. Thanks for saving me a seat." She turns and shoots me her sweetest smile. Her mixture of sweet and sassy is too tempting for me right now.

"Of course." I brush the hair from her face, tucking it behind her ear before I lean my lips against her ear. "You look stunning, by the way."

"Thank you." Her eyes lock with mine, seeming to accept my compliment easily. "I had to dress up for that presentation, but I took my heels off as soon as it was over," she adds, pointing to her bag where a pair of black high heels are poking out.

She makes me smile. Logan is a fucking stunner, but she's still such a tomboy at times.

"Did you finish your paper?" I ask.

"Yeah. I sent it in this morning, but I had so much schoolwork to do yesterday that I couldn't get to it until about ten o'clock last night." I can tell she's overwhelmed, and judging by the bags under her eyes, I don't think she got much sleep from all the studying she had to do.

"Did you finish yours?"

"Yeah, I knocked it out pretty early yesterday."

"And let me guess, you're still not going to tell me what you wrote about?"

I shake my head as a mischievous grin forms on my lips, causing Logan to playfully rolls her eyes at me.

Professor Kenny comes in and spends the next hour explaining this week's assignment. I have to focus the whole time just to keep myself from reaching across my desk and touching Logan. I've never been one for public displays of affection, but with her, I want everyone to know just how much I like this girl. I can almost feel her warmth radiating from here as I keep my hands locked in my lap, trying to concentrate on Kenny's instructions.

When class is over, and all one hundred students decide to exit simultaneously, I reach across and lace Logan's fingers with mine, holding her hand as we walk through the crowd. Whispers surround us, but I don't care. I'm sure it must be weird for people to see me with a girl in public, but I want everyone to know. But, most importantly, I want Logan to know how much she means to me. She squeezes my hand in hers as she relaxes, leaning her body into mine as we walk.

"I have to get to practice," I tell her when we make it to a clearing, away from the rush of students leaving class. "Are you headed to Double G to meet up with Marc?"

"Yeah, but only for a little bit. I have a huge Econ test tomorrow morning that I'm stressed about, and I need to study for."

Well, shit. I was hoping Logan got all of her studying done yesterday so that I would maybe be able to stay with her tonight. Especially since we leave tomorrow, it was going to be my only chance to see her.

"But, that's the last important thing for my week, so maybe I can see you after? I have a late class tomorrow, but Wednesday, maybe?" she asks as her green eyes search mine.

"Actually, the team is flying to Michigan first thing tomorrow morning. We have a division preseason tournament this week." Her expectant smile immediately falls.

"When will you be back?"

"Late Friday, early Saturday," I shrug. I'm trying to act casual, but I'm dreading leaving her behind. I'm not ready for her to know just how badly I need to be with her, though the way she's looking at me makes me think that maybe she feels the same.

"Why didn't you tell me? I would've asked you to stay over last night if I knew I wasn't going to see you all week."

"I know you would've, which is exactly why I didn't tell you," I give her a knowing smile as I place my hands on either side of her face. "I wanted you to be able to study and not worry about me."

"Speaking of worrying, how did you sleep last night?"

"Do you really want me to answer that?"

She sighs in my hands. "Eli, I wish you would've told me that yesterday was my only chance to see you."

I laugh before quickly grazing my lips across hers. "I didn't want to distract my little grad student."

"So a whole week, huh?"

Separating my lips from hers, I wrap my arms around her shoulders, pulling her in for a hug. I nuzzle my face into the crook of her neck, filling my nostrils with her scent as her hands gently stroke my back.

"We went all last week without seeing each other," I remind her, even though I know that answer is bullshit. Things are different between us now.

"Yeah, but things are different between us now, right?" she asks, repeating my unspoken thoughts.

I smile into her neck as I assure her. "Yeah, baby, they are."

I continue to hold her tightly in my arms as she rubs her hands over the length of my back.

"I'm going to miss you."

"I'm going to miss you too," she says into my chest with so much sadness in her tone that it makes my heart hurt. But it also makes me content, knowing she wants me to be around as much as I want to be with her.

"Don't make plans for Saturday. We have our first preseason game at home, and I need you to be there. Will you come?" I pull away to look at her, but keep my arms draped over her shoulders.

"If you want me to be there, I'll be there," she assures me with a sweet smile.

"I don't just want you there, I *need* you there." I press my lips to hers, wanting her to feel how much I'm going to miss her this week. She smiles into my mouth, obviously enjoying my neediness.

I continue to kiss her, and I kiss her hard, right there in the middle of campus. Grabbing her hip, I press her tight little skirt into me, closing the space between us. As I cup her face with my hands, she grips the bottom of my shirt in her fists, making me wish we were in her room or mine so I could peel this sexy little outfit off her. But unfortunately, that's going to have to wait until this weekend. I usually love going on the road for hockey, but now, I would much rather stay home and in bed with Logan.

Since practice ended, I've been trying to pack for the week, but I'm having a hard time keeping my mind off Logan. I want to know what she's doing, I want to know what she's wearing, and I want to know if she's thinking about me as much as I'm thinking about her.

I'm trying to maintain my resolve. I'm trying to be responsible by staying home to allow Logan space to study, but I can't hold myself back any longer. I'm not going to see her all week, and it's already eleven; how much more studying could she really have?

I decide to find out as I grab my suitcase and car keys to drive over to Logan's dorm.

The light in Logan's room shines through the crack under her door, so I know she's awake. I knock but don't wait for her reply before I open the door.

"Fuck," I hear myself say when I spot Logan standing next to her dresser.

She's wearing this sexy little matching set of grey Calvin Kleins. The top is in the shape of a sports bra, but judging by how her tits are bouncing around, I doubt it's workout-approved. The bottoms are shorts. I guess if you want to call them that. They're panties in the shape of shorts, but small enough that the bottom of her perky ass cheeks are peeking out. She was in the middle of putting her hair up when I barged in, so I feel like I'm getting a private little show with her arms up above her head and body on full display.

I know my eyes are bugged out of my head right now, and my jaw is practically on the floor, but I can't help myself as I keep on staring at her. I've never seen this much of her skin before, and I can't wait for the day that I see all of it—in my hands. I've been trying to be a good guy since I met her, but I'd be lying if I said I didn't think about burying myself in her at least once a day.

"Sorry, baby." I attempt to pull my gaze from her but fail miserably.

"What are you doing here?" she excitedly asks, a giant grin plastered across her face. She doesn't seem in the least bit fazed that she's barely dressed as she comes prancing over to greet with me with a hug.

Her body wraps around me, as I feel myself already hardening beneath my joggers. I made sure not to wear jeans tonight—I learned my lesson on Saturday. Snaking my arms around her back, I pull her in closer to me before leaning down to place a kiss on her collarbone, over her tattoo. The warmth of her barely-covered skin mixed with her sweet scent is sending me into overdrive.

"Are you done studying?" I ask as she pulls away. She finishes throwing her hair on top of her head in a messy way, and I swear it feels like I'm watching a live ad for Calvin Klein right in front of my eyes.

"I am," she says before noticing my gaze drifting down her body. "Shit!" She tries to cover herself while grabbing an oversize tee from her dresser and throwing it on over her matching set. She clearly forgot that she was in only her bra and underwear when I walked in.

I, however, will never forget.

I laugh as her cheeks begin to flush.

"Nothing I'm not going to see eventually," I tell her with a sly grin as she rolls her eyes at my arrogance. "Honestly, I was kind of hoping you were still wearing that sexy little outfit from today so that I could be the one to take it off of you." I saunter over to her, pulling her hips into me. Her cheeks deepen in color, and her dimples pop out while she tries to hold back her embarrassed smile.

"What are you doing here? I thought you were leaving for the airport in the morning." She pecks my lips before leaving my grasp and taking a seat on her bed.

"I am. I have to meet the buses at five, but can I stay over? I mean, if you're just going to bed now, anyway."

"Of course," she beams. "You don't have to ask. I want you here."

"Thanks, baby." I close and lock her door behind me before pulling off my shirt and slipping out of my shoes, leaving me in only my joggers. I make sure they're hanging low on my hips so she can see my lowest ab muscles because, quite honestly, I'm trying my best to tempt her. I don't care if I have to be up in a few hours; this is my only night with her all week.

"Well, damn," Logan says with her eyes wide, locking her gaze on my bare chest. "I guess we aren't sleeping tonight," she adds, though I can't tell whether or not she's joking.

"Tempted?" I playfully ask as I plug my phone into her charger and set my alarm for four-thirty. She stays quiet as her darkened eyes continue to wander my body.

"I'll try not to wake you when I leave. It'll be early." I lean over and kiss the top of her head as she sits on her bed.

Logan reaches to her bedside lamp, clicking it off as I climb in the bed behind her, to my spot, as I like to call it, and pull her down beside me.

I'm reminded of her little Calvin Kleins when her ass presses into my cock as she cuddles up to me, her back against my bare chest. The fabric of my sweatpants is so thin that I can feel the curve of Logan's round ass on me. We are held together so tightly that even the smallest of movements is turning me on. Wrapping my arm around her waist, I slip my hand under her shirt so I can feel her warm skin in my palm.

I'm sure that Logan can feel my heartbeat quickening against her back. She has to know what she's doing to me right now as she arches and presses herself into me again. She squirms under my touch as my hand explores her exposed stomach, causing her to grind harder against my package. I suck in a sharp inhale from the contact.

"Are you ready for your test tomorrow?" I ask in a breathy voice. My head leans against hers as I close my eyes and feel every little movement Logan makes with her body.

"Mmm-hmm," she sighs. Her ragged breaths tell me that she's as turned on as I am at this moment.

Moving my hand to her hip, I guide her as she grinds against me. I'm rock hard right now, and I know she can feel my size through my sweatpants.

"Are you ready for your tournament?" she asks, but really it just sounds like she's trying to catch her breath.

"Mmm-hmm," I hum in response. It's pretty evident that neither of us wants to talk right now, so I don't know why we are trying to.

I snake my hand up her stomach until I find her little bra. Pulling the top down, I expose one of her tits, even though her T-shirt is still covering her. I rub her nipple with my thumb before pinching it between my fingers, causing Logan to throw her head back against me, moaning in pleasure. Just watching her unravel under my touch is turning me on like you wouldn't believe.

Reaching for the hem of her shirt, I drag it up as Logan helps take it off the rest of the way and tosses it to the floor. Her back is still to my chest, and as much as I want a better view of this little gray outfit, I'm reveling in the sensation of her ass stroking my dick.

When Logan lets her red hair out of its bun, it falls across her shoulders, and my lips part at the sight. I love watching her this way, feeling turned on, and confident with me. Putting my head to the back of her neck, I kiss my way down to her shoulder, leaving my lips to linger, as I inhale her scent. We're both short of breath as we rub our bodies against one another.

I trail my fingertips down her side, dipping with every curve, and taking in every perfect inch of her body.

Placing my hand on her lower stomach, I press my fingers into her skin before sliding my pinky finger just under the thick branded waistband of her tiny panties. I push her body firmly into me, making sure she feels just how hard I am for her right now.

"Fuck, Logan. Do you feel what you do to me?" I breathe into her neck as her head falls forward, whimpering at my words, unable to respond.

I'm plenty experienced, but not when it comes to being sexual with someone I have feelings for, and I'm finding myself somewhat nervous right now. I want this to be good for Logan. I want her to feel taken care of and cherished, but also sexy and wanted when she's with me.

I lower my fingers into her underwear, ready to feel the warmth between her legs. "Has anyone ever touched you here?" I ask in a ragged, almost shaky voice, my fingers lingering just above her slit.

Her breathing hitches as she shakes her head. "Only you, Eli," she softly says, and I almost come just from those three words alone.

Chapter 53

Logan

I can feel the spot between my legs throbbing in anticipation as Eli's hand slides further into my underwear. No one has ever touched me here before, besides myself of course, and I'm a little nervous. He's done this so many times before, with so many women, but before I can even get lost in those thoughts, Eli's fingers slide down and graze my clit, instantly clearing my mind.

He hisses a sharp inhale between his teeth as I let out a whimpering moan from the contact, tossing my head back onto him and pushing my ass into his erection.

"Fuck, baby. You're so wet for me," Eli breathes into my ear.

Once again, I find myself drifting off into my mind. Am I too wet? Should I be embarrassed? Is that a good thing?

Eli must notice my hesitation, now that I've stopped moving with him. "Stop overthinking, Logan. You're so sexy right now. You have no idea," he whispers, building up my confidence as he slowly circles his finger against my swollen bud.

He feels so good that I turn my mind off, close my eyes, and revel in his touch. He rubs, and circles, and flicks, and fuck it feels so much better than when I touch myself. He knows exactly what to do. He holds me close with his other arm across my chest as his expert fingers continue to explore me, gliding, teasing, pinching. I open my legs wider, giving his talented fingers better access to me. He runs his long middle finger over my slit and into my soaking folds as his thumb continues to focus on my clit.

A groan releases from deep in his throat as he begins to explore me deeper. "You feel so good on my fingers, Logan."

I'm pretty sure that making me feel good is making Eli even more turned on, as the growing thickness pressed against my ass would appear to confirm.

I feel sexy when I'm in his arms. He makes me feel wanted and craved. A sudden surge of confidence takes over as I reach behind me and slide my hand into Eli's sweatpants. I stroke his length over his briefs, and it jerks in my hand.

"Fuck, Logan," he growls into my neck. I could somewhat feel his size when he was pressed against me, but now, stroking him with my fingertips, I can feel just how large he truly is.

I continue to touch him, wanting him to feel as good as I do right now. I'm tempted to reach into his boxers and feel his skin on mine, but I want to do that when I can see him in my hands—in all his glory, not when my back is to him.

He continues to rub me between his fingers, my swollen clit begging for more. He quickens his pace, deepening his pressure as I stroke his dick with a matching tempo. Our breathing is ragged as the pressure builds in my stomach, begging for release as I grind against his hand, meeting his movements.

Eli abruptly stops, pulling his fingers from me as I snap my head to look at him, confused by what just happened.

He starts removing his sweatpants but leaves his briefs in place. "Sorry, babe, but you're about to make me come, and I need these sweatpants to be clean for my trip."

I laugh but feel my cheeks warm at the thought of my hand having that kind of power over him. He leans over and presses his lips to mine, letting them linger there for a moment. He drags the tip of his nose across my jaw before gently tugging at my ear with his teeth.

"Your hand feels so good on me," he moans into my ear, his tone deep and warm.

"So does yours." I confidently grab his hand and guide his fingers back where they belong—on my clit.

Eli chuckles as his lips form into a smile on the skin of my neck before I find him with my hand once again.

He continues his previous movements. Rubbing me with a rhythmic pace, gliding his fingers over me. I keep my hand in place, grasping his dick and letting him find the tempo he likes as he thrusts into my touch. He's moving quicker in my hand while his fingers pick up speed and pressure on my favorite spot. I feel the edge nearing as I grip his opposite arm with my other hand, needing to steady myself.

The room is filled with mixed moans and heavy breaths as we both near our euphoria.

"*Eli*," I cry out, my release approaching.

"Me too, baby."

His words bring my release as I reach a high I've never experienced. My eyes squeeze shut with white blurry vision, my mouth gapes open, and my head falls back, pressing into Eli's chest. Eli's fingers continue their movements as I ride out my orgasm before melting into him, keeping my hand wrapped around him. A few more thrusts into my palm, and I hear my name coming from Eli's lips before I feel a warm wetness seeping through the material in my hand.

A few sedate moments pass, but Eli keeps his fingers on me, and I can feel myself pulsing in his hand.

"Fuck. Watching you like that..." he stops, unable to find the words.

As I start to come down from my high, a bit of embarrassment floods me. I've never come from someone else's touch before, and I'm slightly self-conscious about how I may have looked.

"Seeing you like that...that was fucking hot, Logan," he whispers into my ear, before gently biting my shoulder and instantly taking away any worry I may have had. This man makes me feel sexy and desired, and I need to be confident in how he sees me.

He pulls his fingers from me as I pinch my legs together, trying to ease the ache of emptiness that lingers.

Eli lifts himself off the bed and turns me onto my back, hovering over me. He nudges my legs open with his knee as he presses himself onto me, perfectly lining up his wet boxers with my underwear.

"Was that okay for you?" Eli asks, brushing the hair away from my face as he looks at me with concern.

Was it okay for me? Is he kidding? His fingers are magical, and I've never experienced such a release in my life. He has plenty of sexual experience, so I don't know why he's doubting his abilities with me.

"Yeah, baby. That felt really good." I reach up and place my mouth against his smiling lips, reassuring him. "How was it for you?"

Eli looks down in the space between us, eyeing his wet briefs. "Yeah, I'd say you felt pretty fucking good," he says with a chuckle, as I try to hold back my satisfaction with his answer.

Reaching around his neck, I pull his mouth to mine, exploring his tongue, and memorizing his lips for when he leaves me this week.

"I gotta run to the bathroom," I tell him as he hovers only inches above me.

He lets out a frustrated growl, dropping his head to my shoulder as he presses his already hardening dick against me. I laugh to myself. What was that—two minutes and he's ready to go again?

Slipping out from underneath him, I throw on his oversized shirt to cover my mostly naked body and head to the bathroom to clean myself up.

When I return to my room and peek through the crack in my door, I find a fully naked Eli with his back to me, taking off his briefs to replace them with his clean joggers. His ass is right there on full display for me to see. It's firm and round, and I feel myself overheating at the view. I've never seen a hockey player's ass and thighs before, but holy shit, they're amazing. I guess I can thank all his lunges on the ice for my perfect visual right now.

I stay silent as Eli changes. I don't want him to know I can see him, mostly because I don't think we will get any sleep if we start something again. Eli needs to sleep. He has to be up in just a few hours, and I'm worried he won't get much the rest of the week.

I wait until Eli is fully dressed before I walk into my room. When I do, he pulls me into his arms and kisses the tattoo on my collarbone, even though his shirt is covering it. He's formed a new habit of kissing me there.

"That looks good on you," Eli says, referring to the shirt of his that I'm wearing.

Lifting his tee up and over my head, I place it next to his discarded briefs. He's going to need to take it tomorrow on his trip, and if I sleep in it, he won't be able to.

"And you look even better in that," he adds, eyeing my matching gray set.

I blush as I try to hold back my grin. "Sleep," I remind him, glancing down at the time on my phone.

When we climb back into bed, he pulls me on top of him, so I'm lying with my head on his chest and my body fully on top of his. He holds me with his strong arms, making me feel small as he places a gentle kiss on my forehead.

"Night, Logan," he says, his lips pressed to my hair.

"Goodnight." I memorize his tone and inhale his scent, trying to lock them into my memory to get me through the week without him.

When I wake up the next morning to an empty bed, my heart instantly sinks, remembering that Eli is gone. I now fully realize how terrible he must've felt all those times I left him alone in bed. I let myself loath in self-pity for a few minutes before reaching for my phone to check the time.

A sudden rush of adrenaline hits me, remembering that I forgot to set my alarm for class. I have a huge Econ test this morning that I cannot be late for. My heart rate quickens until I find my phone and read the time— seven forty-five. I would've needed to wake up at eight, so thank god for my internal clock waking me up in time.

I have fifteen more minutes I can use to mope around in bed before I need to get up. I roll over to find a more comfortable position but spot a note sitting on Eli's side of the mattress when I do. It's just a little piece of paper resting on a folded item of clothing, but as my eyes scan the words, my stomach fills with butterflies.

Miss you already.
You look better in my shirt than I do.
P.S. I set your alarm for you.
-E

I quickly grab my phone and check my alarm. Eli set it for eight.

What the hell did I do to deserve him?

My heart flutters at his thoughtful gesture as I grab his shirt and inhale his masculine scent that lingers. I rest my head on it and close my eyes, hoping to capture those last fifteen minutes of sleep as I imagine that Eli is lying next to me.

Chapter 54

Logan

"Is that from lover boy?" Ali teases, glancing over my shoulder to look at my phone before walking around the table to sit across from me.

"Yes, it is," I tell her proudly.

"They're done playing? How did it go?" Marc asks between mouthfuls of chow mein noodles.

With the hockey team on the road, Friday night on campus was surprisingly quiet. Marc, Ali, and I decided to get away from the dorms for the night and head to Marc's parents' house just off campus. His parents are flying in from Indiana tonight to watch Eli's game tomorrow, and Marc wanted to come by and get the house ready for them. We had been talking about getting Chinese takeout all week and finally gave in tonight as we all sit around the dining room table, digging into the takeout boxes.

"Good. They won," I inform Marc, glancing down at my phone as Eli's texts flood in. "4-3."

"Awesome, that's a big tournament for them to win, even if it is just preseason."

My phone dings again, and I feel the smile form on my lips from just seeing Eli's name on my screen. I thought about adding a little red heart emoji next to his name, but I think I would be too embarrassed if he ever saw it.

"He wants me to tell you that Zanders got a five-minute major at the end of the third, Eli scored the game-tying goal, and Cam scored the winner." I read Eli's text aloud to Marc.

"Whatever that means," Ali chimes in before taking a massive bite of Kung-pow chicken.

“Good. Fuck Zanders,” Marc says, shaking his head. “Evan Zanders is this prick who plays for Ohio State. He was the one who threw EJ into the boards illegally and shattered his ankle a few years ago. He’s a dirty defenseman who has had it out for EJ since they were kids playing travel hockey.” Marc directs his explanation to me, knowing Ali could not care less about sports.

“I can’t stand that guy,” Ali chimes in. “Don’t get me wrong, I have absolutely no idea what either of you guys are talking about, but fuck that guy. Right?”

Marc and I both laugh, shaking our heads at Ali’s honesty. Not that I know much more about hockey than she does, but I’ve been trying to learn. Every night this week, when Eli has texted to tell me how his games went, I Googled whatever I couldn’t understand, and I feel like I’m getting a pretty good grasp on the game in general.

“Exactly, Alison. Fuck that guy,” Marc confirms with a proud grin on his face.

She smiles right back at him, mouth full and all.

“You know, there was a time when I was the one that EJ would call when he was on the road,” Marc says, pulling his attention back to me, pretending to be hurt by his brother’s lack of communication with him over the week.

“I think I’m more his type.” I shrug, giving Marc a knowing grin.

He laughs but shoots me a proud smile. He’s made it pretty clear this week how happy he is that things have been going well for Eli and me.

Marc told me that he could see the change in his brother since we’ve been spending time together. He also said how much he noticed a difference in me. Said I seemed more confident, and I have to agree with him. I’m not fully there, but having this support system of people who understand me has really helped me feel like myself again.

“Okay, so a five-minute major is a really bad penalty, right? You have the whole five minutes to play five on four regardless of if you score or not?”

“Spot on, girl. Look at you, you’ll be an expert in no time,” Marc says while trying to steal a piece of chicken from my plate with his chopsticks. “You’re about to know more about hockey than you do basketball, which is saying a lot.”

I swat his sticks away with mine. “Just trying to figure it out, so I have some idea of what’s going on when I finally get to see Eli play. Hockey isn’t very popular in California.”

“You’re coming tomorrow, right? Ali, you too?” Marc asks, looking between us.

“Yeah, I’ll be there,” Ali says. “And we both know Logan will be there, cheering on her man.”

“Okay, chill. He’s not my man.” He is *so* my man, but it feels a little weird to say that in front of Marc.

“That make-out sesh in the gym last week said otherwise. That boy was trying to claim you in front of everyone.” Ali wiggles her brows suggestively.

“Can’t argue there.” I shrug with a smug smirk.

“I really need some more guy friends,” Marc huffs, shaking his head.

My phone vibrates in my lap as Eli’s name pops up on the screen, indicating another new text.

E: *Also, I was named tournament MVP...so what’s my prize?*

“Eli was named Most Valuable Player of the tournament,” I inform my friends as I continue to stare at my phone with a proud smile plastered on my face.

“Good, he’s by far the best player in the division. I’m glad he’s playing like it,” Marc adds.

L: *What do you want your prize to be?* I reply to Eli, knowing full well his mind is probably racing with all the naughty things he wants to request.

E: *You.* He quickly responds, surprising me by going the sweet route and keeping his dirty thoughts to himself. Well, knowing Eli, it was meant to be both dirty and sweet.

I can't help the full tooth-displaying grin from spreading across my face. This guy makes me insanely happy and continually reminds me of how much he wants me. Part of me was worried about him going on the road, especially with his past, but with the amount of time he spent calling or texting me, I can't imagine he had an opportunity for much else.

L: *You already have me.*

E: *I like the way that sounds.*

E: *Boarding the plane. Can't wait to see you tomorrow.*

L: *Me too. Fly safe.*

"Jesus, isn't your face sore from smiling so much?" Ali teases, pulling my attention back to the present.

"Shut up," I tell her as we giggle with each other.

"You guys should try to get there early tomorrow. Even though it's only a preseason game, the arena is still going to be packed." Marc pushes his plate away and leans back in his chair, trying to stretch out his full stomach.

"Really? But doesn't that arena seat like...thousands?" I ask, unconvinced.

"Yeah, but this school and city are all about hockey. It's a huge deal here. If you thought EJ was popular already, just wait until you see him after a game. He's practically a local celebrity here."

"Great," I sarcastically add. I'm glad Eli is well-loved around campus, but I know the pressure he feels from everyone to be and play a certain way. I just want him to be able to enjoy playing the game he loves and not have to worry about the rest. On top of that, the number of women who gawk over the guy is a little disconcerting. Eli has made it pretty evident that he doesn't have eyes for anyone else, but I still don't love watching other girls cling all over the man I have feelings for.

"Will there be scouts from the NHL there tomorrow?" I ask, needing to prepare myself for the fact that Eli could leave at the drop of a hat as soon as he gets picked up by a big-league team.

"Probably not tomorrow, but most likely soon. Once the regular season starts." Marc keeps his gaze on me, trying to gauge my reaction.

Well, at least I won't have to say goodbye to him tomorrow, but still, it's coming.

Ali clearly picks up on my concern as she eyes me from across the table.

"Have you guys talked about what you're going to do if he leaves?" Both her and Marc keep their focus on me.

"No. I haven't wanted to think about it, to be honest. Plus, this thing between us is so new that I don't want to put pressure on him. I want this for him, but on a selfish note, it makes me sad to know that he's probably going to leave soon."

"Well," Marc sighs. "I've never seen my brother like this before, so I wouldn't get too in your head thinking things are ending before they even really begin." He gives me an encouraging smile, trying to ease my concern.

Marc knows better than anyone that I'm used to people leaving me. It's not my parents' fault that they left, but still, they did. Let's not forget to mention Zac. Marc was the first person I allowed into my life without fear that I would lose him. Next was Ali, then most importantly was Eli. The hard part about Eli was that I knew the second I started to fall for him that he was going to leave at some point. But regardless of those fears, I haven't been able to hold my feelings back, which I know will eventually cause the heartbreak of a lifetime when he does go.

"Are you sure you guys don't want to just crash here?" Marc asks us, pulling me out of my daze, as he gets up to throw away the empty takeout boxes.

Ali looks to me for an answer. "I um...No, I think I'm going to head back to the dorms. I'm sure your parents are looking forward to having time alone with you and Eli. He's going to come here when he lands tonight, right?"

Honestly, the only reason I want to leave is that I know their parents will be here soon, and I think that Eli should be included when I meet them. Otherwise, of course, I would stay. I would love to see Eli as soon as he's back in town.

"I would assume so. We usually stay at the house when our parents are in town."

"Cool. Well, I'll grab a ride back with you, Logan." Ali grabs her purse and heads towards the door.

Marc stops me in my tracks by grabbing my arm and pulling me in for a hug. "Stop getting in your head about it," he tells me, obviously noting that I've been off since we talked about Eli's future.

"I'm trying." I shrug in his grasp. When he releases me from his arms, I can tell he's unconvinced. Not that I blame him, so am I.

"See you both at the game," Marc yells out as Ali and I walk down the front walkway towards my car. "Love you, Logan," he adds in his normal volume as I turn around to give him an appreciative smile, always being thankful for his friendship.

I've been lying awake in bed for hours. It's hard to sleep when you're excited about what's to come the next day. Not being able to see, or touch, or hold Eli all week has sucked, and I can't wait for tomorrow when I finally can. We've spoken every day, anytime he wasn't playing or I wasn't in class, but it's not the same as seeing him in person.

I've never felt like I needed someone, so I was surprised at how tough the last few days were. 'Needy' is the last word I would use to describe myself typically. I don't know what's going on with me, but I'm trying to come to terms with the fact that it's okay to need someone in your life. Because right now, I'm learning just how much I need Eli, and that's a little scary to admit.

Eli's shirt has been my choice of sleepwear over the last few nights. His scent still lingers, and I like the oversized fit. When Ali barged in and saw me wearing it last night, she teased me a bit, but ultimately it made her get all mushy. She's been loving my updates on all things Eli. Says it makes her feel like she's watching a Hallmark movie. Even though she doesn't believe in sticking with one person at our age, she's still happy that I'm happy.

I toss and turn in my bed, settling on my back, hoping to find a position that I can fall asleep in when I hear a light knock on my door. It opens before I can respond, and I already know it's Eli. That's how he always enters my room—a quick knock to announce himself, but he doesn't wait for me to answer. It's dark in here, but the glow from the moonlight shining through my window illuminates the room just enough that I can see Eli's perfect frame walk through my doorway.

He drops his things after closing the door behind him and climbs right into bed with me. His long body drapes over mine, pressing me into the mattress with his weight. He slides his arms under and around my back, his face nuzzles into the crook of my neck, and I've never felt more comfortable. I instantly wrap both my arms around his shoulders, holding him tightly to me, relishing in the feeling of having him in my arms again.

"Hi, baby," he says into my neck. His breath is warm and tickles my skin as he speaks.

"Hi." I stroke his shaggy hair with one of my hands.

Glancing over to my door, I notice Eli's bag sitting in the entryway, which makes me smile from ear to ear. He didn't even go home before he came to see me.

"I thought I was going to see you tomorrow?" My lips graze against his temple.

“I didn’t want to wait.” He turns to kiss my collarbone, where my tattoo is inked. “You’re wearing my shirt,” he adds as he hovers his head a few inches from me, eyeing my choice of pajamas.

I’m glad the room is dark right now, so he can’t see the redness creeping up my cheeks. I know he left it for me, but I don’t know if he expected that I’d actually wear it.

“Did you wear it all week?” He turns his head to look at me. The glow from the window allows just enough light for me to see Eli’s flawless face. His eyes are soft as they search mine, waiting for an answer.

I nod my head in response.

He tries to hold back the shit-eating grin creeping across his face, but he fails miserably. His eyes wander from my lips to my eyes and back again before pressing his mouth to mine. It’s warm and soft, and I’ve missed him so much.

“Fuck, I missed you,” Eli says as he pulls away to rest his forehead on mine, keeping his eyes closed.

“Me too.”

He lets out a sigh of satisfaction as he hides his face back into my neck, breathing in deeply.

“You smell so good. I’ve been around disgusting hockey dudes all week. You have no idea how good you smell right now.”

Continuing to stroke his hair, I hold him with my other arm as his breathing slows and steadies. I mean, I hold him as much as I can. He’s a big guy, and even though I’m tall, my arm still doesn’t wrap all the way around him.

“You’re going to meet my parents tomorrow,” Eli reminds me in an almost sedated voice. I can tell he’s getting close to drifting off to sleep.

“I know,” I whisper.

I’m looking forward to meeting Eli and Marc’s parents tomorrow. I’ve been looking forward to it since Marc and I first became friends when he told me just how close his family of four was, but I'm definitely more nervous now that Eli and I are involved. I hope they like me because I know how important their sons are to them, and I want them to know how much their boys mean to me. Both of them— the one who's my best friend and the one who's currently sound asleep in my arms.

Chapter 55

Logan

"What are you supposed to wear to a hockey game?" Ali asks as she bursts into my room to check herself out in my full-length mirror.

"I don't know. I've never been to one, but I would assume something warmer than that." I tilt my head, internally questioning her choice of wearing a crop top to an ice rink.

"Well, you look nice," she compliments as she catches my reflection in the mirror behind her.

I wasn't sure what I was supposed to wear, but I want to look somewhat put together when I meet Marc and Eli's parents. I opted for a maroon mock neck sweater with my tight black jeans, layered with my camel-colored duster jacket. I was going to pull my Vans on but thought I should look a little nicer, so I settled on my black ankle boots. I don't have any school gear, so I'm hoping the maroon of my shirt is enough.

"You nervous?" Ali asks as I follow her back into her dorm to change.

"A little." I pull a cream-colored sweater from her closet and hand it to her to switch into. She pulls off her crop top and swaps it for the sweater, looking much more prepared to sit around an ice rink for a couple of hours.

"Don't be," she reassures. "They're going to love you. Both of their boys adore you, so I'm sure they will be too."

"Thanks, Ali." I give my friend an appreciative smile. "But they're going to love me less if I miss their son's first game. So, let's go. We're running late." I grab her purse off the desk and open her door, urgently ushering her out.

Marc was right. The arena is packed already. I knew we were running a little behind, but we're still here twenty minutes before the puck drop. A crowd of deep red and gold swarms around us as we try to enter the rink, and I can't believe how many people are here already. This town truly is all about their hockey.

A few random spots of purple catch my eye in the crowd, but the sea of maroon and gold engulfs the Northeastern fans.

"Do you see Marc?" Ali asks as her little body dips around, standing on her tiptoes, trying to find our friend.

"I don't," I tell her, having a much easier time seeing into the crowd due to my height. Marc had texted me the location of his seats, but I can't seem to find him in the audience. "Let's just sit up there." I point to a pair of seats that are somewhat close to us and not in the rowdy student section, though they are next to it.

The seats around us quickly fill as more and more Minnesota fans enter the arena. I'm still shocked that this many people would come to a college preseason game. I'm quickly starting to grasp the pressure Eli feels by not only being on this team and being their star player, but also their captain.

"Is Maddison number thirteen?" Ali asks.

"Yeah, he is. How'd you know?"

"Because most everyone in that student section is wearing a number thirteen jersey. And a lot of the rest of the crowd is too." She points out Eli's number peppered throughout the stadium.

"Damn. I didn't realize it was going to be like this. I mean, I heard he was good, but this is wild." I eye the crowd, spotting Eli's number repeated over and over.

I'm glad Eli has fans, but I'd be lying if I said I wasn't intimidated by just how many people love the guy. I knew he was popular, but this is more than I expected.

My phone dings in my lap, and Marc's name flashes across the screen.

M: *Where are you?*

L: *We just picked a random spot. I couldn't find you. I can't believe how packed it is.*

M: *Crazy, right?*

L: *Totally. I'll meet up with you after the game.*

The arena lights dim as shrieks and shouts surround us while the red and yellow strobe lights dance across the ice. The music slowly creeps up as the announcer welcomes the crowd. The Northwestern hockey team is on the ice for warmup, but you can only spot them through the darkness when a strobe light flashes over their end of the rink.

"Alright, U of M fans! We've been waiting all summer for this! Please welcome your University of Minnesota Golden Gophers!" the announcer booms over the speaker system. The team begins to spill onto the ice while the music and cheers rise in volume.

I keep my eyes peeled for Eli's jersey. Number thirteen is the last one to leave the player's tunnel and step onto the ice, and the crowd stirs when he does.

"There he is!" Ali yelps beside me, nudging me as if I hadn't already spotted him.

He's pretty hard to miss. I mean, he's huge. I know he's a tall guy coming in at 6'4", but with the added inches from his skates and the bulk from his pads, he looks like a giant compared to most other players on the ice. From what I've learned about hockey, someone with his build would most likely be a defenseman, but Eli is a forward. And apparently a pretty damn good one at that.

After the national anthem, the starting five guys of each team line up on the blue line as they're being announced. The Northwestern fans make a bit of noise, but nothing compared to the howl from the crowd as U of M's players are introduced.

"Last, but certainly not least. The university's all-time high scorer, your captain. Ladies and gentlemen, Eli Maddison!" the announcer bellows as the crowd erupts in shrieks and screams.

Girls around me are literally squealing as Eli skates forward, gives a quick wave, and returns to the blue line next to his teammates.

This is crazy. I've never heard an arena at this noise level. The crowd was loud as the other players were being announced, but it was deafening when Eli's name was called. Marc was right. He is a local celebrity.

"That's your boyfriend!" Ali teasingly howls into my ear, trying to rise above the volume of the crowd, as we stand with the rest of the fans and clap for our team and my guy.

"He's not my boyfriend!" I yell back, trying to get my voice to project enough for her to hear.

She rolls her eyes at me just as she has all week whenever she mentioned that Eli was my boyfriend, and I shut her down. I mean, he's not, so it would be weird for her to call him that. Eli and I haven't talked about it yet, and I don't want to pressure him to make this thing official. I don't even know if he would want an official girlfriend when he might be leaving for an NHL team soon anyway. I'm confident in where I stand with him, the rest is just a bonus.

He lines up for the opening face-off against one of Northwestern's players, but Eli towers over him. Eli wins the drop with ease, passing it off to a teammate as he makes his way down the rink. The way Eli moves on those skates is beautiful. He's graceful and strong as he glides over the ice with ease. When the puck makes his way back to him, I'm shocked at how well he handles it with his stick. It's like it's an extension of his body, and when Eli's first shot ricochets off the goalpost, the crowd stands, gasping in anticipation.

Watching him quickly skate down the rink to get back on defense is nothing short of breathtaking. Despite his size, he's the fastest guy on the ice, and he moves with more fluidity than any of his teammates or opponents. When he bodies a player in purple into the boards, I wince at the contact, hoping he doesn't hurt himself out there. He causes a turnover from the Northwestern team, passes it off to one of his linemates, and switches out from his shift.

"Damn," I say under my breath, unable to find any other word that would help express just how impressed I am right now.

"Shit. Maddison *is* good," Ali responds as I keep my eyes glued on number thirteen, watching him take a seat on the bench as his coach pats him on the helmet.

"How turned on are you right now?" Ali teases.

"Extremely," I admit, my mouth feeling dry.

Eli's first goal comes towards the end of the first period. Patrick steals the puck from the Northwestern forward and passes it up to Eli. He uses his speed to beat the defenders, then fakes out the goalie by leaning one way before maneuvering the puck to the opposite side of the goal and tucking it into the back of the net with ease.

The eruption of the crowd is mind-blowing as Eli's teammates charge him with hockey hugs, slamming him into the boards in excitement. While the arena fills with 'Maddison' chants, Eli skates past the bench where his team stands, bumping gloves as he goes by. He looks up to the Jumbotron as they replay his goal before the camera pans back to him in the present, and I get to see his face for the first time, which makes me smile from ear to ear. He seems so happy and in his element out there on the ice, but he also looks insanely sexy in that uniform.

"Maddison is so fucking hot," a girl behind me says to her friend. "It's happening this year. He's on my college bucket list."

Ali turns to gauge my reaction.

I can't help but let out a laugh as Ali joins in, both of us knowing that for the first time in his college career, Eli Maddison isn't looking to get with any other girl.

That is until her friend responds and my smile falls.

"We hooked up last year," her friend says. "Might be the best dick I've ever had."

When Ali notices my blank expression, she nudges me with a sympathetic smile on her lips. "Don't worry about it," she says, trying to get my mind off the fact that the girl sitting behind me has done more, physically, than I have with my man.

Eli scores again in the second period and adds an assist in the third, which is extremely impressive. Though, what I find more impressive is when he lands himself in the penalty box for getting in a minor fight. It isn't the fight itself that I like, but the fact that when one of Northwestern's big defensemen starts wailing punches on one of Eli's smaller teammates, Eli steps in to defend him. The Northwestern d-man gets booted from the game, and Eli lands himself in the box for fighting, but when he makes it back to his bench, he's greeted with appreciative pats on the back and fist bumps from all of his teammates.

We win 5-2, and the crowd buzzes with excitement over the potential of what this season could bring. The most surprising thing I found from my first hockey game was the fact that Eli *hadn't* gotten picked up by an NHL team yet. He's by far the best player on the ice. It's not even a question of how talented he is.

M: *Meet me outside of the player's tunnel. It's behind section 112.*

"Marc wants us to go meet up with him," I inform Ali as we make our way through the crowd towards the section he mentioned.

There are quite a few Minnesota fans headed in that direction, but I'm able to spot Marc's height and tanned skin through the crowd when we reach the tunnel.

"Hey." Marc wraps me in a hug. "What did you think?"

"Eli is insanely good."

"Right? He's the best one out there, that's for sure. And he played better today than I've seen him play in a long time."

"Marcus," Ali interrupts to greet him while trying to suppress a grin.

"Ali," Marc responds, holding back the same smile.

I watch for a moment as my two friends hold eye contact with each other, being way more friendly than they've been in previous weeks.

"Let's go. My parents are waiting for EJ outside the locker room." Marc nods towards the tunnel, making his way down the hall as Ali and I follow behind.

Down the corridor, there's a huge crowd standing outside of the locker room, waiting for the players to emerge. Parents and families are waiting around for their boys to come out, but there are plenty of fans and students down here as well. I recognize Marc's parents from his pictures and spot them ahead, among the crowd, waiting for Eli. Alyssa is also down there with her group of girlfriends, all wearing Eli's number on their shirts, and a couple of them have signs in their hands as well. Their attire is making me second guess whether or not I should've worn something more team-spirited than the plain maroon top I chose.

"I'm going to wait back here," I tell Marc as I stop in my tracks, staying towards the edge of the tunnel, far behind the crowd swarming the locker room entrance.

"Are you sure?" He turns back to question me.

"Yeah, go hang with your parents. I'm fine."

When he joins the crowd ahead of us, Ali nudges me. "What's up?"

"Nothing. I just don't think Eli is going to want me to be waiting for him the second he comes out of the locker room. You remember what happened when Cam and Patrick almost caught us holding hands."

"I don't think that's true. He was kissing you on campus just last week."

"I know, but this is different. I don't think he wants these people to know yet, and I'm trying to respect that."

Ten minutes of waiting and the players start to trickle out from the locker room. They're all freshly showered and back in their suits and ties. Patrick files out, saying hello to a few people before going over to Alyssa's clique and giving them each a hug. Cam makes his way through the doors and finds an older couple, who I assume are his parents, judging by their matching ginger locks, before embracing them both. It seems like most of the team has exited the locker room, but Eli still hasn't, and the crowd hasn't lessened, so I assume that most everyone down here is waiting around to see him.

When he does finally emerge, my jaw slacks at the view. He looks so handsome in his navy-blue suit. It's perfectly tailored to fit his muscular build, and the lines accentuate his tall frame. His crisp white shirt is unbuttoned at the top, and his brown shoes perfectly match with his belt. His hair is wet from his shower, and he looks so damn good he should probably be on the cover of a magazine.

When he comes out, the crowd stirs, and my suspicions are confirmed that everyone was waiting for him as a few people rush him the second he appears.

He looks around for a moment until he finds his parents and Marc, dodging the crowd as he heads in their direction. Even though he has spotted his family, he continues to sift through the audience with his eyes, looking around. He gives his dad a quick hug and a pat on the shoulder, then gives his stepmom a swift kiss on the cheek, all while continuing to search through the crowd. He leans over to Marc to say something in his ear as Marc quickly turns in my direction, pointing up the hall. As Eli's eyes find mine, his face lights up, and a huge smile dons his perfect lips as he begins to slip past the crowd to head towards me.

Most people are watching his every move, which is making me nervous, but I'm more excited to see Eli than I am worried about what anybody else thinks.

His long legs bound towards me, and before I realize what's happening, he wraps me in his arms and lifts me up in a hug. Tightening my arms around his shoulders, I close my eyes, pressing my cheek against his. He nuzzles his head into my neck, and I cup the back of his wet head with my hand as he holds me in the air.

"Hi, baby," he says into my nape.

"Hi," I whisper in return.

He tilts his head and kisses my tattooed collarbone, his new favorite spot, before placing me back on my feet.

"Good game." I look up to him, beaming with pride.

"Thank you." He eyes my body up and down. "You look gorgeous," Eli tells me, taking away any worry I may have had about not wearing the team's gear.

My cheeks begin to heat as I'm suddenly reminded that the entire team and all of his fans just saw him hug and kiss me. As I look around, at least thirty sets of eyes are on us, but Eli doesn't seem to notice or care as he cups my face with both hands and leans down to place his lips on mine.

"Hey, Ali," Eli says as he keeps his eyes on me, tucking a strand of hair behind my ear. He slides his forearm around the front of my shoulders, turning me and pulling me in close to his chiseled body. He holds me firmly to him with my back to his chest before resting his chin on the top of my head.

"Hey, Maddison. Nice game." She wears an approving smile as she looks between Eli and me.

When I glance up, Alyssa's face is the first one I see, and it's plastered in disbelief and disgust. She's holding a sign with Eli, Patrick, and Cam's numbers on it, but she's about to drop it as her eyes burn into me. I spot Patrick next, whose brows are furrowed in confusion, then Cam, who has a genuine smile on his face. Most everyone else who I recognize as students are staring at us in shock and surprise.

Marc makes his way to Eli and I with his parents following close behind. Eli drops his arm from my shoulders but slides his hand down, grazing the small of my back.

"Nice game, son," Eli's dad says with a proud grin on his face as he pats his son on the back. He and Eli look so much alike. Even though Eli's dad is technically his uncle, they look as if they could be biological father and son. He's equally handsome and just as tall.

"And who might this be?" Marc's mom asks as she looks to me with a questioning but excited expression. Marc's mom is also beautiful but surprisingly petite. Marc's biological dad must've been where he got his height, but the rest of him is all her. His mom has the same deep tan skin and shiny black hair as her son.

"This is...um..." Eli stumbles. We haven't really talked about how we'll introduce one another, so this is a little awkward. He scratches his brow with his thumb before he looks to me as if I could help him answer. He clears his throat as he starts again. "This is..." he pauses.

"Mom, this is my best friend, Logan," Marc interjects, saving his brother from the embarrassment he's causing himself.

"Oh my god! Logan! Marc has told us so much about you!" She beams as she wraps me in her arms for a hug. "I was hoping I would get to meet you this weekend."

Eli keeps his hand on my lower back the entire time I'm wrapped in his stepmom's arms.

"Though, Marc did not mention that you were so beautiful. Or that you were even a woman for that matter." She cups my face with her hands, taking me in.

"See, I'm not the only one who didn't know," Eli tells Marc in a knowing tone, as Eli pulls me close to his side again. Marc just responds with a shrug when all eyes land on him.

"It's so nice to meet you...Mrs. Maddison?" I question, not knowing the correct name to call her. I know Marc's last name is Jones, but she is married to Eli's dad. It's all so confusing.

"Please, call me Mary." She clasps her hands under her chin and looks between Eli and me, beaming with excitement as she puts the pieces together.

"And I'm Jack," Eli's dad says as he reaches past his wife to shake my hand.

"Nice to meet you both," I say, catching the sly grin Eli's dad shoots him. Jack looks between Marc, Eli, and me before letting out a chuckle, obviously finding humor in the fact that his son finally stuck with one girl, and it just so happens to be his other son's best friend. Eli playfully rolls his eyes and shakes his head as he wraps his arm around my shoulder, pulling me in closer to his body.

"And this is Ali," Marc says, changing the subject. "She's in school with Logan and me, getting her MBA."

"Lovely to meet you." Mary gives Ali a sweet smile.

"You too."

"Well, you girls just have to come over to the house for dinner tonight," Mary states, glancing between Ali and me. "I made plenty of food for everyone."

"I would love to, but I have dinner plans already," Ali tells Mary, regretfully.

"You do?" Marc questions her.

"Yes, I do."

"That's too bad. Next time?" Mary asks, genuinely disappointed as Ali nods in agreement. "Well, Logan, what do you say?" Mary turns her attention back to me.

"She's not going to let you get out of it, Logan," Jack says. "She's been dying to meet you, so you should just give in and say yes. It'll make your life easier."

Marc shrugs in agreement as Mary swats at her husband playfully.

I look up to Eli as he quickly nods his head in approval.

"Dinner sounds great," I tell Mary.

"Wonderful! I'm looking forward to having another woman at the house. I'm surrounded by too many boys."

"I'm going to take off," Ali says to the group as she quickly squeezes my hand to say goodbye.

"Oh! Let me get a picture of the four of you real quick!" Mary pulls out her phone.

"Mom, come on," Marc says in an annoyed tone, rolling his eyes.

"I don't—" Eli begins to complain until I nudge him in the ribs with my elbow.

"Just one," she begs of her sons.

"Just do it so we can go eat," Jack says to his sons from behind his wife, which makes me laugh.

Jack gives me an appreciative smile that I understand his humor.

Eli unwraps his arms from my shoulders and instead drapes it across my back, cupping my side and proudly pulling me into his. I snake my arm around Eli's strong muscular back as Marc stands on my other side and throws his arms around Ali and my shoulders. We all smile while Marc's mom takes more than a few photos.

"That should be enough, mom," Marc says as he releases both Ali and me from his grasp, though Eli keeps his hand wrapped around my back, ever so slightly rubbing his thumb against me.

"I really do have to get going, but it was so nice to meet you both." Ali turns to Marc's parents.

"You too, dear," Mary says before Ali goes to leave. Marc gives her a questioning squint, but Ali just shrugs in response before walking towards the exit.

Eli releases his grip on my side, sliding his hand down my forearm before lacing his large fingers between mine. I don't miss the dirty looks that Alyssa and her minions shoot me as they walk past us to leave, but honestly, I don't give a shit.

"Logan, you riding with me or EJ?" Marc asks.

"I'm just going to drive myself, I think."

"You sure? I can take you to the house and drop you at your dorm later," Eli chimes in.

"That's okay. There's no point in either of you having to drive back to campus tonight. I can drive myself." I'm assuming the boys are staying at their parents' place tonight, and after last night when Eli bailed on them to stay with me instead, I want to ensure that he doesn't have a reason to end up in my dorm again tonight.

"Well, let's go. I'm starving." Jack begins to walk up the tunnel to head towards the car. "And Logan, I hope you're hungry," he adds. "Mary makes the best pot roast of all time. Ain't that right, baby?"

It makes me smile to hear the name that Eli and I use for each other come from his dad's lips in reference to his stepmom.

"Yes, baby, that's right!" Mary exclaims as she tucks herself under her husband's arm, walking out of the player's tunnel together.

Chapter 56

Eli

That was the best I've felt during a game in a long time. My head was in it, I was moving well, and I felt like I could really read the ice today. The great night of sleep I had last night didn't hurt, and I knew there was a pretty little red-haired thing watching me today. That alone was motivation enough. I kept looking to Marc's seats, assuming she would've sat there, but she never did. Somehow though, I still knew she was in the arena. The fact that I felt that calm during a game, it's like I could sense that Logan was close to me.

I don't think I could've been happier than when I finally saw her waiting for me outside of the locker room. I was hoping she would've been the first face my eyes landed on, but it was such a Logan thing to do for her to stand away from the crowd as if she wasn't the person I most wanted to see. She looked fucking gorgeous, as she always does, but today especially.

I felt a little guilty for the dirty looks she got from some of the girls in that tunnel after I kissed her, but it was about time everyone knew she was mine. However, my fumbling ass sounded like an idiot when I tried to introduce her to my parents. I wanted to tell them that she was my girlfriend, but Logan and I haven't talked about that yet, so I didn't know what to say. I didn't think that introducing her as just Logan would've said enough about what she means to me, but instead, I couldn't say anything.

I've spent most of my life avoiding having a girlfriend. The idea of someone else counting on me sounded dreadful. I've never wanted to be tied down to just one girl, but with Logan, I want nothing more.

The smile spreads on my lips from just seeing her little white Honda pull up in front of my parents' house.

"You didn't have to wait for me," she says, walking up the driveway.

"I wanted to." I grab her hand, intertwining my fingers with hers. "You good?"

"Yeah, why wouldn't I be?"

"I don't know." I shrug. "You just met my parents. I wasn't sure if you were feeling nervous or anything."

"I was, but I feel better now. Are you good?" She laughs at me and my apparent anxiety. It's not that I'm worried my parents won't like Logan. I mean, it's impossible not to. To be honest, they'll probably end up liking her more than me. On a more serious note, my concern isn't that Logan won't fit in. It's more so that this makes me think of her parents and that I won't ever get the chance to meet them. I don't want her to feel sad being around my family, knowing that I'll never get to do the same with hers.

"I'm good if you're good." I lean down and place a kiss on her forehead.

I open the front door for her before ushering her inside.

"Holy shit." I follow her eyes towards the large glass window facing the backyard. "I didn't know your parents' house was on a lake!" she exclaims, all the while keeping her gaze locked on the scenic view.

"You've never been here when it's still light outside, huh?"

"I guess not. Damn," Logan says as I pull her away from the foyer and towards the living room where my family is hanging out.

"Logan, the Warriors and OKC game just started," Marc informs her from his spot on the couch opposite of my dad, both of their eyes glued to the television screen.

Logan quickly releases my hand and plops herself down on the couch between my dad and brother, all three of them now intently watching the basketball game on TV.

I guess I don't have to worry about Logan being comfortable around my family.

I follow my nose towards the kitchen, where Mary is putting out boards filled with meats and cheeses on the counter. I snatch a slice of salami before taking a seat at the kitchen island.

"Nice game, EJ. You looked good out there," Mary proudly tells me as she garnishes the cheese boards.

"Thanks, I felt good."

"You looked calm. You looked like your old self, only better."

"Yeah, I've been feeling better lately. Less anxious."

"I'm happy to hear that. And Logan is adorable." She eyes me, silently telling me she knows the reason that I feel so at ease lately.

"Yeah, she's the best."

"When did that start?"

"We met the weekend before school started. But I just recently got my shit together," I tell Mary before shoveling a handful of sliced prosciutto in my mouth.

"Well, do me a favor, and don't fuck it up." She points the cheese knife at me in a playful manner. "I finally get to have another woman in the house."

"You had Lauren, whenever she decided to come around." Though we both didn't like Lauren for Marc, and honestly, I could count on one hand the times she was around my family in the three years they were together.

"Please. You know how I felt about her with Marc. This is different. I can already tell how much Logan means to you. And the fact that she and Marc are so close too, I just like the whole situation."

"Me too." Standing, I quickly kiss her on the cheek. I love Mary. Even though I refer to her as my stepmom or by her name, Mary knows that she's my mom. And she totally understands the fact that I keep the title of 'Mom' for my birth mother.

"I'm gonna go change," I tell her before taking the stairs two at a time to head to my room here.

When I come back down wearing my jeans and a tee, I find Logan, Marc, and my dad still sitting in their same spots on the couch, watching the game.

"Westbrook is a beast," Marc says to no one in particular.

"Westbrook is a crybaby," Logan chimes in as Oklahoma City's point guard whines about not drawing a foul on his layup.

"She's not wrong," my dad laughs from the corner of the couch.

Walking around the back of the sofa, I bend down behind Logan, wrapping my arms around the front of her shoulders and leaning my chin on the back of the couch.

She holds my forearm with one hand and uses her other to gesture towards the TV. "Now, Steph...Steph is a beast," she says as number thirty hits a deep three-pointer.

"That's right, girl." My dad holds his fist out for Logan.

As she bumps her fist against his, I can't help but shake my head and smile, watching three of my favorite people bond in front of my eyes.

When the halftime commercials start playing, Logan taps against my forearm for me to release her from my grip. "I'm gonna go see if Mary needs help with dinner." She gets up from the couch and makes her way to the kitchen.

Walking around the sofa, I sit down in Logan's vacated spot between my dad and brother.

"So..." my dad begins. "You're in love with your brother's best friend."

"Jesus, Dad. Want to say that a little louder?" I sarcastically ask as both Marc and our dad laugh at my discomfort.

"And no. I'm not in love with her. It's only been a few weeks."

"Bull-fucking-shit," Marc chimes in, obviously not believing me.

"Son, you look at her the same way I look at Mary. That's love, kid."

Is it? I've never been in love before, so I don't know what it's supposed to look or feel like. But whatever I feel for Logan, I know I've never experienced it before. I think about her constantly, I always want to be around her, and I want to be the best version of me that I can be for her.

Fuck. Maybe my dad is right.

"She's not even officially my girlfriend, yet," I add.

"Well, what the hell are you waiting for? Honestly, I think I like her more than the two of you," he jokes, referring to Marc and me.

"That's not even a question. I definitely like Logan more than you guys," Marc adds, bantering back with our dad.

"Aren't you going to tell me what a terrible idea it is? Or that she's going to be a distraction for me or some shit like that?"

"EJ, I only ever said that about those random girls that always hung all over you because they didn't mean anything to you. This is the first time I've seen you care about someone outside of the three of us. To be honest, I was worried that you never would. But, you're different with her, I can tell."

He's right. This is the first time he's ever seen me care for someone because it's the first time I ever have. I've never even thought twice about another girl before, but with Logan, she hasn't left my thoughts since the first night I met her.

"You don't think it's a bad idea to have a girlfriend while I'm trying to chase this dream of making it in the NHL?" I mean, I was planning to ask her to be my girlfriend regardless, but still, I would like to hear my dad's take on it. I'm always down for listening to his advice. I care about his opinion more than anyone else's.

"Son, I need you to listen to me," He sits up straighter and turns towards me, obviously feeling very serious about what he wants to say. "There is no dream worth achieving if you don't have the people who matter the most standing next to you when it happens."

Well, that just hit me like a ton of bricks.

When I think about it, if I got called up to the league tomorrow, Logan might be the first phone call I make.

"So, don't be an idiot," my dad adds with a smile.

"Boys, dinner is ready!" Mary calls from the kitchen.

I take my usual seat at the dining room table across from my dad and next to Marc. The only difference is that tonight I have Logan sitting between my brother and me.

"This looks so good, Mary," Logan tells my stepmom. "I haven't had a home-cooked meal in weeks."

I pass her the salad and mashed potatoes before taking my portion, and it makes me smile to see that she's not shy with the amount of food she adds to her plate.

"Do you cook much, Logan?" Mary asks.

"I used to. Back home, when I had a kitchen to cook in." She laughs. "It's a little different now that I'm in a dorm."

"I think I remember Marc saying that you are from northern California?" my dad asks my girl.

"That's right."

"Your parents must be dying with you being so far away," Mary says as my heart begins to race.

"Mom!" Marc objects.

"Mary!" I protest at the same time.

I cannot believe she just said that. I glance over at Marc to see that he's wearing the same mortified expression as I no doubt am right now.

Logan's face is blank as I reach my hand to her thigh and rest it there, holding her. I look down at my plate while shaking my head, wishing we could just erase the last ten seconds.

"What?" Mary asks, confused.

"It's okay," Logan tells me as she squeezes my hand that's resting on her leg. "Actually, my parents aren't around anymore.

They've both passed away." My mouth drops in shock that she's being so open with my parents.

Mary closes her eyes and rests her head in her hands, trying to cover her regretful expression.

My dad looks from Logan to me and back again. His expression softens as he looks at my girl.

"I am so sorry, Logan. I cannot believe I just said that," Mary says, full of remorse.

Logan lets out a little laugh, instantly washing the room with relief. "Don't even worry about it."

My dad is looking at Logan with the same impressed and proud expression I have on my face.

"This pot roast is so good," Logan adds before taking another bite.

I squeeze her leg again, letting her know how proud of her I am, as Marc nudges her with his shoulder, silently saying the same thing.

The rest of dinner is filled with much more light-hearted topics—mostly grad school talk and questions about my upcoming game schedule.

"You guys have a lot of travel coming up," my dad mentions as Logan keeps her eyes locked on her plate. I hadn't told her yet that most of this month would be spent on the road, starting this week. "You're leaving on Monday again?" he asks.

"Yeah, which means we'll be playing at home most of November," I clarify, hoping to reassure Logan.

When Mary stands to start clearing the table, Logan stands with her, taking my empty plate along with her own.

"I got it." I take the plates from her hands, placing a kiss on her temple before she retakes her seat next to Marc, with my dad still sitting across at the table.

"So, Logan..." he begins, my ears perking up. I'm across the kitchen, putting the dishes into the sink, but I can still hear every word he says. "What are your plans for Thanksgiving?"

"Oh, that's a great idea, Jack!" Mary exclaims as she walks back behind my dad's chair, putting her hands on his shoulders.

"Um...I don't know. I haven't really thought about it," Logan tells my parents.

"If you're free, we would love for you to come to Indiana with the boys. We do a big Thanksgiving celebration, and all of the family comes to town," my dad says. "Plus, it's Marc's birthday."

Logan looks to me, standing in the kitchen, then back to Marc, who is sitting beside her.

"I was going to invite you," Marc tells her. "I just kind of figured you would be coming along."

She looks back to me as I quickly nod my head in approval. I would love to have Logan back in my hometown, around all my cousins. Though I already know, I'm going to have to fight some of them off. I only have male cousins, and they're going to go crazy having a cute girl around for the weekend.

"That sounds great. I would love that," she says to my parents with a huge smile across her face.

Fuck, I love that smile. And my parents love her, which is not surprising in the least. The fact that my dad just invited her to our biggest family get-together of the year says a lot. Marc's ex was never invited to these kinds of things.

"I'm going to make a drink and go watch the fourth quarter. Anyone want anything?" Marc stands from the table.

"Yeah, I'll do a whiskey neat," my dad requests as he also gets up and heads towards the living room.

"EJ?"

"Fuck it. Yeah, I'll have just one." I grab Logan's hand, bringing her to the living room with me.

"I'll take a glass of wine. Thank you, sweetheart," Mary chimes in as Marc makes his way to the bar cart.

"Logan, you want a glass?" he asks as I take a seat on the couch and pull Logan as close to me as possible before swinging my arm around her shoulders.

"Sure, that sounds good, actually. Just a small pour, though, please."

"Do you like red or white?" Mary asks her.

"Red would be great if you have it."

"That's my girl. Marc, open up that Pinot, would you?" Mary says. If anyone is going to be allowed to call Logan 'their girl' besides me, it's these three people right here.

Mary sits on my dad's lap as Marc hands us all our drinks. My stepmom clinks her glass with Logan's and I laugh to myself at how much my family likes her already.

The game has been over for at least an hour, and the five of us have been sitting around, talking, as my parents get to know Logan a little better. It's obvious that Mary is swooning over her, and my dad is clearly impressed. My parents and Marc are on their second drink when Logan uses my leg to push off of as she stands up from the couch.

"Well, I should get going. It's getting late."

"Are you sure? You can just crash here," Marc offers.

"I can't. I have an early morning tomorrow," she says, but I know she's full of shit. I'm pretty sure she feels guilty that my parents haven't been alone with my brother and me yet, but she doesn't realize that they would rather her be here with all of us. They're happy to have her a part of our family. In fact, I think they're stoked.

"It was so great to meet you." Mary stands to hug Logan. She squeezes my girl so tightly that I'm not sure Logan can breathe. "I'm looking forward to our next visit. I need to take you to the

Mall of America to do a little shopping next time. And I can't wait for you to come to Indiana for Thanksgiving, of course."

"Me too," Logan tells her with a genuine smile.

"Keep my boys in check, will you?" my dad playfully instructs as he wraps his arms around her.

"Always," she assures him, which makes me smile.

"I'll see you in class on Monday." Marc walks with us to the front door. "Love you," he adds as he pulls her in for a quick hug.

I've heard him say those words to her plenty of times before, but today after that talk with my dad and seeing Logan around my family, I feel a little different when he says it. Not that I'm jealous or upset by it. In fact, I'm happy that my brother and Logan are so close. It's just that I want to be able to say it too, with a different meaning, of course. But it's too soon, and that'll freak her out.

"Love you too," she tells him.

Wrapping my fingers around hers, I walk her down the drive to her car. I turn and lift her up, placing her on her trunk as I stand between her legs.

"You're the fucking best." I brush a stray hair behind her ear.

"They're great."

Leaning down, I gently kiss her tattooed collarbone, realizing that I'm an idiot. I've loved this girl ever since she told me about her past, the same night she told me about this tattoo. I remember when she told me that the 'I love you' script was from the only two people she had ever truly loved and wanting to be the third. Every time I placed my lips on it, I was silently telling her that I was already there.

"You sure you can't stay?" I ask, leaning in and lingering my lips just above hers, trying my very best to tempt her into spending the night with me.

"I can't, baby. I have a workout with Ali in the morning."

I playfully roll my eyes at her fib because I know that's not the real reason she doesn't want to stay. I know it's because she's trying to be respectful by giving my parents time alone with my brother and me. But she's a cute little liar, so I'll let her get away with it this time.

"I'm going to miss you. Can I come over tomorrow night when my parents fly out?"

"That sounds perfect." She wraps her arms around my neck, wanting my lips on hers.

She kisses me soft and slow. Bringing my hand up and cupping her face, I take over and set the pace. She tastes fucking fantastic as my lips glide across hers. Placing my other hand on her thigh, I slide it up, gripping her hip and pulling her closer to me. I lean forward, quickening the pace of our kiss as my tongue is granted access into her perfect mouth. It moves with hers as our breathing quickens, my body pressed right up between her legs.

After a few minutes of heavily making out like a couple of teenagers, I begrudgingly pull my lips away from hers but keep our foreheads connected, ragged breaths swirling between our mouths.

"Okay, I'm about to walk back inside with a hard-on if we keep this up," I whisper, causing her to laugh.

Logan cups the sides of my face after brushing my shaggy hair away from my eyes. "I'll see you tomorrow." She graces me with one more kiss before hopping off the trunk of her car.

"Bye, baby." I regretfully open her door for her to get in.

"Bye." She reaches up on her tiptoes to give me one last swift kiss. Closing the driver's side door, she offers me a small wave before driving off, back to her dorm.

I quickly adjust myself before walking back inside my parent's house.

"Did you do it?" Mary asks.

"Do what?" I take my seat back on the couch.

"Did you ask her to be your girlfriend?" She playfully swats my arm for making her spell it out.

"Chill. No, not yet. I don't even know if she would want that," I say, knowing full well that I'm full of shit.

"Don't be an idiot," Marc chimes in. "Of course, she does. She might not admit it, but I think it would make her feel better to have the security."

I hadn't really thought of it that way before, but it makes sense. Logan has had people continually leave her life. Obviously, I want her to be my girlfriend— I already think of her that way. Plus, I want everyone to know that she's mine and I'm hers. But, most importantly, I want Logan to know that I'm not going anywhere.

"Well, if you don't do it soon, I'm trading both of you in for her. I always wanted a daughter, anyway," Mary adds.

"How the hell am I getting dragged into this? EJ's the one needing to man up," Marc protests.

"I don't know," Mary responds. "I just added you in for dramatic effect." My dad kisses her temple as we laugh at her honesty.

"Alright. Well, then help me come up with a plan for how I'm going to ask her."

I don't miss the proud, beaming smile that my dad shoots me from the other side of the couch as Marc pats me on the back in approval.

Chapter 57

Eli

As soon as my parents left for the airport, I jumped in my truck to head to Logan's dorm. I could see Marc laughing at me from the front porch as I drove off, pulling out right behind my parents. He thinks I'm obsessed with Logan, and I think he might be right.

Marc and I stayed up pretty late last night, hanging out and playing video games. I hadn't seen or talked to him much since Logan and I got together, and I missed my brother this week. When I filled him in on how I was feeling about her, he didn't seem all that surprised. Marc knows me better than anyone. However, he was a bit surprised that Logan had told me everything about her parents and her ex, but I can tell he's happy that she feels secure enough to let me in.

The fact that my brother and my girl are best friends just makes my life that much easier. I'm looking forward to the times spent together with my two favorite people, but right now, I'm looking forward to a night alone with Logan. There's something I need to do, and I've been thinking about it all day.

"Hi, baby," I say as soon as I open Logan's door. Before she can even respond, I wrap my arms around her and lift her up in my embrace. She wraps her long legs around my waist and swings her arms around my neck as I walk into the room with her attached to me like a little koala.

"Hi." She plants a single kiss on my jaw, igniting my whole body.

I set her back down on her feet and quickly place my lips against her collarbone.

"You look good." I allow my eyes to wander her body.

"Eli, I'm in my pajamas," she laughs, unconvinced.

"Well, you always look good," I remind her. "But I'm going to need you to change. I'm taking you somewhere."

"What? It's after ten already."

"Yeah, and your first class got canceled tomorrow. Marc already told me. So, I know you don't have to be on campus until noon."

She eyes me for a moment. "You're such a stalker that you know my schedule."

"You love it," I remind her, brushing her off. Because I know that she loves it— she loves my attention to her details.

She tries to hold her smile back, but her dimples are far too noticeable. "Where are you taking me?"

"You'll know when we get there." A sly smirk slides across my lips.

"You love keeping things from me, don't you?"

"Only because you get all cute and flustered when you don't know what's going on."

She playfully rolls her eyes at me. "What should I wear?"

"Just put on some workout clothes."

"Eli, I am not working out at ten o'clock at night." She crosses her arms in front of her chest, being her naturally stubborn self.

"We aren't. I promise. Just change, and I'll meet you outside." I kiss her forehead and leave her alone in her room. Closing the door behind me, I wait patiently in the hallway for her.

When Logan comes out of her room, fully suited up for winter in her wool coat, scarf, and beanie, I can't help but laugh. She's fucking adorable, and I find it hilarious that my California girl can't handle the cold.

"I don't want to hear it," she says. "When you don't tell me where we are going, I have to prepare for anything."

"How cold do you think it is outside? It's only October, baby." I laugh at her annoyance, leaning down to kiss her scowling lips as I continue to chuckle against her.

When we leave the dorms, and Logan realizes that she overestimated the chill, she peels off the scarf and unbuttons her coat. I try to hold back my knowing smile, but I can't.

"I hate you," she laughs as I intertwine my fingers with hers. I bring her hand to my lips and pepper it with kisses as I try to contain my amusement.

We start walking towards the center of campus, and Logan surprisingly doesn't ask too many questions about where I'm taking her.

"Did you have a good time yesterday?"

"I had a great time," she tells me. "I loved getting to see you play. You're so good, and you have so many fans."

"Yeah, but I only care about one fan." Logan smiles to herself, resting her head against my shoulder as we continue to walk hand in hand.

"And what about last night? With my family."

"They're great. I had so much fun with them. It was nice to have a family dinner again."

"They loved you. I mean, I had no doubt. I knew Mary was going to be in love with you, but my dad," I give her an impressed glance, "he can be a little harder to crack, and I think he likes you more than he likes Marc or me."

"I doubt that." She laughs.

"I don't know. He has a major soft spot for you already. The fact that he invited you to Thanksgiving; he never asked Marc's ex to come to a family function."

"Is it okay that I said yes? If it's too much too soon, I can maybe go home with Ali or something that weekend?" She looks to me with concern.

I stop us in our tracks as I turn to face her. "Are you kidding me? I can't wait to take you home with me."

Her worried expression softens at my words. "Me too. And I'm excited to see Indiana. I can add another state to my list," she adds as we continue to walk deeper into campus.

"Don't get your hopes up. Indiana is not all that exciting," I warn.

"You're just saying that because you're from there. I'm looking forward to it regardless."

Indiana might not be the most fun state in all of America, but it is beautiful in the fall, and it's home. Thanksgiving weekend is one of my favorite times of the year, and I cannot wait to bring Logan back to the Hoosier state with me and show her off.

"So, you and your dad are really close. I could tell last night."

"Yeah, we are. My whole family is, but I have a special relationship with my dad. I trust his opinion more than anyone else's." Logan's expression is soft, and I can't help but stare into her pretty green eyes.

"Oh, I meant to send these to you last night." I break my gaze from her sweet smile. "Mary took these after the game."

Pulling out my phone, I bring up the photos app before handing it over to Logan. Her smile grows as she admires the picture of herself, Marc, Ali, and me that Mary snapped after my game in the players' tunnel. Her eyes dance around the photo as she takes it in, glancing back and forth between the two boys who love her more than anything and the feisty little New Yorker who always has her back.

I continue to lead us to our destination as she keeps her eyes on the picture. Taking a finger, I swipe to the previous one that my stepmom had sent me. It's my new favorite photo, and I already set it as my lock screen. Mary must have snapped it when I took off towards Logan after finding her hiding away from the crowd outside of the locker room. The picture is the moment that I lifted her up in a hug, with my head nuzzled into her neck. One of her arms is wrapped around my shoulders, and the other is burrowed in my hair. Her eyes are closed, and her cheek is pressed tightly against mine.

Logan's eyes soften when she looks at the photo of the two of us. She's biting down on her bottom lip, tying to hold her smile back, but her dimples are popping out as she stares.

"I love this," she says, looking up to me with the sweetest and softest expression. "Can I send this to myself?"

"Of course." I nudge her shoulder as we continue to walk. I'm glad these pictures have been a distraction. Logan has yet to notice where I'm taking her.

Logan types her name in my phone, and before I can remember and take it from her, the amusement begins to sweep across her face. Her eyes are bright when she sees the little red heart emoji I have next to her name. I had put it there the day that Marc gave me her number. She was so pissed off at me that day, and we had only ever kissed once at that point, but I already knew my heart was with her that I couldn't help but add it next to her contact information.

I guess I should be embarrassed right now, but fuck it. Logan knows how into her I am.

She doesn't say anything about it, but she also can't hold back the satisfied smile she has on her face as she sends the pictures to herself.

"Alright, we're here." I stop us in front of the main entrance to the gymnasium.

"What are you talking about?" she asks, looking towards the door. "We can't go in there."

"Sure we can. I have a key."

"Eli, what are you doing?" she whispers as if someone could hear her. I put the key into the bolt, unlocking the large glass doors leading into the lobby of the gym. "We can get in trouble for this."

I laugh at her sweet innocence. "Baby, it's fine. Trust me. We aren't going to get in trouble." I lead her inside and lock the door behind me.

Interlocking my fingers with hers, I guide her through the dark lobby and turn into a pitch-black hallway, heading towards the court.

"What's going on?" Logan asks as I lead her further into the arena. We can't see shit, but I know where I am.

Suddenly the lights begin to come on, one by one, as the furthest seats in the arena come into view first. They quickly light up the next section, then the next, until the court itself is fully illuminated.

I watch as Logan takes in her surroundings. Her eyes widen and her mouth parts as she looks around and up to the empty stands. This gymnasium is enormous. It almost seats as many as the hockey rink. She turns in a circle as she continues to acclimate herself with where we are, but she's clearly confused by what is happening right now.

We are standing directly in the middle of the university's basketball court. The center circle is painted a deep maroon with a large yellow 'M' logo inside. One of the baselines says 'University of Minnesota,' and the other says, 'Golden Gophers.'

"Thanks, Tony!" I yell out, to nowhere in particular. I know Tony, the maintenance guy, is here somewhere up in the rafters, but I'm not sure where.

"No problem, Maddison! Just lock up when you're done!" he shouts back.

"Eli, what is going on?" Logan asks, confused, as her eyes land on the rack filled with brand new basketballs.

"Well..." I walk up to her and drape my arms over her shoulders. "You said that playing basketball made you think of your dad." I tuck a strand of hair behind her ear. "You got to meet my dad yesterday, so I was hoping you could introduce me to yours."

I look down at her as her green eyes soften, losing their confusion. She lets out a ragged sigh, leaning her forehead on my chest, hiding her face. When she looks back up to me, her eyes are glossed over, about to spill tears, and I'm praying that they're good tears. I had some major fears that bringing her here would make her upset. She would've been playing on a court just like this at the University of Oregon if she hadn't given up her scholarship to stay home and take care of her mom.

I wipe her cheek with my thumb as I search her face, trying to read her expression.

"I don't deserve you," she whimpers as she looks up to me. Her green eyes are even more vibrant from the red that surrounds them.

"Oh baby," I chuckle as I pull her into my body, nuzzling my face into the crook of her neck. "Don't cry. What happened to my tough girl?" I tease, trying to lighten the mood.

"You're turning her into a softie," she laughs into my chest as relief washes over me. She's okay. This is going to be good.

Lifting her face from my body, I kiss her temple, then her cheek, then her collarbone, over her tattoo. I don't know if Logan has figured out that I've been telling her I love her every time I kiss the black ink, but if she does know, she's not giving it away.

We walk over to the player's bench to strip off our outer layers. I try to keep my gaze to myself, but Logan is only wearing a sports bra with her little spandex pants, and she knows how I feel about her tits, so it is what it is. I can't keep my eyes off her, and she can't expect me to.

Grabbing her hand, I lead her to one end of the court, leaving her at the three-point line. I walk over to the rack of basketballs and bounce pass one over to her as she catches it with ease.

"Oh, man," she awkwardly laughs. "I'm so rusty."

She dribbles a few times, crosses it over between her legs, then pulls back and takes a shot from the three-point line. She sinks it, nothing but net.

Rusty, my ass.

I rebound the ball with a proud grin on my face as I pass it back to her.

"So, tell me about him."

"What do you want to know?" she asks as she dribbles around the arch.

"What was his name?"

"His name was John Leo." She shoots with perfect form and makes another three-pointer.

I rebound and pass the ball to her again. The smile on my lips grows, watching her in her element.

"What was he like?"

She holds the ball against her hip as she thinks about her dad.

"He was so cool. He was honestly the best dad I could've asked for. People thought he was intimidating, but he was really soft when it came to my mom and me. He was supportive of me, but he also pushed me to work hard."

She does work hard. I see how much effort she puts into school, and I would imagine that translated to other aspects of her life, basketball included.

"My dad and I were really close. We shared a love for sports. He wanted a son so badly, but he got me instead," she laughs to herself. "Hence the name, Logan."

"I'm sure he was stoked to have a daughter, regardless."

"He was. But he raised me as he would have a son. Put me in every sport imaginable. He made sure I could handle myself. My mom was so upset." She laughs at the memory. "She thought I was going to be a girly girl, but that was far from reality." She lines up and shoots the ball, sinking another three as I stand directly under the net, continuing to catch her made shots.

"He ended up loving being a girl dad," she adds as she catches my pass.

I love this conversation. I can see exactly what Logan means when she says her dad raised her as a son. She's such a tomboy but still has this soft and feminine side to her that I'm guessing she inherited from her mom.

"What did he do for work?"

"He was in the wine business, but his true passion was coaching."

"Did he also play basketball?"

"No, actually." She laughs again while casually dribbling the ball between her legs as if it were as easy as walking. "He played football, but he picked up and learned the game when he realized that I was so into it at a young age."

Watching her move with the ball in her hands this way is mesmerizing. She's obviously extremely talented, and the fact that she hasn't played in years and still has it, it's ingrained in her. She clearly downplayed her ability. She shoots again and hits another shot. The ball doesn't even touch the rim.

I laugh to myself as I recall the night I first met her. She had caused three spilled drinks that night, and I thought she was clumsy. This girl is far from clumsy. In fact, she's ridiculously coordinated.

"One more question." I hold the ball in my hands, standing under the net. "Would he have liked me?"

Her expression softens as she cocks her head to look at me.

"He would've loved you, baby."

A proud grin spread across my lips as I walk up to her, holding the basketball. I stand directly in front of her, between her and the hoop, as I place the ball in her hands.

"How about a little one on one?" I ask my pretty girl.

"Really? Are you sure?"

"Hell yeah, I'm sure. And I'm planning to kick your ass."

She laughs. "That's cute, baby. Game to ten, play by ones?"

Hearing her talk shit while she effortlessly crosses the ball over behind her back is seriously one of the hottest things I've ever seen. I love that she's an athlete, and a damn good one at that. I've only ever played basketball for fun, but I'm a division one athlete. I can handle a little one on one with my girl.

"Sounds good. Ladies first." I nod towards the ball in her hands, lowering myself into a defensive position. She leans down with the ball at her hip, a huge smile dancing across her lips. She seems so light and happy here with a basketball in her hands. She looks like she's home.

Logan takes a few dribbles to her right, but I stay with her until she crosses the ball over quickly and smoothly, catching me off balance. She steps back and takes a jump shot from around the free-throw line. Unsurprisingly, she sinks it.

"One-Oh," she says in an arrogant tone as she turns and heads back to the top of the key, expecting me to chase down her rebound, which of course, I do. She's very rarely conceited. In fact, most of the time, she lacks well-deserved confidence. But right now, she's being cocky with her talent, and I fucking love seeing her this way.

I walk right up to her and place the ball in her hands. I don't give her any space as I get into my defensive stance. She takes this as a prime opportunity to quickly blow past me, easily beating me to the hoop for a lay-up. Not just any lay-up, no that would be too easy. She does a reverse lay-up, just because she beat me so badly and has enough space to do so, just because she can.

I can't help but laugh as I watch her kick my ass.

"Two-Oh, baby." She walks past me and slaps my ass as she continues to the top of the key.

I fucking love this.

I'm athletic, and I don't mean I'm athletic enough that I can get by. I mean, I'm a potential professional athlete level of athletic, and right now, Logan is giving me a run for my money on who is more so.

We continue playing, and Logan doesn't let up. She's fucking amazing. She's up 9-4, and she's about to win it right here, and trust me, it's not because I'm letting her. No, I'm fully sweating and short of breath, trying to keep up with her.

I give her the ball for the last play of the game. I know I can't beat her, so I decide just to foul her instead. At least if I'm going to lose, I'll get to touch her this way.

She takes a dribble and a step forward, trying to pass me, but I put my body in her way and wrap my arms around her, holding her back to my chest.

"Foul!" she yells between laughing breaths.

"Cheater!" she adds when I don't release her from my grip, sucking in air as she giggles in my embrace.

Holding her up in my arms, I swing her around in a circle while she holds the ball. When I put her down, we're both out of breath, partly from the game we just played and partly from the laughing fit we're in the middle of.

I bend over, still chuckling as I try to catch my breath, sucking in a deep inhale with a smile across my lips. When I stand up, Logan drops the ball to the ground and swings her arms around my neck.

"Thank you," she sweetly says into my chest.

Fuck. I love this girl.

Wrapping my arms around her lower back, I place my chin on the top of her head as she rests her cheek on my chest. I quickly bend down to kiss her collarbone before asking the question I've needed to ask for a while now.

"I know I couldn't meet him, but he did a really good job raising you." Logan melts into my body, tightening her grip. "And I know I'm not able to ask his permission to date his daughter." I pull her face away from my chest so that I can look into her green eyes. "But I'm hoping this was enough that I can ask if you'd be my girlfriend?"

She drops her forehead into my chest with her arms still draped around my neck. Logan doesn't say anything. She just leans into me.

I'm still waiting for her answer, and I would be lying if I said I wasn't feeling anxious by her lack of a response. I didn't think I would ever ask someone to be my girlfriend, but I figured I'd get an automatic 'yes' if I did.

Finally, she looks up to me with glossy eyes. "How did I get so lucky with you?"

"So is that a yes?" I ask again, needing the confirmation because I'm a needy little fucker when it comes to her.

"Yeah, baby. That's a hell yes."

Chapter 58

Eli

"Why don't we stay at your house tonight?" Logan asks when she spots my truck parked right outside her dorm.

"Really? You want to?"

"Yeah. We always sleep here when we spend the night together. Let's change it up."

I would love for her to stay at my house, in my bed, but I didn't think she would want that again. Also, the last time she was at my house was the night we kissed for the first time, and I said those hurtful things to her. Plus it's a party house, so I just assumed she'd prefer not to sleep there, even though it has been my home for the past four years.

"We don't have to, though, if you don't want to," she adds when I don't respond.

"Of course, I want you to stay over." I bend down and brush my lips against hers.

"Good," she says with a satisfied smile. "I'm just gonna go throw some things in a bag real quick."

"You're bringing a bag to my house? That sounds official. It's almost as if you're my girlfriend or something."

"Or something," she repeats with bright eyes. "I'll be down in a minute. Can I shower when we get to your place?"

My dick twitches at her question. I can just picture her flawless naked body standing under the stream in my shower as the hot water glides over her golden skin. What I would give to be in there with her, cleaning off her sweaty body, touching every inch of her as the soap lathers between us.

"Baby?" she says, yanking me from my heavenly thoughts.

"Um...sorry. Yeah, you can shower at my house."

When we pull up to the hockey house, I open the passenger door for her and swing her bag over my shoulder. I lace my fingers between hers as we walk up the sidewalk. Of course, Logan's bag is tiny because she's low maintenance and doesn't want to intrude on my space. I know that's what she's thinking, but I wouldn't mind if she brought a few more things over and left them here. That way, I'd always have a reminder that she'd be back for them—and for me.

I take a deep breath before opening the front door. I'm not nervous about Logan being here. I want her here, but there are always a lot of people in and out of this place. I'm just glad there's no party here tonight. I don't want her to feel overwhelmed.

Voices are getting louder as we near the living room.

"Hey boys," I say as Logan and I stand in the entryway of the living room. Six of my teammates are sitting around playing video games and yelling at each other when we walk in. One of them pauses their game as they all turn to face us, and the room quiets. Most of them have wide eyes with shocked expressions when they look down at my hand and Logan's hand intertwined together.

"Boys, this is Logan." I nod towards my girl.

"Logan, this is Mikey, Cruz, Goody, Benny, our goalie, and you know Cam and Patrick." I point to each of my teammates occupying the couches in front of the large screen TV. I'm aware that my voice deepened when I said Patrick's name, but I can't help it. I can't fucking stand the guy.

"Hey Logan, how are you?" Cam asks with a genuine smile on his face. He's a good guy, and I know he will make Logan feel comfortable even though she's the only girl here right now.

"Hey Cali," Patrick says with a devilish glint in his eye, as he keeps his stare on Logan.

I could fucking kill him.

"I'm good, Cam, good to see you," she says. "Nice to meet you guys," she adds to the rest of my teammates, ignoring Patrick's greeting, which I fucking love.

I don't miss the looks the boys share between each other or the wide eyes and gaping mouths they have as they stare at Logan.

Trust me, I'm aware she's hot, but I will literally kick all of their asses if they don't get it together.

Half of them seem mesmerized by my pretty girl, and the other half appear shocked that I brought a woman home to stay with me. Though, I don't know why they're so surprised that she's here right now. They all saw her outside of the locker room at our game on Saturday. I know they did because they all gave me shit in the group text today, using words like 'whipped' and 'pussy.' I don't care though, if they had a girl that made them feel like Logan does, they'd gladly be whipped for her too.

"Great to meet you, Logan," Benny, my sophomore goaltender, says in excitement as he stands up to greet my girl, dropping the controller from his hands. The rest of the boys just laugh at him and shake their heads at his obvious infatuation.

"Keep it in your pants, Benny," Mikey says to him as Logan joins in on the laughter.

"Sorry, Logan. Benny hasn't gotten laid all year. Don't mind him," Goody teases.

"Shut the fuck up, Goody!" Benny smacks him in the head with a couch pillow.

"Wanna go, kid?" Goody wears an excited smile as he jumps up from his seat and lunges towards Benny, tackling him to the couch. Most of the boys' attention is redirected as they all cheer on their favorite to win the spontaneous wrestling match going down in my living room right now.

"So, is this a thing now?" Patrick asks while pointing between Logan and me, taking a sip of his beer. Everyone besides Cam is too distracted to hear his question.

Logan stays quiet, allowing me to answer.

"Yeah, it is," I confidently tell my least favorite teammate. "Logan is my girlfriend." Honestly, I'm just hoping that him knowing she's mine will cause him to back the fuck off and stop eye-fucking her every chance he gets.

Instead, it causes him to spit his beer back into his cup. "You're fucking kidding me," he laughs in disbelief. "You're joking, right?"

"Shut the fuck up, Patty," Cam sternly warns.

"I just find it funny, that's all," Patrick says, shaking his head with an amused grin dancing across his lips. "Maddison convincing Cali that he can stick to one woman. I can't wait for all your road bunnies to find out you have a girlfriend back home." He turns to me with an evil grin.

I can feel my body stiffen and my blood beginning to boil as Logan's grip on my hand tightens.

"Watch your fucking mouth, Patrick," I warn as I take a bounding step towards the couch, but Logan gently pulls me back to her side.

"Let's go," she whispers with her face next to my bicep as she holds me back.

I shake my head at Patrick as I let Logan lead me towards the stairs.

"You're a fucking asshole, Patty," I hear Cam say in disgust as we walk away.

I close my bedroom door behind us before setting Logan's bag on my bed for her to unpack the few things she brought with her. My temperature is still rising from our encounter downstairs.

"Don't worry about him," Logan says in her gentle way. "I'm not listening to him, so you shouldn't either." She runs a soothing hand down the length of my arm.

Her touch calms me the way it always does as I try to push Patrick's words to the back of my mind and not let them ruin my only night this week with my girlfriend. She and I both know I have to leave for a two-game road trip tomorrow afternoon, and this is our only time together.

My eyes stayed glued on Logan as she pulls a shirt from her bag and walks over to my closet. She takes one of my empty hangers off the rod and slips it through her shirt before hanging it up. I can't help the satisfied smile on my face by seeing her so comfortable in my space.

She walks back to the bed, pulling out a few more things from her little bag to refold them, and I can't ignore the peace I feel by having her here with me.

I walk up behind her as she's folding a pair of jeans, wrapping my arms around her abdomen and placing my chin on her shoulder.

"I like having you here."

"I like being here." She leans her head back on me. I keep my grip on her middle as I bring my nose and lips to her neck. She still smells like vanilla, but it's mixed with sweat from our basketball game, and her natural scent smells like fucking heaven to me.

I sway with her in my arms. Her head is leaning back on me, and my face is in the crook of her neck as I bask in the moment. Her moving with me, us standing at the foot of my bed, her body molded perfectly to mine. I don't ever want this to end.

I kiss her shoulder, trailing my lips up her neck until I wrap them around her ear and tease it.

She moans into me as her body melts further into my touch. I use my fingertips to unbutton her jacket as we continue to sway together. I let my long fingers dance around her abdomen for a moment until they find the waistband of her tight leggings.

Before I can dip my fingers in, Logan stops me with her hand.

"I need to shower first."

"You're going to have to shower when I'm done with you, so you may as well just wait," I whisper into her nape.

I press my hardening package against her ass, trying to tempt her into letting me touch her.

"I'm gross right now," she whines.

"There's nothing gross about you." I gently suck at the skin of her neck.

She pulls my fingers out from her waistband as she turns around to face me.

"I'll be quick," she says, referencing the shower.

"Me too." I cup her ass cheeks and pull her into my hardening bulge, referencing something *other* than a shower.

She just laughs at me while shaking her head.

"Towels are in the cabinet next to the sink." I squeeze her ass one more time as I kiss her lips. "Make sure you lock the door. Too many pervs in this house."

"Tell me about it," she says as she playfully nods in my direction. She grabs her toiletries and heads to the bathroom across the hall, where we met for the first time.

I leave my door open so that I can keep an eye on the bathroom door. There are too many guys who live in this house, and Patrick being home is reason enough to keep my gaze glued to that door.

Slipping off my shirt and shorts, I throw them in the hamper, so I can jump in the shower when Logan is done. As I continue to glance towards the bathroom, I quickly tidy up my room. There's not much to clean because I usually keep my place somewhat organized, but I want it to be perfect for her. I throw the few things sitting on my nightstand into the drawer below it. It's funny because you'd assume I would maybe hide the condoms in my top drawer, but there aren't any in there. That's because I've never had sex in this room. I've never even had a girl in this room besides the night Logan slept here when we first met, but I've definitely never hooked up with someone in my bed before.

My phone dings on my dresser, and I quickly glance towards the bathroom door to check on Logan before reading my incoming text.

L: *I forgot my clothes. Can you bring them to me?*

I'm picturing her naked body in my bathroom just feet away from me as I glance down to the folded pile of clothes she had made on my bed. I pick them up, piece by piece, as I examine what she's planning to sleep in. First is a pair of cozy looking pants, and the next is an oversized sweatshirt. But below those is a little pair of silky black panties. Fuck. Is she going to wear these tonight? I hold them up to check them out. They're teeny-tiny and practically see-through. I've felt Logan's ass in my hands and on my dick. There's no way it's going to fit in these.

I grab her panties but leave the rest of the bulky sleepwear on the bed as I look through my drawers. I pull out one of my hockey T-shirts that I know will be plenty big because then, she won't need to wear any pants.

I gently knock on the bathroom door. "Baby, it's me."

Logan cracks the door ajar, and my lips literally part open at the sight of her. She's wrapped in a towel with her hair dripping wet. I've seen her like this before when we were in her room, but the view will never get old to me.

My briefs begin to tighten just from looking at her while her eyes drag down my body, following every crevice of muscle, her pupils dilating when they land on my growing package.

When I'm looking at her, I can almost see perfectly down the towel wrapped around her body. Hooking my pointer finger around the top of it, I pull it a few inches away from her chest, giving myself a better visual.

"Hey!" she playfully scolds.

"What? You're the only one who can look?" My grin is all arrogance.

I hand her the clothes I brought her, and she looks at them with skepticism.

"No pants?"

"You don't need them," I tell her with a smirk.

She rolls her eyes at me, but I know that she loves my boldness.

"Thank you." She closes the door to change.

I lean on the wall across from the bathroom, waiting for her to emerge so that I can take my turn in the shower, and when she does open the door, I can't help but smile.

She looks so fucking cute, drowning in my shirt with her bare legs. Her hair is wrapped up in a towel sitting on top of her head. I've seen my stepmom do this with her hair after a shower before, but seeing my girl like this while wearing *my* shirt and coming out of *my* bathroom—it's my new favorite visual.

"You gonna shower?" Logan asks, eyeing my body up and down.

"Yeah, you gonna join?" I arrogantly question as I lean down and brush my lips against hers, knowing she won't but wishing that she would.

"Don't tempt me," she says, which is vastly different than the 'hell no' or the playful swat on the arm I was expecting. So, that might not be too far off in the future... noted.

When I come back to my room after the quickest shower of my life, with my towel wrapped low on my hips, I find Logan sitting on my bed with her bare legs and a book in her hands. Her wet hair is brushed out, lying across her shoulders, and she has those cute little reading glasses on that make her look like a sexy librarian.

I'm going to need to come home to this view more often.

After closing and locking my door behind me, I grab a pair of briefs from my top drawer. I drop my towel with my back to Logan, knowing that her eyes are no longer on her book. Just to be sure, I take a peek over my shoulder and can't keep the cocky grin from spreading on my lips when I catch her eyes on me. That is until she averts her gaze back to her book, her cheeks turning pink when she realizes I caught her staring.

Wearing only my briefs, I climb into bed. Honestly, I don't like wearing anything when I sleep, but I don't know how Logan would feel if I got into bed wearing only my birthday suit.

I take a seat next to my girl, sitting up on my side, with my back against the headboard. Looking over at her, she has a suppressed smile trying to fight its way through. I can tell because her dimples are far too noticeable.

"Why are you so smiley over there?"

"Nothing." She shakes her head, keeping her lips tight, fighting back her grin.

It's obviously something.

"I just like that I'm the first girl to sleep in your bed." She keeps her eyes on her book, but her lips lift in a sweet smile. "I'm glad I get to be your first for something."

She didn't mean to say that in a way that would hurt me, but still, my chest stings from her words. I wish she were my first in many ways, the way I am for her, because she deserves to have all of me. I mean, she does have all of me, but maybe she doesn't see that.

"Hey," I say in a more serious tone. "Come here."

Logan sets her book and glasses down on the bedside table before I guide her hips over my lap. She straddles her legs around me but doesn't sit down. She stays positioned on her knees. I know she's as aware as I am that she's only wearing those tiny panties, and I'm only wearing my briefs, but still, I can feel myself growing from just knowing that her barely covered pussy is hovering only inches above me.

"Yeah, you're the first and only girl I've ever had in my bed." I tuck her loose hair behind her ear. My hands trail down her shoulders before grazing the length of her arms.

"You're also the first and only girl I've ever *kissed* in my bed," I remind her as my fingers skim her thighs upward, finding their way to the hem of the shirt of mine that she's wearing before I press my lips to her warm mouth.

"And my first and only girlfriend," I add as I lift the bottom of her shirt and push her hips down to sit on me. When her body makes contact with mine, Logan and I let out matching gasps from the sensation. She leans her forehead against me, her lips lingering just above.

"All of this is a first for me." I roll Logan's hips against me. The thin fabric can't hide much as my cock hardens from her perfect movements. "I've never done any of this with someone I care for."

She cups my face and presses her lips to mine with fervor and passion, apparently satisfied with my words. She continues to rock against me, and I can feel her already present warmth through the thin fabric. Her lips explore me as I guide her hips, continuing their ideal tempo grinding against my dick. I can't help myself as I reach a hand into the space between us, diving into her tiny black underwear and finding my favorite spot as I glide and tease it with my fingers. And the noise Logan makes into my mouth as I do is enough to unravel me on the spot. She's fucking soaked already, and I want nothing more than to slide inside of her.

Continuing my movements, she writhes in my lap, ragged breaths swirling between us. If this is how she reacts to my fingers, I can't wait until the day I watch her unravel from my tongue and my dick. She will be screaming my name, not just moaning it between precious breaths.

Her hands tug at my hair, steadying herself. Logan's lips are on mine, but we're no longer kissing. The heavy breaths and gaping mouths make it too difficult to do so. Instead, I'm concentrated on making her feel good with my fingers, keeping my eyes glued to her bouncing tits hidden behind her shirt.

She must've caught my gaze because Logan confidently lifts the shirt up and over her head, revealing her perfectly formed body to me. My eyes widen as I take in her in while Logan leans back slightly, allowing me to do so. I palm one of her tits with my other hand, and she throws her head back in pleasure as I continue to tease her with my fingers. She lifts her hips, begging for more contact.

The sight of her alone is enough to make me come. Not to mention the sensation of her pussy riding on top of my dick, sliding over me as she grinds on my lap.

"Logan, you're everything..." I say, but before I can add the 'to me,' Logan rolls her hips in the perfect position, taking away my breath and my words.

"Fuck," is all I can manage to say when my breath returns.

I move my mouth to her tit because, quite honestly, if I don't focus on her pleasure, I'm going to come right now. I can't help it with her. I don't know what it is, but I feel like I'm being touched for the first time, and I can't control myself.

My tongue flicks, laps, and teases her taut nipple as Logan lets out a moan. The sound causes me to groan against her, and the vibration of our bodies is mind-blowing.

Suddenly, Logan's fingers reach the waistband of my boxers, and I pull my mouth away from her in shock. My stomach tightens, knowing that her hand is so close to my dick, and my breathing is coming out in short ragged spurts.

I keep my eyes on her face as she stares at my brief-covered cock.

"Can I?" she asks in a whisper before biting down on her lip, as she barely slips her fingertips into my waistband.

"Please," I beg of her, fully expecting my voice to crack. I feel nervous with her. This feels like it's about to be my first time having a woman stroke my dick.

She sits further back, almost on my knees, causing my fingers to leave her warmth as she runs her hands over the top of my boxers. Keeping my eyes locked on hers, she keeps her eyes on my hardening bulge. She swallows before putting a hand on either side of my hipbone, fingertips dancing around, building up the tension. She begins to tug, so I lift myself up off the bed as she pulls my briefs down. Her eyes widen, and her mouth drops open as I come into view. Her eyes darken over, almost blacken, as she takes me in.

I know I'm well-endowed. However, I don't know if she realizes this because I don't know if she has anything to compare it to. But judging by the look of shock on her face, I would assume she realizes just how blessed I am down there.

She continues to look down at my rock-hard guy, standing at attention and begging for her touch. Her plump lips part and I can't help but imagine them being wrapped around me one day. As eager as I am, I'm going to let her take her time and figure out what she wants to do. I cup her face, and as I'm about to lean in to kiss her, she slides her fingers down my shaft.

I throw my head back on the headboard as I hiss an inhale.

"Fuck," is all I can say on my exhale.

She grips me with the perfect amount of pressure as she glides her hand down my length. Keeping my eyes closed, I take in every movement she makes. As her fingers make their way up again, she uses her thumb to wipe the bead of moisture from the tip, causing me to jerk in her grasp.

"Oh my god, baby," I growl between clenched teeth, trying not to come on contact from finally having her skin on mine.

She scoots closer, hugging me with her thighs, as her tiny black panties and my guy meet. Just losing that one layer of fabric from my briefs is about to send me over the edge. She continues to grind against me as her hand keeps its movements, sliding up and down my shaft, while her pussy adds to the friction. She grabs my chin with her other hand and presses her mouth to mine. I try to focus on her lips, exploring them and tasting her, because if not, her body is going to make my explode.

Her confidence in bed with me is one of my new favorite things about her. I love watching her take control and feel sexy. However, I need to take some control back because I want to make her to feel as good as I do right now.

Sliding my hands around, I grip her ass, picking her up with me as I fall forward and lie her on her back. I'm hovering over her, butt ass naked, as her soft legs wrap around me. I'm so fucking tempted to rip these little panties off of her, but I know that once the barrier is gone, I'll be far too tempted to push myself into heaven. And I'm not going there until she tells me she's ready, no matter how many times a day I think about what it will feel like.

I lean back on my knees while I'm between her legs with my ass sitting against my heels. I can't believe my perfect girl is in my bed right now, almost entirely naked, with her legs generously opened for me. I let my fingers explore her frame as they run over her smooth skin. They form a trail across her collarbone, circling her breasts, and over her curvy hips as I memorize every rise and fall of her flawless body.

I'm the luckiest son of a bitch to love this woman and hopefully have her feel the same about me one day. I want her to feel just how much I love her because even if I can't say it, I can show her.

Slipping my hand into that silky black fabric, I find her again. At the same time, I surround her nipple with my mouth, continuing to tease her body with my fingers and my tongue. Lacing my other hand through hers, I hold her arm above her head against the mattress.

"*Baby*," she cries out between strained breaths as she arches up and into me.

"Does that feel good?" I look up at her through hooded eyes. Her head is thrown back against the bed, and her eyes are squeezed shut as she bites down on her lower lip.

"So good," she breathes as a satisfied smile creeps across my lips, grazing her tit.

She pushes her heels to the back of my thighs, silently begging me to come closer. As I do, my rock-hard dick glides against her silky black panties, her folds on either side of me.

"Fucking Christ, Logan," I growl into her neck as I repeat the motion again.

Above our heads, she keeps one hand intertwined with mine, pushed into the mattress, as she finds my cock with her other. I gently bite down on her shoulder as her fingertips tease me until finally, they grip around my dick. I dip my opposite hand back into her panties, needing to get her to the edge with me because, quite honestly, I'm already there.

My chest is pressed down on hers so tightly that I can feel every rapid rise and fall her lungs make. My cock has the perfect position—sliding over her barely-covered pussy while her hand strokes me. I continue to rub and circle Logan's clit with my fingers, remembering what she liked from the last time I did this.

The room is mixed with moans and whimpers as Logan's legs tightening around me. I can tell she's close, and I need to get her there so I can release.

"*Eli*," she cries out, arching into me, her eyes rolling back and her lips parting open. Watching her come is enough to make me join her, even if I wasn't already there. I love watching what only I can do to her. I love seeing her this way because of me.

"*Fuck*." I jerk in Logan's hand, reveling in my release as every muscle in my body contracts. I probably should've warned her that I was about to come all over her stomach, but from the speed and pressure her hand moved against me, I think she already knew.

After a few moments, I look down between us, at my seed covering Logan's abdomen, and not to sound like an egotistical maniac, but it does something to me. It reminds me that she's mine.

Logan's pussy is still pulsing on my fingertips as I stare at the beautiful girl beneath me.

"Told you that you were going to have to shower when I was done with you." My smirk is all arrogance.

Her cheeks begin to pink as she chuckles, shyly swatting my arm as if she didn't just take me to heaven with her hand. I lean down to my girl and kiss her lips, then her tattoo.

Chapter 59

Logan

E: *Call you tonight after my game.*

I've been sitting on this random bench in the middle of campus, texting with my boyfriend. It's been five days since Eli asked me to be his girlfriend, and four days since I've seen him. The team left Monday afternoon for a two-game road trip, and I've missed him ever since.

I'm trying to get used to him being gone, but it's still hard not being able to see him for days at a time. However, this week alone has allowed me to get ahead on my school work so that I can spend the weekend with Eli when he gets home tomorrow night.

I'm admiring the little red heart emoji next to my boyfriend's name as I read his texts when I'm pulled from my daydreams.

"Hey. You're Logan, right?" a female voice asks me.

Looking up, I find a girl that I recognize from Marc's pictures. I also met her once at a hockey house party, but I have no desire to pretend like I want to talk to her.

"Yeah, I am." I don't elaborate on the fact I know who she is.

"I'm Lauren. We met at a party a few weeks ago. I used to date Marcus."

She takes the liberty of sitting on the other side of the bench from me without my permission.

"So, you and Marcus have gotten really close," she declares.

I don't respond because I honestly have no idea why she's talking to me. I know what she did to my best friend. I know she cheated on him and broke up with him without explanation. What I don't know is why she is sitting across from me, pretending like we can be friends.

"I've heard around campus that you guys have become really good friends," she adds. "I was just wondering how he's doing?"

"He's great," I state without expanding on my thoughts. I'm not going to divulge any information to this girl, but I'm sure as shit going to make sure that Marc sounds good when I do respond.

"That's wonderful. That makes me so happy to hear," Lauren says. Her words are kind, but I can tell she's full of shit. She has ulterior motives, but I just don't know what they are yet.

"Do you know if he's seeing anyone?" she asks.

And there they are.

"That's not my place to say."

"Can you at least just tell me if he's dating that girl from New York? The one from the party."

"Ali?" I ask her, confused. "Look, Lauren, I'm sure you're nice and all." I don't even believe myself when I say it. "But I'm not going to tell you anything about Marc. If you're so curious, you should just ask him yourself." I end the conversation with that, but she doesn't leave my bench.

"But why does it matter if he is?" I ask, unable to keep my curiosity at bay. "You're the one who broke up with him."

She lets out a heavy sigh. "I know I did, and I've been second-guessing that decision lately. Marc won't respond to any of my texts, so I thought maybe he was seeing someone, but no one else on campus seems to have the answer. I figured you'd be my best shot at finding out."

She wants to get back together with him? Fuck that.

I stay silent, with my eyes fixed straight ahead, hoping she'll leave now that she's said her piece.

"I heard you've been hanging out with Maddison," she begins anew, this time in a knowing tone that I don't like.

I stay quiet. There's no way I'm letting this girl know anything about Eli and me. I already don't like her for what she did to Marc after being with him for three years, but she's also friends with Alyssa, and I don't need any information getting back to her.

"I would just be careful," she spitefully adds.

I snap my head in her direction, unable to keep my eyes focused off into the distance as I had before.

"Woman to woman, I was around Marc and his brother for years. Maddison gets around...a lot. He has girls in every city they play in."

I know about Eli's past, Patrick just reminded me of it only days ago, but still, I don't love hearing about it from someone who's not Eli.

"He's never stuck with one girl before, so I wouldn't get my hopes up that he's all of a sudden going to change his ways for you."

"I think you should go," I tell her.

She stands up, swinging her backpack over her shoulder. "Just giving you fair warning. Do with it what you will."

She's obviously pissed off that I wouldn't give her any information on Marc, so she's trying to hurt me by reminding me of Eli's past. I don't care if she spent the last three years around Eli. She doesn't know him like I do... right?

"See you around, Logan," she concludes as she walks away with a satisfied grin on her lips. She's worse than the typical mean girl. She's worse than Alyssa. At least with those girls, you know what you're getting, but with her, she's sneaky. She comes off sweet and innocent, but in reality, she's a snake.

I fucking hated every minute of that. I've never once doubted Eli since that day at the pond, and I don't like Lauren trying to put doubts in my head. I've been proud of myself that I've been able to separate the relationship I had with Zac from the one I have with Eli. Even when Patrick tried to fill my head with reminders of Eli's old life, I ignored it. I could've easily taken the distrust that I gained from Zac into my relationship with Eli, but I didn't, because Eli hasn't done anything to make me not trust him since we got together. I know he has a muddy past with women, but I can't hold that against him now.

"Your ex is not very nice," I tell Marc as I sit on the floor and lay my books and notes out on the coffee table in front of me.

Ali and I decided to take our Thursday night study session to the grad dorm's common area, hoping for a change of scenery from our rooms. Marc also decided to join this week. He and Ali had been waiting for me on opposite couches in the common area while I ran and grabbed my third coffee of the day.

"'Bitch,' Logan. I think the word you're looking for is 'bitch,'" Ali corrects.

"Sorry, you're right. Marc, your ex is a bitch," I restate.

Marc chuckles. "What did she do?"

"She found me on campus this afternoon and asked me if you were seeing anyone."

"Yeah, and when Logan wouldn't give her any information, she started spewing all this shit about your brother. Trying to get her to doubt that Maddison could be faithful," Ali chimes in, fired up.

"Such a bitch," Marc agrees, shaking his head in frustration. "Logan, don't listen to her. She doesn't know shit."

"Besides, she's the one who cheated. What does she know about being faithful?" Ali spits as Marc's face falls. "Shit. Marcus, I'm sorry."

Marc shakes it off. "No, you're right. Honestly Logan, don't even think twice about what she said. She knew the old EJ, and she didn't even know him very well. She barely came around my family in all the years we dated. He's different with you. Everyone who knows him can see that."

"She said she's been texting you," I say to Marc.

Marc quickly looks to Ali as Ali averts her gaze from both of us.

"Yeah, she has. But I never respond."

"She wants to get back together with you." Ali uncomfortably adjusts herself on the couch, sitting back and resting her head on the cushion behind her.

"Don't worry. There's no way in hell that's happening. EJ is the only one of us who has a giiiirlfriend," he teases, dragging out the word and changing the subject.

"Shut up," I respond between laughs. "I've been meaning to ask, who helped him come up with the idea of asking me that way? It was really cute."

Marc throws his hands up in defense. "Don't look at me. That was all EJ. Because *someone* never told me they played basketball," he playfully scolds. "You always just said you were a fan, but you failed to mention that you were a stud."

I shrug in response. "Different life."

"So that was all him?" I ask, surprised.

"Yep. You should've seen my mom. She was practically melting into the couch when he told her what he was planning to do."

I bite my bottom lip, trying to hold back my grin, as Ali nudges me with her foot, telling me that she told me so.

I grab my notes to organize them, with a satisfied smile on my lips. I can't believe that Eli came up with that idea all on his own. I already felt special, but now even more so.

After about an hour of silence and passing around our notes, studying for tomorrow's test, Ali leans back into the couch with a heavy sigh.

"Okay, I need a five-minute break." She pulls out her phone to scroll mindlessly.

"Me too," Marc adds, standing from his seat and stretching his arms towards the ceiling.

I glance down at my phone, hoping to see a missed call or text from Eli, but there's still nothing. Their game should've been over by now, but maybe they went into overtime. Or perhaps he's waiting until he's alone in his hotel room to call me, but I'd be lying if I said I hadn't been glancing down to my phone every few minutes over the last hour, waiting for him to call or text.

"No word from EJ, yet?" Marc asks.

"Not yet."

"Oh, Cam just posted to his story. Maybe their game just ended," Ali says while she scrolls through Instagram.

Marc and I make our way to Ali's couch, sitting on either side of her as we watch Cam's Instagram stories take over her screen.

"Two-Oh, baby, let's go!" his voice rings out as he keeps the camera on himself. He's clearly in the locker room and covered in sweat, still wearing his uniform from the game, but his story was posted just over an hour ago.

"Oh nice, they won," Marc states, not noticing my concern.

Eli usually at least texts the second they're done playing to say hi and tell me how he did. I'm getting a little worried that it's been over an hour already since their game ended, and I have yet to hear from him.

Worried about what exactly, I'm not sure.

Cam's next story automatically plays, and Ali has to turn down her volume from the music blasting through her speaker. He posted this one only five minutes ago. He's at a party, and a big party at that. "Penn State knows how to throw down!" he says, taking his camera on a tour through the house where the party is being held on another campus. My heart begins to race as I spot Eli's teammates scattered throughout the crowd of drunken college students.

I recognize Goody playing beer pong with a pretty little brunette hanging on him. Then Cam pans over to Benny, the goalie, who is awkwardly standing alone with a beer in his hand. Next, Patrick is wedged between a blonde's legs as she sits on the counter, his tongue shoved down her throat. Lastly, Mikey is on a couch with a barely dressed girl tucked under each of his arms.

Cam continues to scan the house with his phone, being sure to take his time and show off all the beautiful women who are there. I feel my mouth dry and my heart race as I wait for Eli's face to make an appearance on Ali's screen, but it never does. There are plenty of closed doors that Cam passes by, and I don't know where Eli is, but I don't have a good feeling as Patrick and Lauren's warnings about his road girls begin to flash through my mind.

"No Eli," I flatly state as Ali eyes me. She is clearly thinking the same thing I am, though Marc doesn't seem fazed by his brother's absence and lack of communication with me.

If he weren't at the party, but instead alone at the hotel, I would've heard from him by now.

My mind begins to go to all the terrible places it shouldn't as my phone starts vibrating on the coffee table. I let out a long sigh of relief, seeing Eli's name on the screen.

"Thank god." I get up to grab my phone, putting Eli on speaker.

"Hi, baby!" I enthusiastically say to greet my man on the other line while plopping myself back on the couch next to my friends.

"Hey, bro!" Marc adds into the speaker.

But there's no response. The line is dead quiet. After a moment of continued silence, I realize that Eli must've dialed me by mistake without realizing it.

I turn up the volume just in case I can't hear him, and as I do, swirls of strained and short breaths begin to come through from the other end, my eyes widening in shock at the sound.

I should say something, anything really, but I can't. I'm speechless.

Distant pants and breathy exhales continue to fill my ears.

"Eli?" I somehow ask as my voice breaks, hoping he realizes that he's on the line with me and can hear whatever is happening on his end.

Still, no words.

Heavy and ragged breaths continue to flood through the line as my jaw slacks. I look to Ali. Her eyes are just as wide as mine, and I know she's having the same thought that I am right now.

That Eli just pocket dialed me while with another woman.

Chapter 60

Logan

My eyes are stinging with unfallen and unwelcome tears as I continue to listen to whatever the hell is happening on Eli's end of the line. I urgently stand, with my phone in my hand, but have no idea where I'm going. Everything that Patrick and Lauren had warned me about, combined with Eli's lack of communication tonight, is putting this puzzle together for me as my mind races with ideas of what my ears are listening to.

"Logan?" Eli's voice shakes through the phone.

"Eli?" I ask again as my brow furrows, but instead of a response, I just hear a sharp and shallow intake of air.

I'm so confused right now.

I look to Marc, sitting on the couch next to Ali, who is *finally* concerned as he mouths a couple of words to me, though I can't tell what he's trying to say. Eli's erratic breathing continues to swirl through my speaker and into my ear.

"*What*?" I silently mouth to Marc as I look at him, lost.

He grabs a page of my notes from the coffee table as he frantically scribbles his message down for me.

'*Panic attack?*' his words read as he holds the paper up for me to see.

I instantly close my eyes as Eli's hard-earned breaths flood the line. Of course, that's what's going on, and I should've known that. Yes, his breathing is short, ragged, and staggered because he's trying to catch his breath. He probably feels a pressure so tight on his chest that he's convinced himself he can't fill his lungs with air.

Because of outside influences, I had convinced myself that Eli was with another woman, which caused me to assume what I heard on the other line was sexual. I'm so mad at myself for letting my mind wander. Eli has done nothing to deserve having me question his faithfulness. In reality, he's suffering as he's clearly trying to catch his breath on the other end.

I would let out a sigh of relief, but I don't feel any relief as I listen to my man struggle on the phone.

Taking him off the speaker, I frantically make my way to the stairs and head to my dorm room, leaving my friends and books behind. I would take the elevator to be quicker, but I'm afraid I'll lose the connection if I do.

"Eli?" I ask again when I hear another sharp gasp of air.

"Where are you?" I ask as I reach my hall, running down the corridor to my door.

He doesn't answer, but instead, the strained pants continue as he tries to suck in air, unable to calm himself down.

"Are you in your hotel room?" I ask, hoping to get his mind off the pressure he feels in his chest that's causing him to be short of breath.

"Yeah," he says in a shaky gasp.

Taking a seat on my floor, with my back against my bed, I close my eyes and listen to him. It hurts my heart to hear him this way. I've never seen or heard Eli in a moment of utter weakness, and it's the worst feeling knowing that he's in so much pain, and I can't be there to help him. Eli is the epitome of strength, whether it be his body, talent, or his commanding presence, but right now, I can tell he feels small.

"Can you describe it to me?" I ask. "Your hotel room."

After Eli told me about his panic attacks that day at the pond, I spent some time researching ways to help him. Because, of course, my first instinct, when faced with a problem, is to study.

I think I remember reading somewhere that describing your surroundings can take the focus off whatever is causing your anxiety and shift it towards something else. Or I could be making it up, I don't know, but I'm desperate here. I'm trying my very best to avoid telling Eli just to breathe because that's exactly what he's attempting to do.

"How many beds are in your room?" I ask as the line stays silent for a moment while I wait for his response.

"Two," he states on a short suck of air.

"What color are the walls?" I look around my room, searching for ideas of what to ask, but having no idea if this is actually helping him right now.

"They're gray." I hear him fill his lungs a bit more.

I got two words out of his last response instead of just one, and his breathing seemed a touch steadier. Maybe this is helping, or perhaps I'm making things worse. I'm so out of my fucking element here.

"Can you describe the pictures on the walls?" I look at the framed photo of Eli and me that Mary took. I printed it out and placed it next to the picture of my parents sitting on my bookshelf.

"There's a...sunset," Eli says while taking a longer and deeper inhale. "And a street sign," he adds on the exhale.

Words. More words. Less sucking of air. I think we are getting somewhere.

Listening, Eli inhales deeply, slowly and steadily releasing the exhale. That sounds better already. I wish I were there with him. I wish I could hold him. He once told me that he hadn't had a panic attack since we met, that I calm him. Which is really sweet, but I have no idea what it is about me that does it for him. Otherwise, I would use whatever it is right now.

I need to keep his focus off the anxiety he is feeling and distract him with something, anything. But, as I look around my room, I'm all out of ideas for questions about his surroundings. I decide to be a bit narcissistic as I ask, "And what color is my hair?" knowing it's one of his favorite physical things about me, and hoping that maybe, just maybe, thinking about me will bring him the peace he needs.

Eli lightly chuckles on the other end. It's my new favorite sound as a wave of relief washes over me.

"My favorite color," he says, followed by another deep, steady breath and a slow exhale.

"And my eyes?"

"My other favorite color," he states, and I can't help but smile. Not only because he is the sweetest, but because I can tell he is feeling better.

I continue to listen to him as his breathing normalizes with deep inhales and exhales.

"Eli, are you okay?" I ask, hopeful.

He sighs. "Better now," he says, his voice still shaky, "I'm sorry."

My brows furrow in confusion. "You have nothing to be sorry for, baby. I just wish I was with you right now."

"Me too."

"What happened?" I ask, wondering what the hell brought this panic attack on, seeing as he's been free from them for about a month.

"I don't want to talk about it," he says with finality.

That's a weird response for him. He's been pretty open with me since we got together. He's not really one to keep things from me, but he probably doesn't want to relive the anxiety he just calmed himself from, so I let it go.

"Okay," I sigh. "Have you slept at all this week?"

"Not really, no. Just a few hours here and there," Eli tells me, which is the other reason I'm using to convince myself as to why he doesn't want to fill me in on what caused his panic attack. He must just be exhausted.

"Do you want me to stay on the line until you fall asleep?"

"Please," he sheepishly responds.

Climbing into my bed, I put Eli on speakerphone before setting my phone on the pillow next to me. I lie down and close my eyes as we catch up on our day, steering clear of the topic of his panic attack. Eli starts to sound drowsy in his responses after a while, so I don't ask any more questions. I just stay on the line, allowing him to fall asleep as I listen to his slow and steady breathing. It's wild to me how much I appreciate hearing his normal deep breaths after having to listen to him fight for shallow ones just a bit ago.

When a knock sounds at my door, I make sure that Eli is sound asleep before hanging up my phone, as Marc peeks his head through my doorway.

"Hey, come in." I sit up on my bed.

Marc takes a few steps into my room before putting my notes and books that I left downstairs on my desk.

"How is he?"

"He's okay now. He just fell asleep."

"What happened?"

I take a deep sigh. "I don't know. He won't tell me."

Marc lightly shakes his head. "Don't take it too personally. EJ can get in his head sometimes. It's probably hockey-related. He's hard on himself."

Staying silent, I nod in agreement. I'm trying to be understanding and remember that Eli has never had a partner. He's never had to be open before, so maybe he's just not used to communicating when something is going on with him.

"What do you think about going to my parents' house this weekend? It might be nice to get away from campus. I know EJ has the weekend off from hockey, and Ali can come too," Marc suggests.

"That sounds like a great idea."

"Cool, we can head there after our test tomorrow. I'll text EJ to let him know in the morning."

I give my friend an appreciative smile. Getting off campus really is a fantastic idea. Whatever it is that Eli is dealing with right now, it's most likely caused by the pressure he feels from people he doesn't know or care about. Being secluded with just the four of us sounds like the perfect plan.

"It'll be okay," Marc says, obviously noting my worried expression.

I tilt my head as I look to my best friend, thankful to have him.

"Love you, Marc."

"You too, Logan." He shoots me a half-smile before leaving my room.

I lie back in bed, trying to get some sleep, knowing I have a test the next day, but I'm having a hard time relaxing. My nerves are shot from listening to Eli struggle for air on the phone earlier. I just wanted to be there and take care of him. I wanted to make him feel better.

This is exactly what I came into this school year hoping to avoid. For once, I didn't want to think about anyone else. I wanted to be selfish and focus on myself and school. Now, here I am, unable to sleep because I'm worried about Eli. I don't care though; Eli is the best thing that's ever happened to me, so if that means losing a bit of sleep or not doing quite as well on a test, that's fine. He's worth it.

Chapter 61

Logan

After I most likely bombed my test this afternoon, I headed straight back to my dorm so that I could pack up for the weekend. I made sure to connect my phone to my Bluetooth speaker as soon as I walked through my door, so I can listen to my current favorite songs on repeat as I began to pack my bag. Spotify must've picked up on my preferences because the second my speaker was connected, John Mayer's angelic voice began to fill my room.

I can't imagine we will do much besides hang around the house this weekend, so I'm only bringing my comfiest loungewear. However, I did make sure to pack a couple of pretty pairs of underwear since Eli will most likely be seeing them.

After last weekend, I basically made up my mind that I was ready to have sex with him. I haven't told him that, of course, because I didn't want to make a rash decision right after he asked me to be his girlfriend. But I've always wanted to wait for someone I trusted and someone I was hopefully in love with. I couldn't trust someone more than I do Eli, and even though I would never admit it because it's far too early and I will freak him out, I think I'm starting to fall in love with him.

Shit, who am I kidding? I *am* in love with him, and I have been for a while now. I don't know if it was the day at the pond or when he took me to play basketball as a way to learn about my dad, but I've fallen, that's for sure.

I've never been in love before, so I suppose you could question how I know that I am now, but I don't have the words to explain it. I just know that I am. I'm more confident when I'm with Eli, I think about him always, and I want the best for him. Not to mention that I feel different when I'm with him. I feel more...me.

So, in the words of my guy, John Mayer, whom I have been happily playing on repeat for a couple of weeks now as I let my feelings wash over me, 'Anything less than I love you, is lying.'

While zipping up my duffel bag, I hear a knock on the door, and it opens before I can respond.

"Hi baby," I say as the smile on my lips grows from seeing Eli enter my room. I haven't seen him since Monday, and he looks just as handsome as ever.

"Hey," he replies tonelessly before bending down and quickly pecking my lips. "Ready to go?" He takes my duffel and swings it over his shoulder, walking out of my room before I can respond.

Okay, what the fuck was that? Eli has never once said 'hey' to me, not to mention his monotone voice and the fact that he barely even looked in my direction or embraced me after we've been apart all week. What was that about?

Down in the parking lot, Marc and Ali both have a look of confusion and worry plastered on their faces, matching the one on mine. They must've already encountered Eli this afternoon.

The drive to the house in Eli's truck is incredibly awkward. Marc and Ali are sitting in the back, and I'm in the passenger seat. The ride has been entirely silent as everyone picks up on the weird vibe Eli is putting out. Not once has he looked in my direction or even put his hand on my thigh like he usually does. He just keeps driving with his right hand on the steering wheel while leaning into his door, seemingly trying to create as much space between us as possible.

When we pull up and he parks, Marc and Ali hop out with their bags as quickly as possible to head inside. Eli doesn't open my door, which is fine; I can do it myself, even though he typically insists. I walk around the hood of the car, to his side, as he slings both of our bags over his shoulder.

"Are you okay?" I ask in a concerned tone.

"I'm fine," he snaps as he walks into the house, not even waiting for me.

Eli drops our bags at the base of the stairs and finds his way to the kitchen. I feel a little stunned right now because I'm used to all the small things that Eli usually does to make me feel special, and today he hasn't done any of them.

As I walk past the living room to head towards the kitchen, I find Marc and Ali already sitting on the couch, obviously avoiding the bomb that is Eli James Maddison. I look over to Marc with a questioning glance, who simply shrugs in response as if to say he has no idea what's going on with his brother.

When I make my way into the kitchen, I watch as Eli pulls out two beers from the fridge, popping the top on both, before taking a chug from one.

"Eli, what's going on with you? What happened yesterday?" I'm careful to keep my tone sweet and non-accusatory as I stand on the opposite side of the island from my boyfriend.

"Logan," he warns, closing his eyes in frustration. "I just need a minute," he growls harshly as he walks out the back door with both beers in his hand.

I watch as Eli makes his way down the back porch and towards his parents' dock on the lake. He chugs his beer the entire time, and when he reaches the end, close to the water, he places his empty bottle on the railing. He leans forward with his elbows on the dock as he begins his second drink.

Through the daze, I find my way back into the living room, where my friends are looking at me with wide eyes. They obviously both just heard the way Eli spoke to me.

"What the fuck?" is all I can manage to ask as I stand in the entryway, feeling somewhat stunned and speechless.

In the time that I've known Eli, he's only spoken to me like this once, and that was after a night of drinking. Eli was completely sober this time when he snapped at me, and this time, just as the last, I did nothing to deserve it.

"I haven't seen him like this in a while," Marc says in a concerned tone from the couch. "You still don't know what happened yesterday?" His brows furrow with worry.

I shake my head in response as the pit in my stomach grows. "He wouldn't tell me." I don't know what's going on with Eli, and I'm a little afraid to find out.

The back door slams shut as I close my eyes, hearing Eli's footsteps somewhere behind me. Keeping my back towards him, I refuse to let him see how much his attitude is affecting me. The quick steps I hear in the distance let me know that he's taking the stairs, most likely two at a time.

I let out a heavy sigh, feeling flustered and unsure of what to do.

"Why don't we go for a walk?" Ali suggests, being the good friend that she is, as she stands up from the couch.

"That sounds like a great idea," I tell her with an appreciative smile. "Let me go grab my sweatshirt."

When I notice my duffel bag missing from the base of the stairs, I quickly realize that Eli took it upstairs with him. I let out another nervous breath as I make my way up, having no idea where I'm going. I've never been upstairs here before, and this house is enormous. There must be five or six bedrooms up here, at least. Plus, I don't know if Eli took my bag into his room or dropped it in a guest room. Honestly, I wouldn't be surprised by the latter. It doesn't seem like Eli wants me to be around him tonight.

I crack open a couple of doors, first finding one of the guest rooms, then the laundry room, neither of which contains my bag. On my third try, when I pop my head into a bedroom, I find Eli sitting at the foot of a bed with his elbows on his knees and his face in his hands. This room must be his. I try to quietly duck out before

I'm noticed, but before I do, I spot my duffel bag sitting next to his by the bathroom door.

When I tiptoe inside, he looks up to me, rolls his eyes, and lets out a heavy sigh.

"Fuck, Logan. I said I needed a fucking minute!" he yells, and I can feel my body physically back away from him. The movement is vastly different from the magnetic pull towards him that I typically experience. He's angry right now, and I have no idea why. I've done nothing to deserve being spoken to this way.

My eyes are wide with shock, and my heart is beginning to race as I walk over to my bag and search through it until I find my sweatshirt.

"You took my bag, and I needed my sweatshirt." I zip my bag up with my back towards Eli. Slipping the sweater over my head, I quickly bound towards the door to leave, continuing to avoid eye contact with Eli.

Before I walk out, a sudden jolt of bravery takes over. "And just because I'm your girlfriend now does not give you the right to speak to me that way." I turn to look him in the eyes, wanting him to know how serious I am.

He pulls his gaze away from mine as he stares straight ahead. "Well then, maybe you shouldn't *be* my girlfriend anymore."

My stomach drops from his words. "What did you just say?" I ask in shock and disbelief as I close the door to his room, not wanting Marc or Ali to hear our conversation, but Eli doesn't respond.

"Are you seriously threatening to break up with me right now?" I take a step towards him. My voice isn't even laced with sadness. It's all anger. Because that's what I am right now—I'm angry that he would even suggest that. I know he doesn't mean it, he's saying it out of spite, and that makes it even worse.

"Maybe we should," he says with a shrug. "I'm going to fuck it up eventually, just like I do with everything. May as well end it now." His voice has no emotion as he refuses to look in my direction.

"What the fuck happened yesterday?" I ask again, this time with much less compassion and a whole lot more urgency.

"Jesus, Logan! Stop fucking asking that! Take a fucking hint!" he shouts with wide eyes and red cheeks, anger burning inside of him. He snaps his head in my direction, finally looking me in the eyes. The eyes looking back at me are not the ones I've spent the last few weeks falling in love with. No, those warm whiskey-colored eyes are nowhere to be found. These ones are dark and mean, just like the emotion behind his words.

I feel just as pissed off as I do defeated right now as I let out a heavy sigh. I wish I could convince myself that this is the alcohol talking, that this isn't Eli saying the words, but he only had two beers, and that's not even enough to get him buzzed.

"Let me know when *my* Eli is back because I didn't sign up for this version," I snap before turning on my heel to leave.

"Maybe this version is the real me," he spitefully retorts with my back towards him and my hand on the doorknob. "Maybe the last few weeks were all an act, and you were too naive to notice."

I slowly turn to face him, taking in his hateful words. "Well, then I wish I could be naive forever because I miss that version. That Eli would never speak to me this way, and he sure as shit wouldn't keep things from me."

"You should leave." He pulls his gaze from mine, unable to look me in the eyes.

"I *will* leave. And I don't just mean this room. I will leave *you* if you continue to talk to me like this. I've never allowed a man to speak to me this way, and I'm not going to start now."

I punctuate my words with a slam of his door behind me.

Chapter 62

Logan

"To be honest, I didn't think you had it in you," Ali tells me, surprised and impressed.

"Neither did I." I've felt more sure of myself since Eli and I got together, and today I was confident enough to stand up and not take his shit. I'm proud of myself, but I don't feel any less sick about the conversation that Eli and I had upstairs.

"Maybe you *should* leave," Ali suggests as we turn the corner and near the boy's parents' house. "I'll go with you."

We've been out walking for about an hour, trying to give Eli and I both space to cool off. I didn't have to fill Marc and Ali in on what happened upstairs. They could hear the whole thing. When I quickly made my way downstairs, and towards the front door, I asked Marc to stay behind while Ali and I went on a walk so that Eli wouldn't be alone. As mad at him as I am right now, I didn't want him to feel like everyone was against him if he decided to come downstairs to an empty house.

"Yeah, I think I should," I agree as we walk up the front porch. "I'm going to go grab my bag from upstairs, then I'll call an Uber."

My heart is racing when I step inside. I'm not sure if Eli has come downstairs yet, and I'm not sure where his mood is at. Most of me doesn't believe what he said about wanting to break up, but there's a little part of me that is scared he was sincere. As much as I don't want to end things, *I* was serious about breaking up with him if he continues to speak to me the way he did today. As much as it would break my heart to not be with Eli anymore, I've learned that my self-respect is too important.

“I’m going to head back to my dorm,” I tell Marc when I find him sitting on the couch, watching highlights from a couple of NBA games that were on earlier.

“Are you sure?”

I shrug in response. “I think it’s for the best. He seems like he needs some space.”

He nods his head in agreement, standing from the couch. “I don’t want you to go, but I’m not okay with the way he talked to you. I’ll grab EJ’s keys and drive you back. Ali, you staying or going?”

“I’m going too,” Ali says with regret.

“Actually, Marc, I’m going to call an Uber. I don’t want Eli to be left alone.”

It takes a minute for him to agree, but Marc gives me an appreciative smile when he realizes I’m just looking out for his brother.

“I’ll be right back. I’m going to grab my bag.”

“Do you want me to get it?” Marc interjects, obviously concerned that my duffel is in the same room as Eli.

I shake my head. “I’m not afraid of him,” I tell Marc confidently as I make my way upstairs.

My heart begins to race with every stair I take. I don’t know what mood Eli will be in, and judging by the last conversation we had, it’s best if I’m in and out of there before any words are exchanged.

I barely open his door as I look inside. Eli is no longer sitting on the bed, but thankfully my bag is still on the floor next to his bathroom. I can hear the shower water running, and I’m glad that Eli is preoccupied so that I can quickly grab my things without being noticed.

As I near my bag, I hear a whimper coming from behind his bathroom door. I furrow my brow in confusion as I press my ear up to his closed door, trying to listen. It’s hard to tell with the water running, but I believe I hear a ragged inhale. Not the kind I heard last night when Eli had a panic attack. No, this time, his strained breathing is the result of him crying.

I quietly crack open the bathroom door just enough to peek my head inside, and the sight before me breaks my heart.

The fogged-up shower glass makes it difficult to see properly, but I can still make out Eli's frame. He's sitting on the shower floor, completely naked, with his knees pulled up to his chest and his forehead resting on his crossed arms. He's mostly silent, but his body is ever so slightly shaking from him crying.

"Eli?" I ask quietly and with caution, but he doesn't respond.

I step one foot inside the bathroom, unable to help myself, as I feel the magnetic pull he has on me once again. The closer I get, the larger the pain in my chest becomes. Eli's large muscular body looks so small, hunched in the corner of the shower.

He may be crying softly, but it's still loud enough to break my heart.

Closing the door behind me, I fully enter the bathroom, keeping my eyes on the man I love as he suffers alone. I've never seen Eli cry before, and I doubt it happens often, but I hope I never have to see his sad tears again. The sight of him curled up on the shower floor is heart-wrenching. He looks so small and weak. As upset as I am with how he spoke to me earlier, I love him too much to leave him alone in this moment.

I pull off my sweatshirt, taking my top with it, leaving me in only my bra. I slip off my running shoes and slide out of my yoga pants, revealing the little black thong underneath. He's seen me in about as little clothing as I have on now, and I've seen Eli completely naked before, just a few days ago, but this moment is different. There's nothing sexual about what is happening right now.

As I open the glass shower door, I fully expect Eli to scold me for not giving him space, but he doesn't say anything. In fact, he doesn't even look up at me. I don't care if he doesn't want me here right now. I'm not leaving him alone to suffer in silence. Whatever is going on with him, I don't need to know. I just need him to be aware that I'm here for him.

Allowing the hot water run over my body, I make my way to the far side of the shower, where Eli is hunched over. I wedge myself between his large body and the shower wall as I slide myself down the cold tile to sit behind him. With my legs bent on either side of him, I wrap one arm around his abdomen, and the other I lace across his chest as I press my cheek against his wet back.

His body is stiff, so he might not want this, but I don't know how else to make him feel better than to hold him right now.

Suddenly, he grabs ahold of my arm that's draped across his chest and laces his fingers between mine. As he leans his forehead against our intertwined hands, his cries turn to sobs. His body shakes in mine as I hold him close to me.

I squeeze my eyes shut as the noise he makes pains my ears. I grip him tighter, trying anything I can to make him feel better. Hopefully, he mistakes the tears falling from my eyes onto his back as water from the shower because I'm trying to be strong right now, but I can't. It's breaking my heart to see him this way.

His body continues to heave in my arms. "Please don't leave me," he begs between sobs.

My tear-filled eyes widen in shock. That was the last thing I expected Eli to say. When I walked in here, I assumed he wanted nothing to do with me tonight, and now his sad words are like arrows to my heart. I've never seen him like this before, and quite honestly, I never thought I would.

"I'm sorry," he cries into my arms.

I don't know what to say. I'm not going to say, 'it's okay' because it's not. But, also, I'm not going to try to prove a point while Eli is breaking down.

Instead of responding, I place a couple of kisses on his back because I want him to know I'm listening even though I don't know what to say.

"I don't know what's wrong with me," Eli says on a suck of air as he tries to catch his breath. He turns his head and body into mine as he finds the crook of my neck, hiding his face. I wrap his arms around his shoulders, keeping him close to me.

"There's nothing wrong with you, baby." I gently run my palm over his tattooed arm, trying to soothe him.

I know that Eli has a hard time controlling where his mind wanders, anxiety can do that, but I didn't realize it would make him emotional too. Whatever is going on, it's clearly consuming him.

I continue to hold his naked body in my arms while we sit on the shower floor until the hot water runs cold. Eli stopped crying a while ago, but I could just sense that he needed to stay where we were for a bit longer.

Finally, I decide it's time to get up as I peel myself off of him. Kissing his forehead, I stand before turning off the water. I walk out of the shower, finding the nearest cabinet, hoping to find towels hidden inside. Thankfully, I do, and I grab one for myself, wrapping it around my bust as I take another out for Eli. Holding it open for him, I turn around and find him standing a few feet behind me, looking sheepish and maybe a bit embarrassed.

"Thanks, baby," he shyly says, wrapping the towel low on his hips.

I try to keep my eyes averted from his chiseled body because I want to be respectful. And if I'm being honest, the argument we had earlier is still playing in my mind, and I feel less comfortable around him than I usually do.

I turn on my heel to leave the bathroom, but Eli's hand gently grips my hip to stop me. He turns me around to face him before his strong arms wrap around my shoulders, holding me to his body. My hands find his lean back as I gently stroke the length of it.

"I'm sorry," he whispers into the crook of my neck as my eyes squeeze shut at the tone of his voice. I know he's sincere, I can tell, but it still doesn't erase the pit in my stomach caused by his earlier words.

He gently places his lips on my tattoo before releasing me from his hold. I file out of his bathroom as he follows closely behind.

Shuffling through my duffel bag, I find an oversized tee and a short pair of shorts. Without looking back at Eli, I head into the bathroom to change into my dry clothes, needing a moment of privacy.

As I look at myself in the mirror, I can't help but think about today. I want to forget about our argument earlier, I do. I love Eli, and I know that, but one of my biggest fears is having the people I love leave me. People always leave me. Opening up to the three people in this house has been so hard for me because I feel like everyone I care for leaves me at some point. The fact that Eli threatened to do just that, especially when he didn't mean it, that scares me. My walls were down because he broke through them, but after that argument, I can feel them coming back up.

Back in his room, I find Eli still in his towel, sitting on the edge of his bed while keeping his gaze on the ground.

"Can I tell you what happened yesterday?" he asks sheepishly, scratching at his brow with his thumb.

"Only if you want to." I kneel on the ground and begin to reorganize my bag, trying to keep myself busy so I don't look in Eli's direction.

He lets out a heavy sigh. "There was a scout from the Dallas Stars at the game against Penn State."

My head snaps in his direction as his gaze lifts off the floor to meet mine.

"I played like shit. Worst I've played in years. He left after the second period." Eli keeps eye contact with me, trying to keep his expression neutral, but I can tell he's upset.

Standing up, my shoulders slack as I look at him with sympathy. He just had a shot at his life-long dream and blew it only hours ago. No wonder he had a panic attack last night.

"Why didn't you tell me?" I ask as I walk over to stand between his legs.

"Because I was embarrassed." He shyly pulls his gaze away from me, looking down towards his lap.

Pushing his wet hair from his eyes, I lift his chin, forcing him to look at me, and suddenly I'm reminded that these beautiful mocha eyes are my favorite things to look at.

"You don't need to be embarrassed with me. I'm proud of you, regardless. You could be the fucking waterboy for all I care, and I would still think you're the best." Eli chuckles, finally giving me a smile. "I just want you to be happy."

He nods his head in my hands as he gives me an appreciative grin.

"Is that what caused you to be so upset in the shower?"

He shakes his head. "No, that had nothing to do with hockey. But that was also really fucking embarrassing, so let's not talk about it."

Nodding my head in response because I don't know what else to say, I turn to walk away, but Eli takes my hand and pulls me back to stand between his legs.

He closes his eyes as if he's trying to force himself to be open with me.

"The thought of being without you, that's what caused that reaction, Logan." He opens his eyes, looking at me with sincerity. "Playing like shit caused me to get in my head and have a panic attack, but being an asshole today, I don't know it's like I'm trying to blow up the rest of my life, too. It's not an excuse, but sometimes when the anxiety builds up, I take it out on the people around me. It's something I need to work on."

"I'm so sorry, Logan," he says, searching my eyes with his.

My phone dings on his dresser and I pick it up to find a couple of missed texts from Marc.

M: *You okay up there?*

M: *I'm assuming you're staying. Ordered pizza, and it's down here if you guys want some.*

"Marc and Ali had pizza delivered." I set my phone back on his dresser. "Want to come downstairs with me?"

Eli shakes his head. "No, I just want to be alone tonight. I'll get it together tomorrow. I promise."

I give him a half-smile before bending down and kissing his temple. Before I can turn to leave, Eli grabs my hips and pulls me to sit across his lap, his arms snaking around my waist.

"I'm sorry, Logan," Eli whispers into my neck.

"I know, baby." I stroke his wet hair with my hand.

After polishing off the extra-large pizza that Marc ordered, sans the two pieces I saved for Eli, Marc stands to go find another bottle of wine.

"What the hell do your parents do for work, anyway? You guys are loaded," Ali asks without filter.

In true Ali fashion, she says what's on her mind, but I've been wondering the same. The fact that this is their second house and it's this large, plus it's on a lake, I can only imagine what their home in Indiana looks like.

Marc laughs from the wine fridge as he pulls another bottle off the wall. "Our dad is a financial advisor, but my mom is actually the breadwinner. She made some smart investments when she was younger. That's how they met."

Ali and I look at each other, swooning at the thought. We both think that Marc and Eli's parents are the absolute cutest together.

"You sure you don't want a glass, Logan?" Marc asks as he refills Ali's.

"No, I'm good, thanks. I'm going to get to bed."

I don't feel like drinking tonight. I'm already drained from the night I had with Eli. I'm emotionally exhausted, and I'm ready to pass out. I didn't tell Marc and Ali what happened upstairs in the shower, that's between Eli and me, but they know me well enough to know that I have a good reason to stay tonight.

"Goodnight, guys." I head upstairs with a plate of pizza in my hands.

"Night, girl."

"Goodnight, Logan. Love you," Marc calls out as I make it to the top of the stairs.

When I open Eli's bedroom door, I find his beautiful body laid out on the bed, wearing only his briefs. His back is to me as he sleeps soundly, most likely just as exhausted as I am from the night we had. I quietly place the plate of pizza on his nightstand, just in case he wakes up and is hungry, before picking up my duffel bag and tiptoeing towards the door to find a place to sleep for the night.

"Where are you going?" Eli asks.

When I turn back around to face him, he's sitting up in bed, confusion plastered on his handsome face.

"I was going to find a guest room. You said you wanted to be alone tonight."

He shakes his head. "That doesn't mean you, Logan. Please stay with me," he requests with an edge of desperation.

I've never been any good at saying no to this boy, even though I still feel uneasy about the way he spitefully threw breaking up in my face. My confidence in myself and our relationship is definitely shaken, but that doesn't keep me from setting down my bag and climbing into bed with him.

My stomach has been in knots all night. I'm having a hard time figuring out my emotions. I feel so bad for Eli that his shot at his dream didn't go as planned, but it's also a reminder that he can be gone any day. But then, he was crying in the shower, begging me not to leave him, when in reality, he's the one that's going to leave me when he gets called up. I don't know. I'm just confused, I guess.

Eli drapes his tattooed arm over my waist as he lays his head on my chest, needing me to hold him. I listen as his breathing slows and steadies until he's fast asleep. Keeping my eyes closed, I try to join him, but my mind doesn't want to shut off. It's swirling around, taunting me by reminding me that people always leave me. That I don't belong anywhere. That this will all be snatched away when Eli gets called up to play professionally. My insecurities continue to play on repeat as my stomach drops with the thought of what it will feel like when Eli does actually leave me, not just threaten it.

Chapter 63

Eli

I'm not surprised in the least when I open my eyes the next morning and find that the spot next to me in bed is empty. I fucked up yesterday, I really did, and I could sense how off Logan was afterward. Even though she tried to make me feel better and bring me peace when I was struggling, I could tell that I drained her.

My only real fear about being in a relationship with Logan is the possibility of adding anything negative to her life. She's had it rough and deserves nothing but ease for once. After that day at the pond, I promised myself that I would stop with all the bullshit, that I would go above and beyond to make her feel special and taken care of. I can honestly say that up until yesterday, I've done just that. But with a few hateful words, I may have thrown everything down the drain.

As I lie in bed with my eyes glued to the ceiling, I replay our argument in my head for what feels like the hundredth time. Why the fuck would I speak to her that way? Why the fuck would I tell her to leave me alone? She's the only person I ever want to be around. Why on earth would I ever threaten to break up with her? I would never, and could never break up with her. I love her. I need her. And I just planted doubts her in her head about whether or not I actually wanted to be with her. I've spent the last month trying to get her to trust me, and just like that, I may have broken it.

Even though Logan is tough on the outside, there are parts of her that are fragile on the inside.

I felt like absolute shit yesterday, but that's still no excuse for saying the things I did. After playing like garbage at Penn State on Thursday, combined with the embarrassment I felt after needing to hear my girlfriend's voice just to calm myself down, I felt the worst

I have in a long time. So, in true Eli fashion, I decided to try to make the people around me feel as terrible as I did.

I spoke to Logan like she was my punching bag and would just bounce back after every hit I threw. Except, she surprised me by threatening not to come back at all if I continued. As much as I hated hearing those words leave her mouth, I needed them. They brought me back to reality and reminded me that she could leave at any moment. That she's independent and doesn't need me, but instead, she *chooses* me.

I was pretty embarrassed after my breakdown in the shower yesterday, but after my panic attack the night before, and the lack of sleep all week, I just couldn't control my emotions.

Finally, after wallowing for long enough, I decide to peel my sorry ass out of bed, needing to go find my girl and hoping that she still is. I apologized countless times last night, but the words don't mean much if I can't prove them.

It's early, and the house is dead silent. Marc and Ali must still be asleep, and Logan, I don't know where she is. I'm hoping she didn't feel the need to go find another bed after I fell asleep. It broke my heart when she came in to grab her bag and leave last night, not realizing that I wanted her with me. Of course, my selfish ass was blessed with a restful night of sleep because I had my girl by my side, but I don't know if Logan got any rest after I drained her with my attitude.

Scanning the living room, I find the couches are empty. I make my way to the kitchen, but Logan is nowhere to be found. As I turn to head back upstairs to search the guest rooms, I spot Logan's pretty red hair out in the distance through the back window.

She's out on the edge of my parents' dock, leaning on the railing, exactly where I was drinking away my sorrows yesterday. She has on a pair of cozy sweats and what looks to be one of my sweatshirts, judging by the number thirteen on the hood, and her ears are snugly tucked into a beanie. I would take her picture right now because she looks fucking perfect, standing in front of the scenic lake as the fog begins to lift, wearing my clothes, but I think I would always remember this picture as the morning after I threatened to break up with her. Maybe though, I need a reminder of how terrible I feel right now, so I decide to snap the image on my phone through the large glass window.

I snag a blanket from the couch after pouring a couple of cups of coffee, making sure to add a little creamer to Logan's. I also made sure hers was extra hot because I'm sure that my California girl is freezing outside right now.

As I cautiously make my way down the dock to her, I catch Logan swiping a hand at her cheek with her back towards me.

Fuck.

I've made her cry twice before, but those were good tears. I can almost guarantee that these are not.

Sliding her mug of coffee in front of her, I leave it on the railing between her elbows. I kiss the back of her head while she keeps her gaze forward on the lake.

"Hi, baby," I say in a cautious tone behind her.

"Hi," she says without turning around. "Thank you," she adds in reference to the coffee as she tries to stifle her sniffling. She wraps her bare hands tightly around her mug, confirming my suspicions that she's freezing right now.

Unfolding the blanket in my hands, I wrap it tightly around her. Crossing my arms around the front of her shoulders, I pull her back into my chest.

A small wave of relief washes over me when I feel her melt into my touch.

I lean my forehead on the back of her beanie. "Thank you for taking care of me last night," I tell her. "And the night before."

She doesn't use words but instead nods her head in acknowledgment as she tries to sneakily wipe away a fallen tear.

"Logan—"

"I'm fine. I'm just really tired," she says, cutting me off.

"Did you sleep at all last night?" I tighten my arms and tilt my head around to look at her. Her nose and eyes are red from the lack of sleep and this morning's tears.

Again, she doesn't respond.

I sigh against her as my forehand falls to her shoulder. "This is all my fault. I'm so sorry, Logan, I really am. I don't know what the fuck I was thinking yesterday."

"I know. It just freaked me out, that's all. But I'm moving past it," Logan says, being the sweet and understanding person that she is.

I kiss her shoulder before lifting my gaze to look out towards the lake in front of us. "What freaked you out the most," I ask, trying to figure out which fears of hers I caused that I need to ease.

"That you're going to leave me." Her voice comes out sheepish as she drops her face, looking down at her coffee mug, continuing to warm her cold hands with it.

Fuck. I've spent the last few weeks fighting to show Logan that we belong together. That I'm hers. That I'm not going anywhere. And in a matter of one conversation, I've convinced her otherwise.

Squeezing my eyes shut, I try to find the right words to say. I want to tell Logan how much I love her. How much I need her. How she makes me a better person. But I can't tell her I love her right now because I don't want her to think it's a Hail Mary in an effort to make her feel better or forgive me. I want to tell her when the timing is right. When she knows I'm sincere.

"I'm not going anywhere," I say instead. "You're the best thing that's ever happened to me, Logan." I kiss the side of her head and linger my lips there, hoping for a response, but instead, she remains silent.

I don't know what else to say. There's not really anything else I *can* say. I just have to prove to her that I didn't mean any of those spiteful words I said last night.

"You're the best thing that's ever happened to me, too," she surprises me by saying as my body begins to relax.

She turns around in my embrace, causing my arms to drape across her shoulders. She's fucking beautiful this morning without any makeup on, cute little beanie covering her head. Every time I look at her, I'm reminded how lucky I am, but especially today. Thank god that Logan has a forgiving heart when it comes to me, but still, I need to stop taking advantage of it.

"Hi," I say again as I look down at my pretty girl.

"Hi." She gives me a smile. It's the first I've seen from her in a while.

I lean down to place my lips on hers, wanting to feel them and needing the reassurance. I make sure to kiss her long and sweetly, trying to tell her how much I love her without saying the words. She's a combination of vanilla and coffee this morning, with a touch of mint from her toothpaste. She tastes like heaven, same as always, but I appreciate it all a little more today.

Moving our mugs down the railing a bit, so I don't knock them off into the lake below us, I tighten my grip around her shoulders. I lean into her hug as Logan strokes the length of my back. I love it when she does this, it's soothing and caring, but she has no reason to take care of me today. Today needs to be about her and reminding her how important she is to me.

"Are you hungry?"

"Always," she says into my chest, causing me to chuckle.

"I can make you breakfast."

She pulls away from my embrace to look at me with a skeptical expression. "You're going to cook for me?"

"Yep. Anything you want."

"Pancakes?" she asks with a raised brow.

"I can do pancakes." I quickly nod, trying to convince her. Granted, Mary did the cooking for us boys growing up, but I've lived on my own for the last four years, so I've picked up some skills in the kitchen along the way.

"Blueberry pancakes?"

"Okay, now you're pushing it too far," I sarcastically say, earning another smile from her as a bit more of the pressure lifts off my chest.

"But, anything for you." I kiss her cheek then collarbone before pulling away to hand her her coffee mug. "I think we have blueberries in the refrigerator."

We walk back up the dock together, towards the house, carrying our coffee. Logan has the blanket wrapped around her like a cape and it drags behind her on the ground. I was hoping to hold her hand so I could make myself feel better, but Logan keeps both of her hands clutched around the warmth of her cup. I can tell she's still a little out of sorts, but I'm hoping she's starting to feel like herself with me again.

Logan sits on one of the tall chairs at the kitchen island as I whip up some batter for her blueberry pancakes. She looks exhausted as she rests her head in her hands and watches me pour the batter onto the griddle. It's pretty apparent that she needs some sleep.

"Morning, Logan," I hear my brother say. "EJ," he adds to greet me. As I turn around from the stovetop, Marc swings his arm around my girlfriend's shoulders, flipping me the bird with the hand that's draped over her. I can tell he's trying to hold back his smile, but Logan can't help it as her dimples become more prominent.

"Yeah, I deserve that," I admit with a shrug and a grin. I already know I'm going to get an earful from him about last night, but I'm just glad he's not doing it first thing in the morning.

"How'd you sleep?" Marc asks Logan.

"Good," she lies while simultaneously shooting me a secretive glance, imploring me to stay silent. She doesn't like to burden the people around her, and for once, I'm glad because I already feel terrible, and I don't need Marc to make me feel worse.

"Do you want some pancakes?" I ask my brother.

"Please." He takes the seat next to Logan.

I set a plate of perfectly grilled pancakes in front of my brother and my girl before grabbing the syrup I heated up out of the microwave.

"Thanks, baby," she says as I set the sticky sugar in front of her, but her eyes aren't as bright as they typically are when she calls me that.

"Good morning, friends!" Ali exclaims as she bounds down the stairs wearing her workout clothes, her headphones draped around her neck.

"Logan, you look beautiful as always," she says, right as Logan takes a mouthful of her breakfast. "Maddison, you done being a little bitch?"

"Jesus, Ali," Marc says under his breath, shaking his head.

I look to Logan as she bites on her bottom lip, trying to hold back her amusement. But I can't help it as I let out a chuckle.

"Yes, ma'am." Ali is a ballbuster for sure, but I'm glad she has Logan's back, even when it's me that her anger is directed towards.

"Good, stop being mean to my friend," she adds. "Logan, I'm going for a run. Want to come?" Ali rips a banana off the bunch from the fruit bowl in the center of the island.

"No, I'm going to stay in. I think I'm going to take a nap." I walk over to Logan with a fork in hand, ready to help her polish off her plate of pancakes.

"Alright, see you guys when I'm back." Ali puts her headphones over her ears and turns to leave. She quickly and slyly squeezes Marc's arm before running out the door.

After breakfast, Marc reaches his hands up, stretching out his stomach. He grabs Logan's empty plate along with his own and places them in the sink.

"I'm going to be watching the Clemson and Auburn game if you guys are looking for me." He makes his way towards the living room. If I happen to have a Saturday off from hockey, our favorite thing to do is to watch college football all day.

Logan stands from her seat. "I'm going to go get some sleep." She heads towards the stairs, and I follow her like a lost puppy dog, needing her to tell me that everything is okay between us.

"Want me to come with you?" I pathetically ask.

She shakes her head. "No, you should hang out with Marc. Thanks for breakfast." She turns to face me halfway up the staircase.

I give her a poor little half-smile in return before she continues up and out of sight.

"She hates me," I tell Marc as I plop myself down to lay on the couch opposite of him in the living room.

"Stop being so dramatic." He can't help but roll his eyes. "Logan will come around when she's ready."

"Okay, let's hear it." I keep my eyes on the TV, watching the opening kickoff of the football game.

"Hear what?" Marc asks.

"The lecture you planned out for me for treating your best friend the way I did last night." I hate every word that comes out of my mouth as I remind myself of what I said to Logan yesterday.

"I'm not saying anything about it."

"Well, that's a first."

"I already know you're beating yourself up over there right now. You love her too much not to be." Marc turns to give me a sympathetic smile.

I nod my head in agreement because he's right. I am.

"But Mom will literally kill you if she ever finds out that you spoke to Logan that way."

"Fuck," I say as the realization hits me. "I know. No joke, she'd disown me."

"So, you going to tell me what caused you to have a panic attack and be an asshole to everyone yesterday?"

I once again keep my gaze glued to the TV. "There was a scout at the Penn State game on Thursday. I played like shit, and he left after the second period."

Out of the corner of my eye, I can see Marc snap his head in my direction. "Shit, man. What team?" he asks in reference to the NHL team I have no shot of getting a call from.

"Dallas."

"Fuck. That would've been a good fit for you too."

"Tell me about it," I say sarcastically.

"It'll work out. You're too good not to make it, man. Anyone can have an off day and we still have Senior Showcase coming up."

Marc is right. Even though Thursday was a huge shot at getting some attention from a team whose offensive system would've worked well with my strengths, the biggest opportunity I'm going to have is at Senior Showcase in Chicago. Every NHL team sends their scouts to watch the weekend of play between the country's top seniors, and I need to impress.

"You're going to bring Logan, right?" Marc asks.

"I haven't brought it up yet, but I'm assuming she will come." As long as I don't do something else to fuck up my relationship before then.

Marc and I continue to watch the game without saying another word, and after the first quarter, Auburn is up 10-7, but I haven't paid much attention to the game. All I can think about is Logan. What else is new? But, right now, I'm just worried I took it too far last night. She didn't hold my hand, she didn't want me to cuddle with her as she took a nap, and she didn't even kiss me before she went upstairs. I know she's off, but I don't know how to fix it. I'm trying to listen to Marc's advice and give her the space she needs until she's ready to come to me, but it's really fucking hard to keep myself on this couch when I know Logan is right upstairs.

As if she could hear my concerns, Logan comes shuffling into the living room, looking all cute and sleepy, with the same blanket from earlier wrapped around her. She finds her way to my side of the couch before she climbs on top of me and lays her head on my chest.

"Couldn't sleep," is all she says as she makes herself comfortable, snuggling into my body.

The smile on my lips grows as I wrap my arms around her back, my entire body relaxing from having her here with me. She soothes my concern, without even realizing, by wanting me near her so that she can rest.

I kiss the top of her head as she finds the right position to fall asleep, and I remember once again that I'm the luckiest son of a bitch in the world. I stroke her back with my fingertips until I hear her breathing steady, telling me that she's fast asleep in my arms.

I look over to Marc, who gives me a knowing grin because, of course, he was right. He knows both Logan and I way too well, but man, am I thankful for it.

Chapter 64

Logan

"Babe, these are so good," Eli tells me from the couch.

"Yeah, Logan. Don't tell my mom, but I think yours are better than hers," Marc adds, regarding the peanut butter cookies I baked.

Eli insisted on cooking us all dinner, so I thought I would pitch in with dessert. He obviously feels terrible about how he treated everyone yesterday, so he's trying to apologize through our stomachs, which I would say is totally working. He made baked potatoes, grilled veggies and salad for dinner. Plus, he cooked steaks for us outside on the grill. They were delicious and perfectly medium-rare. Add being an excellent chef to the list of things that Eli is annoyingly talented at.

I feel better tonight than I did last night. It took me a little bit to warm up again, but it's hard for me to stay upset at Eli for long. I can tell how bad he feels, and he's been trying to make it up to me all day. He wouldn't let me help with anything for dinner, including doing the dishes. When I worked out this afternoon, after my nap, he brought me a water partway through, then came back with a towel ten minutes later. I couldn't help but laugh when I caught him walking by the window and glancing inside the gym every few minutes after that.

I'm trying to put him out of his misery by touching him as much as possible because I've learned that's how he feels reassured. But I can tell Eli is still beating himself up over last night.

"Glad you guys like them. It's my mom's recipe." I put the rest of the warm cookies on the coffee table in front of the couch.

I take a seat on Eli's lap, and he visibly relaxes from the contact. He wraps one arm tightly around my waist and uses the other to bring another cookie to his mouth.

"What do you guys do around here for Halloween?" Ali asks from her seat on the floor. "We're definitely doing something. It's my favorite holiday, so I'll throw my own damn party if I have to."

"Oh, no. There's a party. Biggest party of the year is Halloween weekend at the hockey house," Marc adds as he looks to his brother. Eli's body tenses below me.

"Perfect. We're going, right?" Ali questions, looking around at the three of us, but both the boys' eyes land on me.

"What?" I ask, not knowing why they're looking to me for an answer.

"We don't have to go. I have to make a brief appearance, but I can leave after I do," Eli tells me, trying to sound reassuring.

"That's ridiculous. Why wouldn't we go?"

"Well, you're not really into parties, so I just assumed—"

"Yeah, but it's Halloween. Of course we're going. Besides, I'm going to need a few drinks after midterms this week."

"Oh, shit! Logan's getting drunk next weekend!" Marc teases, knowing how terrible I am at holding my liquor.

"Hell yeah, I am. I hope you're ready to take care of my drunk ass," I tell Marc as I recall some of my sloppy nights abroad.

"I'll take care of your drunk ass," Eli says with a chuckle before kissing the side of my head.

"Is it on Friday or Saturday?" Ali asks.

"It's on Saturday, after our regular-season home opener. You're coming to the game, right?" Eli looks towards me.

"Of course." I swing an arm around his neck and quickly place my lips on his smiling ones.

"Logan, I already know what you're dressing up as, so don't even worry about it. I'll take care of everything," Ali tells me with excitement.

"That sounds terrifying."

"Halloween is my Super Bowl. Please, just let me have this," she begs.

"Nice sports reference, Al." Marc nudges her, impressed.

She shoots him a proud smile over her shoulder.

"Fine. But I don't do slutty for Halloween." I usually go the funny route for Halloween, but I haven't even begun to think about a costume this year. Plus, if all of Eli's old hookup buddies are going to be there, wearing little to nothing, maybe it's for the best if Ali dresses me.

"She can do a *little* slutty," Eli chimes in, wiggling his eyebrows.

I playfully swat his chest as Ali shoots him a wink, which absolutely terrifies me in regard to whatever it is she has planned for me to wear.

"Marcus, what are you going as?" Ali asks.

"I'm not sure yet. Lauren always made me do a couple's costume with her, so I've never really had to think about it," he says. "But I'm looking forward to doing my own thing this year."

"Babe, why don't we do a couple's costume?" Eli asks me in his sweetest of tones.

"Because couples' costumes are cheesy as hell. No offense, Marc."

"None taken." Marc quickly puts his hands up.

"But I like being cheesy with you," Eli says, causing me to smile as I tighten my grasp on him.

"Gross," Marc chimes in.

"Sorry, Maddison. I already called dibs on her. You can have Logan next year," Ali adds, causing my smile to fall, reminding me that Eli won't be here next year. That I'll still be in grad school, and Eli will be off playing professional hockey, being successful, and having even more girls throw themselves at him than already do now.

Clearing my throat, I climb off of Eli's lap, making my way towards the kitchen to grab a glass of water. "We need to figure out our study schedule this week," I say to Marc and Ali, changing the subject.

"Well, we should probably skip Double G on Monday to join that study group for Econ," Marc says as I walk back into the living room, standing in the entryway and leaning my shoulder against the wall.

"And Tuesday and Wednesday are office hours for marketing. Then we have our Thursday night study session as usual. That should get us prepared enough for midterms," Ali adds.

"So, I'm not going to see you all week?" Eli asks me from across the living room.

"Of course, you will. You can come stay over whenever you want. You know that. This is just a busy week for school." I give Eli an apologetic smile.

"Well, in that case." Eli stands up from the couch. "We will see you fucking nerds tomorrow." He grabs me and throws me over his shoulder with ease as he carries me up the stairs. My middle is bent over his collar, and my face is perfectly lined up with his ass as Eli holds onto me by my legs.

"If you guys are gonna go fuck, can you at least try to be quiet about it! I need some sleep!" Ali yells out in an amused tone, obviously joking because she knows that Eli and I haven't had sex yet.

"Jesus Christ, Alison." Marc shakes his head.

"Better go grab your headphones, Ali!" Eli yells back to her, causing her to cackle on the couch.

"Eli James!" I smack his ass while he continues to walk us up the stairs, but Eli can't help but laugh at his own joke.

"Kill me now," Marc adds in the distance.

My strong, muscular man carries me as if I were as light as a feather straight to his bedroom. He kicks the door closed behind him before bending over and laying me on the bed. He climbs right on top of me, his mouth finding me with urgency as if he needs my lips on his right now.

His warm mouth peppers my body, covering me in kisses. He doesn't miss a beat as he lifts my shirt up and over my head, leaving me in only my little bra and leggings. His mouth finds me again, and his graceful tongue glides against mine. He can't seem to get enough, and neither can I as my hands find the hem of his shirt, pushing it up and needing it off of him.

Eli sits up on his knees, my legs open around him, as he peels his shirt off to reveal his perfectly toned abdomen and arms. I love his body, everything about him. I love his tattoos, I love that V that dips into his jeans, but mostly I just love him. All of him. Even the difficult parts that he's not used to letting another person see. I love those parts too.

"Can I ask you something?" I say before my mind can stop me. Something has been eating at me for a few days now, and I think it's best if I ask while we still have some clothes on.

Eli looks down at me, confused and maybe a bit concerned. "Of course."

"Does it bother you that we haven't had sex yet?" Feeling the need to cover up, I cross my arms over my chest.

The question has been swirling in my mind for a few days now since Patrick and Lauren reminded me that Eli has girls waiting for him wherever he goes. My last boyfriend cheated on me because I couldn't get there with him physically. I've done much more with Eli than I ever did with Zac, but Eli is a lot more experienced, so it just makes me worried that maybe I'm not doing enough. I'm mad at myself for even letting the concerns seep their way in, but still, they've been there since the night I convinced myself he was cheating on me when, in reality, he was having a panic attack.

"Where is this coming from?" Eli sweetly asks with concern as I shrug in response.

"Come here," he says as he pulls my arms, uncrossing them and bringing me forward.

My legs wrap around his waist as he sits on the bed, and my chest is right in Eli's face, but he's being respectful, keeping his eyes on me, trying to soothe my concern.

"Does it bother *you*?" he asks as he tucks a piece of my hair behind my ear.

"Sometimes," I shrug. "I'm just worried that what we're doing isn't enough for you."

Eli's head falls in defeat. "Logan, you're literally *everything* to me. How do you not see that?"

I stay silent because I don't know what to say.

"Do you feel pressured?" he asks, worried. "Does it feel like I'm pressuring you?"

"No! No, not at all." I quickly shake my head. "It's me. I'm just getting in my head about it."

"Well, get out of there," he teases, lightening the mood. "I love every part of this. I love getting to take my time with you." His eyes and hands run over my body.

"I'm getting there. I promise."

Eli shakes his head. "Baby, there's no rush," he reminds me as he cups my face and presses his lips to mine.

As his mouth leaves me, he pulls back but keeps his hand on the side of my face, his eyes searching mine. My fingertips begin to trace the crevices of his muscles before swirling around the black ink on his arm. I have no idea how I got so lucky that this man wants me, chose me. But whatever it is, I'm not going to question it. I'm just going to enjoy it while it lasts.

Eli's gaze follows my fingers as they explore him. "You done?" he asks with an arrogant smirk. He knows how much I love his body and his tattoos, and he's giving me shit for it.

"Not yet." I continue to memorize every rise and fall, keeping my eyes and hands glued to him.

His eyes flicker closed, and even though he's teasing me about it, I know he loves when I touch him this way.

While Eli's eyes are shut, I allow my lips to find his neck, kissing him, needing him. I work them over the spot below his ear, and Eli throws his head back in a low moan. Continuing to kiss his body, I sit in his lap and find the button on his jeans with my hands.

I don't really know what I'm planning to do right now. I came into this weekend wanting to tell him that I was ready to have sex, but after last night, I don't think I'm quite there.

All I know is that I was shocked when I finally saw his manhood last week, and I want to see it again. I want to hold it in my hand, maybe use my mouth. I'm not sure. I've never done that, but I want to do all the new and scary things with Eli. I just want him to feel good, and I love seeing how his body reacts to me.

I was surprised when I saw his size. I mean, I don't have much to compare it to, but still, I know he's well endowed. I guess I should've expected it. I mean, the man is 6'4", but frankly, I don't see how what's between his legs is supposed to fit inside of me one day.

I pop open the top button of his jeans, but his hand stops me before I can get to the zipper.

"What's wrong?" I ask, looking down at him, confused.

"Nothing," he says with a sly little grin. "But I want to make *you* feel good." His voice is raspy and his eyes are darkening over.

"You always make me feel good," I remind him as he lies me back on the bed and hovers over me.

"Yeah?" he asks in a seductive tone as his lips once again find my neck, working their way down to my chest.

"Mmm-hmm."

"Well," he kisses my collarbone. "You took care of me the last two nights, so tonight, I'm taking care of you."

His words are sweet, but they're said in a sinister way. A sexy, devilish way. Whatever he means by them, I'm all in.

"Can I take care of you, baby?" he asks in a whisper, leaning into me and rubbing his body over mine.

The only response I can manage is a moan as my hips jerk up into him, needing the friction.

"Is that a yes?" he chuckles into my neck, pressing himself down between my legs. I really want these leggings off. And those jeans of his—I want those off too.

"Please," I beg in a desperate breath.

"What do you want me to do?" His lips trail all over my chest, my neck, my jaw.

"Anything."

"Anything?" he repeats, needing confirmation.

"Mmm-hmm." I stroke my hands down the length of his lean and muscular back.

Eli's hand finds its way into the band of my leggings. His fingers dance around before they dip into my pants and grab onto my hip.

"I really want to taste you, Logan," Eli says while his head is in the crook of my neck, covering me in kisses. He grinds himself down between my legs again, his grip on my hip tightening.

My body freezes with nerves, and Eli senses it right away. He lifts his head to look at me.

"We don't have to. But I think you'll like it."

If he's anywhere near as talented with his tongue as he is with his fingers, I don't think 'like' will be a strong enough word.

But still, I'm nervous. It's something I've never done before, and it's a vulnerable position. Honestly, I wish I were a few drinks in right now so I could turn my brain off and let loose because I want to do this, I do.

"I want to," I shyly tell him before my mind can overthink anymore.

His concerned expression quickly softens then turns dark as the devilish grin rises on one side of his lips. Goddamn, he looks so hot right now, and sexy, and wicked. The fact that he's this excited to go down on me, I can almost guarantee that he's going to be good at it.

Eli pulls himself off of me as he sits back on his knees between my legs. His hands caress my body until they find their way to the top of my pants. Licking his lips, he bites down on the bottom one as he pulls down my tight leggings, leaving my panties in place.

Arching my back, I lift my ass as he tugs them down. Once they're off, I bend my knees and close my legs, leaning them against the bed. When he spots this, Eli can't help but let out a sinister little laugh. His large hands caress my lower legs, taking their time as they travel up. When he reaches my knees, he gently opens them, placing one of my legs on either side of him. He palms each of my thighs, running his hands down, closer and closer to my favorite spot.

I'm already warm with anticipation when his thumb grazes against my clit. And even though I still have my panties on, I'm so turned on and sensitive right now that it causes me to throw my head back against the mattress and push myself into his hand.

"You're fucking soaked already, baby," Eli groans.

Well, no, duh. Eli can walk into a room, and I'll be fucking dripping for him.

He climbs back on top of me, his mouth finding mine. Our tongues dance together as my wet panties jerk up into him.

"Too many clothes," I say into his mouth as my hands fumble with his jeans.

Eli arrogantly chuckles as he gets off the bed, finally undressing a bit more.

As he does, I look over to the mirror over his dresser. It's perfectly positioned that I can see myself sunken into his bed. I almost don't even recognize the girl looking back at me. But, that's my face, that's my body, and that's my red hair. I look different, though. My cheeks are flushed, and my chest is pink from Eli's sweet assault. My black bra is pushing my chest up, causing my girls to look bigger, and my smooth hair is running wild over the pillow below me.

I look better, though. I look more confident, maybe even sexier. I look on the outside, how I feel on the inside when I'm with Eli.

"Admiring yourself?" Eli asks with a sly grin as he catches me staring at the mirror.

I don't respond but continue to watch my cheeks deepen in color.

"You should be. You're fucking gorgeous, Logan." He climbs on top of me wearing only his boxer briefs.

They're plenty tight that I can see just how turned on Eli is right now.

He kisses my jaw, down my neck, and over my chest. He quickly unfastens my bra, pulling it down to reveal my breasts. I watch it all in the mirror, and the picture I see looking back at me, with Eli on top of my body, is even better now.

Eli's warm mouth surrounds my taut nipple as he flicks and teases it with his tongue, giving me a taste of what's to come.

His lips continue their path down my body as they take their time, killing me with anticipation. He peppers my abdomen with kisses before his lips linger just above my panties. My stomach tightens as his warm breath swirls over me.

"I'm going to make you feel so good, baby," Eli whispers in the sexiest of tones.

Oh, I have no doubt.

His words alone make me whimper as Eli's smirking lips linger above the apex of my thighs.

His face is right above my core, but still he continues with his slow torture. Bending my legs on either side of his face, he teases me with wet leisurely kisses on the inside of my thigh. He takes his time, being sure to continue slowly killing me as he does.

"Eli," I beg as his wicked smirk makes another appearance, grazing against the soft skin of my leg.

He stands at the foot of the bed and pulls me closer to the edge. His long fingers slip into my panties at the hip, swiftly and gracefully pulling them off me. The cool air hits me as my naked body lies on full display for him to see. His lips are parted, and his pupils are dilated as he stares down at me. My legs stay open, causing his eyes to darken and hood as he takes me in.

I thought I would feel uncomfortable, being fully exposed like this, but the way Eli is looking down at me like I'm the most delicious thing he's ever seen, it's hard not to feel good.

"You're fucking perfect, Logan," he says on an exhale before he licks his lips. He looks so dark and sexy right now. He looks like he's about to devour me.

His fingers find me first as they glide over my sensitive spot, causing my eyes to close in pleasure. When I open them again, I watch as Eli's wet fingers find their way to his mouth, tasting me on one hand as he touches himself with the other, all while his brown eyes stay locked on mine.

Holy shit. This is the hottest thing I've ever seen. Eli looks like pure sex, and I'm tempted to tell him to just take off his briefs and fuck me right now.

He gets on his knees, keeping eye contact with me. Bending my legs, he hooks his arms around my thighs and pulls me closer to his face. His thumb teases my clit, and my mouth falls open as I watch him.

Suddenly, Eli's warm and skillful tongue presses down on my center, and every nerve in my body fires at once.

"*Oh my god,*" I moan much too loudly as my head falls back to the mattress, but I have no control over any part of my body right now, so I can't help the volume.

His talented tongue flicks and laps and teases as my mouth gapes open, my eyes screwing shut.

How does he feel this good? I feel like I'm having an out of body experience. This is incredible.

Eli's warm mouth continues its welcome assault as I moan his name. It causes him to groan against me, and holy shit, the vibration from his lips is out of this world.

I look down at him between my legs and holy hell, it's the most fantastic view. His shaggy brown hair falls over his eyes as his expert tongue continues to work its way closer to my orgasm.

When Eli looks up to me through dark hooded eyes, I almost lose it right there.

His hand finds its way to my breasts as he pinches my overly sensitive nipple. The combination of his movements sends me into overdrive as my head falls back against the mattress, arching myself into his mouth, begging for more.

"Do you like that, baby?"

I can't respond because I have no words, but he takes my silence as a yes.

Eli's tongue quickens its pace as it flicks over my clit. The hand that was on my chest is no longer there as Eli's fingers tease me along with his mouth. The combination is about to send me over the edge.

Suddenly I feel a sharp pinch when Eli's finger slides inside of me, causing my body to uncomfortably jerk.

"You okay, Logan? Do you want me to stop?" He pauses to look up at me.

I let myself adjust for a moment as the dull pain disappears. Instead of saying anything, I push Eli by his shaggy hair back down to continue his mouth's magic.

He chuckles against me before he sucks my clit and pumps his finger inside of me.

Holy fuck.

Gripping the sheets in my white knuckles, my moans and pants become louder and louder. I want to scream because something needs to release, but Eli and I aren't alone in the house.

"*Eli,*" I cry out as my body jerks and arches, twisting and tightening, unable to control my volume.

I feel his satisfied lips smirk against me from hearing his name leave my mouth as I beg him for more.

I'm so close, and Eli can tell. His movements are becoming quicker and firmer. His finger is moving inside of me at the perfect tempo, matching the pace with his tongue.

Looking into the mirror again, I watch as Eli ravishes my body. I tug at his shaggy hair as he unravels me with his tongue. Every muscle in my body contracts at once as my vision blurs, and my head falls back as I experience the most insane orgasm I've ever had.

I ride out my high as Eli's tongue and fingers continue their movements. My orgasm feels like it might go on forever, but eventually, my heavy breathing begins to slow. My skin is hot from my head to my toes as I start to come off my high. My body is limp, absolutely lifeless after that orgasm ripped through me. I lie there, sated, as Eli climbs onto the bed next to my naked body, his lips glistening with my arousal.

"New favorite flavor," he says before he licks them clean.

Chapter 65

Eli

I fucking love waking up to this girl. Especially when she's sleeping naked, sprawled on top of my body like she is today. She could barely even form a sentence last night when she got up to walk to the kitchen, needing some water, after I made her come two more times with my tongue. I use the term 'walking' loosely. She had trouble with that too.

I love seeing her that way. I love watching her come undone from my touch. What only I can do to her. Mostly though, I just love her, but I haven't told her yet.

I opened my eyes about ten minutes ago, but I haven't moved yet. I didn't want to wake Logan. Her dark red hair is messily spread across my chest, and her face is buried in my neck. Her toned body is on top of mine, keeping me warm and a little turned on.

"Hi," she lazily whispers into my nape.

A smile forms on my lips from hearing her voice, realizing she's awake. "Hi. How did you sleep?"

"Mmm," she hums, content.

Chuckling, I turn to kiss her forehead, running my hands down the length of her back and over her bare ass, holding it in my hands. "Ready for coffee?"

"Can't talk. Can't walk," Logan mumbles.

I laugh again, flipping her naked body over so she's lying on her back.

"I'll go make you some," I tell her with a smile, hovering over her before leaning in and kissing her tattooed collarbone.

Regretfully peeling myself off of her, I slip on a pair of sweats over my briefs, skipping the need for a shirt. Before I leave, I turn back to get one last glimpse of my sleepy girl. Plush pillows and blankets surround her, but the only thing covering her is a thin white sheet, draping her lower half. Her perky tits are out on full display, and her hair is running wild around her. She looks fucking perfect right now as I click a mental image and store it in my mind for forever.

"Maddison," Ali says to greet me as she walks into the kitchen behind me.

"Bertoli."

"Last name, huh?" She takes a seat at the kitchen island.

I make my way to the coffee maker, turning on the magic machine.

"You call me by mine. I thought it only fair to call you by yours."

"Well, I'm not gonna call you 'EJ,' and we both know you like that Logan is the only one who calls you 'Eli.'"

I give her a shrug. "Touché."

"So even though we are kinda-sorta friends now, I'm still gonna call you 'Maddison.'"

"Aww, Ali," I say in my highest of tones. "I think we are kinda-sorta friends now too," I tease, causing her to roll her eyes at me.

Grabbing the creamer from the fridge, I put a splash in Logan's coffee. She hates the bitterness of black coffee, but that's the only way I'll drink it.

"So, are you going to make me some of those pancakes you made for Logan yesterday?" Ali asks from her seat at the island.

"Absolutely not."

"What the hell? I thought we were kinda-sorta friends now?"

"Yeah, and I don't make breakfast for my kinda-sorta friends."

"No, you just make breakfast for pretty little things you're in *love* with," she says, dragging out the word, teasing me, and stopping me in my tracks.

"Whoa, what?" I ask, taken aback.

"What?"

"Who said I was in love with Logan?" I ask in an almost whisper. "Did Marc say something?"

"How am I the smartest *and* the funniest in our friend group? Seriously, I can't do everything around here."

I stay silent, waiting for her to answer me.

Ali rolls her eyes. "No, you caveman. No one said anything. But you're pretty obvious. It's been apparent for a while. What I don't get is why you haven't told Logan yet."

It's not that Ali is wrong. In fact, she's one hundred percent correct that I'm in love with Logan. But still, I want Logan to be the first to hear the words from me.

"Has she said something about it?" I ask, my voice even quieter, hoping Logan can't hear me from my room upstairs.

"I'm not saying a word." She holds her hands up in defense. "Even though you and I are kinda-sorta friends now, she's still my girl, so I'll pick her over you every time. Sorry, Maddison." She shrugs, not seeming all that sorry, which makes me laugh.

"I actually really appreciate that about you, Ali. I've never told you that, but I'm glad Logan has you."

"Maddison, are you getting soft on me?" she asks, giving me shit.

I scoff. "Fuck no."

She gives me a knowing smile. "I'm glad she has you too."

I hold out my fist across the kitchen island as Ali connects hers with it.

"Honestly, thank god that Logan and Marc have the two of us. They're too sweet sometimes," she says.

"Damn straight. And thank god they're as nice as they are. Could you imagine four of *us*?" I motion between her and me. I know I can be an asshole, and Ali is as fiery as it gets.

"Oh, hell no!" Ali says with a laugh, shaking her head.

Ali has been growing on me more and more, and I've been finding myself hoping that something truly is going on between her and Marc. She's feisty as hell, and Marc needs someone like her to have his back. He's too good of a person sometimes and needs someone to defend him the way Ali does for Logan.

"So, you gonna tell me what's going on with you and my brother, or what?" I blatantly ask before turning around to put the creamer back in the fridge.

"What are you talking about?" Ali asks as her olive-toned face pales.

"You know what I'm talking about." I lean down on the kitchen island across from her, resting on my elbows.

"Did Marc say something?" she quietly asks, worried.

"I'm not saying a word. Even though you and I are kinda-sorta friends, he's still my brother, so I'll pick him over you every time," I repeat her exact words in an obnoxious tone, giving her a hard time the same way she did me.

"You asshole." She tries to hold back her laughter but fails miserably.

"Good morning, my friend!" my beautiful girl says as she makes her way into the kitchen, looking all cute and worn out from last night.

Logan wraps her arms around her tiny friend's shoulders, hugging her, all while keeping her soft gaze on me.

My needy ass clears my throat, needing some attention.

Ali rolls her eyes. "You guys did plenty of *hugging* last night, I'm sure." She's sure to use air quotes around the word 'hugging,' as Logan makes her way around the island to me.

"Morning, baby," Logan says sweetly, wrapping her arms around me, and leaning her warm cheek against my bare back.

I hold onto her arms with mine, reinforcing her grasp on me. I fucking love when she hugs me like this. Even though I'm 6'4" and will quite literally never feel small, this makes me feel taken care of and oddly protected. I totally get why girls like to be the little spoon.

"I was going to bring you coffee in bed." I look over my shoulder as she keeps her arms wrapped around my waist.

"Well, I heard voices, so I decided to come down."

"What did you hear?" I ask as my heart begins to race, recalling my earlier conversation with Ali about me being in love with Logan.

"Um. Nothing. Just voices." Logan eyes me, seeming all sorts of confused.

Taking a deep sigh of relief, I turn and pull Logan into my arms, pressing her chest tightly to mine before I bend down and place my lips on hers.

"I like that shirt on you," I tell her as I let my eyes wander over her frame. She's wearing my shirt this morning, the one I left on the floor from last night. I love the way she looks in my clothes. She always looks better than I do. Logan doesn't say anything. She just stares into my eyes with a sweet little smile on her lips.

"Man, you guys are going to have the prettiest babies," Ali chimes in from across the island.

"Okay, Ali. Slow down," Logan quickly says, releasing from her grip and leaning down on the island next to me.

"Tell me I'm wrong," Ali adds in a knowing tone, tilting her head to the side.

"We would have pretty babies, baby." I move behind Logan, pulling her into my chest. Crossing my arms around the front of her shoulders, I place my chin on the top of her head.

"Can we talk about something else, please?" Logan begs, seeming exceptionally uncomfortable with this topic of conversation.

"Yeah, sure. Maddison was just telling me how he was going to make pancakes for us again today." Ali lips turn up with mischief.

I narrow my eyes, shaking my head at her, and knowing exactly what she's trying to do.

"Really?" Logan asks with bright eyes, turning her head to look up at me, hopeful.

I could never say no to this pretty green-eyed girl, and Ali fucking knows it. "If you want them," I tell Logan, looking down at her sweet face.

"Yes, please," she says with an eager smile. "Ali, just wait until you try these. They're so good."

"Mmm, can't wait." Ali's tone is all smug as she looks directly at me.

"You're evil."

"Never said I wasn't."

Chapter 66

Logan

Midterms kicked my ass this week. I don't think I've ever consumed so much caffeine in my life, and that's saying a lot. I think I did okay on my tests. I kept my head down and studied all week. I missed Eli, that's for sure, but I made a promise to myself that my education would be my priority right now. Eli was great, and he understood. In fact, he was my biggest cheerleader all week. He made it a point not to come around if he knew I was studying, which was hard for both of us but also really sweet of him.

However, he did come over just to sleep next to me most nights. When I was ready for bed, he would come by late, then walk me to my first class each morning. One night, I needed to pull an all-nighter, and Eli stayed awake with me most of the night, quizzing me with the flashcards I had made.

He's the best and made sure to prove that his attitude last weekend was a one-off.

Now that midterms are behind me, I'm looking forward to letting loose this weekend. The fact that I'm excited about having a few drinks tonight should tell you exactly how stressed out this week made me.

I slept in today, and Eli left for pregame morning skate before I was awake, but he left a note for me that he was excited I'd be coming to watch his game. I was hoping that his parents would be back in town, but his dad got pulled away for work last minute, and Mary doesn't like to leave Jack behind.

My lazy ass is still lying in bed on this late Saturday morning, trying to get as much rest as I can before the Halloween party tonight. As I'm mindlessly scrolling my phone, I hear a knock at the door, and it opens before I can respond.

"You're still in bed?" Eli laughs as his eyes find me between my sheets. "Hi, baby." He walks into my room, his hands hidden behind his back.

I would respond if I could, but I can't. Eli looks so fucking good right now that he's left me speechless. He's wearing a dark hunter green, almost black suit. It's perfectly fitted for his tall frame, with a crisp white shirt underneath. He has a skinny black tie around his neck, and his shoes and belt match perfectly. His shaggy brown hair is pushed away from his face, thanks to a little hair product.

This is the first time I've seen Eli in a tie before because, quite honestly, he doesn't need one. He's pretty effortlessly polished as is. However, he looks incredibly sexy with that tie around his neck.

How this beautiful man is mine is beyond me.

"Earth to Logan," Eli says with amusement, pulling me out of my daze.

"Hi," I say in response when my brain and mouth finally decide to connect.

I cross my legs at the ankles, under the sheets, trying to calm the effects this man has on my body.

"What are you doing here?" I sit up, leaning my back against my headboard. "Shouldn't you be at the rink?"

"I'm on my way, but I wanted to stop by first. We got our new jerseys this morning." He makes his way over to my bed, his hands still concealed behind him. "You don't have to wear it." He pulls the maroon fabric from behind his back as he takes a seat. "But I've never had someone I could give my away jersey to. It's kind of a girlfriend thing that some of the guys have done over the years." Eli shyly holds the jersey in his lap.

Okay, this is cute. Eli looks so nervous right now, but I have no idea why. Of course, I'm going to wear it. I didn't even know this was a thing, but I love that it is. I felt guilty that I still didn't have any team gear to support Eli, so I went to the school store this week and bought a mustard yellow beanie with a maroon 'M' on the front and a matching pom-pom ball on top. But this, this is so much better.

"You don't have to wear it," Eli repeats when I don't respond.

"Of course, I'm going to wear it," I tell him with excitement as Eli's nervous expression instantly washes away. "I love this."

Taking the jersey from his lap, I hold it up. It's absolutely massive, unsurprisingly so, but I don't care. Even if this thing is practically a dress on me, I'm going to wear it with pride.

My hand grazes over his stitched name at the top of the back side, then over his captain's patch on the left shoulder. This jersey is such nice quality. Even though most of the arena will be filled with number thirteen jerseys, it's pretty evident that this one is the real deal.

"Thanks, baby."

"Thank *you*," he says. "I might actually have a decent game knowing you're watching me and wearing my clothes," he adds with a sly little grin.

He leans across the space between us, pressing his full lips to mine.

"You'll come see me in the player's tunnel after?"

"Sure, if you want me to be there."

"Logan, when are you going to figure out that I *always* want you to be there?" he asks with a sweet little heartfelt smile on his lips. "Need. I think 'need' is a better word. I need you. Always."

Leaning over, I wrap my arms around my needy boy's neck, looking him in the eyes.

"I need you too, baby," I begin, reassuring him. "And I love when you're all soft and sweet like this, but I'm going to need you to flip the switch and turn into hard ass Eli now. You have a game you need to go out and win."

The wicked smirk begins to form on Eli's lips. "Yes, ma'am."

I press my mouth to his, exploring him, needing him. He cups the sides of my face with his large, strong hands as his full and pouty lips find mine.

Needing to get to the rink, he stands from my bed, kissing my forehead as he does.

I slap his ass when he turns to leave. "Now go kick some ass, thirteen!" I yell with enthusiasm.

His head falls back, and his deep chuckle radiates throughout my room as he makes his way to my door.

"I lo—" he begins. "Later. I'll see you later," he says, correcting himself as he hurries out the door.

"Look at you!" Marc says, impressed, as I walk up to him in front of the hockey arena.

I give him a little twirl, showing off my team-spirited outfit. I wasn't sure how to make this jersey look good since it's about double my size in order to fit over Eli's pads when he plays, but I don't care. I might be drowning in this right now, but I love it. I'm wearing a black hoodie with black leggings and my black Adidas on my feet. I slipped the hood through his jersey, and added my new beanie on top with my curled hair draping down around my shoulders.

"Doesn't she look great?" Ali asks in encouragement as she walks up behind me. She looks great too, wearing a Golden Gophers' tee under her black leather jacket with a pair of sleek blue jeans and her signature Doc Martens. She might not like sports, but she's still down to support Marc's brother and my boyfriend.

The arena is packed, unsurprisingly so, but Eli already has his allocation of seats for players' families reserved for us since it's the first game of the regular season, so we didn't have to worry about getting there early this time. The teams are already both on the ice, warming up when we walk in.

Once again, the stadium is full of maroons and golds, but there are quite a few more spots of green from the Michigan State fans than I expected.

We dip through the crowd as I follow closely behind Ali, who is trailing Marc. He takes us all the way down to the acrylic glass encasing the rink on Minnesota's side of the ice. Eli's family seats must be in a prime location if we are going all the way down to ice-level. I keep my head down, bobbing and weaving through the crowd as I walk behind my friends.

Suddenly a loud bang shakes me and I snap my head up, startled. Eli's smug little smirk is waiting on the other side of the barrier that he just purposefully smacked into to scare me.

"Hi, babe!" he yells, projecting through the glass. "You look hot!"

Eli looks just as hot wearing the same jersey as me, except he's in the home version in yellow, and it's filled out with his pads. His eyes are bright but calm as he holds his gaze with mine.

"You scared the shit out of me!" I tell him with a smile, holding my hand across my chest.

"Hey, Logan!" Cam says with excitement, skating up behind Eli, wearing the assistant captain's 'A' patch on his left shoulder.

"Logan!" Goody calls out, dragging out my name as he barrels into both Cam and Eli, not slowing down. He throws an arm over both his teammates' shoulders as he gives me a kind grin through the glass. "Oh! You're wearing the *girlfriend* jersey," he adds in a knowing tone, giving his captain shit.

"Get outta here," Eli tells him with amusement as he playfully throws Goody's arm off of his shoulder.

"Oh, Logan. Baby," Goody says to Cam in a mocking voice. He grabs Cam on either side of his helmet as he begins to pull him closer. Cam catches on, realizing that Goody is pretending to be Eli and me as he puts his hands on either side of Goody's face looking like they're pulling each other in for a kiss.

"Go fucking warm up." Eli pushes them both towards the rest of the team. He's trying to hold back his amusement, but the corners of his lips are turning up from his buddies giving him a hard time about me.

"I'm gonna score a goal for you," Eli says as he returns his attention to me through the glass.

"How many?" I smugly ask.

"How many you want?" He raises an eyebrow, surprised.

Instead of words, I hold up two fingers. Eli could honestly ride the bench all day, not playing a single minute, and I'll be just as excited to be here and support him; I really don't care if he scores, but this is a fun little game to play with him.

Eli's cocky smirk makes its timely appearance. He can be a conceited little punk sometimes, which, to be honest, I love, especially when it comes to hockey. He is so good, and sometimes he doubts his abilities, so when he gets cocky about his talent, it just reminds me that he knows how great he truly is.

"I'll get you three," he arrogantly says with a devilish little grin.

Eli looks at me, his expression changing to soft and sweet, as he puts his gloved hand up on the glass as if he wished he could touch me through it. I quickly return the gesture, holding my hand up on the other side of the barrier, before he turns and skates to join the rest of his team in warm-ups, gliding smoothly along the ice.

Once again, I can't believe that man is mine.

When I look back for Marc and Ali, I find quite a few fan's eyes on me. I still don't love the attention, but I also don't know if I care all that much anymore.

Ali waves me over to our seats, which are right up on the glass, directly behind the Minnesota bench.

"Holy shit! These seats." I turn to Marc, settling in between my two friends.

"Right? The players get to pick their families' seats for the season, and Eli always gets first choice," Marc informs me. "He usually just gets three for my parents and me, but he made sure to reserve a fourth for you this year."

My heart does that flutter thing from Marc's words as he explains why the seat next to Ali is unoccupied today.

"How is Michigan State?" I ask.

"They're good, but we should still win this one."

I did a little research this week about Eli's conference. Minnesota is really the best among them, with Ohio State coming in at a close second. Minnesota should be able to make it through the league without too much trouble from the other teams.

"Go get 'em, EJ!" Marc yells through the glass.

"Let's go, babe!" I project as Eli skates away from the bench to the center of the rink for the opening face-off.

"Sports!" Ali chimes in.

About halfway through the first period, Eli scores, making it 1-0 in Minnesota's favor. It's a beautiful shorthanded goal, and the crowd erupts when the puck hits the back of the net. The cheers for my boyfriend radiate throughout the arena as Eli skates by the bench, giving fist bumps to his teammates.

"Nice goal, thirteen!" Marc yells to his brother as Eli takes a seat on the bench directly in front of us.

Eli doesn't turn around, understandably so, but he holds up a single index finger so that I can see through the glass, making me laugh.

"What's that about?" Ali asks, nodding in Eli's direction.

"Eli promised me some goals, so he's keeping track apparently." I try to hold back my amused smile.

"How many is he going for?" Marc asks.

"Three." A laugh slips from my lips.

Marc can't help but join in. "That arrogant asshole. He promised you a hat trick?"

“You don’t think he will do it?” To be honest, a hat trick is a little insane to promise. One goal, I get it. Two, okay, maybe because he’s Eli, but three? That’s a big ask.

“Oh, no. He will do it,” Marc states. “The guy is nothing if not determined.”

Eli’s second goal comes just minutes later when a shot from the blue line bounces off the Michigan State goalie, and Eli is there to clean up the rebound, tucking the puck into the back of the net. When he makes his way back to the bench, he once again keeps his back to us as he holds up two fingers, reminding me that he’s only one goal away from his promise of a hat trick.

Marc, Ali, and I can’t help but laugh. Honestly, this game between Eli and me is almost more entertaining than the actual hockey game going on right now.

In the second period, Eli goes scoreless. Though, his team is up 3-1 already. During the third period, Eli takes every opportunity he has to score. He hits the goal post twice, plus the goalie has a fantastic save against him.

I can tell that Eli is starting to get frustrated as time is beginning to wind down on the clock. He really doesn’t have to score, his team is up 4-2 at this point, but Eli is determined to get the hat trick he promised.

“It’s not gonna happen,” Ali says as the game clock continues to wind down.

With just under three minutes left, Eli has a one-on-one breakaway and gets tangled up with a Michigan State defenseman. The player in green falls to the ice as Eli shoots towards the empty net. Michigan has already pulled their goalie, hoping to have a man advantage on offense, but before the puck slides into the vacant goal, the referee blows the whistle and calls a penalty.

“Tripping. Number thirteen. Minnesota,” the referee clearly states as he ushers Eli to the penalty box to serve the two-minute sentence.

"Bullshit!" Marc yells as he stands from his seat.

"Terrible call!" I shout, standing next to him.

The crowd around us stares, a bit confused as to why we are so upset when we are clearly about to win the game with ease. Honestly, this penalty doesn't mean anything for the home team, but I really want Eli to get his third goal.

Looking across the ice to Eli, sitting in the penalty box, he shakes his head and laughs at Marc's and my evident frustration at the meaningless call.

With three minutes left, and Eli serving two of those in the penalty box, our little hat trick goal is almost guaranteed not to happen.

Eli stands in the box as the last ten seconds of his penalty wind down. Patrick steals the puck from one of the Michigan State forwards and passes it up the ice, perfectly timed for when Eli gets released from the box. Eli maneuvers the puck down the rink, using his speed to beat the lone Michigan defenseman, and takes a shot on the empty net with twenty seconds left of the game.

In true Eli Maddison fashion, he fucking scores.

The three of us jump up from our seats, screaming and cheering for my man. The crowd erupts with 'Maddison' chants as hats begin to fly onto the ice. Apparently, when a player gets a hat trick, you throw your hat onto the ice in celebration. Eli gets pounded into the boards with hockey hugs before he skates back over to the bench.

On his way, he grabs one of the hundred or so hats lying on the ice. Bobbing and weaving past his teammates, he makes his way to the back of the bench and taps the glass in front of me with his stick. He tosses the hat over the glass, and it lands perfectly in my lap. When I look back up to Eli, he wearing the most arrogant smirk across his lips.

Minnesota wins 5-2.

"Why the hell haven't you boned that yet?" Ali asks quietly, in reference to Eli.

"Great question," I tell her as I watch my stud of a man skate off into the locker room. At this point, I don't know what I'm waiting for. I love the guy, and he's basically dripping with sex, so the fact that I've held off for this long is a bit baffling.

The crowd outside of the locker room is smaller than it was last time. There aren't as many students here, which I'm assuming is because almost everyone who would be down here is back in their rooms getting ready for tonight's Halloween party.

Still, I don't feel too comfortable bombarding Eli the second he emerges, so I stay towards the back, where I was standing last time. Marc doesn't ask questions. He and Ali just stand with me. I think he knows by now that I don't love the attention or looks I've received from Eli's fans, especially the girls, once people learned that I was his girlfriend.

When Eli comes out of the locker room, all freshly showered, he doesn't even scan the crowd. He just looks up the hall, exactly where I was last time, and as his eyes lock with mine, a peaceful smile takes over his face.

He looks so good right now with his white collared shirt unbuttoned at the top, and his sleeves rolled up a few times, showing off his tattooed forearm. His suit pants are hanging low on his hips, and his hunter green suit jacket is slung over his shoulder. His hair is still wet from the shower, so the shaggy parts are pushed away from his face. He looks incredibly sexy and effortless with one hand casually tucked in his pocket as he walks my way.

He doesn't even look like he just played a grueling sixty minutes of hockey. To be honest, he looks like a model walking a fucking runway as he makes his way towards me.

"*Fuck me*," I say to myself.

"I think that's what he's trying to do," Ali laughs.

Okay, maybe I didn't say that to myself, but thankfully I said it quietly enough that Marc didn't hear.

"Hi baby," Eli says with a smile as he leans down to place his warm lips on mine. "I like that jersey on you."

"Nice game, bro," Marc says as he and Eli share a quick hug.

"Thanks, man."

Eli wraps his tattooed arm around my shoulders, pulling me into his body before kissing the top of my head.

"Good job out there," I add as my hand glides down from his lower back to his ass, giving it a little tap.

"Thank you. Was three goals enough for you?"

"Eh, four would've been nice." Eli smiles down at me, pulling me in tighter to his chiseled body.

"I'll work on that," he says, bantering back with me. "You guys coming over now or what?"

"Nope," Ali says quickly. "We have to go back to the dorms and get ready."

"So, what is Ali dressing you up as?" Eli asks, looking down at me.

"I don't know. She won't tell me."

"Nope, and I'm not telling you either, Maddison. It's a surprise."

"A terrifying surprise," I chime in, under my breath.

"Marc, are you coming over now, man?" Eli asks his brother.

"I gotta grab my costume, so I'll just come with the girls when they're ready."

"Bring an overnight bag," Eli says, directing his attention back to me. "I want you to stay over."

I nod my head as the smile on my lips grows, thinking about getting to stay at Eli's house again tonight. I like staying there with him, in the space no one else has ever been privy to before. But, to be honest, the party itself is a little nerve-wracking. The last time I went to a party at the hockey house, Alyssa was a bitch to me, and later, Eli took her upstairs before he came to his senses. Not to mention, the house will be littered with people who cause Eli's anxiety to spike without even realizing it. We don't have much of a track record for parties together, but we are 0-1 so far. Though, I would like to think our communication is much better at this point that we could handle a party as a couple.

I guess we will find out tonight.

Chapter 67

Eli

As I make my way downstairs, I find that the house is the most packed it's been all year, unsurprisingly so. We throw the best parties on campus, but our Halloween parties are legendary. Students from other schools make the drive just to attend the annual event.

The team cleared out the living room last night to make room for the makeshift dance floor, and we had the freshmen set up the DJ booth this morning. The house has been bumping with music for a while already, and the kitchen is overflowing with booze ready to consume.

Behind the costumes, I recognize the regulars. Plenty of the same girls who frequent the house are here, but there are a lot of new faces, too. Girls from other schools, I would assume. They're all dressed in little to nothing. Some are Playboy bunnies and others are naughty schoolgirls, mostly the cliche "sexy" Halloween costumes, but I could not give a fuck about a single one of them. The only one I care to spend time with tonight is my pretty girl with dark red hair, so if she could get here soon, that'd be great.

"A fucking hat trick?" a guy from behind me asks. "Are you just trying to make everyone else look bad?"

I'd recognize that voice anywhere.

"Jay, what's up, man?" I turn to face my old mentor, connecting my fist with his. "I didn't know you were coming."

"No way in hell am I missing the Halloween party or your home opener. And besides, you owe me big time for bailing on alumni weekend. I don't know what the fuck that was about, but I haven't forgotten about it."

The last time I saw Jay was the night that I was supposed to meet up with Logan to work on our creative writing paper, and he kept me here for hours on end. Then the next night, I bailed on the alumni party to hang out with my girl in her room after our night at the pond. That's still one of the best nights of my life, so I could give a fuck if my lack of presence hurt Jay's feelings.

"So, let's go. The least you could do is pour me a drink." Jay nods towards the kitchen, but I don't move from my spot at the base of the stairs with a perfect sightline to the front door.

"Don't tell me you're not drinking," he says in an accusatory tone when I don't respond or follow him.

"I am, probably. But I'm just going to wait a bit."

"Wait for what?" He looks at me, utterly lost and confused.

Wait for Logan, but I'm not going to tell him that. "Just seeing how the night plays out," I say instead.

"I don't know what the fuck has gotten into you, Maddison, but I think you need to get laid or something."

Well, that doesn't sound half bad, but I'm waiting for Logan to tell me she's ready.

"Whoa..." he begins but can't seem to finish his sentence with his mouth gaped open. I follow his line of sight, and I'm pretty sure my heart stops beating for a second.

I watch as Logan walks through my front door looking like an absolute snack, my eyes trailing her body as I take her in. She looks insane tonight in the best way possible. Her burgundy hair is offset by the green of her outfit. She's wearing a tight green corset type thing causing her perky tits to be even more noticeable and full, and her tiny little skirt is barely covering her round ass. Her whole outfit is laced in ivy, and the dark green fishnets look sinfully delicious as they grace her toned legs. She's got a bit more ivy wrapped around her neck and even more in her dark red hair.

Judging by Ali being dressed in a full black latex outfit with cat ears next to her, it's evident that Logan is Poison Ivy from *Batman*. And my little villain looks wicked and sinfully sexy.

I would assume that some guys wouldn't love if their girl were dressed to impress with their body exposed like Logan's is tonight, but I can basically kick anyone's ass here if I need to, and I love that Logan feels confident enough to dress up like this. Plus, she's typically so understated with her tomboy edge, so I'm enjoying seeing this other side of her.

"Dibs," a voice says, pulling me out of my heavenly daze.

"What?"

"Dibs on that fiery one right there." Jay nods towards Logan.

"What? No. Fuck no," I state with urgency.

"You guys hook up? You've never cared about sharing before."

"No. No-no. It's not like that with her. Logan is...she's my girlfriend. Stay away from her."

"Excuse me?" he asks, completely shocked. "Girlfriend? You have a fucking girlfriend?"

I don't respond because he already heard me.

"It's all starting to make sense." He lets out an evil laugh, shaking his head. "You're a fucking idiot, man."

"Why?"

"Because you're trying to make it in the NHL. Don't kid yourself. You know she's a distraction."

"She's not, actually. At all. You don't know what you're talking about." Jay has no idea about my panic attacks or how much Logan has calmed me since I met her, and he doesn't need to be privileged to that information.

"It's a bad idea," he says, continuing to shake his head in disapproval. "Why would you risk everything when you're so close? Does she have a magic pussy or something?"

"Watch your fucking mouth," I growl in warning, anger clear on my face.

"Sensitive, are we?"

"I'm serious, Jay. Don't fucking talk about her like that."

I take off towards my girl without saying another word, shaking my head. Talking about the NHL with Jay is causing my anxiety to seep in, and that's the last thing I need tonight. What I need is Logan, and not just because she calms me down, but because I love her and she looks like a fucking dessert I want to devour tonight.

"Maddison, c'mon!" Jay calls out as I walk away from him.

Logan's eyes connect with mine, instantly soothing me as I make it to the entryway.

"Damn, baby." I grab her hand and hold it above her head, twirling her in a circle and giving me the full effect. "You might need to give me mouth to mouth. I think I need to be resuscitated."

"Stop," she says with an embarrassed laugh, looking down at her devilishly sexy costume. "You don't think it's too much?"

"Logan, you look so fucking good," I reassure her with wide eyes and a parched mouth. "I might need to fight a few people off if they don't keep their eyes off my girl, but it'll be worth it."

Her nervous smile fades as I cup the sides of her face and let my fingers burrow into her silky hair. Pulling her lips to mine, I close my eyes and let my mouth explore hers, forgetting for a moment that we are in a crowded room filled with people.

Pulling Logan into my body with an arm draped over her shoulder, she wraps both her arms around my waist. "Nice work, Ali." I hold my other hand out as Ali connects her fist with mine.

"You're welcome," Ali proudly says. "I've always wanted a friend with red hair so I could live out my Catwoman and Poison Ivy dreams."

"Which is the only reason you decided to talk to me in the hallway on move-in day," Logan jokes.

"Exactly," Ali sarcastically says before turning her attention back to me. "I wanted you and Marc to be Batman and Robin, but he vetoed that pretty quick."

"I'm finally free from having to do a couples' costume," Marc reminds us as he walks around from behind me. "So, there's no way in hell I was going to do a couples' costume with my brother."

"What the hell?" I ask with a laugh. "No," I add, unable to hold back my amusement as my body shakes with laughter looking at Marc's costume.

"Stop, baby." Logan playfully swats me in the chest. "Marc, don't listen to him. You look great. *Space Jam* was my favorite movie growing up."

"This is why you're my best friend, Logan. You actually have a sense of humor." Marc adjusts his bunny ears. It's not that I don't think his Tune Squad costume is funny. It's just that this is Marc's first Halloween being single, and I don't know how far bunny ears will take him in regard to getting a woman in bed tonight.

"It's funny, man. I like it. I just don't think bunny ears are going to get you laid, that's all."

"And the *Top Gun* flight suit that you've worn for the last four years is better?" he asks.

"It's worked all four of those years, if you know what I mean." I shoot him a suggestive glance.

"Okay, then," Logan says uncomfortably, releasing me from her grasp.

"Shit. Sorry, baby." I almost forgot that Logan was standing here, and I wasn't just shooting the shit with my brother.

"You're an idiot," Marc laughs as he shakes his head, walking past me towards the kitchen.

"I'm going to go put my bag in your room," Logan tells me as she holds up her overnight bag.

"I can run it up there."

"I'm good," she says bluntly. She walks past me towards the stairs to head up to my room, and I can't quite tell if I upset her by that stupid comment.

"Real smooth, Maddison. Real smooth," Ali says sarcastically, patting my arm like a good boy.

"Fuck you, Ali," I say with not enough bite in my tone to actually mean it as she lets out a cackle and follows Marc towards the kitchen.

I head towards the base of the stairs as I wait for Logan to come back down. The living room is mostly dark, besides the moving lights over the dance floor, and the music is almost deafening. There are so many people here that I'm squished pretty tight up against the stairwell, but I'm tall enough that I can see into the crowd.

Suddenly I feel the zipper on my costume get pulled down my chest, accompanied by a high-pitched voice saying, "Hey there, Maverick," in reference to my *Top Gun* flight suit.

"Alyssa. You've got to stop." Taking her hands off of me, I zip my costume back up.

"Why? I was just peeling this costume off you last year. Don't act like you don't remember." She cocks her head and bites her lip as if that's going to do anything for me.

"That was last year. Things are different now. I have a girlfriend, and you know that."

"Doesn't bother me," she shrugs. "I won't tell if you don't."

I shake my head and roll my eyes. "Alyssa, give it a rest." I keep my stare on her, hoping she sees just how serious I am.

"Hi, baby," Logan says, tucking herself under my arm and wrapping hers around my waist. I drape my hand over her shoulder as she keeps her gaze on me, trying to avoid looking at Alyssa.

"Oh great, it's the new girl," Alyssa adds in an uninterested tone.

I'm about to open my mouth and say something smart, but Logan beats me to it.

"My name is Logan. But you already know exactly who I am."

Shit. I like this feisty side of Logan. I've never seen it before.

"Try to remember my name the next time you attempt to get my boyfriend to sleep with you." Her words are sassy, but her smile is sweet as she leans further into my body.

My mouth gapes before the utterly impressed smile takes over my face.

"Let's go find Marc," Logan says, returning her attention to me as she pulls me down and kisses my lips. My hand intertwines with hers as I follow her to the kitchen, leaving a shocked Alyssa in our wake.

"Baby! That was fucking hot. I need to dress you up as a villain more often."

"I'm just tired of her trying to get with my man."

Pulling Logan back, I turn her to face me. "You know I would never—"

"I know. I trust you." Which makes me smile, that even with everything her ex put her through, and even me being a dumbass at the beginning of our relationship, she still trusts me.

"Well," I begin, pushing a stray stand of hair away from her face. "Territorial Logan might just be my new favorite version." A sly grin forms on my face before I bend down and place my lips on hers. "And what I said earlier, when I was joking with Marc, I'm sorry about that." I search her face, looking for any signs that she may be upset, but there aren't any.

"Don't worry about it, Eli. I'm not. Let's have fun." She wraps her arms around my neck while my hands find the small of her back, pulling her into me.

"Are you drinking tonight?" she asks.

"I was thinking about it. But I was waiting to see what your plan is for the night."

"We should get drunk together," she playfully suggests as the corners of her lips begin to turn up. "That could be fun."

I can't help but laugh at how excited she is for this. She doesn't let loose often, so this could be interesting. If the way she just stood up for herself against Alyssa is any indication of how this night will go, I'm all in.

"I'm down for that. I would love to see a drunk Logan."

"Well, you might be holding her hair back at the end of the night," she warns.

"Deal." I lean down and kiss her again. Taking her hand in mine, I lead her to the kitchen to find our friends and the booze.

"Damn, girl! Look at you!" Cam exclaims as we walk into the kitchen.

"Thanks, Cam. Good to see you," Logan says in response as Cam wraps her up in a hug. He shoots me a look, wiggling his eyebrows, while he has her in his embrace, trying to get under my skin. I know he's only kidding because he's told me how he likes Logan and me together, but still, with Logan looking like that tonight, I don't need anyone else touching her.

"Okay, okay." I break them up, only somewhat kidding.

The kitchen is packed, which isn't all that shocking. The alcohol is in here, so of course, it's going to pull the biggest crowd. Marc, Ali, and Cam are all standing around the kitchen island as Logan and I join them. Goody is here too, by the fridge, with a random chick under his arm, and my sophomore goalie, Benny, is looking a little lonely with a beer in his hand by the sink. Thankfully, I haven't seen Patrick yet tonight, but it's only a matter of time.

"Cheers, guys." Marc hands out the vodka shots he's poured.

"Benny, come have a shot with us," I call out, feeling bad that the kid is by himself.

Benny makes his way over to the island as Goody and the girl he's with join too. Another random chick has found her way here and is now pressed up to Cam as Marc pours a few more shots for our newcomers.

Between Logan and I, Marc and Ali, Goody and his girl, plus Cam and this new chick, everyone looks somewhat paired off besides Benny. Logan obviously notices as she keeps her stare on my goaltender before glancing back at me.

She quickly looks around the packed room. “Pour one more shot,” Logan tells Marc before taking off towards the other side of the kitchen.

I watch as she approaches a girl, standing by herself, dressed up as a fairy of some sort. The girl seems a bit shy and nervous as Logan begins to talk to her until, eventually, a smile takes over her face. My favorite girl is having a full-on conversation with this chick, and you can tell that the fairy is starting to warm to Logan. The girl nods her head, and Logan takes her by the hand as she brings her over to the island to join our group.

“Guys, this is Sarah. She’s a sophomore transfer, so she doesn’t know too many people yet, and she loves hockey,” Logan says as she introduces the girl.

“Sarah, these are a few guys from the team, and that’s Ali and Marc.” Logan points to the little New Yorker and my brother. Ali gives Sarah a small wave, and Marc nods towards her as Logan continues. “And this is Benny,” she says, taking her time. “He’s also a sophomore, and he’s the hockey team’s starting goalie.” All the dots begin to connect as to what she’s trying to do.

“Hey,” Benny says with an excited smile as he stands closer to Sarah.

“Hey,” Sarah responds with wide eyes, looking like she just met some sort of celebrity.

Logan makes her way back to me. Standing behind her, I pull her back into my chest and wrap my arms around her shoulders. “You’re the best,” I whisper into her ear, finishing it off with a kiss to her temple.

“Cheers,” Marc says again, now that all ten of us have a shot in our hands.

“What are we cheersing to?” Goody asks as we all hold our shot glasses up.

“Cheers to the nights we will never remember, with the friends we will never forget,” Cam says, trying not to laugh.

Everyone makes a face of confusion and mock disgust at Cam’s attempt at a heartfelt toast.

“Corny, dude,” I tell him.

“Hella cheesy,” Logan says.

“Lame, Cam,” Marc adds, shaking his head.

“Cheers to getting fucked up!” Cam says on his second attempt.

There are a few shouts and cheers before the ten of us down our first shot of the night.

Chapter 68

Eli

I lost track of the shots, beers, and mixed drinks over an hour ago. I'm plenty buzzed, and my girl is fairly drunk as I watch her dance with Ali in the middle of the dance floor. The room is dark, but the moving lights illuminate Logan's body just enough that I can watch her in all her glory. I'm posted up by the banister, leaning on the wall, with a beer in my hand, enjoying the show she's providing.

Logan is killing me right now, moving her body to the beat. Ali is an okay dancer, but Logan...Logan can fucking move. Her hips are swaying, and her hands are moving, feeling herself and the music. The fact that at one point I thought this girl was clumsy or uncoordinated is insane. Her body moves in perfect rhythm as she allows the music to take over.

I love seeing her this way. I love watching her feel free and confident without a care in the world.

She looks over to me with a little smile on her face as she continues to dance. Keeping my gaze on my girl, I bring my beer up to my lips, enjoying every second of this.

Suddenly, some dude dressed up like a dumb-ass pirate comes up behind Logan, putting his hands on her hips and pulling her into his body. I stand up straight, about to charge over to him, but Logan takes care of it herself. She removes his hands from her as she turns around to face him. Logan shakes her head as she says something to him, but he doesn't seem to want to listen as he continues to lean into her. Logan adds something else before pointing to me, and the guy's face pales when he glances in my direction.

Well, at least he's not a complete idiot.

The pirate quickly takes off, and I settle back, watching my girl handle business.

Logan looks back to me before she starts to make her way over, leaving a buzzed and happy Ali on the dance floor. Logan's steps are a bit wobbly as she walks, thanks to the amount of alcohol she's consumed, but overall, she's in control.

"Hi," she says, wrapping her arms around my neck.

"Hi, baby." My hand finds the small of her back before drifting south, cupping her ass.

"Are you going to dance with me or what?" she asks with a drunken glint in her eye.

"I don't dance, Logan."

She sticks out her bottom lip in a pouty way, which pretty much sways my decision, but she gives in before I do. "Fine," she sighs, though she doesn't seem to care all that much.

Reaching up, she kisses my lips before turning around, her back to my chest and her head leaning back on my shoulder. My forearm drapes across the front of her chest as I hold her to me, and I use my other hand to continue drinking the beer in my cup.

"Oh, god. No." Logan nods towards the dance floor.

My eyes follow hers to find my brother dancing with his ex, Lauren. His fucking bunny ears make him pretty hard to miss as we watch them move together. His hands are on her lower back, and her face is right up against his cheek.

"Nope. No way. Absolutely not." I finish my beer and toss the cup aside before taking a step towards the dance floor.

"No, don't." Logan pulls me back. "Marc is a grown man. He can make his own decisions."

Marc loves to give me his sage advice, but man, oh man, are the tables going to turn when I give him the lecture of a lifetime in the morning about what a terrible mistake he's making right now. But still, I guess he has to figure it out on his own.

"You're right," I sigh, settling back into my previous spot. I keep my eyes on the dance floor as Logan makes herself comfortable up against me, her ass ever so slightly grinding against my dick, and quickly diverting my attention back to her.

"I love this song," Logan says, leaning her head back on me. She closes her eyes as the music takes over.

My hands find her hips before my lips find her neck. I pull her into me, needing the friction. I've basically been turned on since the second she walked into my house, but now with her barely covered ass swaying against me to the beat of the music, I'm having a hard time hiding her effects on my body.

Somehow even with the deafening music, I can hear Logan's ragged breathing as my lips trail her jaw, down her neck, and across her shoulder. Her vanilla scent fills my nostrils as I pull her hips into me and sway with her to the music. We move together in perfect sync as I press myself into her.

Okay, I lied. Maybe I do like dancing.

Logan's hand reaches back around my neck, silently asking me to keep my mouth on her as my warm breath swirls across her soft skin. She continues to move to the beat, slowly grinding her body against mine.

My hands dance around her waist, her hips, her everything. I'm so fucking tempted to dip my hand into this tiny little skirt of hers. However, even though we're hidden in the darkness, in the back corner of the packed living room where no one is paying us any attention, I don't want to risk someone seeing Logan in the way that only I get to see her.

"Upstairs?" I ask in a whisper as my lips trail up her nape.

"Mmm-hmm," she whimpers against me.

I kiss her jaw before guiding her towards the stairs, staying behind her and keeping my hand on her hips, trying to hide the noticeable bulge in my costume caused by Logan's movements.

She hurries up the stairs, and I take them two at a time, both of us obviously wanting to get to my room as quickly as possible. When she reaches the top, I can't help but grab her arm and pull her back to me. I push her up against the hallway and kiss her hard. My hips pin hers to the wall as my hands find her red hair, her pretty neck, and her waist.

Our kiss is heated and hurried as my hands trail down her thighs before cupping her ass and picking her up. She wraps her long legs around me, and her hands burrow in my hair, her tongue gliding against mine. I groan against her, pushing all my weight into her, including my very present erection.

I want to rip this little green number off of her right now, but I need to get her into my room first. Even though It's only a few feet away, it feels too far, but still, it can't happen in this hallway, so I will my feet to move. Carrying her flawless body to my room, I somehow find the door handle to open it, then kick it closed as soon as we are through the threshold.

Turning around, I pin her body up against the back of my door as my hands squeeze her ass and my lips find her neck. Logan's strained breaths fill my ears as my mouth works its way down to her chest.

"Eli?"

"Mmm-hmm," I hum in acknowledgment as my mouth continues to pepper her neck, her collarbone, and her chest with haste.

"I want you."

"You have me," I tell her between kisses as my lips continue their sweet assault.

"No. I want you," Logan repeats, saying the words slower, trying to change their meaning in my mind.

Pulling my face away from her neck, I look at her in the eyes. Her piercing greens tell me exactly what she's trying to convey as they hold my gaze.

Oh. She *wants* me. She wants me...inside of her.

"Tonight?" I ask as I hold her body up and pinned to the back of the door. "You want to have sex...tonight? Like right now?" I ask again, my voice a bit shaky and rushed.

I wasn't sure when this day would come, but I find myself a little shocked that it's finally here.

She nods her head in agreement, but her green eyes are a little red from the booze as she looks at me.

"Baby, we can't," I regretfully tell her as I think about the amount of alcohol that she and I have both consumed tonight.

"What?" she asks, her face instantly losing its color as she gently pushes herself down to stand on her own feet.

"No. Not like that," I say with urgency. "Fuck. I want to. Trust me. God, do I want to," I add, trying to reassure her, but still, her expression looks hurt and confused.

"Logan, you've been drinking, and I want you to make this decision when you're sober." I push a strand of hair away from her face, tucking it behind her ear.

"I *did* make this decision when I was sober. I'm just *telling* you when I'm drunk," she says with a bit of a slur. Enough to reinforce my decision that we can't have sex tonight.

I try not to, but I let out a chuckle as she tries to convince me. "Well," I begin. "I've been drinking too, and I'm pretty buzzed right now." I cup the sides of her face as my eyes search hers. "And I want to be completely sober when we do this. I want to be able to remember every second of it."

Her concerned face softens as she takes in my words. It takes a moment for her to agree, but eventually, a shy little smile takes over her lips as she nods her head in my hands.

"You're too good to me," she says, which makes my heart melt. All I've ever wanted is for Logan to feel cared for and loved.

"And you're too good *for* me," I say in response, which makes her shake her head before wrapping her hands around my neck, pulling my lips to hers.

I can't believe she's ready to have sex with me. I've waited for this day since the night she ran into me and spilled my drink down my shirt. I also can't believe I had to tell her no. Or at least, 'not yet.' I love her too much to do such an important thing when she's drunk.

And I do love her, every part of her. I love her shy side, I love her confident side, and I love all the sides that only I get to see. I want to tell her. It's been on the tip of my tongue for a while now. I almost let it slip out this morning when I was leaving her room, but I don't know when I should say it. Is it still too soon? It's only been a few weeks since we officially got together, and I've never done this before, so I don't know if there's a timeline on when it's acceptable to admit.

I've been meaning to ask Marc. He has more experience with the whole relationship thing than I do. But I do know that I should wait until I'm sober in the same way we need to wait to have sex. It's too important to be tainted with alcohol. Tomorrow maybe, if the timing feels right, I can tell her then.

Suddenly, Logan's skillful fingers find the zipper of my costume as she begins to pull it down.

"What are you doing?" I ask as I watch my zipper expose my white undershirt then my briefs.

"Don't ask questions," Logan commands as her hands explore my body. She leans up and places her lips on mine as her hands slide across my shoulders, under my flight suit, pushing it down my arms.

I slip my arms out of the sleeves before my hands find her face, cupping the sides as my mouth explores hers. Whatever she's doing, I'm here for it. She turns us around, our lips still attached, so that I'm now the one pinned against the door. Her hands trail down my abdomen and reach around to my backside as she pushes my costume down my body, leaving me in only my briefs and a tee.

"Baby, what are you doing?" I ask again, this time much more out of breath.

She leans up on her toes, her lips dragging across my jaw until they connect with my ear. "Stop asking questions," she says again in a seductive whisper before wrapping her full lips around my lobe.

"Yes, ma'am." I close my eyes and drop my head back against the door, reveling in her touch.

Her hands find the hem of my tee as she pulls it up and over my head, exposing my chest and abs. Her lips attach themselves to my neck, covering me in hot kisses as her fingers trail every inch of my body.

Her hand dips into the waistband of my briefs, finding my rock-hard guy, ready for her touch.

"Fuck, baby," I moan, pushing myself into her hand. I keep my eyes closed, feeling every movement as she surrounds me.

After a few pumps, she releases me from her grasp. Her fingers slide against my hips before she pulls my briefs down over my ass. Opening my eyes, I watch as she exposes me, my dick bouncing back to his full glory once the barrier of my underwear is gone. She slides them down my thighs, and I kick them off once they make it to my ankles.

Logan's expert hands find me once again as she pumps and strokes while reattaching her lips to my neck. Her mouth explores my body, her lips dragging over every crevice of muscle. She gets on her knees in front of me, and I jerk in her hand when her tongue licks a line down my lowest abs, dangerously close to my dick.

She settles in front of me with her hands around my cock, and her gaze fixated on it. She takes a deep breath before licking her lips.

"Logan, are you sure?" I ask. But I don't know why I ask. I should really keep my fucking mouth shut. I've been dreaming of the moment when her plump lips would surround me since the second I laid my eyes on them.

"Baby," she warns. "You've got to stop with the fucking questions."

Man, I love sassy Logan. She's fiery and confident as hell tonight.

Before I can respond, her warm mouth surrounds me, taking away my breath and my words.

My eyes screw shut as my head falls back, feeling every nerve fire at once.

"Shit," I hiss between my teeth when I hit the back of her throat.

There's no way in hell she's going to be able to fit all of me in her mouth, but what she can't fit, she uses her hand on.

I know this is Logan's first time doing this, but fuck, she feels good. She has the perfect tempo as her tongue glides along with her lips, sucking and stroking me.

Her head bobs up and down as I open my eyes once again to watch her. Her red hair is messily falling around her as she moves. I gather it in my hands and hold it back for her as I continue to watch her mouth's movements with my parted lips. She sucks her cheeks right at the tip, and holy shit, I almost come right then.

"Fuck, baby. Yeah, just like that," I say between ragged breaths to encourage her. Her warm wet mouth feels fucking fantastic, and the fact that Logan is comfortable enough to do this is a huge turn-on.

My hips begin to thrust involuntarily into her, and I don't want to hurt her, but I can't really control them. Her eyes screw shut, but she doesn't stop as her hand twists and turns at the base of my cock, and her tongue circles the tip before gliding down the shaft.

"You feel so fucking good, Logan."

After a quick couple minutes of literal heaven, I can feel myself throbbing inside of her, ready to release, as her mouth continues its movements.

"I'm gonna come," warning Logan that she should stop if she doesn't want it in her mouth. But she doesn't stop. Not only does she continue her perfect tempo, but she also looks up at me as she does.

When her pretty green eyes meet mine, that's when I lose it. Every muscle in my body contracts as I come. "*Fuck*," I groan, closing my eyes and basking in my release, holding the back of Logan's head to me as I finish in her mouth.

Fucking hell, that felt amazing.

I lean back against my door, out of breath and butt ass naked. My mouth is gaped open, and my body is flushed as I try to catch my breath. Logan stands up as my hooded eyes look down at her.

She stares right at me as she wipes her lower lip with her thumb, fully smirking at me as she does.

My sweet girl has turned dark tonight, and I fucking love it.

"That was incredible," I say in a sedated tone. "I didn't know that's what you had in mind when you told me I would be holding your hair back tonight."

I lean down and place my smirking lips on Logan's. "Your turn."

"What are you going to do?" she asks as I pick her up and toss her on my bed.

"Don't ask questions," I say to her in the same forceful manner as she did earlier, though I make sure to add a playful edge in my tone as I do.

"Yes, sir," she says, which gets my tired guy to perk back up real quick.

"You don't need these, right?" I run my hands up her thighs, over her fishnets.

She doesn't use words. She just shakes her head as her dark hooded eyes look down at my hands.

"Good." I rip the tights off her body, giving myself access to her pretty pussy. I don't want to deal with the rest of her costume, so I push it up and out of the way. As much as I can't wait to peel this little number off her, right now, I just want to make her feel as good as she made me feel.

When my tongue makes contact with her warm wetness, Logan arches her back and cries out my name. The sound is music to my ears, and I wouldn't mind everyone hearing my name leave her lips. I continue my movements, knowing exactly what she likes as I tease her, causing her to scream so loudly that there's no way in hell people can't hear us even with the loud music downstairs.

I flick, circle, tease, and suck as her white knuckles grip my sheets until she completely comes undone from my tongue.

"*Fuck me*," she sighs in satisfaction as I climb onto the bed next to her.

"Can't wait to." My fingers glide against her pulsing clit.

After a few sedate minutes of lying next to each other, I lean over and kiss Logan's pretty mouth, then her tattoo before I stand and redress myself in my costume.

She leans up on her elbows, watching my every movement.

"Enjoying the show?" I ask as I slip my white tee over my head.

"Mmm-hmm," she hums. "Very much so."

I laugh at my cute girl and her honestly tonight. "Let's go." I walk over to her, lying on my bed. Pulling her arms towards me, she whines as I force her to stand. "If we don't go now, we are never going to leave this room. And Ali will have my head if I leave Catwoman stranded without her Poison Ivy."

"You're right," she drunkenly agrees as she pulls off what remains of her ruined fishnets.

I guide Logan downstairs as I hold her hand in mine. The music has gotten louder, and the crowd has gotten larger as we make it to the base of the stairs.

"Let's go outside," Logan projects over the music.

"Are you sure? You're going to get cold."

“Thanks to the mixture of the booze and you making me come, I’m pretty warm right now,” she says, causing my mouth to gape at her lack of a filter tonight.

Drunk Logan is the best.

I lead her out the back door, and the cold air instantly hits us. The back porch is surprisingly empty tonight. Typically, this is a popular hangout spot on party nights, but thanks to the DJ and makeshift dance floor in the living room, the backyard is almost all ours.

There’s a couple of groups of people out here. A few girls huddled around the outdoor heater and another handful of guys passing around a cigarette. There’s also a couple hooking up on one of the outdoor benches. She’s straddling him with her back towards us, and by the looks of them, they’re going to need to get a room here pretty soon.

Except that’s not just some random couple. Judging by the full black latex outfit and cat ears...that’s Ali with her back towards us.

“Damn, Ali! Get it!” I yell out, teasing her the same way should would me if the roles were reversed.

She snaps her head back to look at Logan and me as her eyes widen in shock, revealing the guy underneath her.

“Marc?” Logan asks in disbelief.

Chapter 69

Logan

"What the fuck?" I hear myself say in shock as Ali climbs off Marc's lap.

"Shit," Ali says under her breath as we catch her red-handed.

"Um...hey. Hey guys," Marc adds, adjusting himself before standing next to a wide-eyed Ali.

"What the actual fuck?" I ask again.

"Logan, I've been meaning to tell you..." Ali begins.

"Meaning to tell me? This has happened before?" My eyes are wide as Eli's deep belly laugh radiates next to me.

"Did you know about this?" I ask, turning to my boyfriend.

"It was never confirmed, but I mean...I'm not blind, baby," he says in pure amusement. "You had to have known," he adds through his laughter.

"I had my suspicions, but I figured you guys would've told me if something was going on." I turn back to my two closest friends.

"How long has this been going on?" I ask, but they both stay silent, each looking to the other to answer.

"Since move-in day," Marc says quietly, finally breaking the silence.

"Move-in day?"

"Oh my god, this is good," Eli adds, unable to control his laughter.

"But you hooked up with Cam that night," I remind Ali, but she shakes her head. "And Lauren?" I ask Marc, who also confirms that I'm mistaken.

"You assholes left me stranded at the kickoff party to go hookup with each other?" I ask in shock and disbelief. It's not that I'm upset. I'm just surprised that they would ditch me.

“Shit. Logan, honestly, I’ve felt bad about that ever since,” Marc says with sincerity.

“Don’t feel bad bro, she slept in my bed that night,” Eli’s smug voice adds next to me.

“You guys hooked up at the kickoff party?” Marc asks, looking as shocked as I am right now. “This has been going on for that long?” He motions between his brother and me.

“No.” I shake my head. “No, it wasn’t like that.”

“It was totally like that,” Eli states, being the arrogant asshole that he is. I swat him in the chest, but he grabs my hand and kisses it between laughs.

“So, what is this then?” I gesture between Marc and Ali. “Are you guys like...together?”

“Oh, no. It’s casual,” Ali quickly says with a shake of her head.

“Not everyone falls in love at first sight like you guys,” Marc adds, looking between Eli and me.

Eli stiffens up next to me. If Marc could not use the word ‘love’ in front of his brother, that would be nice. The guy just got his first girlfriend. I’m pretty sure that word would freak him out, being only a month in, which is exactly why I haven’t told him yet.

“I think I need a drink.” I turn away from my friends, heading back inside.

“I’ll go with you,” I hear Ali say somewhere behind me.

“Logan. Logan. Logan,” Ali repeats as she chases me down. “Please don’t be mad at me.”

Stopping in my tracks, I turn to face her. “Mad at you?” I ask with confusion. “I’m not mad at you. I’m just...surprised. Why didn’t you tell me?”

“I don’t know,” she says with a sigh. “You and Maddison have this whole soulmate thing going on, and Marc and I are just having sex,” she shrugs. “I felt a bit silly divulging all of it when you have the real thing.”

Cocking my head to the side, I look at her with sympathy. Just because I have a boyfriend doesn't mean she can't talk to me.

"And, I wasn't sure how you would feel about us being friends with benefits. I know you're protective over Marc," she adds without judgment.

"Yeah, I'm protective over him when it comes to him being with shitty people. Ali, I love you, you know that. And you guys are adults. You can do what you want, and I would never judge you. I just don't want you to feel like you have to hide things from me."

Ali's expression melts in front of me. "I love you too, Lo."

"Lo?" I ask with a chuckle. "New nickname?"

"Maybe? I'm kind of drunk, so I'm just trying it out," she adds, causing us both to laugh, relieving the tension.

"So, friends with benefits, huh?"

"Well, it was just benefits at first. The friends part came later."

"And you don't have feelings for him?"

"It's not like that," she quickly says, shaking her head.

I pause for a moment, trying to figure out if I believe her or not.

"Have you hooked up with anyone else this year?" I ask. "What about that guy Dylan? You guys went on a date."

She shakes her head again. "I left early. And no, there hasn't been anybody else."

Tilting my head, I eye her with skepticism because I'm not sure if she hears herself. "Are you sure there aren't feelings involved?" I ask again.

"It's just sex, Logan."

"It's never just sex, Ali. Not when it's with someone who you get along with that well. And someone you spend all your time with."

There's no way in hell she doesn't have feelings for Marc or vice versa. They spend all their time together. Granted, I'm there most of the time, but still.

"I don't do boyfriends," she adds as if she's trying to remind both herself and me.

"Maybe you should."

We drop the topic of conversation for the moment and find our way into the kitchen, looking for more alcohol. Between my time upstairs with Eli and finding my two friends hooking up outside, my perfect drunken state is beginning to wear off. We bob and weave through the crowd until we make it to the kitchen island where the bottles of liquor are waiting to be consumed. Unfortunately, when I look up, I find Lauren with a couple of her girlfriends standing on the opposite side.

"That's her," one of Lauren's friends says.

My eyes dart upward to see the group of girls staring at my friend. Ali is oblivious or at least pretending to be, as she pours us a round of shots.

"Yeah, I know," Lauren says, looking at Ali. "Slut."

My blood begins to boil as I hear that word leave her mouth in regards to my friend. "What did you just say?" I snap from across the island.

"Logan, I got this," Ali says, clearly aware of the girls talking shit about her in front of us.

"No. Lauren, what did you just say?" I ask again, but she stays quiet, averting her gaze from mine. "What? You don't want to repeat it out loud now that you're being called out on it?" It takes her a moment, but finally, Lauren looks up to me with an evil stare and her lips pressed in a hard line.

"I called her a slut," Lauren repeats, "because she is."

Oh, she did not just say that.

"She's a slut?" I ask with wide eyes, pointing to Ali. "Because she's hooking up with your ex, that makes her a slut?" Lauren keeps her smug expression, not wanting to take back her words. "Your ex-boyfriend that you *cheated* on," I remind her. "If you really want to use that word, I mean..." Chuckling, I motion up and down at Lauren, obviously referring to her.

Lauren's face pales. "And you're a bitch!"

I can't help but laugh. I've never been called a bitch before, so this is fun. "I'm a bitch?" I laugh in disbelief. "Ali, did you hear that? *I'm* a bitch." I turn to my friend, who has a shocked but impressed look on her face.

"Yeah, Lauren, *she's* the bitch," Ali says with extra-heavy sarcasm.

I spot Marc and Eli out of the corner of my eye, watching this whole interaction in the entryway of the kitchen. Their mouths are gaped, but both of them look thoroughly amused.

"Marc, did you hear that?" I call out. "I'm a bitch!" I add with a smile as I point to myself.

"*Such* a bitch," Marc shouts with a deep laugh.

"Fuck you!" Lauren yells at me from across the island, causing Ali and I to burst into more laughter.

"Yeah, yeah." I grab a bottle of vodka off the island and turn to walk towards my boys. "Fuck you too," I casually add as I give Lauren my middle finger over my shoulder and leave the kitchen.

"Who the hell are you?" Marc asks with a laugh as he catches up to me, swinging his arm over my shoulder.

"I'm just tired of everyone messing with my people." I pass the bottle to Marc.

"That's my girl!" Ali says, jumping up and down, shaking my shoulders.

"Nice work, babe!" Eli adds with enthusiasm as he slaps my ass in approval.

"Thanks, baby." I take a chug from the bottle Marc has now handed back to me. My eyes screw shut as the vodka burns going down my throat.

I feel like a boxer between rounds as my team hypes me up in my corner, massaging my shoulders, wiping my bloody face, and spraying water in my mouth. Except the fight was with words, there won't be a round two, and the water bottle is actually vodka.

Eli wraps his arms across the front of my shoulders, pulling me in, before kissing the top of my head.

"Anyone else you want to put in their place tonight?" he asks.

"To be determined." I pass the vodka back to Marc and hold onto Eli's forearm.

Ali lets out a deep sigh of satisfaction as she looks at me with a proud smile before turning her attention to Marc. "Want to go dance?"

He nods his head, putting the bottle of liquor on the closest surface he can find. "We good?" he asks me, obviously referring to me catching him and Ali hooking up outside.

"Of course."

"You're going to grill me with questions tomorrow?" he asks with a knowing smile.

"Absolutely."

He and Ali take off towards the dance floor, leaving Eli and me alone.

"Feels good to say what's on your mind, huh?" Eli questions.

It really does feel good to speak my mind. And I never would've spoken to Lauren that way if she didn't say what she said about Ali first, but I'm glad I stood up for my friend. What else would feel good would be telling Eli that I love him. I'm not going to say it tonight when I'm drunk, but suddenly the admission doesn't feel all that scary anymore.

Leaning my head back on Eli, I close my eyes, feeling sleepy. I figured I would be coursing with adrenaline from the verbal fight I had in the kitchen, but it didn't really affect me that way. I don't know what time it is, but I do know it's well past midnight.

"Well, well, well. You going to introduce me, Maddison?"

When my eyes shoot open at the stranger's voice, I'm greeted by a good-looking guy, not as handsome as Eli, but still, he's attractive. He's tall with light brown hair and piercing blue eyes, and he looks to be a few years older than us.

"Logan, this is Jay," Eli says in a flat tone. "Jay, Logan," he adds, not releasing me from his grasp as he holds me to his body.

As soon as Eli says Jay's name, the dots connect. I remember everything Eli has told me about him. How he was his old mentor and extremely talented, but ever since he didn't make it in the NHL, he's been riding Eli to make sure it happens for him. Which, you would think is an honorable thing for a friend to do, but from what I've been told, he causes Eli's anxiety to spike.

"Hey," I cautiously say, not sure how I feel about this friend of Eli's yet.

"Hi," Jay says with a smile.

"Don't say 'hi,'" Eli interjects from behind me, causing me to laugh and melt into him further. "You can say, 'hey.'"

As I'd previously assumed, Eli has also picked up on the fact that we always say 'hi' to each other, but it's cute to hear it confirmed. Plus, I like how protective he is of our thing.

"Okay?" Jay says with a questioning look. "Possessive much?"

"You have no idea." Eli wraps his arms tighter around my shoulders.

Suddenly a loud crash echoes throughout the house. There's definitely some shattered glass or a broken window in the other room.

"Fuck," Eli says under his breath, looking in that direction.

"Maddison!" someone calls out.

"Better go, Maddison," Jay says. "Logan will be fine with me."

Eli looks from Jay, back to me, completely unconvinced.

"Maddison!" another person shouts.

"Come with me?" Eli asks. I contemplate it for a moment, but to be honest, I feel bold tonight, and I want to get to the root of this Jay thing.

"Go. I'm fine."

He looks to Jay with a pointed glance. "Look out for her, will you? And don't be a dick to her," he adds before kissing my forehead and quickly heading towards the other room.

"So," Jay begins. "You're Maddison's girlfriend," he says somewhat slowly, trying to see how the words taste coming off his tongue.

"Yes, I am."

"How long has this *thing* been going on between you guys?"

"Since the beginning of the school year." The words leave my mouth before realizing that Eli might not want Jay to know these things.

"You know he's probably going to be leaving soon, right? He should be getting called up before the end of the year, and I just want you to be prepared." There's not an ounce of concern on Jay's face, it's all smug.

I don't like where this conversation is going. If I were sober right now, Jay would probably intimidate me, but I'm drunk, confident Logan at the moment, and I speak what's on my mind now, apparently.

"You don't think I know that? I've known that since the day we met. Trust me, I'm aware."

"And you know—"

"I'm just going to stop you there, Jay," I say, cutting him off. "Trust me. Whatever you're about to say, I've thought about it. I'm not trying to distract him or pull his attention away from hockey, and I'm not going to stop him when he finally gets his shot. You don't need to worry."

He lets out a heavy sigh as his self-righteous expression softens. "I'm sure I sound like a jackass, but I'm just looking out for him," he says with sincerity, his intimidating tactic gone. "I was really close to making it when it all slipped away from me, and I just don't want the same thing to happen to Maddison. I care about the kid, even if I don't always show it in the best way."

“Me too, Jay. We are on the same team. I’m not going to stand in his way. But you know there’s more to him than hockey, right?” I ask with raised brows.

“I know,” he replies quickly, not really thinking about my question.

“Do you, though?” I ask again. “I mean, really, do you?”

Jay stays silent, averting his guilty gaze away from me.

“He wants to make it more than you know,” I tell him. “More than you want it for him. More than anyone wants it for him. But don’t you think it’s got to get old when the only thing people want to talk to him about is hockey? Like he’s some kind of meal ticket? He’s a really good guy, and the only thing people see is the arrogant athlete.”

Jay remains quiet but looks at me while taking in my words.

“I’m sure you know how he feels. You were in his same position a few years ago,” I add.

He lets out a sigh. “I didn’t really think about it that way.”

I give him a half-smile, and he returns the same grin, seeming to understand where I’m coming from.

“You know I came over here fully expecting not to like you,” Jay says offhandedly, causing me to laugh.

“And?”

“I’m kind of a fan,” he says, laughing with me. “I’ll ease up on the whole NHL thing.”

“Thank you,” I tell him with sincerity.

“Cali, girl!” someone drunkenly slurs as they wrap their arm around my shoulder. Judging by the nickname, it’s Patrick.

“Patrick,” I tonelessly acknowledge as I remove his arm from my shoulder. He reeks of booze, and his bloodshot eyes have the same blank stare as they did the night I met him.

“Patty,” Jay flatly says to greet him.

Patrick doesn’t respond to Jay but instead takes a strand of my hair, twirling it between his fingers.

"Dance with me?" he asks.

"No," I quickly state, turning my head so that he loses the strand of my hair.

He sighs before looking me up and down, keeping his eyes on my body. "You look so good tonight."

"Fuck off, Patty," Jay chimes in.

"I just want Cali to give me a chance. She never gave me a chance," Patrick slurs, slightly leaning into me.

"I'm with Eli," I quickly state.

"Golden boy, Maddison," Patrick says before taking another sip of whatever is in his cup. "Always gets what he wants. What about what I want?" he whines, causing my skin to crawl. "I just want to dance with you."

"You've always been such a creepy little bitch, Patrick," Jay states.

"Fuck you, Jay. What are you even doing here?"

"Apparently making sure you don't take advantage of any drunk girls tonight. I've heard the rumors."

Jay's words make me feel sick to my stomach as I remember the first time I was at this house with Patrick.

"I don't know what you're talking about."

"Convenient," Jay adds. "So would you rather have me or Maddison kick your ass for hitting on his girl?"

Patrick chugs the rest of his drink while keeping his stare on Jay before dropping the cup at Jay's feet and turning to walk away.

"Fucking hate that kid." Jay shakes his head.

"What's his deal with Eli?" I ask.

"He has some weird rivalry thing with him, but I don't think Maddison is even aware. Patty is jealous of the attention Maddison gets for being the star forward. Patrick is a defenseman, and he's pretty fucking good, but he will never get as much recognition as Maddison, and I think that gets under his skin. Plus, Patrick is just a shitty human, so he's easy to dislike."

"Looks like you're in the clear," Jay changes the subject, nodding towards Eli, who's making his way over to us with his hands behind his back.

"You good?" Eli asks me from behind, dipping his face down close to mine.

"Mmm-hmm."

"Thanks, man," Eli says to Jay.

"It was...*nice* to meet you, Logan," Jay says with a questioning look.

"Felt weird to say that, huh?" I ask with a laugh.

"Yeah, it really did." He gives me a soft grin. "See you later, Maddison," he adds before taking off towards the dance floor.

"He's not so bad." I turn my attention to Eli. "Everything good with that crash?"

"Some dumb drunk freshman shattered the window, so that'll be fun to fix tomorrow. But more importantly..." Eli wraps his arms in front of me and holds out a brown bag he'd been hiding behind his back.

"Where the hell did you get that?" I ask with excitement.

"Marc told me that McDonald's fries are your drunk food of choice, so I had some delivered."

I turn around to face him. "You're my favorite person ever. But how many did you get?"

"What do you think? That I'm an idiot? Of course, I got two orders. I knew you weren't going to share with me," he says with an amused smile. "And I got you a burger."

"Sexy and smart." I reach up on my toes, pressing my lips to his.

"Want to go put on our pajamas and eat them in my bed?" he asks with an excited glint in his eye.

"Oh my god, that might be the hottest thing you've ever said to me," I tell Eli, causing him to laugh.

Chapter 70

Eli

"I'm never drinking again," Logan moans, stretching her body and waking me up.

I peel my eyes open but quickly shut them again as the morning sun pours through my bedroom window, blinding me. I'm still in the position I fell asleep in last night with my head on Logan's stomach, my arms wrapped around her waist, and the rest of my body between her bare legs.

I couldn't be more comfortable.

"Yeah, I'm sure you'll go all of Thanksgiving weekend without drinking with Mary," I sarcastically say with my hoarse voice and dry mouth.

"Besides that. I can't say no to Mary." Logan's hands find my hair, gently scratching my scalp.

"Mmm, hi, baby." I close my eyes again from Logan's gentle touch. "I put some Advil and water on the nightstand for you last night."

"Eli James, you're an absolute angel," she tells me as the corners of my lips turn up. "But any chance you have Tylenol instead? I can't take Advil."

Turning my head, I lean my chin on Logan's stomach to look up at her. "Why can't you have Advil?"

"It gets filtered through your kidneys, and since I only have one now, I just have to be careful. Tylenol goes through your liver," she casually states.

"Oh. I had no idea." I peel myself off her body to dig through my nightstand. Finding a bottle of Tylenol, I take a seat on the side of the bed and get two pills out for her.

Logan sits up with her back against my headboard as she downs the painkiller with some water to help with her hangover.

"Does only having one kidney affect any other part of your life?" I ask Logan with a bit of concern as I run my hand over her bare thigh.

"No, not really. I just have to be sure I live a healthy lifestyle. Which I normally do, when I'm not drunkenly eating fries in my boyfriend's bed at two AM."

"But like health-wise, down the road, you don't need to worry about anything?" I ask, needing the reassurance.

She shakes her head.

"What about kids? Will it affect you being able to have them?" I continue, which surprises even me that I would bring this up. I don't want kids anytime soon, and I've never even thought about them until Ali brought up how cute our babies would be. Still, it would be ironically heartbreaking if the thing that Logan did to try to save her mom would prevent her from becoming one.

"No, it wouldn't affect that." She leans forward in the space between us, wrapping her arms around my shoulders. "Morning," she says with a cute little smile.

"Morning, baby," I say only an inch from her mouth as I slide my hand up her bare thigh and under my shirt she slept in, feeling the warmth of her silky skin in my palm. "How's my little party animal feeling?" I climb into bed with her, tucking us both under the covers as we face one another.

"Hungover," she says with a grimace, causing me to chuckle.

"Did you have fun, though?" I dip my hand under her shirt, grazing my fingertips along her back.

"Mmm-hmm," she hums with a satisfied smile. "Did you?"

"I had a blast."

"What was your favorite part of the night?" she asks, running her hand through my messy hair.

"Besides you blowing me?" I question with a cocky smile, causing her to playfully swat my chest in embarrassment. "I did enjoy seeing you get all sassy and stand up for yourself last night, but I would have to say my favorite part was definitely eating fries in my bed and laughing my ass off with you for a solid hour. I haven't laughed like that in a long time."

Last night when we came upstairs, Logan changed into one of my hockey tees, and I threw on a pair of sweats, getting comfortable on the bed while we scarfed down some fast food and talked for well over an hour. We couldn't stop laughing with each other, and at one point, we were both in tears from the uncontrollable giggles.

Once again, I was reminded that not only am I totally in love with my smoking hot girlfriend, but also that she's my absolute favorite person to hang out with.

"That was your favorite part?" Logan gently asks, her eyes and smile getting all soft.

"Of course it was," I reassure her. "I love spending time with you."

I don't know if it's the sweet, genuine smile Logan has from my words or what that causes me to continue, but I do.

"You're my best friend," I tell her, feeling kinda silly admitting it. But it's true. I could spend every waking moment with this girl and still not have enough time with her.

Logan's green eyes go wide then soft as she looks at me. "You're my best friend too, Eli."

I take a moment to bask in her words before getting playful and giving her shit. "I'm telling Marc!" I quickly say in excitement.

I sit up in bed with my back against my headboard. "Marc!" I yell towards the closed door.

"Shut up!" Logan laughs, trying to cover my mouth with her hand, but I quickly pull it away from me.

"Marc! I gotta tell you something!" I yell again in amusement.

Logan frantically crawls over to me and straddles my lap as she puts her hand more firmly over my mouth. "You're such an asshole!" she says, unable to control her laughter.

"Marc!" I mumble into Logan's hand.

"You're the worst." Logan lets out another giggle, keeping her hand over my mouth. My eyes shine with amusement as I look at the happy girl in my lap.

"Can I tell you something?" she asks, changing the subject.

I nod my head, unable to speak because Logan's hand is still covering my mouth.

She hesitates for a moment, her eyes quickly darting between mine.

"I love you," she tells me, catching me off guard.

Holy Shit.

Did she really just say that? Did I hear her correctly? Judging by her pretty green eyes frantically searching mine, I must've.

Logan drops her hand for me to respond, but I can't.

I never once considered what it would feel like to hear those words leave Logan's mouth. Honestly, I only ever thought about what it would be like for me to tell Logan that I loved *her*. I wanted *her* to know she is loved. I wanted *her* to know she is cherished. But now that the time is here, the words won't come out. I'm speechless.

Hearing her say those three little words, the words I've had on the tip of my tongue for so long now, feels like an overwhelming out of body experience.

I feel light but full.

I feel a bit sick to my stomach, but in the right way, like I have butterflies floating around in there. Pterodactyls. Pterodactyls might be a better way to describe it.

I feel calm, the way I always do with her. An overwhelming peace takes over as my stomach and chest continue to flip inside out. It doesn't make sense. Trust me, I'm aware.

I feel a bit scared. Scared that the only thing that calms all my fears and anxiety is wrapped up into one beautiful woman who is currently sitting in my lap. But I feel safe, like she's exactly where I need to be.

More than anything, I feel like I'm home with her. She's my home, where I'm centered and grounded, the best version of me, and I never knew how much I needed to hear those words—that she loves me.

She loves me. Fuck. The most selfless girl I've ever met, who loves hard, but has never been in love before. She loves *me*. She's in love with *me*. I don't deserve it, but I'll absolutely, one hundred percent take it.

Logan continues to look at me, waiting for my response, worry beginning to form on her face, but I still can't say anything. It's like there's something stuck in the back of my throat. Emotions, that's what's stuck back there. I feel them welling up, causing my lungs to be short of air and for my eyes to sting with tears.

What the fuck is going on? Just fucking say something. Put her out of her misery.

There's a tightening in my chest, and I can't seem to get the words out, so I decide to tell her in the way I've been telling her for weeks. I wrap my arms around her waist as I pull her to me, placing my lips on her tattooed collarbone as a couple of unwelcome tears escape my eyes.

If you would've told me a year ago that I would be sitting here with the girl of my dreams and never once thinking about another chick since I met her, I would've told you that you lost your goddamn mind. Hell, you could've said this three months ago, and I wouldn't have believed you. But here I am, feeling like a completely different man as I hold the girl I'm utterly in love with in my lap, crying like a little bitch, and needing this forever.

I hold her for a few moments, with my lips on the black inked words, until finally, Logan gasps in realization.

She wraps her arms around my neck, burying one of her hands in my hair, holding me to her.

"Why didn't you tell me?" she asks in a shaky voice when she realizes I've been silently telling her for weeks.

"I was," I say with my head burrowed in her neck, hiding my face. "In my own way, I was telling you."

Logan lifts my face to look me in the eyes. Her piercing greens are full of hope and love as she searches mine, wiping a traitorous tear from my cheek.

"I love you, Logan," I finally tell her, feeling exponentially lighter as the words come off my tongue.

She lets out a little chuckle as the satisfied smile takes over her lips.

"I really fucking love you," I add as I look at my favorite girl.

Logan wraps her arms around my shoulders, leaning on me and burying her face in the crook of my neck. I hold on to her as tight as I can, needing her and filling my nostrils with her sweet vanilla scent.

"I've loved you almost as long as I've known you," I quietly add as I stroke her back.

"You could've told me."

"Yeah, I'm sure that wouldn't have freaked you out," I say sarcastically with a halfhearted laugh. "Imagine if I would've told you if I loved you after you came over when I found out my birth father was dying. Or if I would've told you I was *in* love with you the night at the pond. I would've sounded insane."

Logan sits up on my lap, looking me in the eyes, my hands dropping to her hips as she shakes her head.

"I loved you then," she tells me, brushing the shaggy hair out of my eyes and wiping away the last of my almost-dried tears.

She cups my face as she presses her full lips to mine, exploring me with her perfectly pouty mouth.

I fucking love this girl with everything I am, and I finally get to tell her.

"Well, now I'm not going to shut the fuck up about it. I love you. I love you. I love you," I say between peppered kisses, leaning forward and flipping Logan onto her back as I hover over her. Logan laughs and yelps as I continue my sweet assault, kissing every inch of her face, neck, and chest as I say those sacred words I've held in for far too long.

"I love you, Eli."

The words cause me to pause as she runs her hands through my hair.

I don't think I'll ever get sick of her saying that to me. I already loved the way my name sounded coming from her lips, but now with those three words in front of it...fuck, it sounds good.

"About what you said last night—" I begin, but she cuts me off.

"I want to."

I was hoping it wasn't just the alcohol talking last night when she told me she was ready to have sex, but I needed the confirmation, just in case.

Nodding my head, I search her face for any sign of hesitation. She doesn't look nervous or scared at all. If anything, I'm the nervous one here. I've never done this before. Sure, I've fucked plenty of girls, but this...this is different.

She opens her bare legs as I press myself onto her. My lips find hers, and my palm dips under the hem of her shirt, gliding across her warm, soft skin. Our tongues move together as Logan wraps her arms around my neck, pulling me into her and needing me closer. I find one of her tits with my hand as Logan arches up into me.

I'm already insanely turned on thanks to our vulnerable morning and the thin fabric covering Logan's pussy. My morning guy is standing at attention, under my sweatpants, as my hips begin to grind down into hers. My lips drag across her jaw and down her neck as Logan's panting breaths fill the room.

It's one of my favorite sounds, like music to my ears.

Suddenly, voices begin to echo through the hallway outside of my room, telling us that the guys from the team are beginning to wake up. Loud, obnoxious voices are ruining our moment as they talk about how hungover they are or who got laid last night.

"I got my dick sucked by two different chicks!" one of my teammates yells out, causing both Logan and I to awkwardly laugh and wince in embarrassment.

"Maybe we don't do this here," Logan says with a halfhearted chuckle as I drop my head to her shoulder in defeat.

"I'll move out," I tell her. "I'll move out right fucking now."

I'm only half kidding.

Realizing that we aren't going to do this right now, I let out a heavy sigh. "Coffee?"

"Coffee," she agrees with a nod before leaning up and kissing my lips once more.

After getting dressed, I guide Logan down the stairs, my fingers intertwined with hers, finding my brother at the dining room table as the rest of the guys begin to clean up the living room.

"Where's Ali?" Logan asks Marc as she takes a seat across from my brother.

"Probably back at her dorm."

I pour two cups of coffee for Logan and me. I bought her some creamer and hid it in the back of the fridge so she would have coffee she enjoys whenever she stays over here.

"When did she leave?" Logan asks as I set her morning caffeine fix in front of her. She stands from her seat so I can sit down, pulling her hips to me. Even though there are plenty of open seats at the table, she and I both know that I'd rather be sitting with her on my lap.

"I don't know," Marc casually says with a shrug.

Logan takes a sip of her coffee, obviously trying to bite her tongue.

"Go ahead," Marc says. "Ask your questions."

"Why didn't you tell me about you guys?" Logan quickly asks.

Marc lets out a heavy sigh. "I don't know, Logan. To be honest, when we hooked up the first time, I had no idea that you guys were going to become such good friends. Otherwise, I probably wouldn't have done it. But I didn't tell you when it happened because I didn't want you to think of me differently." He pauses for a moment. "I've never just had meaningless sex. I've always been a relationship guy, but I wanted to try the whole 'no strings attached' thing for once. Lauren kind of fucked me up for a while, and I wanted a casual distraction, and that's what Ali was looking for too."

"Marc, I would never judge you. You're a grown man. You can do what you want. I just feel stupid for not knowing all this time," Logan says.

"Why didn't you tell *me*?" I interrupt. "I tell you everything."

"Oh, like how you told me that Logan slept in your bed the night you guys met or how you were basically obsessed with her the second you laid your eyes on her?" Marc sarcastically asks.

"Exactly." I let out a laugh, remembering how I tried to hide my feelings for his best friend from him, though that didn't last long.

"I didn't tell you because I'm the 'relationship' sibling, and you're the 'fuckboy' sibling," Marc says to me. "Sorry, Logan," he adds when my girlfriend's expression twists from being reminded of my past.

"I didn't want to hear 'I told you so' when I decided to just do the fucking part and forget about the relationship part after all the shit I gave you over the years," Marc tells me with honesty.

"I was wrong," I quickly state, shaking my head.

"Wrong about what?"

"Just having random meaningless hookups. It's nothing compared to the real thing." I tighten my grip around Logan's waist. "You were right."

Logan stays silent, zoning out with her coffee mug held up against her lips.

"Logan, what's on your mind?" Marc questions.

"I'm just thinking about all the times I left you and Ali alone together, and you guys were probably boning," she laughs, washing away the serious tone of our conversation.

"Plenty," Marc says with raised brows. "I will say that."

"I almost caught you guys," I tell my bother before I take a sip of coffee. "I knew something was going on then."

"When?" Logan snaps her head around to look at me.

"The night Jay was in town. The night before the alumni game, when I showed up at your dorm at like one AM and Ali came out to give me shit. Marc came out of her room too. That's when I knew."

"Do you have feelings for her, Marc?" my sweet girl asks.

"No," he plainly states. "I don't."

Logan and I give him the same pointed glance, not believing his words.

"It's not like that," he says, shaking his head. "I could barely stand her the first couple weeks I knew her, and now she still drives me absolutely insane half the time. She has no filter. She does and says whatever she wants—"

"So what? Do you want another Lauren?" I ask, cutting him off. "At least Ali can handle herself. Lauren needed you to do everything for her, and she took advantage of you most of the time. Not to mention she's a total bitch."

"Ali would be good for you," Logan says, chiming in.

"Okay, Mr. and Mrs. 'we have what everyone is looking for,' this is just sex," he says, holding up his hands in defense. "Meaningless sex. Let it just be that. You know how Ali is, she doesn't do relationships, and that's exactly why this 'friends with benefits' thing works for us."

"So, you'd be okay if she started seeing other people?" Logan asks, unconvinced. "There have been a couple of times you seemed less than thrilled that Ali had other plans."

"Yes. I'd be fine with that. I think I reacted that way because I'm used to being in a relationship, but as soon as I remembered what this thing between us is casual, I was fine with it."

"I just can't believe I didn't know. I'm such an idiot." Logan shakes her head in disbelief as Cam comes strolling in the kitchen, pouring himself a coffee and taking a seat next to Logan and me at the dining room table.

"Logan, you beautiful girl," Cam says with a chuckle. "Even I knew. That first night we met after our beer pong game, Ali bailed on me the second Marc walked back into the living room."

"Sorry, man," Marc says with a laugh and shrug.

"All good."

"Okay, bye," Goody says in the distance, walking out his overnight guest, still in her costume. "No sorry," he adds, not being sorry at all, ushering her through the front door. "Yeah, see you around." He closes the door in her face.

She's the third girl that's been walked out this morning by a different one of the guys, and Logan has noticed each time.

"Clinger," Goody says with wide eyes, pointing his thumb over his shoulder towards the front door as he makes his way into the kitchen to join us.

"Do they just kick out all their girls the next morning?" Logan whispers to me.

"House rule. No overnight guests can hang around the next day."

"But I'm an overnight guest."

"No, you're not," I tell her, pressing my lips to hers. "You're my girlfriend." Her concerned expression softens as she wraps an arm around my neck and leans back on me.

"So, Logan, since you're the only girl here, what are you making us boys for breakfast?" Goody asks.

"Aye, watch it," I quickly interject.

"Goody, c'mon, man," Cam says with disappointment.

"What?" Goody asks, genuinely confused why no one is laughing with him.

"That sexist comment just earned you the responsibility of cooking breakfast for the house," I smugly add. "And for getting that broken window fixed today. Congratulations."

"Maddison. Come on, man. I was kidding," Goody whines. "Marc, help me out here." He turns to my brother.

"Oh, no way. I'm on my brother's side here." Marc shakes his head as he stands up from the table to get himself a fresh coffee. "Even if Logan wasn't my best friend, it's the twenty-first century, man. Women do more than cook and clean," he adds, patting Goody on the shoulder.

"I think you owe Logan here an apology," Cam says with amusement, enjoying watching Goody get reamed.

Goody lets out a heavy sigh. "Logan, I'm sorry. I was making a dumb joke." His voice is monotone, and his expression is frustrated.

"You're forgiven, Goody," Logan says with a smile, all of us thoroughly entertained by Goody's uncomfortable apology.

"I like my eggs over easy, by the way," Logan adds, causing all of us to burst into laughter. I drop my head forward, leaning on the back of her head, as I continue to chuckle at my girl giving Goody shit. Even Goody can't help it as his pursed lips soften and turn into a smile.

"Logan, my girl!" Benny exclaims with his arms open wide as he walks into the kitchen.

"Not your girl," I quickly correct him.

"Logan, Maddison's girl!" he tries again. "That cute little innocent fairy you introduced me to last night? Not so innocent, if you know what I mean," he adds with a suggestive glance.

"Aye, the kid finally got laid!" Cam pats Benny on the back as most of us clap for him. He had quite the dry spell, poor guy.

"Did you even last thirty seconds?" Goody asks with a chuckle.

"Absolutely not," Benny quickly says, causing the room to burst into more laughter. "But I did the second time...and the third," he smugly adds.

"Well, I hope you actually see her again. She seemed really nice," Logan says, chiming in and bringing her sweet nature into our guy talk.

Tightening my hold around Logan's waist, I lean down and press my lips to her collarbone. I talked about the women I slept with in the same way these guys are just a few months ago, but now, I could never imagine being so causal with someone. Even if Logan and I would've hooked up the first night we met, I could never imagine kicking her out the next morning then talking about how many rounds we went with the guys.

"I am," Benny says. "I'm going to take her to dinner this weekend when we get back from our road trip. I actually kind of like her."

I don't miss the proud smile on Logan's lips.

"Shit. I forgot you guys are leaving again tomorrow night," Logan says, turning her head to look at me.

"Just a quick two-game road-trip," I assure her. "Then I'm home until after Thanksgiving."

By this point, Logan is used to me being on the road, so I don't think that's what's bothering her. But what she doesn't realize is that I've already considered all of this, and there's no way in hell that I'm not going over to her place tonight.

After breakfast, the team goes back to cleaning the shit show left from the party last night, and Goody works on getting a window repair guy out as soon as possible.

"I can help if you guys need it," Logan sweetly offers as she continues walking towards the front door.

"Absolutely not," I tell her with a shake of my head.

Logan mentioned getting a workout in and studying this afternoon, so I'm not going to keep her here and let her clean up after everyone else's mess.

Pulling her into my body, I wrap my arms around her shoulders as she caresses the length of my back.

"I'll come stay over tonight?" I suggest, saying more than I can with just those words.

She pulls away from my embrace to look at me, understanding what I'm trying to say as she nods her head with a little shy smile across her lips. I lean down and press my mouth to hers, lingering there for a moment.

"I love you," I tell her for what feels like the hundredth time today.

"What did you just say?" Marc asks from behind me in shock and amusement. "Did you just tell her you loved her? Fucking finally!"

I'm trying to hold back my smile as I keep my mouth pressed in a hard line, not turning around to face my brother, and a little annoyed that he's ruining this moment, but Logan is thoroughly entertained as she giggles at my frustration.

"Hey! Did you hear that?" Marc yells to the rest of the house. "EJ finally told Logan he loves her!" he adds with a laugh.

The house behind me fills with shouts and cheers from my teammates.

"You owe me twenty bucks, Cam!"

"I love you too, Logan!"

"Fuck, Maddison, took you long enough!"

Not to mention a few concerning fake sex noises off in the distance.

Logan can't help but laugh as I try to hold back my smile from all my teammates giving me shit.

"I love you too," she giggles, standing on her tiptoes to give me a sweet kiss before turning around to head towards her car.

After watching my favorite girl drive off towards her dorm, I close the front door before averting my attention to the rest of my team.

"You're all fucking dead," I tell them.

Chapter 71

Logan

I spend my day studying—if you want to call it that. My books are open, but I can't focus. The words on the pages are jumbled, black, and blurry, while my mind swirls with other thoughts.

I've never felt like this before. I've loved Eli for a while now, but hearing him say those words back to me felt surreal. When he didn't respond for what felt like hours, I started to internally freak out. I was already nervous about telling him, I didn't want to scare him, but I couldn't hold it in any longer. I had to get it out, and I'm happy I did. I've never seen him look like he did today. He looked calm and at peace, and if me telling him that I love him does that, I will tell him every chance I get, whenever he needs to hear it.

That beautiful man, my favorite human, he loves me...I almost can't believe it.

"Hi, baby," Eli says after a quick knock at my door, walking himself right in as he always does.

"Hi," I respond in a bit of a daze.

How does he effortlessly look this good all the time? It's a bit infuriating that he looks just as good now, with his hoodie, joggers, and backwards hat, as he does in his tailored suit on game days.

But he's mine, so I'll let it slide.

"How was your day?" He makes his way over to me, where I sit on my bed with my books spread open before bending down and kissing my wanting lips with his. "Get some studying done?"

"It was good, and yes," I lie about the second answer. I'm not going to tell Eli that I couldn't focus on the words of my books' pages because all I could think about was the idea of his naked body inside of mine.

I stand and gather my textbooks, putting them back in my bag as Eli takes a seat on the edge of my bed.

"I missed you," he says with sincerity.

"I just saw you a few hours ago," I remind him with a chuckle as I close my dorm room door.

"Doesn't mean I didn't miss you."

I walk over to him, standing between his legs.

He looks up at me with his gentle chocolate eyes as I push his shaggy hair away from his face. "I missed you too, baby," I tell my needy boy.

Leaning down, I connect my lips to his. They quickly part as his tongue glides against mine, coaxing a whimpering moan from me. He cups my face, pulling me into him, needing me.

There's a difference between us tonight. I don't know if it's because we finally told each other how we felt this morning or because we both know what is going to happen later. But whatever it is, the passion and need is stronger than usual—which I didn't even know was possible.

His mouth continues to move with mine as Eli's free hand reaches around my backside, pushing my ass towards him and silently asking me to come closer. I climb onto his lap, putting one knee on the mattress and swinging the other leg over, straddling him. He presses me into him, rolling my hips, as I gasp into his mouth from the sensation.

Eli is already getting hard, and I know I'm warm with anticipation, instantly turned on by my guy. He slips his hand into the back of my shorts, grabbing my ass as he continues to rock my body against his. When his mouth finds my neck, I throw my head back and grind against him harder, needing the friction.

"Logan, I—" Ali burst into my room without as much as a knock, as she always does.

I snap my head back to look at her in shock and frustration as her eyes widen and her mouth gapes, catching Eli and me in the heat of it.

"Ali, you've got to be fucking kidding me," Eli groans, dropping his head to my chest.

The corners of Ali's lips turn up as her cheeks turn pink in amusement.

"Maybe we should start using the sock method," Ali suggests with a giggle.

"Maybe we should start using the *knock* method," I snap in frustration, thoroughly annoyed that my best girl is in my room right now.

"Maybe we should start using the *lock* method," Eli says with a pointed glance and a frustrated tone. "Seriously, Logan, you need to start locking your door. It makes me feel uneasy that you keep it unlocked so much."

"But I like that you can come in whenever you want," I remind him, looking down at his handsome face, his frustrated expression softening.

"Well, give me your spare key then. It'll make me feel better knowing you're locked in here at night."

"Marc has it."

"I'll get it from him tomorrow," Eli says.

Running my fingers through his hair, I look down at my favorite guy, my eyes exploring him, lost in this moment together as I lean down to place my lips on his.

"So, what are you guys up to tonight?" Ali asks, reminding us that she's still in the room.

Eli lets out a heavy frustrated sigh.

"Ali, I love you, but read the fucking room," I tell her.

"Yeah, I'm..." She awkwardly backs away towards the door. "I'm just gonna go." She throws a thumb over her shoulder, pointing towards her room before rushing out and closing my door.

"We are moving. We are moving to the middle of fucking nowhere," Eli says, his voice beginning to rise. "Where no one knows who the fuck we are! Where I can have sex with," I place my hand over his mouth to quiet him, "my fucking girlfriend!" Eli yells, his words muffled into my palm.

"So romantic." I chuckle at his frustration before pressing my mouth to his, wanting to get back to our moment, and trying to fill the aching need I have for him.

"Let's get out of here," he whispers against my lips.

"Where would we go?" I wrap my arms around his neck. There's no way in hell we are having sex for the first time at the hockey house. There are way too many people there.

"Let's go to the house off-campus," he says. "The last thing I need is my fucking brother knocking on your door tonight."

I nod my head as Eli kisses my tattoo, just as he always does, but now that I'm aware of what it means to him, the butterflies in my stomach flutter more than they usually do.

"I love you too," I tell him, causing him to smile against my skin.

Climbing off his lap, I gather a few things, packing an overnight bag. I slip off my shorts, replacing them with leggings before throwing on a pair of running shoes. I honestly don't care what I wear tonight. It won't be staying on for long anyway.

"I didn't know you printed this out." Eli holds up the newest addition to my framed photos. It's the one of the two of us with Marc and Ali after his game when I met his parents for the first time.

"Yeah, I just added that one," I tell him as he sets it back down next to the other two prints on my bookshelf.

"I love this one of us," he says, pointing at the next one, my favorite picture— the one of Eli and I after that same game. "But we need more pictures together. I need to fill my phone up with your pretty face for when I'm out on the road," he adds, making me smile.

"And these are your parents, right?" He points to the third photo on my shelf.

"Mmm-hmm," I confirm.

"We've never really talked about your mom. What was she like?" he asks with sincere curiosity as he looks at the photo, causing me to pause.

"I don't want to talk about her."

Eli snaps his head around to look at me, his expression concerned. "Shit. Sorry, I didn't mean to bring it up. We don't have to talk about her." He bounds over to me, wrapping his arms around my shoulders and pulling me into him. My body melts into his touch as he strokes my back with his large hands.

"We don't have to discuss anything you're not comfortable with," my sweet man says. "But just know that if you ever do want to talk about her, I'll happily listen."

My mom would have absolutely adored Eli, and it's not that I don't want him to know about her, but I have a tough time talking about her and that time in my life. The only time I've mentioned her in the last eleven months since she passed was when I told Marc about her on a drunken night in Spain and when I told Eli about everything that night at the pond. I don't know that I've even processed that she's really, truly gone, but I'm definitely not going to start working through that tonight.

"Ready?" I ask, changing the subject as I swing my overnight bag over my shoulder.

"Yep." Eli kisses my forehead, grabbing my bag from me as he does.

My fingers intertwine with Eli's as he walks us down the hall towards the elevator. As the letters and numbers on the elevator wind down, the nerves begin to set in as I silently stare at the metal doors, waiting for them to open. When they do, they reveal my best friend on the other side.

"Hey guys," Marc says as Eli and I exit the elevator. "Where are you going?"

"We're gonna go stay at the house off-campus for the night," Eli informs him as we head towards the lobby doors.

"Oh, I'll come with you."

"No!" Eli and I quickly interject at the same time.

"Well, damn," Marc says, taken aback. "I didn't really want to go anyway."

"We just need a night alone," Eli tries to soften our blow as he ushers me outside and towards his truck.

The nerves begin to build again on the drive over to the house as my knee involuntarily bounces while I stare out the window. The weather quickly shifted from a crisp fall day to a stormy night. The rain begins to pelt down on Eli's truck, drowning out the music on the radio, as the windshield wipers move at their quickest pace.

"Logan." Eli puts his hand on my bouncing leg, instantly settling it. "We don't have to do this. There's no rush."

Placing my hand over his, weaving our fingers, I look at him while he keeps his eyes on the road. "I want to. I'm just nervous. But, they're good nerves, I promise."

One of the corners of Eli's lips turns up. "Don't be nervous," he says, pulling up to the house. "It's us. There is nothing to be nervous about when it comes to us."

Unfortunately, the driveway is fairly far away from the front door. This big-ass house has a big-ass walkway, which I distinctly remember from the first night I was here and stuck in a storm.

"We gotta make a run for it." Eli grabs my bag from his back seat. "Ready?" he asks with an excited glimmer in his eye.

I nod my head as a smile creeps across my lips.

"Let's go," he adds, opening his door the same time as I do, both of us making a dash for the house.

Even though he and I are quick with our long legs, we both end up soaked, and the rain is freezing. Eli swiftly unlocks the door and ushers me in, but it's too late. I'm drenched and shivering.

"Well fuck," he says as both of us laugh at our misfortune, our clothes and hair dripping rainwater onto the entryway floor.

"I'm so cold," I tell him with chattering teeth and a happy smile.

"What's new?"

He bends down and scoops me up as I wrap my legs around his middle and grasp onto his neck with my arms.

"Where are you taking me?" I ask as he hurries up the stairs with my body clinging to his.

"To warm you up, my cold, California girl." He quickly presses his lips to mine.

Eli heads straight through his room and into his bathroom before setting me back on my feet. He tosses my wet bag onto the tiled floor before turning the shower to the hottest setting.

"Get naked," he commands with dark eyes. And even though he told me to do it, he assists as his greedy hands find the waistband of my tight, wet leggings. He pulls them down my legs, and I kick them off when they reach my ankles.

Since he is helping with mine, I deem it only fair to help him get undressed as well. I tug at his damp hoodie, and when it makes its way over his head, his hat goes with it.

Eli's hooded eyes find mine as he cups my face, but my eyes wander to his chiseled torso, watching his chest rise and fall with rapid breaths.

"I love you," he says between heavy inhales. He closes his eyes and rests his forehead against mine, taking away any remaining nerves.

Crashing my lips against his, I dip my hand into his joggers, pushing them down and finding his cock. As I wrap my hand around him, Eli moans into my mouth, and his body jerks in my grasp. He simultaneously finds my stomach with his hands, lifting my sweatshirt up and over my head, forcing us to break off our kiss.

My body shivers, partly from the cold, but mostly from his touch as Eli's lips connect with the delicate skin of my chest. Though, there's nothing delicate about his mouth's movements. He nibbles and sucks, causing that sweet sting that is sure to leave a mark. He easily unfastens my bra, letting it fall to the floor, his thumbs circling over my taut nipples.

He kisses the length of my neck, flicks my nipple with his tongue, and drags his lips down my stomach as he gets on his knees in front of me. His fingers slide into my thong at the hips, tugging it down my legs until it hits the floor.

Eli's lips part and his breathing turns shallow as he stares at my center. I burrow my hands into his hair as his warm tongue makes contact with me.

"*Fuck*," I moan, my head falling back to the bathroom wall behind me.

Eli's skillful mouth works its magic, getting me even more soaked than I already am.

He reaches behind me into the shower, testing the temperature of the water before he stands and picks me up again, wrapping my long legs around his waist. His rock-hard erection slides against my swollen clit as he holds me up, causing me to shudder against him.

Eli walks us under the warm stream as my eyes close to keep the water out. His hot breath swirls against my neck as he presses me against the cold shower tile, the mixture of temperatures causing goosebumps to rise all over my body. His hips pin me to the wall as his lips find me with fervor, panting breaths swirling between us, and his cock sliding against me.

Eli sets me down before he turns the shower head towards us, trying to keep me warm before once again getting on his knees in front of me.

He lifts one of my legs over his broad shoulder, resting it there as he sucks and flicks my clit while one of his fingers pumps inside of me. I tug at his shaggy hair, needing to steady myself as he continues his welcome assault. My toes curl as I look down at him, needing to watch him ravish my body, my lips parting at the view.

He's so fucking good at this, always knowing what my body needs.

The pressure builds, and Eli can sense it as his pace quickens against my center. Whenever I moan his name, it causes Eli to groan against me, sending a vibration straight through my core.

He looks up at me while his tongue glides against my clit, but quickly closes his eyes again from the water beating down on us. Pulling his finger out of me, he stands, causing me to whimper from the loss of contact, being so close to my release.

"I need to watch you come, baby." His tone is deep and low as he leans down to my ear, his erection pressing into my stomach.

His words heat my entire body, washing away the cold from the rain. I watch as the water forms a path down his rapidly rising and falling chest, drawing my eyes all over his perfect frame.

Eli turns me around, pulling me into him as he wraps his tattooed arm around my waist, pressing my back to his chest. I can feel his erection against my lower back as we stand under the stream, the water beating down on our wanting bodies. Reaching my hand around, I grip his length, needing him to feel as good as I do right now.

He groans against me, his forehead falling to my shoulder. "Not yet," he pants as he backs his ass away, forcing me to lose him from my grasp. "I need you to come first."

He grabs the shower head from its bracket as he rubs his free hand against my clit, circling and teasing until he spreads my folds with his finger and thumb. Placing the shower head in my hand, he guides it to my swollen bud as the water pulses against my bundle of nerves.

My head falls back to Eli's shoulder, my knees buckling from the sensation, but he keeps me held upright.

"Hold this here," he instructs as he leaves the shower head in my hand, pulsing against my clit, while his fingers enter me again. He's using two this time, as a warm up for what's to come, and it feels absolutely incredible.

His free arm wraps around my waist, holding me up, because I certainly can't do it on my own right now.

"*Oh my god*," I cry out as the stream beats against me in combination with Eli's touch, my legs turning to Jell-O from the pressure of both.

I've gotten myself off in the shower this way before, but now with Eli's fingers in the mix, the sensation is almost too much.

"Are you going to come, baby?" Eli asks. Though, I think he already knows the answer to that question, thanks to my shaky limbs and contracting abdomen.

Biting my bottom lip to stifle the cries, I nod my head to tell him yes. I reach above me, wrapping my arm around his neck, needing to steady myself.

"Logan, are you going to come?" he asks again, his wet lips brushing against my cheek.

"*Yes,*" I cry out. "I'm going to come," I whimper as Eli's devilishly mischievous lips graze against the side of my face.

I pull the shower head away from me because, quite honestly, the pressure is too much, and I feel like I'm going to combust, but Eli isn't having it.

"No, baby. Keep it here." He moves my hand back and even closer to my clit, causing the water pressure to assail my already sensitive nerves. My legs begin to shake, and my entire body tightens. I fall forward, but Eli secures his grip around my waist to hold me up as I unravel and cry out his name. He holds onto me as I ride out my orgasm, letting it rip through my entire body.

"I could watch you come all night." Eli presses himself against me, reminding me how hard he is right now. Removing his fingers from me, he takes the shower head that I dropped in the heat of the moment, and places it back into its bracket before setting me on my feet again. My breathing is ragged, and my heart is pounding from both that glorious orgasm and the perfect image of the naked specimen standing behind me.

I turn around to face him, my chest heaving, as the water continues to wash over us.

"I want you," I remind him, staring into his warm brown eyes.

I can see him searching my face through the stream, most likely looking for any hesitation or second thoughts, but there aren't any. I want this. I want to do this. I love this man with everything I am, and he's exactly who I've been waiting for.

Eli presses his lips to mine as he reaches behind me, shutting off the water. His muscular body lifts mine with ease, carrying my soaked frame to his bed. I'm drenched, and so is he, not that either of us gives a shit, as he lays me on his mattress.

He peppers my neck and chest, biting and sucking, then licking to ease the sting. The smooth skin of his erection slides against my thigh as he continues his mouth's assault. He works his magic down my body as he pushes my bent knees towards my chest and presses his tongue against my sex.

My head falls back to the bed as my eyes screw shut from the sensation. He feels fucking amazing as he always does as his tongue flicks against my clit. Somehow, I feel like I might come again already as Eli's masterful mouth teases me.

"Eli," I manage to say between heavy breaths, trying to tell him I want him inside of me. I attempt to pull him up by the forearms, but he stays put between my legs.

"I know, baby," he says against my aching center. "I just need to make sure you're nice and wet first."

Eli peels his dripping body off of mine and walks back into his bathroom. I'm warm with anticipation and absolutely fucking soaked as he comes back into the room with his joggers in his hands. He reaches into the pocket and pulls out a foil packet before tossing his pants to the side.

My breathing hitches when I see the condom.

Okay. This is happening. This is really happening.

When Eli comes back to the bed, he leans down and places his warm lips on mine. His kiss is sweet and caring, full of love, calming me down.

He climbs on the bed, nudging my legs with his knee. I generously open them as he holds his body up on his elbow, hovering above me. He looks down at me once again, his eyes quickly scanning my face before I lean up and press my lips to his. He smiles into my mouth as I remind him that this is what I want.

Eli tears the foil packet with his teeth, keeping his gaze on mine the entire time. I watch as he takes the condom in the space between us and rolls it on.

He leans down and finds my mouth with his, parting my lips and allowing his tongue to explore mine. He cups my face and slides his hands into my wet hair as his feverish kiss continues. The silky condom brushes against my hip, causing my body to shudder. Eli breaks our mouths' connection as he leans his forehead against mine, our eyes remaining closed as the panting breaths swirl between us.

"Are you nervous?" He whispers.

I don't feel like I can speak, so instead, I nod my head against him.

"I'm nervous too," he admits as my eyes shoot open to look at him.

"Why are you nervous?"

"Because I've never done *this* before," he shyly admits, his warm eyes peering down at mine.

I know what he's referring to, so I don't need him to clarify. He's never been with someone he cares about before. It's always just been about fucking random girls for him. Suddenly, I don't feel so afraid, knowing this is a first for both of us, just in different ways.

"Don't be nervous, baby. It's us. There's nothing to be nervous about when it comes to us." A smile overtakes his lips as I repeat his earlier words.

"I love you," he says, his words immediately relaxing me.

Chapter 72

Logan

Eli slips his tattooed arm behind me, between my back and the bed, his hand gripping my shoulder from behind. His erection glides across my pelvic bone as he lifts himself a few inches above me. My entire body tightens from the sensation, knowing exactly what is about to happen.

"Baby," Eli softly says. "You have to relax. It's going to hurt like a bitch if you don't relax."

I let out a nervous laugh. "Thanks, babe. That's really going to help me to calm down," I tell him with sarcasm, which only causes him to laugh with me.

I'm glad he's laughing. I'm glad I'm laughing. I just want us to be ourselves right now, and if joking around helps with that, then I'm all for it.

"I'm sorry," he chuckles as he bends down and kisses my lips. "Here." He leans his body on mine, using his free hand to wrap one of my arms around his back. "Hold onto me."

I wrap my arms around Eli's back, under his arms, holding onto his shoulder blades.

He bends down and kisses my tattoo as his fingers circle my clit. He kisses his way up my neck, across my cheek, until his lips make contact with mine, instantly settling me. Eli grips his length as he leans up a bit, rubbing himself over my bundle of nerves and silently telling me what is about to happen.

He lines himself up with my center and very slowly pushes into me.

The pressure takes my breath away as my mouth gapes, but I keep my eyes open, looking at Eli. His mouth falls open from the sensation, and his eyes flutter, but he keeps his gaze locked on me.

It's borderline unbearable, and he's not even in all the way, but I'm trying not to tense up and make things worse.

My fingers dig into the flesh of his back, trying to relieve the pain as Eli continues to push himself into me, filling me and stretching me, but I know he's attempting to be as gentle as he can.

"*Fuck*," he breaths out on an exhale.

Once he's fully inside of me, he drops his head to the side of mine, both of our chests rapidly rising and falling. His fingertips are digging into the top of my shoulder, and I can tell he's trying to hold himself back.

My eyes screw shut once he's no longer looking at me as I try to adjust to the feeling of him being inside of me. Biting my lower lip, I attempt to work through the foreign discomfort. Eli stays still, giving me time to adjust.

"Logan, you okay?" Eli asks as his breath tickles the skin of my neck.

I don't think I can speak just yet, so I nod my head against him.

He lifts his face to look at me, his brown eyes searching mine, trying to make sure I'm alright. I don't want him to worry about me, I can do this, so I wrap my hand around the back of his neck and pull his lips to mine. As our mouths explore each other's, Eli pulls back and slowly presses into me again. My eyes squeeze close from the sting as he gently thrusts into me.

Keeping our lips connected helps distract me from the uncomfortable feeling. Eli's fingers continue to dig into the back of my shoulder as he keeps his tempo slow. I squeeze his back every time his hips grind down into mine, and as difficult as it is, I try to stay relaxed. He pulls his lips away to look at me once again as he continues to slowly pump inside of me.

He looks like he wants to lose control, but he's trying so hard to keep it slow. His lips alternate from being gaped open and him biting down on them as he attempts to stay gentle with me. His breathing is strained and ragged, uneven and short. Even with his slow pace, I've never seen him like this, and I don't think I'll ever get tired of seeing his reaction to being with me.

With each thrust and heavy pant, the discomfort is lessening. I feel like I need to move a bit and adjust, so I bend one of my knees on the side of Eli's body. When he notices this, he grabs the back of my thigh and uses it as an anchor, pressing it into my chest with each slow drive. He takes his arm from behind my back and laces his fingers with mine, holding our hands next to our heads, pressed into the mattress, as his gaped mouth lingers above me.

"Talk to me, Logan," he moans. I realize now that I have yet to say a word since he entered me, but I finally feel like I can speak.

I'm not really one to talk dirty, and I don't think that's what he's asking for. I'm pretty positive he wants me to speak so he can make sure that I'm alright. I'm also not going to be that girl that continually says, 'I love you' while losing her virginity. Even though it's true, that just seems a little intense in an already overwhelming experience. I don't want to make tonight some big romantic show. I want to keep things as light as possible and enjoy it as much as I can. So, I decide to try to lighten the mood instead.

"How was your day?" I ask, the words a bit strained as they leave my mouth, wincing as he pushes into me again.

Eli's forehead drops to my chest in laughter. "I fucking love you," he says between laughs and heavy breaths. He leans up and kisses my smiling lips with his. "A lot better...right now," he adds, struggling to get the words out between thrusts.

"You're okay...*fuck*...you're okay, though?" he asks, needing the confirmation.

I could not love this guy more. He's doing everything he can to keep it slow for me, and the only thing he's concerned about is how I am. I didn't know he was who I was waiting for, but I feel so lucky to be this comfortable with him and love this man as much as I do.

"Yeah," I gasp as he pushes into me again. "I'm good." I kiss his damp forehead just to reassure him. Even though it's still uncomfortable, I want him to enjoy this and not worry about me.

I never expected to feel pleasure my first time, and I don't. Not sexually, anyway. But I absolutely love watching Eli unravel from finally being inside of me.

"*Fuck*," he groans, his eyes rolling back. "You feel so fucking good, Logan." He takes the hand that was interlocked with mine and wraps it behind my back, curving around my waist, anchoring himself as he holds onto my hip.

He continues his movements, every once in a while placing a kiss on my skin or throwing out a curse word caused by the sensation.

The mixture of his hips meeting mine and the rain pelting against the windows outside causes a heavenly combination to overtake me as I let myself get lost in this moment and enjoy watching him this way. I knew I needed to trust someone to allow myself to completely let go, and I couldn't trust anybody more than I do, Eli.

"I'm so close," he says, but I could already tell, due to his short breaths and contracting muscles. "I love you so much, Logan."

Even though I thought I wasn't going to say it in the heat of things, to lessen the dramatic effect of it all, maybe he needs to hear the words right now, and I sure as hell feel them, so why not share.

"I love you too, Eli." I run my hands through his unruly hair, holding onto the back of his neck.

He moans at my words as his head falls to my neck with a few more thrusts until his entire body tightens and jerks, my name falling from his lips with a couple of breathy 'fucks' thrown in there too.

I could watch this over and over, Eli coming undone from being with me, and I fully plan to.

His hot, heaving body falls on top of mine as I wrap my arms around his shoulders and hold him to me while he catches his breath.

"Fucking hell," he says into my nape, causing me to laugh.

Eli lies on me for quite some time, his warm body pressing me into the mattress as I hold him in my arms and stroke his wet hair with my fingers. Eventually, he leans up and places his soft lips on mine.

"Are you okay?" he gently asks with concern.

I give him a nod with a smile.

His lips linger on mine as he slowly pulls out of me, causing me to wince from the sudden emptiness. It's plenty wet down there, and I'm not sure if it's from my arousal or if I bled, but I don't want to find out just yet. Either way, it's fine. I highly doubt that Eli is going to give a shit if I got blood on his sheets.

He quickly discards the used condom before sliding back into bed and pulling the covers over our naked bodies. Putting his arm under me, he rolls me onto his body, so I'm lying on top of him with my head on his chest, but the swift movement causes me to whimper against him.

"Shit. Did I hurt you? I was trying so hard not to hurt you." Eli lifts his head to look at me with concern.

"I'm just a bit sore. I'll be alright."

He strokes my back with his fingertips and plays with my hair as we bask in the moment together. I could lay like this all night, wrapped up with my man, but I'm also starving and need to pee.

"Baby?"

"Yeah?" Eli quickly asks.

"I'm hungry."

"Thank god," he says, his body shaking with laughter. "I'm fucking starving, but I didn't want to rush you and ruin our romantic moment."

"Pasta is romantic," I tell him. "Pasta, and bread, and butter."

"I love when you talk dirty to me."

I very slowly and cautiously peel myself off Eli's lean, muscular body, looking to the sheets next to me as I do. Surprisingly there isn't any blood, but I guess everyone's first time is different.

I make it to the bathroom with a bit of a limp before I quickly pee and wash my hands in the sink. When I look up in the mirror, I can't help the smile from creeping across my lips.

I feel so lucky. So goddamn lucky that Eli was my first. I've heard stories of girls who lost it to guys who didn't give a shit about them, making their sexual experience solely one-sided. It's partly what made me wait all this time. But I'm so glad I did. And not just because Eli loves me, but because he cares about me and respects me, which was evident tonight.

"Shit," Eli says from the bathroom doorway. "I didn't mean to go that hard." His naked body bounds over to me, standing behind me, as his fingers delicately graze the red marks peppered across my chest.

"That's okay. I kind of like it," I tell him, referring to the red skin that is sure to turn into hickeys tomorrow. "At least you kept them low so I can hide them."

Wrapping his arms around my middle, he bends down to kiss my collarbone before leaning his chin on my shoulder.

"Was it okay for you?" Eli sincerely asks, looking at me through the mirror as he holds onto my naked body. "Was that how you imagined it?"

God, I love him. This big-ass arrogant dude is just a soft teddy bear when it comes to me.

I turn around to face him, wrapping my arms around his waist. "It wasn't about how. It was about who." I reach up on my toes to kiss his worried lips. "But the 'how' was great too."

"I love you," Eli says, smiling down at me.

“I love you too,” I tell him, enjoying his embrace for a few moments. “Now go make me some dinner.” I slap his bare ass as Eli’s deep belly laugh echoes across the bathroom walls.

I take my time gathering myself and my thoughts before heading down to the kitchen, wearing Eli’s shirt. As I walk down the stairs, I spot him in front of the stove, shirtless, his lean back facing me.

When I get a little closer to him, I find scratch marks on his back that I must have put there when we were having sex. I remember grabbing onto him, trying to relieve the pressure, but I didn’t realize I was that rough.

“Eli, I scratched the shit out of you.” I walk up behind him, grazing the red marks on his upper back.

“I know. I felt it,” Eli says without turning around as he heats a pot of water on the stove.

“Sorry, baby.” I wrap my arms around his middle and press my cheek to his bare back.

He drapes his arm over mine. “Don’t be. I liked it.” He turns around and presses his warm lips to mine. “I have a very important question for you. Are we thinking legit pasta or Kraft Mac and Cheese? Because I have options, and I excel at both,” my arrogant boy says as he lifts me up and gently sits me on the kitchen island.

“Kraft Mac and Cheese,” I quickly answer without hesitation.

“That’s my girl.”

“Remind me where you’re headed this week?” I ask as Eli puts the noodles into the boiling water to cook.

“Tuesday, we play at Purdue, which will be cool because my parents aren’t far, so they’re coming to watch. Then Friday, we’ll be at Ohio State.”

“Ohio State. Isn’t that where that guy who broke your ankle plays?”

“Evan fucking Zanders,” he says in a low voice. “Yeah, he plays there.”

"Are you worried about that?" I ask with concern. He might not be, but I certainly am. The last thing I want is for Eli to get hurt again.

"Worried?" he asks, turning around to face me, standing between my legs. "No. I just gotta keep my head up when I'm out there because he's a dirty motherfucker. He's been on my ass for years. But he's good, so is his team, and there will probably be at least one NHL scout there that night. He and I are both on their radars."

His words hit me as I'm reminded that Eli can leave at any moment. As soon as he gets that call, he'll be on the next flight out, leaving me here. I pull my gaze away from his as the unwelcome thoughts swirl around my mind.

"Don't worry," Eli says, tucking my damp hair behind my ear. "If I start to feel panicky, I'll call. I'll be alright."

Perfect, now let's add Eli's panic attacks to my list of concerns.

"What time are you leaving tomorrow?" I ask, trying to get my mind off things.

"I gotta meet the bus at six tomorrow night."

"What about school? You guys miss so much school. Doesn't it affect your grades?"

Eli looks at me with a smug glance. "Baby. I'm a division one athlete with a full-ride scholarship. As fucked up as it sounds, we get special treatment. And our professors are picked for us, knowing which ones favor athletes. So no, I don't really need to worry about school."

I knew this. I was well aware when I was offered a full-ride to play for the University of Oregon that I wouldn't have to worry too much about my classes, but still, it's crazy to know that some of us have to work so hard in school while others get a free pass.

"That's wild that they just let you guys graduate like that."

"Well, I don't know if I'm going to graduate," Eli casually says with a shrug.

My brows furrow in confusion. "What are you talking about?"

"If I get picked up by a team, I'm out of here. I might not make it to May."

"You're not worried about getting your degree?"

"Not really." He shrugs. "If I get an NHL contract, that's going to pay me a whole hell of a lot more than some job I can get fresh out of school with a kinesiology degree."

It's really going to happen. He's going to leave, and it can happen any day. I knew this, but I don't think it ever really sank in. But now, hearing him say that he might not be here in May when I still have another year and a half of school, it's overwhelming. As sad as I'm going to be, I want Eli to be happy, and fulfilling his lifelong dream will make him happy. So as selfish as I would like to be, I can't. I love him too much to want anything less than for him to succeed.

"What's on your mind?" Eli asks, pulling me out of my daze.

"Nothing." I shake my head. "Just thinking about how much I'm going to miss you this week is all."

"I'm going to miss you too," he says before pressing his lips to mine. "Always do. But it's just a short week, then I'm home, and we are off to Indiana soon."

Turning back to the stove, he takes the cooked noodles off the burner.

"Speaking of Thanksgiving, who all am I going to be meeting that weekend?"

"Oh, you'll be meeting everyone. The whole family will be there," he says as he finishes up our dinner. "Marc and my parents. Then there's Mary's two brothers, my uncles. Uncle Drew is married to my Aunt Molly, and they have three boys, Gavin, Gabe, and Garrett. Then my other uncle, Tommy, is married to my Aunt Grace, and they have twin boys, Sam and Scotty."

"Don't worry. I'll remind you who is who all weekend," Eli adds over his shoulder with a sweet little smile.

"That's a whole lot of testosterone in one house."

"Tell me about it."

Eli returns to me, standing between my legs, wrapping his arms around my waist, and hiding his face in my neck. I drape my arms around his shoulders, stroking his shaggy hair as he leans into me.

"I already know a few of them are going to go crazy having you there all weekend. Not to mention my aunts, they're going to be obsessed. They all wanted daughters, and everyone ended up with a shit ton of boys."

"What about your dad's side of the family? Are any of them going to be there?"

He shakes his head against me. "He doesn't have anyone on his side. It was just him and his sister, my mom before she passed."

Oh, I had no idea.

"Is anyone else bringing their significant other, or is it just me?" I ask, quickly changing the subject. I'm not sure how Eli feels about talking about his mom, and I just want to keep things light tonight.

"The cousins are all single except Gabe, but I'm not sure if he's bringing Liam or not this year. They've been together for a long ass time, but besides that, no one has ever brought anyone else home."

"Oh, so this is kind of a big deal then," I say in a teasing tone, lifting his head to look at me. "Are you nervous?"

"No, not at all," he confidently states, shaking his head. "I'm a little nervous we're going to scare you off, but besides that, I'm excited for you to come home with me."

He kisses me quickly before returning to the stove and scooping our mac and cheese into bowls. I love watching Eli in the kitchen. Even if it's as simple as boxed pasta, I can't help but admire my sexy shirtless man standing in front of the stove, cooking for me.

"Almost forgot," Eli says. "You'll meet Max too, our golden."

"You guys have a dog?" I ask with excitement.

"Yeah, but don't get any ideas." Eli holds up his wooden spoon to me in a playful manner. "I'm his favorite, and I don't need you trying to steal any of his attention away from me."

Oh, I'm going to smother the shit out of that dog. Eli will be lucky if he gets any of *my* attention that weekend, let alone Max's.

"What did you do last year for Thanksgiving?" he asks as he hands me my bowl of cheesy carbs.

Last year I was sitting in my mom's hospital room, eating a microwaved turkey dinner from the hospital cafeteria. At that point, my mom didn't know who I was half the time due to the meds she was on, but I'm not going to bring that up right now. I don't want to put a damper on tonight.

"Not much," I say instead.

"Are there any Thanksgiving traditions that you guys did growing up? Anything we should do this year that you're used to?"

"I always ran a 5k on Thanksgiving morning. I looked forward to the annual Turkey Trot in our hometown."

Eli gives me a skeptical glance. "My little athletic freak, you ran a 5k to start your day of eating?"

"Mmm-hmm," I hum with a smile, my mouth full of pasta. "Do you have any traditions?"

"We do a Maddison-Jones football game on Thanksgiving afternoon. It's a big deal and highly competitive, so get ready to cheer me on for that. Signs are encouraged," he adds with heavy irony. "Plus, Marc's birthday is that weekend, so that'll be fun."

I slowly hop off the kitchen island as we make our way to the couch, our mac and cheese in hand. Taking a seat on the sofa, I kick my feet up as Eli sits next to me. He grabs the remote from the coffee table before taking my legs and gently swinging them over his lap instead.

"What do you think about skipping school tomorrow and just hanging here until you have to leave?"

Eli pauses with his forkful of pasta partway to his mouth. "Logan Jo Leo, are you suggesting that we ditch?" he asks with wide eyes. "Who are you, and what have you done with my girlfriend?"

"It's Logan *Josephine* Leo," I remind him, even though I know he just likes to shorten it because he thinks it flows better off the tongue. "Classes obviously don't matter for you, and I don't have anything too important tomorrow. We could still go to creative writing if you want to?"

"Nope," he quickly says, shaking his head. "The only reason I even like that class is because you're in it, but you can't be naked there. So, home it is."

"Alright, my little LJ, what do you want to watch?" he asks, holding the remote up to the television, turning it on.

"I have two more episodes of this season of *New Girl*. Can we watch that?" I ask as sweetly as possible, hoping to get my way. "I'll explain what's going on."

"Baby, you just let me have sex with you. You could pretty much have anything your little heart desires right now," he says, making me laugh with my mouth full. "But I have a confession. Remember that night when I showed up at your dorm, and you were pissed off at me? The night after we kissed for the first time."

I nod my head suspiciously, having no idea where he is going with this or why this has anything to do with the show I want to watch, except that he watched a few episodes with me that night.

"Well, I told you I drove there, and I couldn't drive home until I sobered up," he reminds me. "Yeah, I walked there from my house." His lips turn up in a devilish grin.

"You little liar!" I say with a gaping mouth, though the corners are turning up in amusement.

"I couldn't tell you the truth! You were going to kick me out!" He puts his hands up in defense.

I take a pillow off the couch and playfully smack him with it, causing him to throw his head back in laughter.

"You persistent little punk," I add, trying to hold back my grin.

"Yeah, and that persistence paid off, I'd say." He runs a hand up my bare leg before leaning over and kissing my lips with his.

"And since we are on the subject of being truthful," he says, his lips lingering just above mine. "I've seen this season of *New Girl* twice already."

My mouth hangs fully open. "Do I even know you anymore?"

Chapter 73

Eli

Allowing the hot water beat down on me, I stand under the stream in the locker room showers, with my hands on the tile wall and the water coating my exhausted body. The pulsing pressure feels amazing on my tight muscles. I've been going hard the last couple of weeks between important division games and longer practices, plus I've been staying late on the ice to get some extra repetitions in. My body can feel it. But I have to keep my head down and grind because Senior Showcase is only a little over a month away.

This morning's game felt good, and the pregame wake-up sex felt even better. It's been a couple of weeks since Logan and I first slept together, and it's gotten better each time. And by better, I mean for her. It's been fan-fucking-tastic each and every time since the start for me, but it's different for girls, and it's been more enjoyable for Logan the more we've done it. Regardless, Logan has taken it like a champ. But still, I'm looking forward to the day that I don't have to hold back with her.

"No Logan today?" Cam asks from the shower next to mine.

"No, she's here. But I have some friends in from out of town, so she and Marc gave up our family seats to sit in the student section today."

"I was wondering who that cute little blond kid was, sitting right behind the bench," Cam says through the squeal of the shower head. "Well, tell Logan that she was missed."

I give him a sideways glance. "Why are you creeping on my girlfriend anyway?"

"She's my friend," Cam says with a shrug. "And she always hypes me up when I'm on the bench between shifts. I missed my pep talks today."

What the fuck? "She doesn't do that for me," I tell him with furrowed brows.

"Maybe because you don't need it, NHL prospect. Whereas my 5'8" scrawny ass gets thrown into the boards by every giant asshole defenseman in the league. Sometimes I just need a little encouragement."

My guy, Cam. I try to look out for him on the ice, but we are rarely on the same shift. Of course, Logan would notice when he's getting beat up and needs a little pep talk. I fucking love that girl.

"Well, I'll tell her you missed her." I shut off my shower. "Have a good Thanksgiving, man."

I comb my fingers through my wet hair, trying to push it out of my face before throwing on my game-day suit. I toss my dirty jersey in the equipment bin and pack the rest of my gear in my gym bag. Snagging my phone and keys from the top shelf of my locker, I quickly eye my two favorite pictures that are taped to the back of my stall, right where I can see them before every game—one of me and my girl and the other of my family.

When I step out of the locker room and into the player's tunnel, I'm surprised to hear it as quiet as it is. There's still a crowd waiting, but not as large as usual. Most students must be leaving for break right now, just as Logan and I are about to do.

I don't even scan the crowd. I already know where she is.

Just as I suspected, Logan is tucked away, up the hall, away from the crowd in her usual spot. She looks so fucking cute right now, wearing my maroon road jersey that literally drowns her frame.

"Hi," she says as I make my way to her. Her pretty green eyes shine when she locks her gaze with mine.

"Hi, baby." I wrap her up in my embrace, kissing the top of her head as I do.

"Good game. That shorthanded goal was pretty," Logan says with a tap of my ass.

"Do you know how hot it is when you talk hockey to me?"

"Eli," a voice behind me says.

I turn around, keeping my arm around Logan's shoulder, finding Trev just behind me.

"Trev, glad you could make it, man." I swing my arm over him in a hug.

"Hey Stace." I turn to the pregnant woman next to him, quickly pecking her cheek. Just as I do, a little forty-pound boulder tries to take me out by the knees.

"Little man!" I scoop up the blond boy at my feet, holding him to my chest.

"You...you...you the fastest one, Maddison," Ian says as he smooshes my cheeks together.

"Oh, yeah? I bet you're probably faster than me by now."

"Yeah, I...I...I the fastest," he says, proudly poking himself in the chest.

Ian has a little stutter that his parents are worried about, but the kid is a stud. He will be just fine.

"Baby, you remember Trev from the coffee shop?" I ask Logan while nodding towards Trev.

"Yeah, of course. Hey, Trev," she says, hugging my friend.

"And this is his wife, Stacey, and their son, Ian."

"I...I Maddison. You call me Maddison," Ian corrects, making me laugh. I forgot that Trev told me Ian now prefers to be referred to as 'Maddison' instead of his own name.

"Well, Maddison," Logan begins, pointing to Ian's chest. "That's a cool jersey you got on there." Ian is wearing the tiny jersey I sent him with my last name on it. You know, since it's his name now, too, apparently.

Ian doesn't respond. Instead, his pale cheeks turn rosy as he lifts his shoulder, touching his face to it and giving Logan his sweetest smile.

Little flirt.

"I almost didn't believe Trev when he told me that Eli brought someone to the pond. I had to see it to believe it," Stacey says, looking to Logan.

Logan's smile beams. "Your property is so beautiful. I want to get back out there soon."

"Anytime. We would love to have you guys out. If you wait another month, the pond should be frozen over, and there will probably be a fourth." Stacey rubs her pregnant belly.

"You look great, Stace."

"Eli, you sweet liar. I look like I have a basketball stuffed under my shirt and my feet are the size of balloons."

"Still look great," I remind her with a shrug.

"So, this is where my son learned to flirt," Trev chimes in, giving me shit. "It's all making sense."

"You wanna go see the locker room?" I ask the little blond boy in my arms.

He quickly nods his head in enthusiastic agreement.

"Be right back," I tell Logan as I lean over and give her a swift kiss.

Ian lays his head on my shoulder as I carry him to the locker room, and I'm pretty sure Logan's ovaries are doing cartwheels as she watches us walk away.

I take Ian on a tour around the empty locker room while my giant hand engulfs his tiny one. His blue eyes are big and bright as he looks at the player stalls with all the hockey equipment inside.

"What do you think?" I ask, looking down at the little guy by my side.

He doesn't respond but instead continues to hold my hand, shyly putting his other fingers in his mouth and giving me a nod of approval.

"Are you going to play here one day?".

He shyly nods again.

"She...she your wife?" Ian asks out of nowhere, pointing towards the hall.

"Logan?"

Again, he shyly nods.

I bend down, making myself eye level with him. "No, little man, she's not my wife."

I'm not sure if he knows what a girlfriend is, and I'm pretty sure the only other people he's seen kiss are his parents, so it makes sense why he thinks we are married.

Ian's big blue eyes go wide with excitement at my answer.

"Whoa. Just because Logan isn't my wife doesn't mean she's not taken. Get in line, buddy," I playfully tell him with furrowed brows.

"She has pretty hair," he shyly tells me.

"Right? The prettiest."

Picking up the kid, I carry him back to where his parents and my girl are waiting. "I'm gonna need you to stop being such a flirt, though," I whisper. "Your dad is going to kill me if you pick up any more game."

"We'll let you guys go. I know you need to get on the road," Trev says. "Thanks for the tickets."

"Anytime, man," I remind him, giving him another hug.

"Be good," Stacey tells me. "Logan, it was so great to meet you." She wraps Logan up in her embrace. Well, as much as she can. She has a big round belly in the way.

"You too. I'm looking forward to meeting him," Logan adds, motioning towards Stacey's belly.

"Maddison." I bend down to Ian's eye level again. "Let's skate soon?" I ask, holding my fist out for him.

He quickly nods and pounds his fist with mine.

"Bye, Maddison. It was nice to meet you," my sweet girl says to him.

Ian doesn't respond but instead tilts his head and shoots her his flirtiest smile, causing me to roll my eyes.

Little shit.

I watch as Trev and his family walk out of the tunnel together. I'm so appreciative of those three, especially Trev. I might not be here, still playing hockey, without his friendship and listening ear.

"You're so good with him," Logan says as I swing my arm around her shoulders, walking out of the tunnel and back to her dorm together.

"He's easy."

"Do you want kids?" she casually asks as we walk together.

I knew this question was coming. I knew that as soon as Logan saw us together, her mind would go there. But to be honest, I've been thinking about it a weird amount, too, so the question doesn't freak me out at all.

"Yeah, of course," I tell her. "One day."

She nods her head but stays silent.

"How many kids do you want?" I ask.

Even though this would typically be a heavy topic this early on in a relationship, Logan and I are different. There's nothing scary about thinking of my future with her. Not to mention she is going to make the best mom.

"I don't want kids," she says, keeping her eyes straight ahead and averted from mine.

"What?" I ask with a laugh. "Of course, you do."

"No, Eli." She turns to look at me. "I don't."

"Wait, really?" I stop in my tracks. "But don't all women want babies and shit?"

She gives me a shrug. "Not me."

"Why not?" I ask, taken aback and much more flustered than a twenty-two-year-old who doesn't want kids for a long time should be.

She lets out a heavy sigh. “Honestly, baby, after everything with my parents, especially my mom, the idea of having to take care of someone else again sounds terrifying.”

I look at her in utter confusion. “But, it would be different with your own kids,” I say, apparently trying to convince her.

Logan has to be a mom. She would be the world’s greatest mom. And not just the mom that you buy the ‘world’s greatest mom’ mug for. No, I mean the actual greatest mom in the world. She is the kindest, sweetest, most loving, and selfless person I’ve ever met.

Our kids would be lucky to have her.

Fuck. That’s not what I meant.

Okay, maybe that’s what I meant. I shouldn’t even be thinking about these things right now, but I can’t help but assume that if Logan doesn’t have kids, that means I won’t have kids because I’m pretty sure Logan is it for me. No, I *know* Logan is it for me, and I want my kids to be half of her. Frankly, I want them to be all of her, but that’s not how it works.

Most twenty-two-year-old guys would be loving the fact that their girl isn’t pressuring them for marriage and kids, but apparently, that’s not the case for me. How is *she* the one who needs convincing?

“I just don’t want kids. I don’t want to have to worry about anyone else,” she says with a shrug, terminating the conversation.

That’s definitely not the end of that discussion, but I’m going to let it go for now.

Back in Logan’s dorm, I change into my joggers and a sweatshirt, hanging my suit in her closet for when we’re back home. We have an eight-hour drive ahead of us, and I just want to be comfortable.

Logan folds the jersey of mine that she was wearing and leaves it on top of her dresser. She throws a couple more things in her weekender bag before putting it by the door.

"Good game, Maddison," Ali says as she pops her head through Logan's open doorway. "At least I think it was good? I still have no fucking clue what I'm watching. You guys just look like a bunch of horny dudes who like bumping into each other out there on the ice."

"I'm glad my future career makes so much sense to you, Ali."

"Hey." Marc walks up next to Ali, leaning against the doorframe with his suitcase in tow. "You guys ready?"

Logan and I nod in agreement before my girl turns her attention to Ali. "What time is your flight?"

"I need to call an Uber in about an hour."

"Well, we're going to miss you over break," Logan tells her tiny friend, speaking for all of us apparently.

"Are you excited to be going back to New York?" Marc asks. "You're probably homesick by now."

"Yeah, but honestly, I feel like I'm home whenever I'm with you guys."

"Aww, Ali. That was really sweet," Logan exclaims in a high tone, just as surprised as I am that Ali has a sentimental bone in her body.

Ali looks at her, confused. "Oh no. Not like that. I just mean that you three are so fucking tall it feels like I'm walking around with New York skyscrapers all day. Seriously, I don't know if the sun has hit me once since I moved here."

"Well, I'm going to miss towering over you all day," Logan says as she wraps Ali up in a hug.

"Bertoli." I extend my fist.

"Maddison." She connects her hand with mine.

Ali turns to Marc in the hallway, both of them awkwardly looking at each other, not knowing what to do. They each look like they're going in for a hug, but the timing is off, so they pull away until they decide to just high-five instead.

Wow, this is uncomfortable to watch. Those two are even more awkward, now that we all know they're fucking, than they were before.

"Alison," Marc says with a nod.

"Marcus." Ali turns to head off to her dorm room.

"Ali," Marc interjects before she gets to her room. "Call me and let me know that you landed safely, okay?"

Ali gives him a smile and a nod in agreement before ducking into her room and closing the door behind her.

Logan looks to me, obviously having the same thought that's swirling around my mind right now.

"What?" Marc looks between Logan and me, both of us biting our tongues and wearing the same knowing expression.

"Nothing," Logan says with a shrug, trying to hold back her smile.

"Shut up." Marc shakes his head.

"We didn't say a word," I remind him.

The eight-hour car ride flew by thanks to the constant conversation with my two favorite people, not to mention Marc's killer road trip playlist chock-full of hip-hop and R'n'B from the early 2000s. I kept Logan's hand intertwined with mine as I drove, only letting go when I had to fill up with gas, or if she needed a bathroom stop.

There's just the tiniest bit of daylight left when I pull up in front of my childhood home.

"You're kidding me," Logan says with wide eyes as she leans forward to look out the window, taking in the massive house in front of her. "This is where you guys grew up?"

"Logan, it's Indiana." Marc sits forward in the space between our seats. "Houses are practically free here compared to California prices."

"But still, this place is...this place is massive."

She's not wrong. Our childhood home is huge. It's a six-bedroom house with a den that may as well count as a seventh, not to mention the pool out back or the firepit and half basketball court.

Yes, my parents are financially very well off and can afford a place like this. But more than anything, my parents bought this house so that our families could get together under one roof. Family has always been at the forefront of any plans they made, and that idea has been passed down to Marc and me. It's the most important thing to me.

"Ready?" I ask Logan.

I don't see any of the extended family's cars in the driveway, so they probably won't be here until later. At least Logan won't be bombarded the second she walks through the door.

"Logan!" Mary exclaims, throwing open the front door before bounding towards my girl. She wraps her arms around Logan, keeping her held tightly against her short body. "I missed you."

Even though Mary has only met Logan once, she's not lying about missing her. Every time I've spoken to her since, the first thing she asks is how my girl is doing. When Mary and my dad came to my game at Purdue a couple of weeks ago, the only topic they wanted to discuss was her. Not that I mind. Logan is my favorite subject, after all.

"Fuck us, right, mom? You know us, your actual children," Marc sarcastically says, noting the total lack of attention the two of us are getting right now.

"Yes." Mary holds on to Logan, rocking her back and forth in a hug. "Fuck you guys," she adds with a smile.

"Thank you for having me," Logan says to Mary, once released from my stepmom's embrace.

"Oh, sweet girl, thank *you* for coming. I'm looking forward to you being here this weekend."

Mary gives Marc and me a hug as we walk into the house. A quick hug, definitely nothing compared to the one she gave Logan.

"Oh my god!" Logan shrieks, bending down to say hi to our dog as Max almost tackles her to the ground. "Hi, sweet boy! Hi, Maxy boy!" Logan says in her puppy voice, giving him pets, as Max wiggles his golden butt and licks her face repeatedly.

'Hi,' huh? I see how it is.

"Hey, Max!" I say in my same high-pitched voice, bending down to his level and opening my arms for him to come to me.

Instead, he completely ignores me and continues to give Logan all of his attention.

"Damn. First my stepmom, and now my dog? No love." I stand and give up.

"Where's dad?" I ask Mary as I set our bags by the base of the stairs.

"He ran to the grocery store, that saint. I forgot green beans, and your dad is now at his third store looking for some."

"Logan, can I get you anything? Coffee, tea, wine?" she offers.

"Oh, I'm good right now. Thank you, though," Logan says with a smile as she walks up behind me.

"I'll take some wine," Marc chimes in.

"You know where it is," my stepmom states, brushing off Marc and turning back to the kitchen.

"Damn, Mom. Do you want to at least pretend you're happy that EJ and I are home this weekend?"

"I'm sorry," Mary says with a laugh. "I love you boys, and I'm so happy you're home. But I've never—"

"We know. You've never had a girl here before," I add, causing Mary to flush in embarrassment as Logan chuckles along.

"EJ, will you show Logan to your room?" Mary asks me. "Logan, we have a bit of a full house this weekend, so I have you in EJ's room. But I can kick him out and put him on the couch if you'd prefer."

I look at my girlfriend with a pointed glance. She already asked me where she was staying. When I told her my room, she got so uncomfortable thinking about sleeping in the same bed as me in my parents' house, but my parents don't give a fuck. In fact, they're probably hoping we make them grandparents this weekend. And if she thinks I'm sleeping anywhere else besides next to her, she's lost her goddamn mind.

"Don't be weird about it," I tell Logan when she hesitates.

"I guess he can stay," Logan tells Mary with a shrug and a smart-ass smile.

"So generous of you, baby." I quickly lean down and kiss her lips.

Placing my hand on her lower back, I guide her to the stairs, grabbing our bags before walking up to the second floor.

"That's Marc's room," I tell her, pointing down the hall. "That's where the twins will probably stay." I point towards another door. "The den is down there," I add with a nod. "The other three cousins usually crash there."

"And this," I grab the door handle to my childhood room, "is my room."

I let Logan walk in first, taking in her surroundings. There's not much here that's too exciting to look at besides a case full of trophies and a few family photos on the dresser. My walls are plain gray, and my sheets and comforter are a blue plaid because, well—masculinity and all that shit.

"Cozy," Logan says, circling my room.

I drop our bags by the door before grabbing her from behind, draping my arms around her middle, and leaning my chin on her shoulder.

"We can have sex there." I nod towards my bed. "And there," I add, motioning towards my bathroom. "And well," I look at my dresser with a sideways glance, "there."

Logan giggles in my arms. "We are not having sex this weekend."

"Says who?"

"Says me," she whispers as if someone could hear her. "We are not having sex in your parents' home."

"You lost your v-card in my parents' home," I remind her with a smug smirk, not worrying about my volume.

She playfully smacks my chest in embarrassment. "Yeah, when no one was there. There are going to be way too many people here this weekend."

"Whatever you say, baby." I shoot with a knowing glance. "If you really think you can hold out that long."

"Me?" she asks with wide eyes and a bright smile. "How about you? You're the one that it's going to be a problem for."

She's not wrong. I'm literally thinking about taking her right here and now, but I have a fucking ego, and I don't lose.

"Fine," I say with an outstretched hand. "Let's make a deal. First one to cave, loses."

"I held out for twenty-two years," she smugly says. "I'm pretty sure I can hold off for a few days."

Logan puts her hand in mine, shaking it. "What does the winner get?"

I quickly kiss her lips, lingering mine just above hers. "They get laid, baby," I tell her with a slap of her ass.

Chapter 74

Eli

"Damn, babe!" Logan shouts from the front porch. "I didn't realize you were *that* slow," she adds with a cocky little laugh. Max is just sitting there, panting and happy next to my girl.

I decided to run a 5k with Logan this morning. I wanted her to feel like she had a piece of home with her this holiday, and apparently, running a little over three miles is how she likes to wake up and celebrate Thanksgiving.

"How are you so fucking fast?" I ask her between heavy breaths. I stand up straight with my hands on my hips, trying to catch my breath as I walk up to where she's waiting for me, outside of the house.

Logan stayed stride for stride with me for about the first mile, then couldn't hold back any longer before she took off, and of course, my dog decided to run with her instead of me.

Traitor.

"Thanks for doing that with me." Leaning up, Logan presses her lips to mine and wraps her arms around my neck, both of us a little sweaty. Me more than her.

"It kind of liked it. Got my endorphins going. You know what else would get my endorphins going?" A smirk slides across my mouth as my hands conveniently find her ass.

"Oh, you're ready to lose your bet already?" Logan leans her sweaty body into mine, knowing exactly what she's doing to me.

"We said no sex in my parents' house. We aren't in my parents' house. We're on their front porch," I smugly remind her.

"No, we said first one to cave this *weekend* loses. We didn't say anything about the location."

I throw my head back in frustration. "Remind me why we are doing this stupid bet?"

"It was your idea."

I don't know why I would make that bet with her. I regretted it about five minutes in when Logan changed right in front of me, slowly peeling off layer by layer and absolutely torturing me. Do you know how hard it is to sleep next to your half-naked girlfriend and keep your hands to yourself? I swear I had a hard-on all night.

With my arms still draped around her, Logan turns around in my embrace, bending over to scratch Max's head, allowing her ass to rub right up against my dick. "Oops," she says over her shoulder, turning to look at me with a sneaky little grin. "My bad."

"Good run, Maxy boy." She opens the front door for him, leaving me without the much-needed friction of her body on mine. Turning around, she shoots me a sweet innocent smile, absolutely killing me.

"Oh, that's how we're gonna play this?" I ask her with amusement, adjusting myself before walking into my parents' home. "It's on, baby."

The smell of cinnamon, bacon, and fresh coffee fills my nostrils as we walk inside the noisy house. Logan and I fell asleep before the cousins got into town last night, and we left for our run before anyone was awake, but from the sound of it, she's about to meet everyone.

"You guys went for a run?" Marc asks, still in his pajamas, as we bump into him at the base of the stairs. "You guys are so fucking weird," he adds, shaking his head, before walking ahead of us into the kitchen, straight to the coffee pot.

As soon as Logan and I walk into the kitchen, the room quiets. My cousins and aunts are all standing around the island, breakfast and coffee sitting ready in the center of it. Every single set of eyes turns to look at us in the entryway, wearing our workout clothes and covered in drying sweat.

Mary's face is the first I spot, beaming with excitement as she brings her coffee cup to her lips, trying to hide her smile.

"Uh, hey everyone," I say to my family. "This is Logan." I motion towards my girl, keeping my other hand on her lower back.

I'm pretty sure my two aunts are about to explode with joy, seeing another woman in this house, as they look back and forth between each other, us, then to my stepmom.

"Logan, this is Gavin, Gabe, and Garrett." I point to my three older cousins standing on one side of the island. "And that's Sam and Scotty," I add, motioning towards the twins. "And Aunt Molly and Aunt Grace."

"Nice to meet you all," Logan says with a sweet smile and a shy wave as the family all greets her with hellos. Or in Garrett and Sam's cases, wide eyes and gaping mouths.

"No Liam this year?" I ask Gabe, wondering where his fiancé is.

"I'm pretty sure his mother would kill me if I stole him for another Thanksgiving, and this is his last one before he's officially a Jones, so no, not this year. He'll be here for Christmas, though."

I grab a couple of water bottles from the fridge for Logan and me, and thankfully, most everyone goes back to minding their own business now that introductions are out of the way.

"Where's Uncle Drew and Tommy?" I ask Mary.

"They're out setting up for the football game later, and your dad is around somewhere."

I pour Logan and myself each a coffee, using the festive mugs that Mary put out on the counter. Everything is orange and brown with turkeys or leaves on it. Mary loves a theme. I've known this since I was three.

I open the fridge, looking for creamer, hoping that Mary bought the one I told her Logan likes. Not only is there one bottle, but there's two.

"Thanks, baby," Logan says when I set her hot coffee in front of her. "Mary, can I help you with anything?"

"I think we are set for now, but maybe later?" Mary's eyes are bright and excited, thrilled to have another woman in the house. And I know she doesn't need help. She and my aunts never let anyone in the kitchen on Thanksgiving, but I also know that Mary will do just about anything to spend time with my girlfriend.

"Morning, everyone!" my dad booms as he walks into the crowded kitchen, grabbing a slice of bacon from the island. "Logan, how bad did you smoke EJ?"

"You don't even want to know," she teases, shaking her head.

"That's our girl." He pounds his fist with hers before kissing my stepmom on the cheek.

Last night Marc went to bed early, but Logan and I stayed up with Mary and my dad to play some cards. When I told my parents what our plan was for this morning, my dad would not stop giving me shit, knowing that I'm not a runner. But he also knows I'd do just about anything to make my girlfriend happy. Logan was pretty sure she was going to kick my ass, and she wasn't wrong. At least I won our round of Euchre last night; my ego needed a little stroke.

"I'm gonna go shower." Logan gives my arm a squeeze before taking off towards my room, coffee in hand.

As soon as she is up and out of sight, all eyes turn back to me.

"Holy shit, EJ! She's fine," Garrett says in excitement.

"So fucking fine," Sam adds with a nod and wide eyes.

Before they can elaborate, Marc smacks them both in the back of the head for me.

"Don't talk about my future daughter-in-law like that," my dad playfully scolds from across the island.

"Jesus, Dad. Really?" I ask with a pointed glance, but he just smugly shrugs in response.

"Mary, she's beautiful," my Aunt Molly says.

"I know, right?" Mary agrees as if she had anything to do with it.

I look at them both with furrowed brows and a confused expression, but they just smile at each other, seeming like they want to squeal with excitement.

Maybe it was a mistake bringing Logan home so soon. My family is already being insane about her. I'm going to be lucky if they don't scare her off by the end of the weekend.

"You guys have shirts made for this?" Logan asks as we walk out to the big empty field in my backyard.

"Told you it was a big deal," I remind her as I throw the pile of blue shirts over my shoulder. Marc is on the other side of Logan, carrying the stack of yellow shirts plus the red one for the all-time quarterback.

This game really is a big deal for our family. I don't know why, but it is. Maybe because there are ten overly competitive dudes under one roof, but all I know is we've been playing this annual football game on Thanksgiving since I was nine.

"What do you guys play for?" Logan asks, carrying a blanket and a glass of pinot that my stepmom poured for her to drink while she watched.

"Losing team does dishes after dinner, but that's not really what it's about," Marc tells her. "It's a pride thing."

"Oh, so you guys just have a bunch of egos that need to be stroked," Logan says with a laugh.

"Exactly."

Uncle Drew and Uncle Tommy went all out this year, spray painting the lines on the field with perfect measurements. They also set up a fourth chair on the sideline instead of just the three that are typically out here for Mary and my aunts.

"Logan!" Mary shouts, patting the open seat next to her and holding up the bottle of red she has with her. "I brought the wine!"

"Good luck." She leans up to me, giving me a quick kiss.

My girl happily takes off, sitting in the open spot between my stepmom and two aunts, before wrapping herself up in the cozy blanket she brought with her. Of course, my dog follows right behind, finding his perfect spot at her feet. Logan looks so fucking cute, bundled up with her little beanie on and a glass of wine in hand. I almost don't even want to play right now just so I could snuggle up with her.

Marc and I hand our dad the uniforms before joining the rest of the cousins on the field.

"Alright, boys," my dad begins as we all gather around. "Sam, you're all-time quarterback per usual," he says, tossing him the red T-shirt. "Gavin, you were last year's MVP, which means you're the first captain. Who do you want to be the second?"

"EJ," he says, nodding towards me.

"Thanks, man." My dad hands me the stack of yellow shirts, giving Gavin the blue ones before lining up with the rest of the family so we can pick teams.

"I'll take Gabe," Gavin starts off by saying, tossing his brother a blue shirt.

"Marc," I respond by throwing my brother our team's uniform.

"What the hell, EJ?" my dad asks, wondering why he's not my first pick.

"Sorry, dad," Marc chimes in. "Beauty before age, old man."

"Jack," Gavin says, using his next pick on my dad.

"Smart kid." My dad catches the blue shirt.

The picks continue, and Gavin takes his dad, Drew. I add my cousin Scotty and Uncle Tommy to my team, leaving Garrett as the last choice. He automatically goes to Gavin's team, giving them five players to our four.

"Shit. We don't have Liam this year." I hold up the last yellow shirt in my hand. "We're one short."

My dad quickly turns around, looking at my girl.

"Logan. You wanna play?"

Logan's eyes go wide with her wine glass to her lips as all eyes turn to her.

"Oh, I don't think that's a good idea," she quickly says, shaking her head.

"Come on," Marc coaxes. "You'll be on mine and EJ's team. We need another."

Logan looks towards me as I excitedly nod in approval.

"I don't want a girl on my team," Scotty says, being the little asshole that he is.

"Shut up, Scotty!"

"Shut the fuck up!" Marc and I snap at the same time.

"Come on," I say to her with a nod and an encouraging smile.

Logan takes her blanket off, putting her glass of wine on the armrest of her chair.

"Logan, you can be all-time QB," my dad says.

"What? No!" Sam interjects. "That's my job."

"Not this year," my dad says. "Sam, give her your shirt."

Sam rolls his eyes before slipping off his red tee and handing it to Logan. I throw him his new uniform, being sure to hit him in the face with it for being such a whiny little bitch.

"I don't know if this is a good idea," Logan says with a pale face as she slips the red shirt over her head.

"You'll be great," Marc tells her with encouragement.

"Do you even know what you're doing?" Scotty asks her in a condescending tone that causes me to smack the back of his head. The twins are being little bitches right now, and I wish they weren't on my team so I could tackle them both for being assholes to my girlfriend.

"Logan's dad used to play football," I tell the family. "You know what you're doing, right, babe?"

"Kind of."

I've seen Logan box, and I've seen her play basketball. Even if she's never played football before, she's athletic enough to get by. I have no doubts that she can handle this.

"If Logan is QB, then Marc and EJ can't be on the same team," Garrett says. "She'll favor them."

"Fine." Marc pulls off his yellow shirt. "Gabe, switch teams with me. Is everyone done bitching now?" he asks in annoyance.

"Everyone knows the rules," my dad begins. "Clean tackles only. I don't want anyone getting hurt." He pauses. "Two-hand touch on Logan, though."

"Maybe no-hand touch on Logan?" I quickly interject. "Just stand close to her. That should be good enough."

Marc and my dad roll their eyes at my possessiveness. I call it protectiveness.

"Baby, you got the timer and the score?" my dad calls out to Mary, and she nods in response. "Yellow, you're on offense first."

I walk over to Logan, who is standing next to my aunts and stepmom as she takes her beanie off and throws her hair up in a ponytail.

"Eli, I don't know if I can do this," Logan begins. "This is too competitive."

"You'll be fine." I run a gentle hand down her back and over her red shirt. "You have Marc and me on different teams. We'll help you out," I tell her, trying to sound reassuring, but she doesn't look convinced.

"Mary, tell her she will be fine," I say to my stepmom, needing some backup.

"Logan, you'll be great. Half of these guys are all talk when in reality, they totally suck."

"Mary!" my dad calls out. "I heard that!"

"Not you, babe!" Mary yells to my dad. "You're the best one! Number one fan over here!" She slyly shakes her head with wide eyes while taking another sip of her wine.

I lead Logan over to the huddle of yellow shirts.

"Okay, we'll start off easy," I instruct my team.

"Gabe, you're center, so you're doing the snap to Logan. Uncle Tommy, this is your route." I show him where to go on the palm of my hand. "Logan, Tommy is your target. He's going to be right there. It's a quick little toss—no big deal. Scotty will be here," I add to the imaginary drawing on my hand. "And I'll be here."

"What about me?" Sam asks.

"Just go long." Sam is usually the all-time quarterback because he has a good arm, and that's about it. So, it's best if we keep him out of most of the plays today.

We line up for the snap, and Marc is covering me. Logan looks scared shitless as she stands behind Gabe.

"Just say, 'hike,' when you're ready," I tell her.

She leans down behind Gabe and takes a deep breath. "Hike," she calls out.

I run a few steps forward, but Marc stays with me. I try to lose him by taking a sharp left, but it doesn't work. He's still on me. I find Uncle Tommy, who Logan is supposed to throw to, but he's pretty well covered by my dad.

Looking back to Logan, panic starts to form on her face as she quickly glances between Gabe, Scotty, Tommy, and myself, but no one is open for her. Finally, she looks up the field to Sam, who is deep in the end zone without anyone covering him.

Logan takes a step back, simultaneously cocking her arm, before releasing a Hail Mary to Sam. It's a long-ass throw and a perfect spiral. My eyes follow the ball until it lands in Sam's outstretched hands in the end zone.

Sam is standing there with a stunned expression after catching Logan's pass. Everyone else has gaped mouths and bugged eyes as we turn back to my girl.

I swear you could hear crickets chirping from the stunned silence that has overtaken this group of guys.

"Logan," I say, filling the void, unable to say any other words. My little tomboy has left me a bit speechless here.

"Sorry," she quickly says. "He was covered." She motions to my Uncle Tommy.

"What the hell?" Garrett says, letting out with a deep startled laugh.

Finally, the group breaks out into shocked laughter, everyone just as surprised and impressed as I am.

"Go, Logan!" Mary shouts from the sideline, wine in hand.

"Where did you say your dad played again?" my dad asks, his face in pure shock.

"He was QB-1 for Stanford," she casually says with a shrug. "We used to play catch."

"Holy shit!" Scotty chimes in with an impressed smile.

"I think I'm in love," Sam says as he makes his way back from the end zone while Garrett nods in agreement.

"I think you just lost your job from here on out, Sam." Marc pats him on the back.

"Your kids are going to be the most athletic freaks of nature," Gabe says to me with a laugh, loud enough for the group to hear.

"Whoa there, Gabe. Let's not scare EJ, talking about babies already," Gavin chuckles. He's the oldest of the bunch, and the idea of having kids is terrifying to him, let alone an actual real committed relationship. But I was in his shoes just a few months ago, so I get it.

"I'm not the one you should be worried about. You might freak Logan out, though." I nod towards my girlfriend, who definitely looks a little shy from all the attention she's getting.

"Alright. 6-0," my dad changes the subject after noticing how uncomfortable my girl is. "Logan, just do that again, but for my team." He throws his arm over her shoulder, walking her to the blue team's huddle.

After losing, thanks to Logan running in the winning touchdown for Marc and my dad's team, everyone headed inside to get showered and ready for Thanksgiving dinner. I let Logan use my bathroom first because Mary is itching to get some time in the kitchen with her since the guys stole her for the football game.

As Logan finishes up her shower, I peel off my sweaty and mud-covered clothes, ready to take my turn in the bathroom. Just as I hear the water shut off, I get an idea for a little payback from Logan's earlier teasing session on the front porch.

I double-check to make sure that my bedroom door is locked because if my plan works the way I think it will, we are going to need some privacy.

With the bathroom door closed, I stand right in front of it, with my hands up on the doorframe and my naked body on full display.

Logan opens the bathroom door and slightly jumps back from finding me right outside, waiting for her. Her stunned gaze wanders from my face, down to my torso, and finally landing on my most prized possession. Her mouth gapes as she takes me in before letting out a heavy sigh.

"Fuck you," she says with a frustrated smile, tossing her head back, trying to advert her eyes from what she really wants to be looking at.

"Oh, please do," I request with a devilish grin.

"You're not playing fair."

"I have no idea what you're talking about."

Her gaze finds me again, and I can tell she's contemplating whether or not she's ready to give in as she bites her bottom lip and allows her eyes to wander my frame.

"Screw it," she says with a defeated sigh as she reaches up, wrapping her hand around my neck and pulling my lips to hers.

Her mouth is warm and needy, finding mine with fervor. Her tongue glides against my lips, asking for permission, which I oh so gladly give to her. She drops her towel from around her bust, letting it pool at her feet as her hands begin to explore my naked body. My greedy hands find her tits as my fingers circle and pinch, earning a desperate moan from my girl.

Her warm naked skin is still damp from the shower, and my hands can't touch enough of it. I pull her into me, needing her body on mine, cupping her perky ass, and loving the friction. Our heated moment continues as Logan's fingers wrap around my dick, slowly pumping it in her grasp.

It's only been about forty-eight hours since her skin has been on mine, but man, did I miss it. She strokes and glides my rock-hard guy as our mouths continue to explore one another's. She feels fucking amazing as she always does. Almost as amazing as this bet I'm about to win. I just have to get her over to my bed and—

"Have fun finishing that off by yourself in the shower," she whispers in my ear, her hand leaving my aching cock before she pats me on the shoulder in victory.

Logan's naked body walks away from mine with a satisfied smile dancing across her lips while I'm just standing here in this bathroom doorway, watching her get dressed with a major hard-on and needing her to take care of what she started. But she doesn't. She throws on her clothes and heads out of my bedroom, leaving me to jerk one out in the shower.

She's good. I'll give her that. But payback is going to be a bitch.

Chapter 75

Eli

"So Gabe," my Uncle Tommy begins, "how's wedding planning going?"

I pass the mashed potatoes to Marc while waiting for Gabe's reply. We all love Liam and knew that the two of them were going to tie the knot at some point. It was evident since the first time Gabe brought him home that he was going to be a part of the family.

"So far, so good," Gabe says. "We have a trip to Ohio in a couple of weeks to hash out the last of the details with his mom."

"That's going to be a fun wedding," Mary chimes in with a genuine smile. "Excited for you two to make it official."

"Speaking of Ohio." Uncle Tommy turns towards me. "EJ, how was your game against Ohio State?"

I finish chewing my piece of turkey that I had smothered in gravy before responding.

"It was alright. We lost 3-2, but it was a good game, and we played well. Ohio State is annoying as fuck, but they're good. I'll give them that."

"Were there any scouts there? Your dad mentioned he thought there could be," my uncle asks.

Logan puts her gentle hand on my thigh, under the dinner table, calming me down. I found out a scout was coming to that game right before I went out for warmups, and I started to feel a bit anxious in the locker room. But I used Logan's trick she taught me about describing my surroundings, and it brought my focus back before any real panic kicked in. The quick pregame phone call I had with her didn't hurt either.

"Yeah, there was a scout from the Chicago Blackhawks there. Their lineup is in need of defensemen, so he was more so there to see Zanders from Ohio, but he did come talk to me afterward and told me he was looking forward to seeing me at senior showcase, so that's positive, I guess."

"Definitely positive," my dad says with a nod.

"Any word from other teams around the league?" Gavin asks as I uncomfortably adjust myself in my seat. Logan tightens her grip on my leg as I take another breath.

"Here and there. Nothing to commit to yet. Senior Showcase will be a big weekend, and NHL playoffs start soon after that when most of the call-ups happen. So hopefully anytime now, but as soon as I get that call, I'm gone."

As soon as the words come out of my mouth, Logan releases her hold on me. I tilt my head to look at her, but she keeps her gaze fixed on her plate before taking another bite of her Thanksgiving dinner. When I look back up, my dad is the first face I see, as he glances between Logan and me.

"We should talk about Senior Showcase," Mary says. "Logan, you're coming to Chicago that weekend, right?"

"Yeah. I'm going to road trip out there with Marc, and our friend Ali is coming with us."

"We met her, right?" Mary asks. "At EJ's game." Logan nods in agreement, both of us eyeing Marc, but he keeps his gaze locked on his plate, trying to avoid engaging in the topic of his fuck buddy.

"Dinner was great," Uncle Drew says once everyone's plates are empty and stomachs are full.

I stand up with the twins to start clearing the table, and Logan stands with us.

"I can help clean up," she offers.

"Oh, no, you don't," my dad interjects. "Winning team doesn't do dishes." He pounds his fist with Marc, enjoying today's victory. "Especially the MVP. So, kick back and relax."

Logan happily plops herself back in her seat, handing me her empty plate with a satisfied grin on her lips.

"How are my two favorite sons?" My dad joins Marc and me, sitting around the firepit outside, hours after dinner and dishes are done. He hands us each a whiskey as he holds his up for a cheers. "Glad you're home. Love you both."

"You too, Dad." Marc takes a swig of the amber liquid.

"So," my dad begins, taking a seat between my brother and me, kicking his feet up close to the fire. "Where's my FDIL?"

"FDIL?" I question with furrowed brows.

"Future Daughter-in-Law," he explains with a laugh, finding himself exceptionally hilarious tonight.

"Jesus, Dad."

"And, I'm out." Marc picks up his glass and takes off towards the house. "Good luck, EJ," he says before leaving me alone with our dad.

"Mary and the aunts kidnapped her somewhere, but you guys all gotta chill with the whole marriage and kids thing."

"I'm just giving you a hard time," he laughs, patting my shoulder, smiling to himself. "But don't act like you haven't thought about it."

He knows how I feel about Logan, so of course, I have.

"We're only twenty-two," I remind him with a pointed glance.

"Almost twenty-three. The same age I was when I became a dad. And if you think Logan is a normal twenty-two-year-old, you're lying to yourself. Not after everything she's been through."

"I know she's not. And by the way, you didn't choose to become a dad at twenty-three. Your sister died, and you were stuck with me."

"And becoming your dad is the best thing that's ever happened to me," he says, looking at me with sincerity.

I give him an apologetic smile, knowing that he does love being my dad, even if the circumstances that caused that to happen were devastating for him.

"She reminds me of her, you know," my dad says, changing the subject.

"Hmm?"

"Logan. She reminds me of your mom, my sister." He takes swig from his crystal glass.

"Really?" I ask, turning my head in his direction. I've never really thought about it before, but from all the stories my dad has told me about my mom, they really do line up with the kind of person Logan is.

"Oh yeah. Elizabeth had that soft and strong thing going too. Tough as nails, but sweet as could be. Kept my head on straight, that's for sure."

"Yeah, that sounds like Logan." I can't help but smile.

"I'm really proud of the man you've become, EJ. Your mom would be too."

"Thanks, Dad."

"But I do need to talk to you about something." His tone completely shifts from sentimental to serious.

"Okay?"

"I just want you to try to be more careful with how you talk about leaving for hockey when Logan is around. I saw the way her face fell at dinner when you mentioned leaving as soon as you got called up."

"Logan knows I'm leaving at some point," I casually tell him with a shrug. "But that's not going to change anything between us."

"Is it not? What's going to happen when you go? Are you going to do long-distance?"

"I don't know." Suddenly, I feel a bit flustered. "She'll probably come with me wherever I end up playing, I would assume. She's not going to want to be away from me, in the same way I don't want to be away from her."

"Have you talked about this with her? Does she know that's what you're planning for? She still has another year and a half of grad school, and from what I know of her already, she's not going to want to give that up."

His questions don't have answers, and he knows they don't. They're asked in a way that they're not actually questions, but instead, they're things he wants me to think about.

"Well, then I guess we'll do long distance, I don't know." My voice begins to rise frantically. "What are you saying? That I have to choose between her and hockey?" I ask with disbelief.

"Absolutely not," he quickly states, shaking his head. "Quite the opposite, actually. I just want to make sure you're aware that there are two of you now. When you're making decisions, it's not just you anymore, EJ. You don't get to be selfish here. Not if you're thinking about a future with her the way I assume that you are."

I don't know what to say to him right now. I'm a little overwhelmed here. I haven't put too much thought into the logistics of Logan and I being together, just that I know we will be. I guess I assumed that she would want to come with me, knowing this is my life-long dream. She has to know that we will be together no matter what, in the same way that I do.

My dad sits forward, resting his elbows on his knees, keeping his gaze on the fire in front of us. "Look, son, I was once in Logan's shoes. My sister was the only family I had, and when I lost her, I had never felt so alone in my life. I thanked god every day for you because you're what kept me going, but it wasn't until I met Mary that I felt like myself again. Like I belonged somewhere, with someone. I would assume that Logan probably feels similarly, so just be aware of how you speak about leaving. She's lost everyone in her life. I don't want her thinking she's losing you too just because you're going to play professional hockey somewhere." His eyes are glossed over but full of sincerity.

This man is a fucking sap when it comes to his family. The same way I am, I guess.

"I knew you had fucking soft spot for her," I tease, lightening the mood.

"Oh, the softest," he laughs.

But because he has me alone right now, which doesn't happen all that often anymore, he continues with all the sweet and sentimental shit.

"I know Mary and I are big fans of hers, and maybe we're a little over the top." He pauses. "Mary more so than me, of course."

"Of course." I playfully roll my eyes.

"But it's not just because we like her, which we do, but it's because we like the man you are when you're with her. She really does bring out the best in you. You're a completely different guy than you were three months ago."

Well, fuck. Now I'm the one who's about to get all sentimental here. Anything to do with my family or Logan will get to me. But, the combination of the two with my dad telling me just how much he likes my girl is about to really fuck me up emotionally.

Thinking about Logan makes me want to be with her, the way it always does. So I quickly stand, patting my dad on the shoulder as I do.

"I love you, Dad."

"I love you too, EJ."

As soon as I reach the back door slider, he yells out to me. "Logan Maddison. Has a nice ring to it, don't you think?" He throws his head back in laughter.

"Fucking hell, old man!" I shout back to him, rolling my eyes but loving the way her name sounds with mine.

When I make it back inside, I find my aunts and Mary gabbing away in the kitchen, but Logan isn't with them. A few of the cousins are playing cards with my uncles at the dining room table, but she's not there either. I wander the house until I make my way into the living room, but all I find is the back of Marc's head as he watches the replay of the Lions game today.

"Hey, man, have you seen Logan?" I ask my brother.

He doesn't reply but instead turns his head to look at me before holding his index finger up to his lips, telling me to be quiet. Then he points down at the couch next to him.

I walk around the sofa and can't stop the smile from creeping across my lips when I find Logan passed out asleep with her head on a pillow leaning against Marc's lap. She's taking up most of the couch with her long legs, but Max found plenty of room next to her, cuddled up under her arm as he snores away.

Gently slipping my arms under her body, I pick her up and take a seat on the couch with her draped across my lap. She stirs for a moment until her head sinks into my shoulder, falling right back to sleep. Max isn't having it as he readjusts, finding his way under Logan's bare feet and dropping his head into my lap, right next to her.

I wrap my arms tightly around her, basking in the feeling of her body on mine.

"So," Marc whispers, trying to hold back his amused grin. "You're gonna go and marry my best friend now too?"

"Fuck me," I quietly say, trying not to wake Logan. "Not you too."

"I'm just giving you shit," he laughs.

We sit and watch the replay of the football game in comfortable silence for quite some time.

"You know," Marc says, breaking the silence. "I maybe haven't said it enough, but I really do like you guys together," he adds, referring to his best friend and me.

What the fuck was in this whiskey tonight that is making everyone in my family turn into total saps?

"Thanks, man. I know she makes me a better man and all that shit," I say with a chuckle, trying to lighten the mood.

"Not just that, EJ. You make her better too. I know you've been a bit of a fuckup in the past," he says with a laugh. "But she's much more sure of herself with you."

Well shit. First, my dad, and now my brother? Is everyone trying to fuck with my emotions tonight?

"I think it's both of us, Marc. I think that maybe she feels like she belongs somewhere, like she has a family with you and me." I reflect back to my dad's earlier words about how he was once in Logan's shoes, not having anyone in his corner until he met Mary.

Marc turns to me, giving me an understanding and grateful grin as I return the same.

"This is really fucking random, but did you know that she never had any pictures in her room when we were in Spain?" Marc asks. "I don't know why, but for a college girl, I thought that was so weird. Then when she moved here, she only had that one of her parents."

"I noticed that, too. But she has a couple more now. With us."

"I know, that's my point," he says. "I think you're right. I think Logan knows we have her back. That we are her family."

We give each other a meaningful glance before Marc changes the tone of this much too sentimental conversation.

"All thanks to me," he says with arrogance. "I am her best friend, after all. And the reason you two even met in the first place."

"Actually, I meant to tell you. She recently told me that I was her best friend." My tone is all smug.

"She did not!" he states in playful shock. "Well, you better wake that traitor up because we are about to have a conversation, her and I." His voice rises in mock frustration, causing both of us to quietly laugh.

We go back to watching the football game, putting the sentimental moments on hold for the time being.

"But to answer your earlier question...Yes."

"Yes, what?" he asks, his eyes still focused on the television.

"Yes. One day I'm going to marry the shit out of your best friend."

"Eli."

"Eli, wake up." Logan's voice is soft as she gently grazes her fingertips across my forehead, pushing my shaggy hair away from my face.

Slowly peeling my eyes open, I find my favorite girl sitting in my lap exactly where she was sleeping while I was hanging out with Marc a bit ago.

"We fell asleep," she whispers.

I look around the living room, but the house is pitch black, and no one else seems to be around.

"What time is it?"

"I don't know, but it's late. Everyone else is asleep. We should get to bed." She begins to peel herself off me.

"In a minute." Tightening my hold on her, I pull her into me, wanting to enjoy this for a moment longer.

Logan melts into my body as she sits in my lap, her fingers playing with my hair.

"I missed you today," I tell her with sincerity.

The corners of her pouty lips tug upward as she tries to stifle her smile, clearly amused by my neediness. "I was with you all day."

"Not really. Everyone was all over you, pulling you in different directions. I feel like I've barely seen you today. So, yes. I missed you."

She can't hold her smile back any longer as her dimples pop out. "I missed you too, Eli." She leans up, placing her warm lips on mine for a moment.

"Do you know how much I love you?" I ask.

"I think I have a pretty good idea."

I run my fingers across her cheekbone, tucking a fallen strand of hair behind her ear as I do. "I don't think you have any idea."

Her eyes search mine for a moment before, once again, sitting up and pressing her lips to mine. Her movements start slow and sweet but quickly turn feverish, both of us needing what we haven't had all day—each other. I cup her face, pulling her into me, but kissing just isn't enough.

I slip my hand under her shirt to feel her warm skin in my palm. Logan's hands find my torso, igniting my entire body with her touch. I pull her into me, needing her closer as our mouths move with intention. My lips find the delicate skin of her neck as I kiss her, sometimes gently and sometimes not so gently.

I allow my fingers to explore her for some time, but eventually, they find their way to where they really want to be—between her legs. I slip my hand into her yoga pants, taking my time as I do. Logan lets out a whimper in anticipation before I've really even touched her, causing a satisfied smile to creep across my lips. My fingers dip south, finding her warmth as she arches into my hand, begging for more.

Her heart rate is accelerating, and her breathing is strained as I circle and tease her, knowing exactly what she likes. The delicate moans of my name in between precious breaths and her needy body pressed into me is the most heavenly combination. She's fucking soaked right now, which doesn't surprise me all that much. I've been just as turned on ever since we made that stupid bet, wanting what I can't have all that much more.

As Logan's beautiful body twitches and shudders from my touch, I somehow find the restraint to pull my fingers from her.

"What are you doing?" she breathily asks. "Don't stop."

I place my lips against her ear. "That was for the cold shower I had to take earlier."

She closes her eyes, and her head falls back in frustration when she realizes that I'm just being a tease.

“You’ve got to be fucking kidding me,” she groans.

“Happy Thanksgiving, baby,” I tell her with an arrogant grin, unable to hold back my laughter. “I’m *so* thankful for you.”

Chapter 76

Logan

"Birthday boy!" I wrap my arms around Marc's shoulders from behind. "Morning." I kiss his cheek, being sure to make an extra loud smacking noise as I do.

"Gross," he laughs, wiping at his face. "Those lips have been on EJ's."

"Mmm, yes they have," I tell him, not elaborating on the fact that they've been on a lot more of his brother's body than just his lips.

"Been on a lot more of me than just my lips, man," Eli chimes in with a knowing smirk as I playfully smack him in the chest. I'm glad no one else from the family is in the kitchen. Marc is used to his brother's filter-less mouth at this point, but I don't need anyone else hearing it.

"How'd you sleep?" Marc asks me.

"Good. That turkey coma was nice."

I also decide not to elaborate that I kind of slept like shit because I was sexually frustrated thanks to the stunt his brother pulled on me last night, which I admittedly deserved. All while Eli slept like a baby next to me. I swear I could see him smirking in his dreams, exceptionally proud of himself for finally winning a round of our abstinence war.

"Good morning, Logan!" Mary says as she strolls into the kitchen. "Can I get you some coffee? Breakfast is in the oven."

"Oh, I'll get it. Thank you, though." Even though I've only been here for a couple of days, I feel quite at home in the Maddison house. I stand from my seat at the island to pour myself a coffee, adding in the creamer from the fridge that I'm certain was bought specially for me. I also pour a black coffee for Eli, not that he needs it. He slept just fine last night, that asshole.

"Can I help you with anything?" I ask Mary.

"Actually, I'm all set. But if no one else wakes up soon, the four of us are going to have to dive into these cinnamon rolls."

"Marc, what do you want to do today?" I turn my attention to my best friend before setting Eli's coffee in front of him. Eli pulls me to stand between his legs as he sits at the kitchen island next to his brother.

"I want to do absolutely nothing. I have that appointment with EJ later, but besides that, once the cousins leave, I just want to chill and watch sports all day."

"Well, that sounds perfect."

"Are you coming with us?" Marc asks.

"No, I think I'll stay back," I tell him as Eli pulls me in closer to his body.

Eli already asked if I would go with them to their tattoo appointment, but I want them to have some brotherly time. Since Eli and I got together, he and Marc haven't spent too much time alone. I don't think they mind that I'm always around, but still, they have their own relationship that I don't want to get in the way of.

"Oh good, we can hang out while the boys are gone," Mary chimes in. "The rest of the family has to get on the road after Marc's birthday brunch. It'll be nice to spend some time with just the five of us tonight."

"Marc, honey, are you nervous about getting a tattoo?" Mary joins us at the kitchen island, coffee in hand.

"No, I think I'll be fine. EJ has a shit ton. I can handle one."

"What made you finally decide to get one?" I ask.

"EJ was going to get one for me regardless, so I figured this would be a good time to get my first."

"What do you mean 'get one for you?'"

Eli pulls his sleeve up, revealing his perfectly chiseled arm covered in black ink. "These all represent something. Mostly family. I was going to get one for Marc anyway, so now we will have matching brother tattoos."

"I love that." I graze my fingers across the bit of bare skin on Eli's arm that will soon be filled with even more black ink.

"Okay, this looks like the last one." Mary picks up a red envelope from the center of the dining room table with Marc's name on it.

This card is from me, so I sit up a little straighter as I watch my best friend open my gift while Eli keeps his hands on my shoulders, standing behind me.

Marc reads the card to himself as a smile sneaks across his lips.

"Read it out loud," Mary requests.

"Happy MJ birthday, MJ. I love you so much. From, Logan." He's wearing a genuine grin as he looks across the table at me.

"I don't get it," Eli chimes in from behind me.

"It's my twenty-third birthday. Which was Michael Jordan's number, so it's my MJ birthday," Marc explains to his brother. "Happy MJ birthday, Marc Jones," he reads again without the abbreviation.

He opens the smaller envelope that was sandwiched in his card, pulling out two tickets.

"You're fucking kidding me." Marc's eyes widen, reading the details on the ticket stub.

"What is it?" one of the twins asks. To be honest, I still can't tell them apart, so I don't know who asked the question. All of the cousins look eerily similar with their tanned skin and black hair. The Jones genes run strong in this family.

"Two court-side tickets for when the Kings come to town to play the Timberwolves." Marc holds the tickets up in explanation.

"Why are you so cool?" Garrett asks me rhetorically.

"Thank you, Logan. This is awesome. I can't wait to watch my favorite team lose in person," Marc adds with a genuine smile.

"I know I bought you two tickets, and I'm supposed to tell you to take whoever you want, but you're taking me, just so you know."

"Obviously."

The doorbell rings, and Jack answers it as the rest of us go back to enjoying what's left of our brunch.

"Looks like there's one more gift." Jack walks back into the dining room with a box in hand.

"Who is it from?" Marc asks.

"I don't know. It just got delivered. Says it's from Brooklyn."

Marc's eyes dart to mine as I try to hold back my amused smile. I already know what it is because I helped Ali pick it out, but I'm excited to see Marc's reaction.

When Marc opens the box, his face splits into a huge shit-eating grin. He can't even pretend like he's not excited that Ali sent him a gift.

Those two are so full of shit.

"For real?" he asks as his eyes land on the basketball jersey, perfectly folded in the box. "Logan, I know you had a hand in this." Marc lifts the vintage Kings jersey from the open box, running his hand over the stitched last name. "Chris Webber was my favorite player as a kid."

Eli squeezes my shoulders because he knows I helped with this gift. But I just helped with the idea. Ali was the one who was excited for Marc's birthday and was full of anxiety, trying to find him the perfect present.

Like I said, those two are full of shit.

Marc grabs ahold of the card tucked underneath as he reads it to himself. His excited smile quickly turns soft, reading whatever Ali wrote on the paper.

"Read it out loud," Mary says again.

"Maybe not this one," Eli interjects, looking out for his brother as Mary eyes us suspiciously.

"I should go call Alison and thank her." Marc stands from the table and heads up the stairs, dialing our friend in New York as he does.

Grabbing the card that Marc left on the table, I read it to myself, allowing Eli to see it over my shoulder.

Happy Birthday, Marcus.

I already know that the best part of your 22nd year was that you met me, but I'm excited to be a part of your 23rd year too.

P.S. Logan helped with the gift, so if you don't like it, blame her.

-Alison

"Those two are so full of shit," Eli says from behind me, speaking aloud my unspoken thoughts.

I grab my empty plate and head to the kitchen to clean it. As I'm scrubbing it down in the sink, Eli walks up behind me and wraps his arms around my waist, leaning his chin on my shoulder.

"Court-side tickets, huh? I can't wait to see what you buy me for my birthday," he teases before bending down and kissing my tattoo.

"I don't need to buy what you want."

"That's true. Sex with you is free."

"Really, though." He turns me around to face him. "Court-side tickets? Can you afford that?" His brows are furrowed with confusion as he leans his body into mine, resting his palms on the edge of the sink behind my back.

"Yes, I can," I tell him without elaborating.

"Okay. How, though?"

"I don't know," I shrug. "Financially...I'm pretty set."

The lines on Eli's forehead deepen with perplexity. I guess I would be confused too if I knew of a grad student who didn't work and could afford those tickets, plus be financially stable.

"Look," I whisper, not wanting the rest of the family to hear us in the dining room. "When my dad died, he had a life insurance policy. And when my mom died, I sold our family home that was owned outright. Plus, I got a payout for my dad's shares of his wine company. So, financially, I'm fine. I'm more than fine, to be honest."

Eli's eyes widen in surprise. "Why didn't you tell me?"

"Because it doesn't change anything. I'm still going to get a job after I graduate as I would've anyway. I'm not going to live off of someone else's money for the rest of my life. I use it here and there, but I just kind of pretend like I don't have it for the most part. I've been meaning to talk to your dad about investing some of it, actually."

His confused expression softens as he takes in my words.

"Logan Jo Leo, are you my sugar mama?" Eli teases, steering the conversation away from its serious nature after sensing that I don't love talking about this subject.

I let out a little chuckle. "I think you'll be just fine once you sign that NHL contract, baby."

"So." Mary strolls into the kitchen with a few more dirty plates as I pour myself a new coffee. "What's up with Marc and this Ali girl?"

Eli and I exchange knowing glances, wondering which one of us is going to answer. "Um...they're *friends,*" he says.

"Oh, so they're fucking," Mary states, causing me to spit my fresh coffee back into my cup. "Logan, do you like her? For Marc, I mean."

"I do. Ali is great. She doesn't take anyone's shit, and she has a good sense of humor. I think Ali would be good for Marc. And she would never take advantage of him, which is something I worry about."

"Wow, she does sound great," Mary says. "Only because she sounds like me."

"What are you reading?" Jack asks me as he walks into the living room.

"It's called 'Managerial Economics.'" I hold up my textbook to show him, stirring a sleepy Max as I do.

"That sounds terrible." He eyes the book as he takes a seat on the couch opposite me.

"Tell me about it," I say with a chuckle.

Now that the boys are at their tattoo appointment and the rest of the Jones family has gotten on the road, the house is finally quiet enough that I can get some studying in. I have finals in just a couple of weeks, so I need to start putting my nose in these books.

"What field do you want to go into when you finish your MBA?"

"I like the idea of money management. Similar to what you do, actually."

"Oh, yeah? Marc wants to do the same," he states. "Well, if you need a job when you graduate, you have one at my firm."

"Really?" I ask, taken aback.

"Of course. Anyone who can tame my son, then kick his ass at football is more than capable of working for me," he says with a laugh. "But regardless of all that, you're exactly the kind of person I would want to hire. You have a strong work ethic."

I give him a grateful smile. "Thank you."

"How much is it pissing EJ off that Max likes you more than him?" Jack laughs, motioning towards the golden boy sleeping in my lap.

"He won't admit it, but I think it's getting under his skin, which is always fun."

"My son doesn't often lose, so it can be amusing when he doesn't get his way."

"Tell me about it," I say, but knowing that Eli and I are just as competitive as one another. You could take our bet of abstinence this weekend as an example.

Jack takes a deep inhale as he adjusts in his seat. "Actually, I was hoping I could talk to you while EJ was out of the house. If you have a minute, of course."

"Yeah, of course. Anything to distract me from Econ. Is everything okay?" I ask of Jack's serious expression. In the time I've known Eli's dad, he's usually joking around or giving his sons a hard time. I've never seen him look this stern before.

"Logan, I would like to know what your intentions are with my son," he plainly states.

"What?"

"I'm just giving you shit," Jack laughs, shaking his head and relieving my worry. "No, I wanted to thank you, and I haven't had a minute alone with you yet."

"Thank me for what?" A giggle slips past my lips, but it's essentially just a sigh of relief.

"Well, a lot of things," he says. "But I wanted to thank you for having that conversation with EJ when his birth father died. He didn't tell me about it until recently, but I just want you to know how much it means to me that he could let go of some of the anger he had towards Jamie before he passed."

"That was all Eli." I shake my head. "He's the one who forgave him."

"Yes, but you're the one who caused him to shift his perspective on the whole situation. You have no idea how thankful I am for that."

I give Jack a meaningful glance, not sure of what else to say about it.

"Jamie was one of my closest friends," Jack adds, expanding on the subject of Eli's birth father. "He and my sister were the only family I had, and when Jamie started drinking after Elizabeth died, it broke me. I wish EJ could have known the kind of man his father was before everything because Jamie really was a good guy. I'm just glad he was able to say goodbye." He offers me a thankful half-smile.

"Me too."

I take a moment, not knowing if I should push the subject, but I've been more than curious about Jack's past, losing his entire family the way I did.

"I didn't know that your sister was the only family you had," I say before I can decide whether or not I should bring this up. I don't know if Jack feels the same way I do, in that it's hard for him to talk about everything. "Eli recently told me. I'm sorry for your loss."

"Thank you. Yeah, she was," Jack says with a nod. "But look at me now. I have this huge family with a smoking hot wife and two amazing sons. But it was a tough couple of years. I was your age when she died."

"Really?"

"Mmm-hmm."

Again, I can't tell if Jack wants to talk about his sister, but he's the only person I've met who has gone through what I have.

"How did you move on?" I shyly ask.

He searches my face for a moment, and I think he realizes why I'm asking.

"I don't know if I ever did, to be honest. But I learned to celebrate my sister's life instead of mourning her death. And it made the daily struggle of being without her that much easier to handle. Mary helped heal me. And the boys, of course."

I give him poor half-smile, pulling my gaze away from him.

"Where are you with all of that?" he asks. "I don't want to overstep, but I've been in your shoes before."

I knew he could tell that I was asking because I don't know how to move on. I haven't done it yet. Something about Jack makes me feel at ease. Like I can be open with him. I don't know if it's because he raised the man I'm in love with or because he understands my grief as almost no one else can.

"I don't know where I am with all of it," I tell him honestly. "I don't like to think about it. Especially my mom. Last year was pretty traumatizing, and I don't like to go there."

He once again looks at me, searching my face before letting out a heavy sigh.

"Logan, I'm saying this from experience. You're going to have to grieve for her at some point. You're going to have to feel it all so you can move on and start celebrating her and the impact she had on your life."

"I don't know if I can. That sounds terrifying."

"It will be," Jack says. "It's going to suck. I can promise you that. But there's a light at the end of the tunnel. You just have to start moving in that direction. Otherwise, it's going to follow you around like a dark weight on your shoulders until you do."

I don't respond, but I know he's right. And I've been dreading the emotions that are going to come when I finally decide to start dealing with my guilt and grief. I don't know when that will be, but I know I'm not ready yet.

"You have EJ and Marc," he adds. "You're not alone in this. And you have Mary and me. If you ever need anything in the fatherly sense or if you just need a friend who understands what you're going through, you can always talk to me. It's hard when you feel like you're the only one who has experienced that kind of loss."

I shoot him a grateful smile. "Thanks, Jack. I appreciate that."

"Well, we appreciate you, Logan. More than you know. We feel very lucky that the boys met you. The man EJ has become since you guys got together is the man I was hoping he would be, and I know a lot of that is thanks to you."

I shake my head. "I'm the lucky one."

"I think we all are."

"Did you have a good birthday?" I hand Marc his second piece of cake as I curl up on the couch next to him.

"The best birthday, just like this cake," he says with his mouth full.

Mary let me make Marc's birthday cake this afternoon while the boys were gone. After that conversation with Jack, I couldn't get my mind back into studying. It was swirling with thoughts that I was afraid to tackle head-on, so instead, I distracted myself with baking. Red velvet, of course—Marc's favorite.

"How weird is it that this is my first birthday we've spent together? I feel like I've known you my whole life," he says between bites.

"Right? I was thinking the same. I can't believe we met in Spain less than a year ago."

"I know Ali thinks that she was the best part of twenty-two, but that's not true." He nudges me in the shoulder. "Meeting you was the best part of twenty-two."

I give Marc a grateful smile. I seriously love this guy, and I'm so lucky to have him.

"What's going to be the best part of twenty-three?" I ask.

"Well, us being one year closer to graduating, and hopefully getting an apartment off-campus together next year. As much as I love the coed bathrooms in the grad dorms, I would really like a kitchen again."

"And being there when EJ finally signs his NHL contract. I'm excited for him," he adds.

I haven't thought too much about what next year's Thanksgiving weekend will look like. Eli might not even be able to come home depending on his hockey schedule. And will he want me to be here if he does? This time next year, will he just see me as his college girlfriend that he left behind? I'm a little afraid to find out what these next twelve months will bring for us.

"Are you fucking serious?" Marc releases a heavy sigh, looking down at his phone.

"What's wrong?"

"Lauren. She's texted me three times today, and now she's calling." He holds up the screen so I can see his ex's name run across the top.

"What the hell does she want?" I ask with disgust. I already didn't like the girl, but after the Halloween party, I think 'despise' is a better word.

"I don't know, to wish me a happy birthday or some shit. I didn't respond to any of her texts, so now she's calling." He quickly declines Lauren's call.

"She sucks."

"Yeah, well, just be glad you don't have to see your piece of shit ex around campus like I have to," he says with an exhausted breath. "Speaking of that asshole, have you heard from Zac at all?"

I quickly shake my head. "Not since the night you and I talked at the hockey house. Which was also the night that Eli and I first got together, so as soon as that happened, I blocked his number. He's reached out on social media, but I haven't opened any of the messages."

"Good. Fuck that guy," Marc states without sarcasm.

"Fuck what guy?" Eli asks as he walks around the couch, taking a seat next to me before pulling me to sit across his lap.

"Zac."

"Oh, *fuck* that guy! I swear to god if I ever meet that motherfucker—"

"Can we talk about something else?" I interrupt, not wanting to relive the worst week of my life from last year. I already started thinking about it after that conversation with Jack, and I just can't handle more today.

“Let’s see the tattoos,” I request of the boys.

Eli holds out his tatted arm, his bandage long removed, as Marc cautiously peels the plastic wrap away from his fresh ink.

“They look so good.”

It’s a simple design that coordinates perfectly with the rest of Eli’s sleeve, but also doesn’t look too extravagant on Marc’s bare arm. They each have two dots, smaller than a dime, one of which is entirely filled with black ink while the other is just an outline. The first circle is filled in on Marc’s because he’s the older of the two, and the second is filled in on Eli’s arm because he’s the younger, while the empty circle represents the other.

“Did it hurt?” I turn to Marc.

“No, not really. The shading kind of sucked. But probably nothing compared to yours.” He motions towards my tattoo. “Right on the bone, that hurt worse, I’m sure.”

“Did it hurt you?” I sarcastically ask my boyfriend. The guy’s arm is covered in ink. I highly doubt a small tattoo above the crease of his elbow hurt him at all.

“No, I like the feeling at this point. It’s reached the stage where it’s addictive.” Eli lifts his arm, revealing the bit of blank skin on the inside of his bicep. “Though I’m not looking forward to filling this spot. I heard this hurts like a bitch.”

“Be right back,” Marc says, interrupting his brother as he gets off the couch with his empty cake plate in hand, heading to the kitchen to put it in the sink. Or to get a third slice, I’m not too sure.

“What do these all represent?” I graze the ink on Eli’s arm. I’ve looked at these tattoos hundreds of times, but I didn’t know they had a family meaning besides his mom’s name.

“Well, the big oak tree represents family,” he says as he rolls up his sleeve over his shoulder, revealing more of his toned arm to me. “The roots more so. This rose right here is for my dad. It’s the rose from the Grateful Dead logo. It’s his favorite band, and he always used to play their music throughout the house when we were growing up. And this funny looking heart that doesn't connect at the tip." He points to the next tattoo. "Mary used to write Marc and me a note and put it in our lunch every day when we were kids. She always used to sign it with this weird looking heart. It was practically her signature, so that's for her."

I trace the black ink. Even though none of these tattoos would go together in theory, they are oddly cohesive as they intertwine on Eli's arm. More so now that I know the meaning behind them. And you would think that a heart and a flower might look feminine, but they don't. Not when they're in black ink and pulled taut due to Eli's muscles.

If this weekend has taught me anything, it's that Eli's family is the most important thing in his life. I once thought it might have been hockey, but it's become evident that I was wrong. This weekend has been great, and I loved spending time with the Maddisons and the Joneses, but I've become even more aware of the fact that Eli will never be able to do this with my relatives. That I no longer have a family that he could spend a holiday with.

"Does it bother you that I don't have a family?" I quickly ask before my mind catches up with my mouth.

"What?" Eli's eyes are wide with shock.

"Does it bother you that you will never get to do this with my family?" I ask, motioning around the house.

"Logan, are you serious?"

I shyly nod.

"Fuck. Come here." He wraps his arms around me, hugging me in his lap. "I would've never brought you here if I thought it was going to make you miss your parents. I would've happily stayed on campus with you this weekend. I don't want you to be sad when you're here, baby."

"No. No, I'm so glad we came this weekend. I had so much fun, but I just feel bad that you'll never get to do this with my family."

"You have a family. I'm your family," he adds in a desperate tone as my heart drops, realizing I may have hurt his feelings. "Marc is your family."

I stay silent because I don't know what to say. Eli will never get to meet my parents, and that's becoming a harder pill to swallow than I expected. They'll never get to meet the man I'm in love with. My first love, and probably my best love.

"Do I wish I could've met them?" Eli breaks the silence. "Of course, I would've loved to have met the people who raised you. Mostly so I could've thanked them, but Logan, you have a family here. I don't want you to feel like you don't."

Eli lifts my face from his shoulder so he can look at me, but I'm having a hard time meeting his gaze. I feel oddly emotional today, and even though I'm not crying, Eli can read me like a book, and I don't want him to feel bad for me right now.

"We don't have to come back for Christmas. If it's hard for you, we can stay on campus and spend the day just you and I."

"No, Eli. I'm fine, I promise. I love being here, I do. I'm just working through some things."

"Can I help you work through them?" he asks, tucking a fallen strand of hair behind my ear.

"It's nothing. I'm fine, baby." I lean in to kiss his lips, trying to convince him of my lie.

Chapter 77

Eli

"Why are you driving so fast?" Marc asks from the backseat.

"I just want to get home." I keep my tone casual as I continue to drive a good fifteen miles over the speed limit on our way back to campus from Indiana, and my hand remains on Logan's thigh as she sits in the passenger seat, needing to touch her as I always do.

"Are you seriously driving this fast so you guys can get home and fuck?" Marc accuses without filter, causing Logan and I to laugh at the truthfulness of his statement.

He's not wrong. It's been on my mind ninety-five percent of the weekend after Logan and I made that stupid bet. Our teasing each other the whole time didn't help either. It just made us want each other all that much more.

But after last night, I could tell Logan was off. She didn't say anything about it after our conversation regarding her family, but I could tell she was sad. Neither of us even thought about messing around last night. I just innocently held her while we slept. It simply wasn't all that funny to tease each other when I knew she was upset.

She seems much more herself today, though, laughing and joking around, being her usual sweet self. The full night of rest must have done her good, and I can tell she's anxious to get back to campus for the same reason as to why I'm speeding down the freeway right now.

"Don't worry, Marc. Ali will be home tomorrow," Logan adds with a giggle.

"But seriously, bro. Don't expect to see us again until Monday," I chime in with a laugh. I fully plan on spending Saturday evening and my entire Sunday buried between Logan's legs, but I don't need to divulge that part.

"Seeing as the last thing I want to think about is my brother and best friend's sex life, how about a little music?" Marc says, before proceeding to blast his playlist through my speakers.

We pass the Minnesota state line, bringing us that much closer to our destination and my inevitable heaven.

"EJ, what's your road schedule look like coming up?" Marc turns down the music so he can hear me.

"We have UMass on Wednesday. Then we fly to Maryland for Saturday's game, and we stay on the east coast to play Rutgers the following Wednesday. We'll fly a red-eye so we can play Nebraska at home the next day."

Logan is already well aware of my schedule as she keeps her gaze out the passenger side window.

"The Nebraska game should be a good one," my brother says.

"Then off for break. I'll be home until after Christmas," I add, hoping that the last part will soften the blow for Logan. She hates when I'm gone, almost as much as I hate leaving her. This is just a reminder that I need to talk to her about what our plan will be if and when I get called up and have to leave.

I turn up the dial to drown out my voice, hoping Marc won't be able to hear me. "Baby, are you going to be okay while I'm gone?" I squeeze Logan's thigh. "This is going to be the longest we've been away from each other."

Seeing her get upset out of the blue last night has me a little worried about leaving her this week. That just wasn't like Logan. But it's the holidays, so I'm sure it's a sentimental time for her to be without her parents. I just want to get this road trip over with, so I can spend four weeks of winter break with her.

This eight-day road trip will be a good practice run if we have to do long-distance for a bit. We have good communication, so I'm not worried about that, but I've never needed to be near someone as much as I do Logan. Having her around me always calms me down, and I'm a little nervous about being away from her for so long. Not to mention, as independent as Logan is, I know she has a hard time when I'm not home.

"I know, I'm dreading it," she tells me. "But I have finals to distract me. I'm going to miss you, though."

"I always miss you," I remind her as I intertwine my fingers with hers, continuing to drive a little too quickly back to campus.

I urgently shut Logan's dorm room door behind us, being sure to lock it as I do. I'm happy it's still Thanksgiving break, and most students won't be back until tomorrow because I have a feeling Logan and I are about to be loud as fuck tonight, and I don't want to be unneighborly. But also, I'm going to be away from my girl for eight days, so I don't really give a shit.

As soon as her door is closed, I grab Logan and pin her to the back of it, needing my lips on hers.

"So, I guess we both won the bet," my overly competitive girl says between feverish kisses and panting breaths.

"Logan, we both fucking lost, and you know it." My forehead rests on hers as my hips hold her to the door. "That was a lose-lose situation. Let's never do that bullshit again."

Logan's hands dart up, quickly unbuttoning her outer layers as our mouths explore one another's, but I stop her movements.

"Let me do it," I beg. "I won't get to see your body for more than a week. I need to memorize it." Turning her back into my chest, I swiftly undoing the buttons of her coat, allowing it to pool at her feet.

But before I really touch her, I pause for a moment. "Logan, are you sure you're okay? Last night you—"

"I'm fine, Eli." She reaches behind, wrapping her hand around my neck, and pulling me into her. "I promise."

My wanting lips connect to the thin skin of her pretty neck, feeling her rapidly rising pulse beneath them. Slipping my long fingers under her shirt, I explore her warm skin, feeling every rise and fall, and worshiping every dip and curve.

From behind, I run my hands up the length of her torso, cupping the lace of her bra. I smile into her neck, knowing exactly what she's wearing, even though I can't see it yet. She's only worn this little number once before, and I swear to god I almost exploded at the sight of it on her toned body. It's a simple black set, delicate lace that barely covers her perfect tits. She would never wear something like this for a long car ride except that she knew exactly what was going to happen when we got out of the truck.

"Fucking tease," I whisper into her ear as my finger hooks over the top of her bra, grazing her taut nipple.

Logan throws her head back on my shoulder, ever so slightly backing her ass into my already present bulge. "There's no teasing tonight. You can have all of me. Whatever you want."

Allowing my fingertips to wander her body, I dip into her waistband ever so slightly, just to confirm she's wearing the matching lace panties. I run my fingers over the texture as my forehead drops to Logan's shoulder with a whimper. A fucking whimper. This woman turns me into putty in her hands. I have no control with her, and she knows it. She has me wrapped around her pretty little finger, and I'll happily live out the rest of my life that way.

"What am I supposed to do for eight days without you?" I ask into her nape, unbuttoning her jeans as I do.

"I'm sure you guys will manage." Her lips lift into a sneaky little smile as she reaches behind her and palms me through my pants.

"I'm going to be jerking off to the mental image of you in this little set the whole time." I push her jeans over her ass, leaving them on the floor for her to step out of.

My hands find her soft thighs, my fingers grazing their length. I tease the fabric over her hips before ever so gently swiping over the warm wetness between her legs that's already seeped through the delicate lace.

Another whimper. I'm fucking done tonight.

Lifting her shirt up and over her head, my hands run the length of her arms as I memorize every square inch of the most beautiful body I've ever laid eyes on. And not just because it's smoking hot and perfectly formed for me, but because it's Logan. The woman I'm unquestionably, undoubtedly, madly in love with.

My middle finger delicately traces the line from the dip between her breast, down her abdomen, until finally I can't take it anymore and I need to see her. Turning her around to face me, my jaw slacks as I take in the golden-skinned beauty in front of me. Shiny red hair falls around her shoulders, cheeks and chest already pink and warm. Not to mention, the black lace that isn't doing much to conceal two of my favorite things.

"I can't get enough of you," I tell her, my eyes finally landing on her green ones.

Her fingers sink into my messy hair, ever so slightly tugging at the roots. "The feeling is mutual, baby."

I bend down, needing to taste her, needing her pouty lips on mine. It's only been a few days since we had sex, and that's not even what's overwhelming me right now. It's seeing Logan in my home this weekend, realizing what I already knew—that's she's it, that she belongs with me. That she's mine forever.

Her hands swiftly unbutton my pants, dropping them to my ankles, the tight briefs not doing much of anything to hide how ready I am for her. She tugs at my shirt, asking me to remove the layer, which I quickly do, revealing my tattooed arm and rapidly rising and falling chest. Her fingers and eyes explore the ink, tracing the delicate lines just as she's done so many times before.

I watch as she does it, knowing that one day the last bit of bare skin will be filled for her.

Picking her up, she wraps her long legs around my waist. I toss her on the bed, watching her bounce with an excited little smile dancing on her lips. I squeeze her thighs, my hands finding her hips as I pull her to me.

I sit back on my heels as I leave the lacy piece on, just for a moment, locking the mental image in my mind—Logan on her back, legs open wide for me, flimsy black fabric covering her pussy.

Curling my fingers around her panties, I pull them off in one fell swoop. Without missing a beat, I push her knees wide, first finding her with the swipe of my finger, her head falling back into the mattress as I do. I dip down, my warm breath causing her to jerk in anticipation, before pressing my needy lips to her center.

"*Fuck, yes,*" she moans, pushing my head down as she does.

My tongue flicks ever so gently, slowly killing her. She writhes beneath me, her hips bucking into my face, begging for more as her knuckles turn white with the sheets in her hands.

"Do you want more?"

"We said we weren't teasing tonight," she reminds me between ragged breaths, her eyes screwed shut from the sensation of my meticulously torturous pace.

"Mmm," I hum against her sex, causing Logan to twitch and wiggle beneath me. "You're right." I plunge two fingers into her as my mouth sucks at her clit.

"*Oh, god,*" she yelps from the sudden intrusion, her hips moving at the same tempo as my fingers, meeting them in pace.

If she's as sexually pent up as I am right now, she's not going to last long. I continue my movements. Sucking, flicking, circling with my tongue while my fingers move with intention—to bring her to the edge.

I feel her tightening around my fingers as she arches up off the bed, my mouth dripping with her arousal. Her clit throbs against my tongue as I watch her come undone. My sweet girl's eyes screw shut as her mouth forms the perfect 'O,' falling apart from my touch—what only I can do to her.

Logan takes a moment to come down off her high as her chest slows, her perky tits spilling out of the black lacy bra I left on—more for the visual, to be honest.

She sits up and crawls over to me, tugging at my briefs and allowing me to spring free. She grips around the base of my aching cock, and I don't know if I've ever been harder in my life. That is until she bends over, taking me in her warm mouth, her tongue swirling around the tip, licking up the already formed bead of moisture.

"*Fuck, Logan,*" I groan from the sensation, my head falling back.

She pulls back and flips her red hair over her shoulder before taking me in again, this time slowly inching until I hit the back of her throat, almost causing me to fall forward from the sensation.

I cup her cheeks as I slide out of her, a devilish little grin on my sweet girl's mouth. The way she tends to look when she knows she has me under her spell. Which, let's be honest, is always.

"I'm going to come way too quickly if you do that again, and I need to be inside of you."

A proud smirk lifts her lips, and her green eyes shine with amusement from what she does to me.

She lies back on her bed, unfastening her bra, and leaving her perky tits on full display. My mouth gapes open from the sight of her. Flushed skin, wild hair, legs open for me—I'll never get tired of it. I'll never get tired of what we have.

Leaning forward, my greedy hands fill with her chest as I connect my wanting mouth with hers. My rock-hard dick slides against her folds, feeling the wetness on either side. I want to put it in. I want to feel her warm walls tighten around my bare skin, but she's not on birth control yet, and she will literally kill me if I knock her up, so condom drawer it is.

I stocked her nightstand full to the brim a couple of weeks ago, so I reach over, pull one out and quickly roll it over my length. I sit back, taking in the view of her as I grip my cock, ready for it to be inside of her.

Teasing the tip against her clit, I give it a couple of slaps as I watch the entire time, my mouth gaping from the view and the sensation. I look up at my girl, her lips spread, eyes locked on the same damn thing.

I slowly push into her, my eyes glued on Logan as hers screw shut from the intrusion. I pull back, rocking my hips into her ever so slightly, taking my time as I do.

"Logan, are you okay?" I ask, just as I always do. Her answers have gotten better each time, but this one is, by far, my favorite response.

"*Fuck.* Yeah, it feels good."

"Wait, really?" I stop my movements, a bit surprised. Things have felt better for Logan the more we've done this, but she's always had a little discomfort.

She pushes her heels into the back of my thighs, starting my movements again. She bites down on her bottom lip as she nods her head.

"No discomfort? No pain?" I ask for confirmation.

"No, baby," she breathes. "You feel really fucking good."

Well, fuck me. Let's go then.

Grabbing her hips, I thrust a bit faster, keeping my eyes on her the whole time. She looks like fucking heaven right now, and she feels like it too, as her head falls back into the pillow beneath her and her tits arch up, close to my face. My fingers dig into the skin of her curvy hips as I push myself into her, but still, holding back a bit, letting her adjust.

"*Harder*," she moans, pushing her heels into me again.

There's no way I heard that correctly.

"What, baby?"

"Eli. Harder. Please," she begs.

Holy fucking shit. You don't have to tell me twice. Well, she did, but you get the idea.

Logan and I have done the sweet and slow lovemaking. We've done the playful shit, but we've never just fucked. Pure animalistic fucking. But the time has come—time to shine.

I fall forward, holding myself up and hovering my lips over hers.

"I'm going to tell you I love you now because we aren't doing the lovey-dovey shit tonight. Okay?"

Logan's eyes widen, then darken from my words, her pupils completely dilated. She takes a swallow as she nods in agreement.

"So, tell me you love me so I can fuck the shit out of you."

"I love you."

"Good, me too," I tell her as I slam into her, her mouth falling open as I do.

I thrust into her full force over and over again, absolutely entranced by the whimpers and moans leaving Logan's lips and filling the room. Her tits bounce with every blow I deliver, creating the most heavenly visual for me.

I fucking love finding new sides to Logan. New parts of my favorite girl that no one else has ever seen, and I don't mean physically. No, what I mean is finding new sides of her personality, new things she likes, and judging by the sounds filling my ears—Logan likes it hard.

Sitting back, I pull her hips to me, bouncing her onto my dick. She's arched almost all the way off the bed as I pummel into her, her needy hands gripping at the sheets, the headboard, me. Whatever she can find, really.

"*Fucking shit*," I breathe as my pelvic bone slams into hers, loving the whimpers that leave her lips every time I do.

Then, because I'm selfish and want to see her this way, but also because I know this will feel good for her, I flip us over, so she's on top, riding me. Her knees are bent on either side of me as she leans forward, anchoring her hands on my chest, as she rolls her hips, causing me to almost lose it right there.

To be honest, I can't believe I've lasted this long, seeing as this is all I've thought about for the last three days. But Logan hasn't come from us having sex yet, I always take care of her with my fingers or mouth, but I have a feeling it can happen tonight, so I'm going to try to last as long as I can and get her there with me.

She moves in slow circles, taking my breath away as I follow her rhythm. I keep my eyes open, watching her bouncy tits and gaping mouth as she rides me. And fuck, does she ride me good.

God, I love this woman. And I love watching her unravel with me. She's usually so put together and sweet; however, she's anything but when we're in bed with each other.

Grabbing ahold of her hips, I slam her body onto me, the loud smacking of our skin filling the room. The tingle at the base of my spine is telling me I'm about to explode as Logan's head falls back, letting me take control of her, bouncing her on me with urgent tempo and force.

"*I'm gonna come,*" Logan cries, her body at my disposal.

Oh hell yes, you are, and so am I.

I sit up, wrapping my arms around her waist, holding her body to mine. Her tits are right up in my face as I lift myself off the bed, thrusting into her. Her arms are wrapped around my neck, her fingers threaded in my sweaty hair as her cries of pleasure fill my ears.

Logan's body tightens around me as her head falls back, basking in the most beautiful orgasm I've ever seen. The pure bliss on her face as her body jerks and trembles, entirely out of control, is enough to send me over the edge. Her moans are loud, and most of them are my name, which is my favorite thing to hear coming from her lips. The second I see her eyes roll back, I give one more heavy thrust as I spill into the condom, every muscle in my body contracting.

I bite down on her shoulder, trying to stifle my grunts and screams, but it's no use. We are both loud as fuck right now.

I drop back on the bed as Logan falls on top of me, both of us out of breath, damp with sweat, and fucking high as hell on each other.

"Water break. Round two in twenty minutes," I tell her between panting breaths with the slap of her ass.

"What?" She pulls her head off my chest to look at me with shock. "How many rounds are we going?

"Let's just say that I don't know if *walking* to class is going to be an option for you on Monday."

Chapter 78

Logan

It's been five days since Eli's been on the road, traveling for his away games, and I'd be lying if I said I was doing okay. There's been a darkness around me, a heaviness on my shoulders since Thanksgiving weekend that I can't seem to shake. The sadness I feel has nothing to do with Eli being gone, though his absence hasn't helped, that's for sure. I was distracted and felt like myself for a couple of days, having him home with me until he left.

I'm used to being Eli's rock, his foundation to steady on when he needs to be centered. I'm the person who is there for him when his mind wanders to dark places. When he can't calm himself down, that's my job.

I've never once felt like I needed that from someone. I'm strong, and I've gone through hell and back in my life that's caused me to be able to stand on my own two feet, but something about the all-consuming grief that's been clouding my mind, lingering just outside, waiting to crash down on me, is making me feel like I need him more than I ever have before.

And I don't like that. I don't like needing anyone but me.

I had my first final today, and I'm pretty sure I bombed it. I've spent the last few days with my head in my books, but my mind couldn't retain the words on the pages. It's like it was too full of other swirling thoughts to add any more into the mix.

As if the thought of this week hasn't been weighing on me already, adding my final exams into the equation is almost enough to make me break.

Almost.

As I'm lying in bed, trying to fall asleep early, hoping that a good night of rest will reset my mind, my phone starts vibrating on the nightstand.

I assume it's not Eli because I already told him I was going to bed, but I don't know who else would be calling me.

I pick up the phone, seeing an unknown number flash across the top of the screen with my hometown's area code. A quick burst of panic runs through me, thinking it could be Zac, but changing his number or using someone else's to get ahold of me seems like a little much, even for him.

"Hello?" I quietly ask as I answer the unknown number.

"Hello. Is this Miss Leo?" a female voice questions.

"Yes?"

"This is Southpoint Self Storage."

Fuck. I almost forgot about this.

"You have a storage unit with us that was prepaid for twelve months. We tried to run your card on file to renew your lease, but it was declined."

"Shoot. I'm sorry about that. I moved across the country and got a new bank account. I forgot to update my card with you guys."

"Would you like to do it now?"

"How much time do I have to decide if I want it renewed?"

"You were paid through this week. We have a three-week grace period, so either the card needs to be charged by December thirty-first, or your storage unit needs to be cleared out. Otherwise, you'll lose the unit, including all assets inside."

"Okay. I'll make a decision this week and give you a call back. Thank you so much."

"Have a good night."

This is the last thing I need to deal with right now. On top of finals and the heaviness that is clearly creeping in, knowing what day Thursday is, having to decide on the storage unit might be the breaking point.

Part of me wants to let it all go. Let all the memories go with whatever is inside. Or I could pay another twelve months. Hold off the inevitable mental breakdown that is sure to occur when I see what's in there. I have the money. I could do it.

But what good is it to keep putting it off? And I think I might hate myself one day down the road if I let it all go without going through it. Every single sentimental part of my childhood is in that locker. All my family pictures, parents' clothes, and anything worth keeping from their lives is in there.

I can't just get rid of it. As much as the two-thousand-mile distance has done for me with regard to creating space between me and what happened to my mom last year, the fact is, it still happened. And everything I have left of her is in that storage unit, waiting for me to go through it.

When I decided to leave for Spain last year, I gathered anything meaningful to my life or my parents and shoved it in that storage unit. I never went through it. I just tucked it away. I couldn't process the emotions that would come from touching my mom's old dresses or seeing pictures of my dad teaching me how to shoot a basketball, so I didn't. I hid it.

I had our family home renovated while I was overseas so that I could come back and sell it. The good thing was that when I walked back into that house after being gone for six months, I didn't recognize it. The colorful walls were now a stark white. The oven that my mom and I had once baked dozens of cookies in was long gone and replaced with a new shiny stainless steel one. The den where my dad and I had watched countless basketball games was now staged as a playroom for hopeful buyers.

I didn't recognize a single square inch, which is exactly what I wanted. I didn't want to relive a single memory from that house. It hurt too much. And that's how I feel about whatever is in that storage unit. Every memory I've tried to suppress over the last year, every single ounce of sadness I've pretended didn't weigh on my shoulders, it's all waiting to come crashing down on me. It's all tucked away inside of those four walls.

I close my eyes, needing some relief from the mental games my mind is playing on me, hoping for some sleep, when my phone dings again.

Squinting at the screen, I see my boyfriend's name with an incoming text.

E: *Hi, baby. I know you're sleeping, but I just wanted to tell you that a scout is coming to Wednesday's game. I just found out. It's the scout from Dallas, the one I played like shit in front of. I'm surprised that he even wants to see me again. Anyway, I'm doing okay. I feel really good, actually. And I just wanted to tell you how much I love you.*

I want nothing more than to be excited for Eli right now, but I can't help it. I'm too selfish in this moment to be happy.

Of course, this is the fucking week he's going to get called up. The week I need him the most.

The next day, after another shitty test, I decide to throw on some workout clothes, needing to get to the gym. I haven't worked out all week, which is so unlike me. I need to clear my head, and a few rounds on the bag will do just that, as it always has. I only have about forty minutes until I need to get to my next exam, but that should be enough time for some gym therapy.

I want to feel angry, and I can do that while throwing punches at a heavy bag. Anger is much better than grief-stricken, in my opinion, and lately, grief has been my only option. But not today. I'm turning things around, channeling my emotions the way I want to feel them.

As I'm throwing my gloves and wraps in my gym bag, Ali comes barging into my room.

"Logan, I need to talk to you," she urgently says, taking a seat on my bed.

"Ali, I can't right now. I really need to get a workout in."

"Shit," she says, taken aback as her gaze catches mine. "Are you okay? You don't look like yourself."

"Yeah, I'm fine. Just needing a gym break from all this studying," I lie with the shake of my head.

"Please, Logan. I really need to talk to you."

Ali has always been there for me. I would be a terrible friend to leave her when she needs me, even though I need nothing more than a therapy session in the gym right now.

"Okay." I toss my bag aside before taking a seat at my desk chair. "What's up?"

"Well," she begins as she awkwardly adjusts the way she's sitting, obviously feeling very uncomfortable. "I just need to get something off my chest, and I don't know the right way to say it, so I'm just going to come out and say it."

"Okay?" I ask with a confused expression and furrowed brows. I've literally never seen Ali this awkward or off her game unless it's about...

"I have feelings for Marc!" she blurts out before quickly covering her mouth like she said something terrible.

I can't help but let out a laugh. The laugh feels good. I haven't done that in a while.

"Yeah, Ali. I know."

"What?"

"You're so obvious. Of course, I know. I've known since the Halloween party that you two were full of shit."

"Fuck. What do I do?" she asks with desperation.

"Why don't you try telling him?"

"Oh, no, I can't do that. No, no, no." Ali shakes her head. "This whole friends with benefits thing was his idea."

"Yeah, probably because you don't do boyfriends," I remind her. "So he was most likely trying to play it safe, assuming you would've shut him down if he suggested more."

“Do you think he wants more?” she asks with expectant eyes, needing the reassurance.

“Ali, honestly, I haven’t talked to him about it. But it’s Marc, and it’s you. I wouldn’t be surprised if the feelings are mutual. You should talk to him.”

“Maybe after winter break. I’m going to sit with it for a minute. I’ve never felt this way. I don’t want to be rash right now.”

“My little cold-hearted Ali is warming up,” I tease.

“Fuck. This is a scary feeling. How the hell do you do this? This thing in my chest is like pounding whenever I see him. What the fuck is that?”

I can’t help but laugh. “That would be your heart, and those would be called feelings,” I smugly tell her.

“Oh, man. They feel awful.” She falls back on my bed in distress. “Fucking awful.”

I eye the clock again, hoping to make it to the gym, but there’s no use at this point. I have to get to my next exam. Channeling my emotions is going to have to wait for another day.

“Are you sure you’re okay, Logan?” Ali asks as she leans up on her elbows, eyeing me. “You haven’t seemed like yourself this week, and I’ve barely seen you.”

“I’m fine. I haven’t been doing great on my tests, and it’s stressing me out. But besides that, I’m all good.”

Well, at least part of that statement was truthful. I have been doing poorly on my exams, but the rest was a bald-faced lie. And in true Ali fashion, she knows I’m full of shit.

“I know you’re lying right now. But I’m not going to push it unless you want to tell me what’s up. If you need to talk, you know I’m always here.”

“I know, but I’m good,” I tell her with a not-so-convincing nod as she eyes me suspiciously.

L: *Hi. I can't answer. I'm at the doctor's right now. I'll call you later.* I text Eli after declining his video call on Wednesday afternoon. I know he needs to get on the ice soon, but I can't answer while I'm sitting in this busy waiting room.

E: *Why are you at the doctor? What's wrong??*

L: *Nothing is wrong—normal check-up. I'm supposed to get my kidney tested quarterly. This is just routine.*

E: *Promise me nothing is wrong*

L: *I promise. Just a check-up. Good luck tonight. Remember how great you are. I love you so much.*

E: *I love you too, Logan. Please text me after your appointment and tell me everything is okay. Marc and Ali said they're worried about you. They said you seem off. Is that why you're at the doctor? What's going on?*

L: *Nothing is going on. I've just been studying like crazy, so I haven't seen them much this week. I'm good, though! Go kick some ass, thirteen.*

Locking my phone, I throw it in my bag and go back to flipping through the pages of an old magazine while I wait for my appointment.

"Logan Leo," a nice-looking nurse calls out to the waiting room, holding a clipboard that no doubt contains my medical history.

"That's me." I stand from my seat and walk over to her. She holds the door open for me as I follow her down the long sterile hallway until she ushers me into an empty room.

"Alright. Take a seat. Just going to do a quick blood pressure check before the doctor comes in."

She puts the cuff over my bicep which inflates until the very average blood pressure numbers flash on the machine.

"Looks great," she says while she removes the cuff. "Dr. Lopez will be with you shortly." She gives me a sweet smile before exiting the room, closing the door behind her as she goes.

I look around the sanitized room, taking in my surroundings. I haven't been to a doctor's office since this summer when I had my last check-up back in California. I typically wouldn't book an appointment during finals week, and I almost canceled mine today because I've just felt so overwhelmed lately. But they were booked out another two months, and I've already been irresponsible by missing my last kidney check-up.

"You must be Logan." An older looking gentleman walks into the room. His white coat covers up most of his frame, but there is a bit of blue from his collared shirt that brings out the blue of his kind eyes. I typically don't love going to male doctors, but I didn't have much of a say when booking an appointment so last minute, and this older man seems nice enough.

"I'm Dr. Lopez, but you can call me Robert."

"Nice to meet you," I shyly say.

"What brings you in today?" He takes a seat on the rolling stool across from me.

"Well, I moved here at the end of the summer, and I haven't seen a doctor yet. I'm supposed to do quarterly check-ups on my kidney, but I'm a little behind on this one." My cheeks warm, slightly embarrassed for waiting so long to come in.

"I see that." He flips through the pages of my medical records on the clipboard in his lap. "You have quite the family medical history," he adds, reading over the notes. "Your father passed from a heart attack and your mother from kidney failure."

Yes. Thank you for the reminder. As if that's not all I've been able to think about this week.

"Your blood pressure numbers look great, though, and you seem to live a healthy lifestyle." His eyes continue to scan the pages on the clipboard. "Well, we'll get a urine test for your kidney check, but Logan, I'm sure you're perfectly healthy." He looks up at me with a kind smile, obviously noting the expression on my face.

Setting the clipboard down, he turns to me. "That's quite an impressive thing for someone your age to do. Donate your kidney to your mother like that."

I give him a casual shrug. "It didn't work."

"Still, a very brave thing to do," he adds with another half-smile, trying to read me. "You've been through a lot. Did you have someone at home helping you out?"

"No, it's just me."

"This is a lot for you to have taken on all by yourself. Have you ever thought about seeing a counselor? Someone you could talk to? I can arrange a referral if you'd like?"

"No, I'm fine. I don't want to talk to anyone," I quickly snap.

He pauses for a moment before he nods his head. "Okay. Well, if you ever change your mind, you let me know. Open offer."

I shoot him a thankful smile, feeling bad for the way I snapped. He's just trying to help. I know that, but this week has been an absolute nightmare already, and I don't want to dig into my past anymore. I just want to move forward and pretend like last year never happened.

"Well, Logan. It was great to meet you." He stands from the stool, walking towards the exit. "I'll see you in three months for your next check-up, yeah?"

"Yes. Thank you, Dr. Lopez."

"Robert," he playfully corrects me.

"Sorry," I chuckle. "Thank you, Robert."

After giving a quick urine sample, I made it back to campus with plenty of time to make it to my last final of the week—managerial economics. But it didn't much matter. I know I did terribly. My mind is nowhere near school right now. It's not even much on Eli, which is unusual. It's all on my mom. What happened last year, what I haven't dealt with yet. I can't stop thinking about it.

The heaviness I feel pushes me into my mattress as I try to fall asleep. The darkness of the room around me is exactly how my mind looks. Dark, scared, and sad. Afraid to tackle this head-on. The grief is creeping in. I can feel it slowly consuming me, reminding me that I have to deal with this.

I haven't shed a tear. Not one fucking tear, and I refuse to start because once I do, I don't know if they'll ever stop. It's going to come on full-force. I can sense it.

The conversation I had with Jack while I was in Indiana has been playing on repeat in my mind. "*You're going to have to feel it all so you can move on,*" he said. I don't think I have much of a choice anymore. It's happening whether I want to acknowledge it or not.

Last year, I didn't grieve. I threw all my shit in a storage unit and hopped on a plane to Europe. I spent the semester pretending like nothing was wrong. I drank away any unwanted emotions, and Marc was the greatest distraction I could've asked for. He probably doesn't realize it, but he was. He was the light in my very dark world. He pulled me out of the depths of grief before I had really even gone through them. But here it is—it's dark again.

My phone dings with a new message from Eli. He doesn't know what's going on with me. I've lied the whole week, pretending like I was okay. I've stayed away from Marc and Ali a fair amount, too, blaming it on school. I don't want anyone to see me like this. They all know me too well, they'll know something is wrong, and I don't want to be a burden on anyone else. I can handle it myself.

E: *I'm glad your appointment went well. I don't need anything happening to you. The game went great. I felt really good. The Dallas Scout is flying to Minnesota to watch our game tomorrow too. This is big, and I'll fill you in on that tomorrow. I'll try not to wake you when I get home. It'll be late. I love you so much, and I can't wait to see you.*

And there it is. The first tear to fall. There's no stopping it now. I'm in it, and I don't know how long it'll take for me to get out. Or if I ever will.

Tomorrow is the day. Eli is going to get called up. It's only fitting that he leaves me the same day my mom did.

Chapter 79

Eli

I finally got a good night's sleep last night after being on the road for eight days. I don't know what I'm going to do if Logan decides stays in Minnesota if and when I get called up. And not just because I can't sleep without her, but because I need her. I always need her. She's the other half to my whole.

She's had me worried sick about her all week. Something in my gut is telling me she's lying about being okay. I can feel it. She sounded perfectly normal on the phone whenever we spoke, but she would never answer my video calls. It's like she didn't want me to see her face or something. She always had an excuse as to why she couldn't answer. Not to mention that Marc and Ali confirmed my suspicions that Logan didn't seem like herself on multiple occasions this week.

Something about this doctor's appointment she had yesterday isn't sitting right with me. Is that why she's been off all week? She said it was a routine check-up, but was that true? Is she afraid to tell me something is wrong? After her kidney, my second thought was that she could be pregnant and is afraid to tell me. Even though we always use protection, there's still that chance. Knowing how sure Logan is that she doesn't want kids, it would make sense why she hasn't been herself all week.

Then there's the thought that she's sad about her parents because it's the holidays. She was upset the day after Thanksgiving, but she hasn't brought up the subject since, and Logan is usually pretty cut and dried when it comes to that part of her past. I don't know what's going on yet. All I know is that after my game today, we are officially on winter break, so whatever is going on with her, we can work through it together.

I give one last lingering kiss to Logan's tattoo, trying not to wake her as I peel myself out of her bed. I would kiss her pretty lips too, but her head is buried under a blanket at the moment. I need to get to the rink for pregame skate, and after Logan's week of finals, I'm sure she needs the extra rest. She was asleep last night when I came in, which I fully expected since it was so late, but even being able to have her in my arms after eight days makes me feel like myself again. Although, with that scout coming today, I wouldn't mind hearing Logan's soothing voice before I hit the ice, but I don't want to add any more of a burden onto her at the moment. I'd rather she get some rest.

I write her a note, throw on my clothes, and give her shoulder a quick kiss before heading to the rink.

During warmups, I've kept my eyes on the four seats behind our bench, but they remain empty. I figured that Logan and Marc would be here by now, but they're not. Maybe they're just running behind.

My eyes drift up a few rows, finding the Dallas Stars scout already in his seat. We had a good talk last night after my game. He told me that he could tell from my season's stats that the substandard game he watched me play back in October against Penn State was a one-off. He let me know what his team was looking for and that he thought I could be the right addition, to which I quickly agreed. Dallas' offensive system plays right into my strengths, and it's a team I've had my eye on for quite some time if I was given a choice.

He also told me that they aren't going to be making any call-ups just yet. They're waiting until the trade deadline to see where their budget cap is at and what their playoff standings might look like. I understand, and if I'm being honest, I'm relieved to hear it. It would give Logan and me a bit more time to figure out our game plan. The fact that he flew out to the Midwest to watch a second game in a row is enough to assure me that I'm at the top of his radar.

I watch as Marc sneaks into his seat right after the national anthem, but he's alone. As soon as starting lineup announcements are done, I quickly skate over, crawl over the player's bench and tap on the glass in front of him to get his attention.

"Where's Logan?" I quickly ask my brother from behind the barrier.

"She said she wasn't feeling well."

"What? What's going on?"

"I'm not sure, man. But you need to focus on this game. Logan will be fine."

"Did you see her?"

"She wouldn't answer her door. I tried. She texted me to tell me she was sick and to go without her."

"Marc, I need you to go back and check on her. Please. Something is going on," I urgently request of him as the referee blows the whistle for me, wanting to start the opening puck drop that I'm clearly absent from.

"Maddison, let's go!" my coach yells, my back still to the ice, desperate eyes locked on my brother.

"I know, I'm worried too. But Ali stayed back. She's right across the hall, and Logan knows she's there if she needs anything," Marc calmly explains. "EJ, you have to get your head in the game. It's just sixty minutes of hockey, and then you can go see her. But this game is too important for you to lose focus." He looks over his shoulder, reminding me that my possible future NHL team is watching from just a few rows back.

"Text her for me, please. Let her know I'll be there as soon as the game is over."

I reluctantly turn around, finding every player's eyes on me as I skate to the center circle to face off against Nebraska. I position myself as I always do, but I'm in too much of a daze to time my stick right, allowing the other team to win the opening face-off.

I skate back on defense as my mind swirls with thoughts of Logan. She had a doctor's appointment yesterday, and now she's not feeling well. Something is going on that she doesn't want to tell me about.

Patrick steals the puck, pushing it up the ice to me, but I'm too distracted in my own thoughts to catch his pass as the team in red quickly picks up the failed connection.

"What the fuck is wrong with you, Maddison?" Patrick yells while covering his zone. "Get your head in the game or get off the fucking ice!"

As much as I hate the guy, he's not wrong.

Intercepting Nebraska's pass, I send it off to our other defenseman to take his time carrying the puck up the ice, allowing us forwards the chance to change out from our shift.

"Where's Logan?" Cam asks as I take a seat on the bench next to him, clearly aware that her absence is already throwing off my game.

"I don't know, man. She's not feeling well."

"Well, she will literally kill you if you blow this shot, so you better get your head in it, man." Cam's words are sternly delivered before he hops over the boards for his shift.

He's right, and his words are all it takes. A reminder that this dream I'm chasing isn't just for me. It's for Logan, too, for our future. She would be just as mad at herself as she would be at me if her absence caused me to play like shit. So, for her, I put her out of my mind for the sixty minutes of play and focus on the game, which is exactly what she would want me to do.

Chapter 80

Logan

I'm a terrible girlfriend. I know I am. And I've never felt more selfish in my life than I do today.

I cried myself to sleep last night as the grief and guilt I've been running from crashed onto me like a tidal wave. When Eli came in late from his red-eye flight, I woke up but pretended like I was still asleep as I kept my back towards him, not wanting him to see my face. I knew as soon as he saw my puffy eyes and colorless skin that he would realize something was seriously wrong with me.

My sadness kept me awake the whole night as the warm tears fell down my cheeks. I quietly wiped them away, being sure not to wake Eli's sleeping body wrapped around me. It was nice to have him with me, but at this point, I don't think there's anyone or anything that could make me feel better other than working through the emotions I need to deal with. And, even then, it feels like I might never be the same.

I was still awake this morning when Eli left, but again, I pretended to be asleep as he said goodbye to me. He has a huge opportunity today, and I knew if he saw me that he would be off his game, and I can't feel any more guilt than I already do on this day.

Today is the one-year anniversary of my mom's death.

Fuck, that sucks to say.

One year ago, everything I worked so hard at, every minute that I spent next to her in the hospital, every painful moment that came from trying to save her, all came crashing down when she took her last breath.

And it was my fault.

It was my fault she died. She was my responsibility, and I failed her. It was my organ that her body rejected. It was my fault. I should've done more. I should've tried harder—anything. Maybe I let the doctors stop her medications too soon. Maybe they would've worked if we just kept trying. Maybe she would still be here if I didn't make the call to let her go. It's my fault.

That decision crosses my mind every day before I shove it down and try to suppress the guilt that comes with it.

I've pretended like I had my shit together, like I was alright. Like I was strong and could handle the hand I was dealt. But it's not true. I'm fucking weak and scared and a coward, running from everything for so long, like it would never catch up with me.

But it did today.

I've been running for a year straight. I ran away to Spain. I shut off any emotion towards that time in my life, any feeling of her. And I hate myself for it. I've acted like she didn't exist for the last twelve months. Like she wasn't the most important person in my whole life. She was my best friend and my mom, and I refused to think about her. I refused to remember her. I refused to let Eli know her.

I'm a terrible daughter, trying to forget about her the way I did. But I can't any longer. It's like the memories that I tried to black out from my mind are all seeping in today, and the force with which the grief is sitting on me is almost unbearable.

Flashes of her sandy brown hair that lightened in the sun run across my mind. The time I dropped my dad's birthday cake that she worked so hard on, then pretended like she didn't like it and was going to redo it anyway so I wouldn't feel bad. Her dresses that flowed in the wind. She always looked like a soft feminine doll floating around on air. I was never that pretty and soft, but she was. The basketball jersey that she sewed for my Barbie doll because I was upset that the store didn't have anything that wasn't pink and frilly. The way she smelled. That one sits with me the most. She smelled like strawberries and sunshine. I didn't even know you could smell like the sun, but she did.

In the last few months of her life, she didn't smell like sunshine anymore. The sterile hospital stole her pretty scent, and overtook it with chemicals. They say scent has the strongest memory ties. I remember those hospital days all too well. Her feminine dresses were swapped for an oversized hospital gown, and her yummy home-baked treats were traded in for terrible microwaved meals from the hospital cafeteria. Our warm California home had been left empty as I practically moved into her 8x8 room, overtaken with loud beeping machines and the constant revolving door of nurses and doctors.

The thing I remember the most? The way she couldn't remember me.

And that's the thing I never want to remember again.

The way her meds were so strong towards the end that they made her memory foggy. The way she asked if I was the nurse on shift on more than one occasion. The way she asked what my name was as I sat and ate my reheated Thanksgiving dinner next to her. I don't want to remember that.

But they're all here, all the memories. The good ones and the bad ones, and they aren't leaving anytime soon.

I wipe at my eyes again, but it's no use. The tears haven't stopped all night. I don't cry, rarely ever, but I truly don't know if I'll ever stop again.

The only hint of relief I've had in the last twenty-four hours was the email from my doctor with my test results. Everything looks good, but do I really care? I'm not so sure.

I look over to my dresser, Eli's jersey sitting right on top, making me feel even more terrible than I already did. I know he needs me at his game, but I can't go. I can't get myself off this bed. It's like a vortex of all-consuming sadness that's sucked me in, and I might never be able to get out.

It's dark here, too. The lights are all on, but all I see is darkness. My chest is heavy. The way I assume Eli's is when he's having a panic attack. Now I know what it feels like, but I think I deserve it, whereas he definitely does not.

The note Eli left me this morning is sitting in my palm, where it's been since I read the words the first time. I open it again, reading it to myself through my blurry, tear-filled eyes.

Hi. You're the best.

I can't wait to see you at my game.

-E

Eli. I love that man more than I've ever loved anyone in my life, but I am anything but the best. To be honest, I feel like the absolute worst right now. He can't see me like this. He doesn't need this. He can't handle this, and he shouldn't have to. No one our age should have to.

The idea of having to take care of someone else has absolutely terrified me. I failed so miserably with my mom, I wasn't ready to take on that responsibility again. But when I met Eli, I knew he needed me, and it's like that part of my natural instincts kicked in because I wanted to be there for him. I wanted to take care of this strong man who sometimes feels weak. Whose mind plays tricks on him and tells him he's not good enough. I was happy to finally be successful at taking care of someone else, but here I am, failing again when he needs me the most.

Today is the day he's going to get called up, and I'm not even there for him. I'm so selfish right now, but I can't do it. I don't know how to do it. I feel broken.

I think I am broken.

I guess the timing works out perfectly for him. He can leave for Dallas and not have to deal with my mess. He doesn't need this, and I don't want this for him. At least I won't have to explain to him why I have to go back to California by myself to clear out that storage unit instead of spending Christmas with him and his family. It won't matter because he'll be gone.

It really is fitting that today would be the day he leaves me. I think I deserve that.

The knock at my door pulls me out of my daze. Well...barely. It's still blurry and dark as hell in my mind right now.

Ali has been texting me, telling me she's across the hall if I need anything after I lied to her and Marc about not feeling well. Though, I guess it wasn't a total lie, I feel the worst I've ever felt in my life, and I don't know if I'll ever feel better. The knocking is Marc. I know it is. He already came by, pounding at my door before Eli's game started, but when I didn't answer, he finally gave up and left for the rink.

I know it's him again, but I don't know why he's here. I already told him I wasn't feeling well, and I don't think Eli's game is over yet. I'm just going to ignore him until he goes back to the arena. I know I'm a terrible friend in this moment, but he needs to be there for his brother right now because I can't.

The knocking continues, and Marc hasn't let up. I don't want him to see me, but I don't know how else to get him to leave. I somehow peel myself off of my mattress, the heaviness on my chest and shoulders pushing my dragging feet into the ground. I take a deep breath and unlock my door, ever so slightly cracking it open to tell him that I'm okay. But when I open my door, it's not my tall tanned-skin best friend waiting on the other side.

No, it's the last person I ever wanted to see again.

"Zac?"

Anger.

Oh, I like this emotion. Much better than grief. I can handle anger.

Chapter 81

Eli

As soon as the final buzzer sounded, I quickly skated off the ice, threw my skates in my bag, tossed my jersey in the dirty bin, and ran out of the locker room. I didn't bother to shower or to stay for the post-game meeting. I know something is wrong with Logan, and I have to find out what's going on. Nothing else matters at this point.

The pit in my stomach is growing the closer I get to her dorm. Usually, a calm takes over me when I know she's near, but not today. Today I feel anxious, worried, and scared.

I charge through the lobby doors, bypassing the elevator, knowing that the adrenaline coursing through me will take me up the stairs quicker than the elevator ever could. I pull out my keys with shaky fingers, finding Logan's spare on the ring, ready with it in my hand as I make it to her floor. But as I sprint down her hall towards her room, I notice that her door is already wide open.

"Logan," I call out when I reach it, turning the corner as I do.

My stomach instantly drops as I take in the sight in front of me. My strong, sweet girl is almost unrecognizable as she sits on the edge of her bed, curled up with her knees to her chest, making herself small.

Her striking green eyes are now dull and vacant as she looks at me with worry. Her golden skin is drained and pale. Her cheeks look a bit hollow, and her nose is pink and raw. She's not crying right now, but I can tell she has been, maybe even for days at this point.

"Fuck. Logan, are you okay?" I ask with urgency as I bound over to her bed. Kneeling in front of her, I tuck her tangled hair behind her ear to give myself a clearer look at her face.

It's now become evident why she never answered my video calls this week. She knows that if I would've seen her like this, I would've jumped on the next flight back here. I should have.

"What's going on?" My eyes dart between hers, trying to read her as I always can.

But today, I can't. She's blank. I don't know where she is, but she's not here.

"Who the hell are you?" a male voice behind me asks.

I glance over my shoulder, finding some guy standing in the middle of Logan's room wearing the stupidest fucking expression on his face. I didn't notice him when I barged in here, but suddenly his presence is all I can focus on.

"Who the hell am I? Who the fuck are you? And why are you in my girlfriend's room?" I ask the douchebag who's wearing fucking boat shoes in the middle of winter, standing behind me.

"Girlfriend?" the prick asks in disbelief.

"Eli, it's not what it looks like," Logan says, pulling my attention back to her. Her voice is almost as unrecognizable as her features.

Not what it looks like? It doesn't look like anything other than some frat boy asking to get his ass kicked for being here right now and causing Logan distress. I know Logan would never cheat on me in the same way that I wouldn't. That's not even a concern of mine.

"It doesn't look like anything." I furrow my brows and shake my head. "Logan, I would never think that," I softly add.

"You never told me you had a boyfriend, Logan," the guy behind me states in a tone that I'm less than thrilled with being directed at my girl. His words cause me to stand up as I quickly do a body comparison, making sure I can take him if and when the time comes.

"Because I haven't spoken a word to you in three fucking months!" Logan shouts, shocking me with the rage that's spewing out of her. "I don't even know why you're here right now!"

I swallow hard, trying to hold back my anger. "You need to leave," I plainly tell him, my blood beginning to boil, seeing Logan as upset as she is, seeing the veins in her neck protruding through her hollow skin.

"You know why I'm here, Logan," the jackass says, ignoring my polite instruction. "I remember what today is."

What the fuck does that mean?

"What's today?" I turn back to a small and frail Logan sitting on her bed.

"Zac, get the fuck out!" she yells, motioning towards her door, her pale face turning red with anger.

Zac? This douchebag dressed like he's getting on a fucking yacht is Zac? Oh, fuck no. That possible ass-kicking? It's inevitable now.

"Zac?" I ask with wide eyes. "You're Zac?" I take a step towards him, putting myself between his body and Logan's.

Again, he ignores me. This guy just keeps making mistakes.

"He doesn't even know what today is, Logan?" Zac asks her over my shoulder in disbelief. "Come on. Is this a joke, Logan?" His tone is patronizing, trying to manipulate my girlfriend, the way I assume he did plenty of times during their relationship.

The way he says her name after every sentence. I hate hearing her name coming from his mouth. He adds it on with a commanding edge when her name should only be said with tenderness.

"Of course, you remember what today is!" Logan shouts, standing from the bed. "It's the same day I caught you fucking someone else, you piece of shit!"

I'm not facing her, I'm facing him, but I'm still proud of her regardless. He's trying to make her feel small, and she won't let him because she's not. She's tough as hell, even if she doesn't look like it right now. But as much as I love seeing Logan stand up for herself, she's obviously not in the right mental space to have to do so.

"Get the fuck out," I sternly tell him with flared nostrils, getting real close to his face. "Now."

Zac gives Logan a pretentious little nod before he turns towards the door to leave.

"Your mother wouldn't even recognize you right now, yelling the way you are," Zac spitefully adds, turning back to look at Logan.

"Don't fucking talk about my mom!" Logan shouts as she takes a bounding step towards Zac. "You barely even knew her!" she adds just in time for me to turn around and grab her, wrapping my forearm around her waist, stopping her from a physical altercation with this piece of shit.

I'm holding her up off her feet as she kicks and flails in my grasp, trying to get to him. I've never seen Logan angrier in my life, but I don't blame her at all. I am too.

"Get the fuck out!" I tell Zac again as I hold Logan back.

Finally, after giving us both one more look over, he turns on his heel and leaves.

I slam the door closed the second he's through the threshold before setting Logan back on her feet. Her face is red with anger, her breathing short and shallow, pacing the room as she tugs at her tangled red hair. Her eyes are wild as I grab her by the waist, guiding her back to sit on her bed before I bend down to make my eyes level with hers.

"Deep breath, baby." She locks her eyes with mine, trying to calm herself down. She inhales deeply before letting out a long exhale, her gaze on me the entire time as she does.

I'm not entirely unaware that the roles are reversed here. I'm usually the one who can't catch their breath, and Logan is the one talking me through it, but right now, she needs me the way I always need her.

Even though Logan is calming her nerves, it's doing nothing for my anger, seeing that motherfucker in my girlfriend's room. Remembering what he did to her. Knowing that the uncertainty she felt in herself when we first met was caused in part by him. Hearing the way he spoke to her makes so much sense as to why Logan was the way she was. A bit shy and awkward, sheltered. He did that to her.

"Be right back."

She doesn't even ask where I'm going. I'm sure she already knows.

My long legs run out of her room, through the hall, and down the five flights of stairs, before throwing open the lobby doors with the rage pulsing through me. I don't know if I've ever been this mad in my life. Seeing the asshole who cheated on my favorite person, who made her feel like it was her fault that he did, is doing nothing but fill me with hatred as the memories of what she's told me about him flood my mind.

It's cold as fuck outside right now, a fresh blanket of snow on the ground, but the fire running through my veins is keeping me plenty warm.

I dart to the parking lot as I spot Zac walking to his car. A rental car, I would presume, seeing as he probably flew here from California. And it's a Hummer. A fucking Hummer. I didn't even know they made those cars anymore, let alone use them as rentals. But of course, that's the rental he chose.

Glad to know his dick is tiny.

"Zac!" I yell as I bound towards him.

He turns to face me with a shake of his head. "Good luck with that one." He nods towards Logan's dorm as I quickly continue towards him, not slowing my pace.

I cock my arm, putting all my anger into my fist as I connect it with his nose, hearing a heavenly crack before I black out for a moment from the adrenaline coursing through me. When the light comes back through, I see blood splattered on the fresh white snow before Zac crumbles to the ground in a whimper, grabbing at his face.

"Stay the hell away from Logan! Or next time I'll put you in the fucking hospital, exactly where you should've been when her mom was dying, you fucking piece of shit!"

Looking at my fist, I can't tell if it's his blood or mine that's coating my knuckles, but I assume from the split skin and welcome sting, it's mine.

"And get some real fucking shoes, you pretentious motherfucker!" I add when I notice the solo boat shoe that slipped off his foot when he hit the ground, kicking it a couple of feet away from him.

I turn away, my heart beating out of my chest, but as soon as I do, it hits me. I know exactly what today is, and I don't know how I didn't realize it before.

"Fuck," I mutter under my breath as I run back towards Logan's dorm, taking the same route as I did before, bypassing the elevator altogether.

I run into her room, but it's empty. She's gone. I step inside and circle the space as my heart begins to race uncontrollably. I grab at my messy hair before realizing that, of course, I know where she is.

She couldn't have left too long ago; I was only outside with Zac for a minute or two. But, of course, Logan is much faster than I am.

As my feet carry me towards the campus gym, much quicker than they ever have before, my eyes begin to sting as I think about the grief that Logan is going through right now. I take a deep breath as I hold onto the gym door, trying to compose myself and be strong for my girl before I walk in.

When I step inside, I realize the gym is completely empty, most likely because winter break has officially begun, but I spot my angry girl wildly throwing punches at a bag as her red ponytail flails around her.

In the times I've watched Logan box before, the first thing I notice is how composed and in control of her movements she is. Today, she's not. It's as if she's trying to get all her thoughts and feelings out of her body and into the bag as quickly as possible.

I can see how weak she is from here, and that's never been a word I've used to describe Logan before.

"Logan!" I yell, trying to get her attention. Trying to distract her from the anger spewing from her fist, but she ignores me. Or she doesn't hear me. I'm not sure.

"Logan Josephine Leo!" I bound towards her angry body, but again she doesn't respond to me.

I cautiously wrap my arm around her waist from behind as I avoid her gloved up fist. "Baby," I softly say, now that I have her in my grasp.

Logan throws a few more halfhearted punches before falling forward, leaning her forehead and fists on the bag as her anger breaks into a grief-stricken sob.

Her body heaves in my arms as her cries fill the empty gym, the place she's always been able to find relief. But today, there's no relief for her as she collapses in my embrace.

I sink to the ground, taking her with me as she continues to cry uncontrollably. I turn her body into mine as she hides her tear-soaked face in my chest. I wrap her up as tightly as I can, knowing that this helps me when she does it, and not sure what else to do as I try to mask the pain I feel for her. She's never once needed me the way I do her, but she does right now, and I have to step up and be strong for her.

I sit here with her for quite some time, not saying a word but letting her feel it all as I gently run my hand over the length of her back. When Logan's cries quiet a bit, I take off my jacket and drape it around her before wrapping her legs around my waist and standing with her in my grasp. She tightens her arms around my neck and buries her face in my shoulder as I carry her against my body back to her dorm.

When I make it to her hall, I spot Marc and Ali standing outside Ali's doorway, faces plastered with concern when they see the broken girl in my arms.

Marc has never seemed more worried in his life, but I give him a look, trying to tell him that I know what's going on without saying the words.

Closing Logan's dorm room door behind us, I sink to the ground with her straddling my lap and my back leaning against the door. She stays hidden in my nape as I remove her gloves, tossing them to the side before gently unwrapping her hands.

Logan gasps for air between cries as her warm tears continue to fall onto my chest, soaking my shirt.

"I'm sorry," she squeaks out.

What? What does she have to be sorry for?

I run my hand over her messy hair, trying to calm her down. "You have nothing to be sorry for, baby."

"I'm sorry I missed your game," she says against my skin.

"I don't give a fuck about my game, Logan. I'm worried about you." I pull her face away from my body so she can see my concern.

Her green eyes search mine for a moment before she climbs off my lap to stand, swiping at her tears.

"When do you leave?" she plainly asks as if she's not in the middle of an emotional breakdown right now.

"Leave for what?" I stand from the floor, completely confused.

She takes a deep breath before looking at me, but I'm having a hard time recognizing the sad girl in front of me. "Leave for Dallas."

I furrow my brows and shake my head. "I'm not going to Dallas. Not yet, anyway."

"But soon," she says, and I can't quite tell if she's telling me or asking me.

"Maybe." I walk up to her, wiping another tear from her face. "I don't know for sure yet. We don't need to worry about that right now, Logan. We need to talk about how you're feeling and what you're going through."

"I'm fine," she states, looking at me with vacant green eyes. The look on her face is almost chilling. It's as if she's being haunted by grief.

"Logan, stop trying to act all tough right now. You're not fine, and it's okay not to be fine."

She keeps her face turned away from me as she takes a seat on her bed, not wanting me to see just how much she's hurting.

"I know what today is," I tell her as her head snaps back to look at me. "Why didn't you say anything?" I gently ask.

Her bottom lip begins to quiver before more tears start to fall from her sad and swollen eyes.

"I didn't want to put this on you," she says with a shaky voice.

I close my eyes before looking up to the ceiling, trying to collect my thoughts.

"Logan, that's what I'm here for. We are a team now. It's not just you anymore. Your pain is my pain."

"No, it's not!" she snaps. "This is my pain! This is my fault!" She pokes at her chest, tears continuing to run down her red cheeks.

"What's your fault?" I somehow ask as my heart begins to race, hearing Logan's frantic tone. Logan has never spoken to me this way before, but I know she's not mad at me. She's angry at herself, but I don't know why.

"It's my fault," she cries, hiding her face in her hands. "It's my fault she's dead."

My jaw slacks, and my face pales as I take in Logan's words. Not only is she grieving for her mom one year after she died, but now she's blaming herself for it all, which is the furthest thing from the truth. Not only did she sacrifice part of her body, but she sacrificed her innocence, her selfish years, her childhood.

I drop to my knees in front of Logan as she sits on the bed, while I attempt to get her gaze to lock with mine. I pull her hands away from her face, keeping them interlocked between my fingers. "That wasn't your fault, Logan. You did everything you could for her. More than everything." My voice is laced with desperation, trying to convince her of my words.

She shakes her head as she stands from the bed, leaving me without her touch. "It is my fault. I should've done more. Tried harder. But instead, she died, and I just fucking ran away to another country and tried to forget all about her." Her hands frantically wipe away the fresh tears that won't stop falling.

"Logan." I stand up and grab her wrists, but she pulls away from my grasp. I wrap my arms around her body and keep her held tightly to my chest, not letting her get away from me. Finally, she melts into me as her sobbing begins again.

I smooth her tangled ponytail as she hides away in my chest. "Have you ever mourned her?" I ask, as her cries become louder. I pick her up and take a seat on the bed with her across my lap as she continues to cry into my shoulder. "It's been a year, and you've never talked about her. You've never let me in."

"Let me help you," I beg of her.

She shakes her head against me. "I don't want this for you. I'm broken, and I don't know if I'm ever going to get fixed."

My eyes screw shut at her tone as my heart breaks a little more. "You're not broken, Logan. Far from it. You're the strongest person I know. Let me be here for you."

She climbs off my lap, creating distance between us, both figuratively and literally.

"I have to do this alone," she plainly states as she stubbornly crosses her arms in front of her chest.

"But you're not alone, anymore. You have me. You have Marc."

"I am alone!" she shouts with wild and sad eyes. "I'm always alone! Everyone always leaves me. You're going to leave me," she cries.

I feel stunned right now. I should've caught this. I should've taken my dad's advice earlier and assured her that nothing would change if I got called up and had to leave. It won't change anything. It can't change anything.

"Come with me," I desperately request as I stand from the bed to face her. "If I get called up, come with me."

She looks at me with confusion on her face before violently shaking her head in disagreement. "I can't just go with you, Eli. I'm still in school. I'm not giving that up."

I let out a defeated sigh. This is the last thing I want to talk about today, but for some reason, thoughts of her mom being gone is convincing her that I'm going to leave her too. "Even if I go, nothing is going to change between us, Logan. I'm not leaving *you*."

"What am I supposed to do, huh? Come visit every time you happen to have a day off from hockey? Fly all over the country trying to catch you on my weekends while I'm in grad school? I can't live my life for someone else, Eli."

"I'm not asking you to live your life for me, Logan! It's not just about you or me. It's about us!" I look up towards the ceiling, trying to calm myself down.

After a moment of silence, I lower my voice back to its normal volume and continue. "I've only ever wanted one thing, and that was to play professional hockey, but that one dream turned into two dreams this year when I met you. I'm not going to apologize for wanting you, too."

"I can't even handle you being on the road for a week. Look at me, look how fucked up I am! I don't want to feel like I need you. I don't want to need anyone but me."

"Why not?" I ask, feeling extremely flustered at the moment. "It's okay to need someone. I need you!"

"This was never supposed to happen," she says with a whimper as she motions between us. "You weren't supposed to happen."

"Well, guess what, Logan. It did happen! And it's the best goddamn thing that's ever happened to either of us! You know it. I know it. Everyone fucking knows it!"

"I was supposed to move here and become this selfish person. Think only about myself for once. That was the point of me coming to school here," she adds as if she didn't even hear me.

She pulls her gaze away from me as she continues to break my heart. I swallow hard, trying to keep my emotions back.

"Selfish is the last word I would use to describe you, Logan. And you don't have to be selfish when you have someone else looking out for you. You made me realize that this year."

Her gaze meets mine momentarily, so I continue. "I used to only think about myself, and I never realized how lonely that was. But when I met you, I knew I couldn't be selfish anymore, and I didn't want to be. Because you always had my back, you always had my best interests at heart the same way I have yours. It wasn't just me anymore, the same way it's not just you."

Logan's tears begin to fall again as I walk over to her and wrap her up in my embrace, and this time she thankfully doesn't fight it. "I'm always going to look out for you, baby. I'm always going to protect you and take care of you. You're not alone anymore," I desperately remind her. "I need you the same way you need me."

"You can't need me," she quietly says into my chest.

"Why not?"

"Because I can't take care of you. I can't take care of anyone. I can't even take care of myself. Look at me." Logan pulls away from my chest, locking her gaze with mine. "I'm a mess."

I am looking at her. I'm always looking at her. She's the most beautiful and best thing in my world. I've never taken my eyes off of her. Even if she thinks she's different now because of the pain she's going through, it doesn't change the fact that she is and always will be the girl I'm desperately in love with.

"I have to go back to California," she says.

"What?"

"I have a storage unit there. I have to clear it out by the end of the year. I just got a call about it earlier this week." Logan wipes at her face again, trying to keep herself composed.

"I'll go with you," I plead.

Logan shakes her head. "You can't. I have to do this alone."

There's that word again—alone. But she's not alone. She's never going to be alone again. Why doesn't she see that?

I release an exhausted breath and start pacing around the room. "Please stop, Logan. Stop being such a fucking martyr all the time. You think you're this burden to everyone around you, but you're not!" I yell. I can't help it, I'm angry and hurt right now.

"You're mad at me," she states in a sad and quiet tone.

"You're damn right I'm mad at you!" I shout, trying to keep the tears from welling up and falling down my cheeks. "But only because I fucking love you, and you're always trying to save everyone. Why can't you let someone save *you* for once?"

She stays quiet. I already know my stubborn girl isn't going to give in on this one, and I don't know how to change her mind. She's leaving me. She's afraid that I'm going to leave her, but here she is, leaving *me*.

"Is there anything I can do or say to change your mind and convince you to stay?" I gently ask. "To stay here with me?"

She averts her eyes from mine before lightly shaking her head to tell me no. I close my eyes and let out a defeated sigh.

"Do you realize how mad at me you'd be if the roles were reversed and I was pulling away from you? I'm trying not to take this personally, but I can't help it."

"I'm not trying to hurt you," she protests. "I'm trying to protect you."

"Protect me from what?" I ask with wide eyes and a raised voice.

"Me! This! The thoughts that are in my head right now. The grief that is literally consuming my entire body. I'm sad and dark and broken, and I don't want this for you. You're too good to feel what I'm feeling."

"Well, guess what? I'm feeling it regardless! Everything you feel, I feel. I know your heart is broken right now, Logan, but you're breaking my heart too."

"I'm not trying to," she whispers through a cry, which shatters my heart even more. "That storage unit has all my parents' things in it, and I need to start dealing with these emotions that I've been hiding away from for the last year. I ran away, and I need to go back. I need to go back home and work through some things."

Bounding over to her, I wrap her up in my arms, unable to handle the distance between us any longer. "Please don't call that place your home. This is your home. I'm your home the same way you're mine," I gently remind her. "I love you so much, Logan. It physically hurts how much I love you. I need you to know that. You might feel like you're alone in this world, but you're my *entire* world."

It's crazy how much I love this woman. So much so that it scares the shit out of me. I've been afraid every day since I met her that I would somehow fuck it up and lose her, and trust me, I've been close. But I feel like I'm losing her right now, and I don't know how to stop it.

"I love you too, Eli. I'll always love you."

I hate the way that sounded. I've always loved hearing her tell me that she loves me, but that didn't sound like she was saying those words. It sounded like she was telling me goodbye.

"Why does it sound like you're breaking up with me?" I ask as my voice cracks.

"I'm not," she says with a shake of her head. "I could never, but I don't know if I'm going to be the same person you fell in love with after all of this. I already feel different."

"I don't need you to be the same. I just need you to be you."

I pick her up and carry her to the bed with me, draping her across my lap as I sit up with my back to the headboard. She leans up and connects her mouth with mine, surprising me. It's the first kiss I've had from her in eight days, and it feels like a hello and a goodbye all at once.

She's salty from the tears, but I can still taste a bit of vanilla on her lips. And it's a reminder that she's still there. My girl is still there.

When she pulls away from me, I can't help but stare at her face, trying to memorize every part of it. Her pretty green eyes that have dulled at the moment. Her dimples that I haven't seen for far too long. Her shiny red hair that hasn't been brushed in days, and her pouty lips that usually say just enough to put my world together. But today, her words are shattering it.

"Don't look at me like that," she says, keeping her gaze on mine.

"Like what?"

"Like you pity me," she meekly adds.

"I don't pity you, Logan. I love you."

She lays her head on my shoulder and allows me to hold her for some time. I don't know how long it'll be until I get to have her in my arms again, so I'm taking every moment I can get.

"I don't want you to go." I tighten my hold on her, burrowing my face into her hair, trying to memorize her scent.

"I have to. I have to do this for me," she softly says as her fingers delicately trace the black ink on my arm.

"How long will you be gone?"

"I'm not sure."

"You'll come back, though, right?" I ask with desperation.

She doesn't respond, and the rest of what's left of my heart shatters into even tinier pieces.

"Please come back, Logan," I beg of her. "Please come back to me."

To be continued...

Acknowledgments

So, this is crazy, huh? Writing acknowledgments for my first ever novel? Wow.

First and foremost, I need to thank my readers, especially those of you who started reading this story, chapter by chapter, as I uploaded it online. Without you, this would have never happened. Thank you for your patience and for eagerly waiting for me to update every Monday and Friday. Thank you for sticking through the cliffhangers and the heartache and trusting me to bring everything around full circle. Thank you for loving on these characters who mean so much to me and hopefully hold a place in your hearts now too. Thank you for your continued support. You guys are everything.

To Becka Mack, my Canadian soul-sister, thank you for being such an amazing and supportive friend. There's no way in hell I'd be here, publishing this book, if it weren't for your listening ear. Our message thread turns my bad days around, and your advice and understanding mean the world to me. You're crazy talented, and your writing inspires me. Thank you for being who you are and for writing books I can't put down. I'm looking forward to that beer, my friend.

To Marc (yes, there's a real-life Marc), thank you for not only being one of my best friends but also my biggest hype man. The way Logan feels about her Marc mirrors how I feel about you. Thank you for being the inspiration for Logan's best friend—there's no better person to inspire that character.

To Izabela, who knew about my writing long before most of my friends or family, thank you for keeping my secret until I was ready to share. You're the first person in my life to read this book. Your encouragement gave me the confidence to share it.

To my publisher, Vanessa, thank you for believing in my writing and taking a chance on me, Eli, and Logan. This whole thing is surreal and it's because of your faith in me, so thank you.

To my mom, who didn't even bat an eyelash when I told her I was writing a book, I love you.

To my brothers, thanks for being stoked for me. And if for some reason you happened to read this book, even though I told you not to, I'm sorry for the smut.

And lastly, to my dad, thank you for teaching me how to work hard. I wish you were here to see this (though, there's no way in hell I'd let you read it), but I know you'd think this whole thing was pretty freaking cool.

Did you enjoy Becoming Selfish?

♥

Leave 5 stars and a nice comment to share the love!

You didn't like it?

♠

Write to us to suggest the kind of novel you dream of reading!
https://cherry-publishing.com/en/contact/

Subscribe to our Newsletter to stay up to date with all of our upcoming releases and latest news!
You can subscribe according to the country you're from:

You are from...

US:
https://mailchi.mp/b78947827e5e/get-your-free-ebook

UK:
https://mailchi.mp/cherry-publishing/get-your-free-uk-copy

CANADA:
https://mailchi.mp/96b9df3ed1ca/newsletter-canada-cherry-publishing

AUSTRALIA:
https://mailchi.mp/f7093b3c6c1a/newsletter-australia-cherry-publishing

Printed in Great Britain
by Amazon

74076284R00350